ONE FINE Beast

UNVEILED I

ELIZABETH COURTRIGHT

Year of the Book
135 Glen Avenue
Glen Rock, Pennsylvania

ISBN 13: 978-1-942430-49-0
ISBN 10: 1-942430-49-3

Library of Congress Control Number: 2015958260

Dedication

To Aria
for the inspiration

and

Beryl
for the encouragement

One

August 1885

The walls of the hospital corridor were stark white, blindingly so, but they didn't bother him anymore. Neither did the tangy, overpowering smell. He was used to it. He'd been here five long months. This morning they'd taken his bandages off for good. This afternoon he was going home.

Leaning heavily upon the round-handled, mahogany cane given to him by the hospital, Gabriel Drayton continued his labored progress down the endless white hall. He'd been doing the same trek three times a day for the last two weeks. The two weeks prior, he'd done it two times a day, and before that once a day. His doctors had told him he would never walk again, but he'd proved them wrong. Then they told him he would always have a limp and he would always have pain. He told himself he could live with the limp, and the pain would hopefully lessen in time. He refused to accept that he might spend the rest of his life confined to a chair.

He'd been racing down the stairway of his home when the ear-splitting explosion threw him. He remembered hurtling through the air, caught up in the wind and debris of it, twisting, landing hard on his right side. He remembered the sharp cracks and rumbles of heavy stone and wood breaking apart and falling, and the harsh jolts of things crashing down on top of him. There were seconds of searing agony, but he didn't remember anything after that.

When he'd woken, he'd been lying on his back and all he could see was white. He was shrouded in it. Everywhere his eyes darted—white, so much white. He had no idea where he was.

"Charlotte! Charlotte!"

He remembered thinking it, but he didn't remember shouting it the way a nurse later told him he did.

He remembered feeling like he was going to cry. He hadn't cried since he was ten years old. He never cried. The white turned blurry, like fog. A fly—he was sure it was a fly—landed at the corner of his eye and skittered across his temple into his hair. It itched.

"Charlotte!"

He remembered hearing a voice saying his name, but he didn't know who it was.

"Where is she? Charlotte! Baby!"

He remembered thinking he needed to get up, and he tried to.

The second time he came awake, he was still smothered by white, but it wasn't solid. It was moving. A face appeared in it—a woman's face. The mouth told him where he was, and then said he should lie still. It wasn't possible to move his left arm, but he could move the right one. He reached up and felt bandages covering his face, his head. There was pain, so much pain. Everywhere pain.

The woman—a nurse—kept talking to him. She was kind, her touch feathery. She took his arm and laid it back on the bed. He tried to speak, but his voice didn't sound like his own. It was raspy, whispery. "Where's my daughter?"

"She's with your cousin, Alex, and his wife. They'll keep her until you're well again, until you can go home," she told him.

Charlotte was okay! Before he drifted away again, he remembered thinking it was strange how the pain didn't matter. All that mattered was Charlotte was alright. She was safe. She was alive!

The whole concept was completely foreign to him. It made no sense. He didn't like Charlotte. He didn't want to have anything to do with her. He remembered well the day Charlotte had come into his life. A lady he assumed was her mother came to his house early one Saturday morning. She pulled the bell repeatedly, rousing him from slumber. It was too early for his butler to be in attendance. Growling in fury, clad only in a dressing gown, he'd raced down the stairs and yanked open the door. He didn't know the lady, or at least, he didn't remember her. She was strawberry-blond, and pretty, in a delicate way.

Her dress, however, was shoddy, not typical for a caller to his home. And she held a funny looking ball of pink in front of her. Before he realized what she was about, before a word was spoken, she thrust the pink thing at him. He recoiled, but then had to grab it. She would have dropped it had he not caught it. He held it up in front of him, under its arms, surprised by how little it weighed and how tiny it was. Its bonneted head flopped forward.

"She's yours. You take care of her," the lady said. "I don't want her."

"And you think I do?" he snapped.

The lady threw papers at him. They fluttered to the floor at his feet, and she stomped off, leaving him standing in his doorway.

He took the pink bundle to his parlor and laid it on his sofa, and then went back to retrieve the papers. One was a birth certificate. His name was written in the space for father. The mother was listed as Mary Smith, a name that meant nothing to him. The baby's name, the paper said, was Charlotte.

Back in his parlor, he stood several feet away from the sofa, staring stupidly at the ball of pink. Then, because it seemed content enough, he left to take his bath and get dressed. He was eating his breakfast when it started to howl. Even from the dining room, thirty feet away, through two sets of closed doors, the wail made his ears ring. He went straight to his butler's lodgings and demanded the butler's wife come do something with it. She said she would only help until he found a nanny.

Charlotte had been his burden for three years now. Three years of wasting his time interviewing nannies, none of whom stuck around for long. Three years of wasting his money to pay them. Three years of expensive tailors and toys and everything else he'd bought, because the nanny said whatever it was, was something Charlotte needed. Three years of being interrupted when he was doing something more important, like reading the newspaper, sleeping, or entertaining. Once, without knocking, she came skipping into his bedroom dragging one of her dolls behind her. "Daddy, is that one my new momma?" she asked.

Silently he cursed the latest nanny for putting such ridiculous notions into her head, and rolled his eyes to the lanky naked blond lying under the sheet next to him.

Ringlet curls bounced under the oversized red bow in Charlotte's hair. He didn't like it when the nanny fixed it that way. It was straight and dark like his, except hers was long. When it wasn't curled it hung to the middle of her back the way it was supposed to. "Go back to the nursery. I'm busy," he told her.

Expressive brown eyes stared up at him. "Daddy, will you read me a story?"

"No. Go away!" he barked.

That same dimwit nanny was the one who ran out of the burning house in the middle of the night, leaving Charlotte trapped in her crib. Charlotte's cries had awakened him.

His home was supposed to be finished now. The workmen were supposed to have put it all back the way it had been. New furnishings were supposed to have been delivered. In his nightmarish daydreams he imagined arriving to a broken-windowed, roofless, floorless frame containing not one single chair. That thought scared him more than anything.

Since he wasn't able to leave the hospital, his cousin Alex was supposed to oversee the reconstruction for him. Alex, however, wasn't the most responsible person in the world. All Alex really cared about were his ridiculous pets—his snakes. Why Alex liked snakes Gabriel never understood. It wasn't like he could actually pet them. The Timber Rattlesnakes were kept in enormous, tightly secured tanks. Sometimes Gabriel wondered if Alex liked his wife, Susan, as much as he liked his snakes. He certainly paid more attention to the nasty poisonous things than he did to Susan. Then again, she was *Susan*. And Alex had paid attention to her at least once. In another month or so, Susan would be giving birth.

Snakes and Susan and whatever else aside, Gabriel did enjoy his cousin's company. Alex knew how to have fun. Hosting parties, toasting shots of whiskey, playing cards all night long and going to the tavern were just a couple of the things he was looking forward to doing with Alex again. Lying down with one of the tavern barmaids was another. He hadn't thought about *that* pleasure for a while, and he wondered, as he continued his slow shuffle down the hall, how difficult it would be for his not-quite-fully-healed, shattered pelvis to…

A young woman was walking toward him, the heels of her boots clacking evenly on the hard white floor. Based upon her fashionable, tailored dress, she wasn't a nurse. Rather she was there to visit another unfortunate soul. She was pretty and she was blond. He'd always preferred blonds. Their eyes met, but only for a second. The lady flinched and looked away.

Trying not to let her reaction bother him, Gabriel hobbled the remaining distance to his room, turned through the doorway and came face to face with himself in the glass on the wall. It wasn't a pretty sight. The left side of his face—from his eye to his ear—was covered in mottled, red and black scars. What little hair on the side of his head that hadn't burned off had been shaved. It was growing back, but it was uneven and patchy. His ear was nothing more than a red-creased lump stuck to the side of his head.

Gingerly, he sat on the bed. At least his clothing hid the rest of him. His entire left side, with the exception of his forearm and hand, was in much the same condition as his head. The scars rounded almost to his spine and continued down his hip, buttocks and thigh. Whatever he did tonight wouldn't involve going to the tavern, and certainly wouldn't involve a barmaid. He would spend the evening, or any portion of it he could stay awake, resting on furniture he hoped had been delivered, listening to Charlotte's chatter.

Fortunately for Charlotte, Susan wasn't as irresponsible as Alex. For all Susan's faults, Gabriel knew she hadn't neglected Charlotte too badly. She'd hired a nanny for Charlotte's daily care, and religiously, twice a week, she'd brought Charlotte to the hospital to see him. She and Charlotte would be there soon to take him home. He glanced at the clock on the wall and caught himself smiling.

The first time Susan had brought Charlotte to visit, he'd been in the hospital for a little more than a week and barely able to move. In those days, especially when the nurses came to change his dressings, bathe him and shift him around in the bed, he'd wished the fire had killed him. Death would have prevented him from having to endure the daily torture. There was no other way to describe it. He hurt everywhere, all the time, but when they moved him… *dear god*… it didn't bear remembering.

Susan had warned him she would bring Charlotte, and although he'd wanted to, he hadn't protested. He remembered hearing Susan's voice outside his door before they came through. She was saying to Charlotte, "You must be nice to your daddy. He doesn't feel well." Susan continued on, explaining about his bandages, preparing Charlotte for what she would see. Gabriel closed his eyes and silently willed them both to just go away.

He hadn't opened his eyes until they were standing next to his bed. When he saw the solemn, wide-eyed look on Charlotte's rosy-cheeked face, his throat suddenly clogged. She reached up and touched the back of his hand with her little fingertips. In his daydreams he could still feel the tickle of it.

"Hi Daddy," she said.

He turned his hand over and she put hers in it.

"Thank you for saving me," she said.

His fingers had closed around her warm, tiny ones.

Gabriel couldn't say he looked forward to her visits. Still, he didn't understand it, but somehow, for some reason, whenever she was there, he forgot his pain. Susan would pick her up and set her on his bed, and she would babble about her toys and other nonsensical things that didn't matter to him at all. But then, after she was gone, he found himself imagining her changing her baby doll's diaper—not that he had any idea how that was done—wrinkling her nose and forcing down peas she didn't like that Susan insisted she eat, arms flailing, jumping around, splashing in the creek with Alex.

During one of her visits he asked whether she liked living with Susan and Alex. She cocked her head to the side, and her little rosebud lips went flat. "It's okay," she said, "but I would rather be with you. I'll be happiest when you're well so you can bring me home."

It wasn't the answer he'd expected, so he didn't understand why his chest felt tight. He didn't understand why he felt... he didn't know exactly what he felt, but he thought, even though it made no sense, it was a bizarre kind of relief.

On another visit Charlotte brought him flowers. They were dandelions, most of which were wilted or crushed from being squeezed in her pudgy fists during the ride. She pressed them into his palm and grinned proudly. "They're yellow like sunshine. They'll make you feel better. I picked the puffy ones too. Susan showed me how to blow on them and make wishes. I wanted to bring one for you to make a wish, but I made all the wishes already."

"What did you wish for?" he asked.

Her brows drew downward, changing her expression into one that told him he was a complete idiot for posing such a question.

"I can't say out loud, 'cause my wishes won't come true!" she said. But then her eyes lit up. "Maybe if I whisper in your ear they will still come true, 'cause that's not out loud."

"Okay." He rolled his head on the pillow to give her easier access to the undamaged side of it.

She leaned over, tickling him as she clumsily pushed his hair out of the way, and then he felt her soft, sweet breath. "I wished for you to walk again."

After she was once again sitting on her rump, looking at him, he found himself swallowing, once, twice. When he was able to, he said, "That's only one. I thought you made lots of wishes."

She shook her head. "I only had one wish. Alex said if you can't walk, you won't be happy anymore. I made my one wish lots and lots of times so it will have to come true."

A week later she held his hand, or rather his thumb, while he somehow managed to drag himself down the hospital corridor.

His musings were interrupted when he heard the high pitch of her voice in the hallway. She and Susan were there. Within the hour he would be home again! His smile grew as he listened to the approaching, rhythmic click of Susan's heels and the light, sporadic tap of Charlotte's. Hand in hand they came through the door.

Gabriel's smile faded instantly.

Oh my god! No! No! No!

Quickly he turned his head, but it was too late. He didn't think… his bandages! Charlotte had never seen him without them!

Charlotte's eyes became huge saucers, her rosebud lips opened wide, her little cheeks balled up. Piercing sound reverberated off the white into Gabriel's skull. It was so damning and powerful he felt the vibration numbing his arms, his legs, his fingers, his toes.

Charlotte was… *screaming…*

Two

1888, Three years later

She was crazy—absolutely crazy—for taking this job! Lilly Hawthorne glanced at the man seated next to her driving the well-appointed buggy. He was friendly enough and had been rather amusing, in a shy, boyish sort of way when he'd interviewed her.

"We're almost there," he said, grinning. Then he clucked at the horses and turned through an elaborate iron-barred gate onto a densely tree-cloaked lane.

His name was Alex Drayton. His hair was dark, coiffed in the latest style, short in the back, longer in the front and hanging a little over his forehead. His eyes were icy blue, but held unusual warmth. His nose was straight and long, his mouth wide and firm, and smiling. His clothes were expensive and perfectly tailored to his slim build.

Two weeks ago, he'd come knocking. He'd told her she'd been recommended by the teacher at the local school and asked whether she would be interested in taking a position as a private, live-in tutor to a six-year-old girl. At first, the idea filled her with excitement. It was the only offer of employment she'd received since completing her studies at the teacher's college. Then he told her the child's name and where she would be expected to reside. She'd been struck dumb, unable to do anything but stare at the young, attractive man sitting across from her in the tiny sitting room of her sister's townhouse. Counting today, she'd met Alex Drayton three times. She liked him. But he wasn't the man she would be working for.

It was warm. The heat of summer lingered long into the late afternoon, yet Lilly shivered. The forest on either side of the drive seemed to close in on her, narrowing with each turn of the buggy wheel.

She really had no choice. Her sister, Julie, desperately needed the money. They both did.

For the last four months Lilly had been watching her sister's waistline increase, while the little bit of money her husband left in the bank before he disappeared, dwindled. Lilly didn't like her sister's husband, Jason Gibson. He was irresponsible, preferring a life of fun and games to the hard work necessary to support a wife and family. She hadn't been surprised upon learning he'd run off.

Both Lilly and their mother had tried to convince Julie not to marry Jason, but Julie wouldn't listen. After the wedding, Jason took Julie to Havertown, a small community not far from Philadelphia. Julie's new home was a good hundred miles from where they'd grown up. Sometimes Lilly wondered whether their mother's illness had been brought on by anxiety over Julie. Weeks after Julie's marriage, their mother got sick. A month later, she was dead.

If only Julie hadn't convinced Lilly they should sell their mother's home, where she and Julie could have returned to a more comfortable existence surrounded by familiar, unobtrusive neighbors. Then again, Lilly wouldn't have had to return from anywhere, because she wouldn't have had the money from the sale of the property to pay the tuition at the teacher's college.

She couldn't believe three years had gone by since her beloved mother had passed. And three years since that awful night when every one of her aspirations had suddenly and drastically changed. The terror of that night she'd buried long ago. Dwelling on the past only led to disappointment and heartache combined with a decent dose of shame. What she needed to do was concentrate on the future and her new position. Julie needed the money to pay off the numerous creditors Jason Gibson had left behind. And the landlord needed to be paid before that nasty man threw them both out onto the street.

Upon moving to Havertown, all of Lilly's initial efforts to find work had been in vain. She'd even made several desperate attempts to find employment *after* meeting with Alex Drayton, all to no avail. But she couldn't afford to allow the nervous knots twisting her stomach to impede her determination.

"You can see the house up ahead," Alex said. He lightly whipped the horses, urging them onward. The lane started to incline. Ahead of them, where the trees ended, a round light appeared. In it, Lilly could see the corner edge of a stone building, and her gaze remained fixed there. The moment full sunlight speared down upon them, she had to forcibly keep her mouth from gaping.

The structure in front of them wasn't a house at all. It was huge, constructed in large blocks of dark grey stone with four rounded spires separating it into three sections. The immense wooden door in the center section was framed by a pillared, stone porch. The few windows she could see were long and thin and deeply set. Julie had told her the place was large enough for twenty families. When she asked how Julie knew, Julie shrugged and said, "I've never been there myself, but that's what *they* say."

They were the residents of Havertown and *they* had a lot to say about Lilly's new employer. About the house *they* were right. It was every bit the medieval castle she'd read about in books, replete with its own dungeon. The only thing missing was a moat. She'd been hoping *they* were wrong. She'd been telling herself everything she'd heard about *him* was grossly exaggerated. And what she'd witnessed on her own hadn't really happened.

"Welcome to Drayton Hall!" Alex grinned.

He helped her down from the buggy and handed her a key, which he explained worked the front door. While she stood there, looking up at the monstrous building, every hope she'd had seemed doomed. Even the key was a heavy iron thing, weighty enough that if she were to drop it, it would surely break her toe.

"I'll take your trunk up to your room and show you around some, but I've got to get going." Alex had previously told her that he and his family—his wife and son—lived a few miles down the road, closer to Philadelphia. Clutching her carpet bag tightly in one fist, and the key to the front door in the other, she moved closer to the stone steps. Alex appeared beside her, stiffly, under the weight of her trunk.

"Would you mind?" he said, glancing toward the door.

"Of course." Lilly spurted up the nine steps to the deep flat porch. She touched the door latch, a thick bar of iron, and hesitated. What if *he* was waiting just inside?

Alex was right behind her. "Turn the key to the right, around twice. And push hard."

The heavy door creaked on its hinges, inch by painful inch. A swath of cold air rushed out to greet her. Lilly crossed the threshold and sidestepped so Alex could pass. The room she stood in was so large her sister's entire townhouse could have fit inside. Not a soul was in sight.

A twinkling shimmer caused her to look up. In the center of the ceiling was a giant chandelier. She guessed it had more than a thousand crystals hanging from it. She'd never seen anything so glamorous. Next her eyes were drawn to a deeply set balcony supported by four marble pillars. From there, twin polished slate staircases curved, like a horseshoe to the lower floor. To her left were two sets of closed double doors. Identical doors were on the wall to the right. Ahead of her, in the darkened recesses below the stairs, past the pillars, was another set. There wasn't one piece of furniture in the entire space. It was magnificently austere. It chanted wealth, arrogance, and a coldness that had nothing to do with the temperature. It was the most horrible place Lilly had ever seen.

She didn't realize until Alex chuckled that this time she hadn't been successful in keeping her mouth from hanging open.

"Don't worry, you'll get used to it," he said. "Come on. I'll show you where your room is."

She preceded him up the stairs to the right. At the top, centered in the long aisle of the balcony, were more double doors. On the far left end was another set. With a quick turn of his head, Alex gestured to the right, and the only set of open doors. "The north and west wings are not used. Your room is in the east wing."

The carpet running the length of the wide corridor looked like it had been dyed with blood. The walls, unlike the lower level, were intricately carved dark walnut boards. Along each were a half dozen closed doors with lamps evenly placed between them. Again, there wasn't one piece of furniture in the entire space.

"Second door on the left," Alex said.

When Lilly pushed the door open, it felt like she'd stepped into a garden. For having so few windows, it was surprisingly bright and colorful. And she discovered her *room* wasn't just a room. It was an entire suite. Alex told her to look around. There was a sitting room, a library, a bedroom with a bed larger than any she'd ever seen, and a dressing and bathing area. Most of the décor was bright yellow and white with sporadic splashes of royal blue. It was simply lovely!

Alex deposited her trunk in the bedroom and joined her in the sitting room. "What do you think? If you don't like it, there's another room at the end of the hall, also fully furnished."

Lilly set her carpet bag down, and carefully controlling her expression to prevent herself from appearing unworldly, said, "This will be fine."

Alex's brows drew together in concentration. "There are some things I'm supposed to tell you. Let's see. Oh, yes, you're expected for dinner at seven tonight. Breakfast is at eight every morning. Don't let me forget to show you where the dining room is. Oh, and..." He gestured for her to follow him back out into the hallway where he pointed to the door they'd passed to get to hers. "That's the nursery." He caught himself and grinned. "Not the nursery. Charlotte says she's too grown up for a nursery now. It's the *playroom*. Her bedroom is through there as well."

He pointed to the first door, closest to the stairs directly opposite Charlotte's room, and said, "My cousin's chambers are there, across the hall."

Lilly's breath caught.

Then he went on, "Hmm... what else is there? Well, whatever it is can't be that important." With a shrug, he started away, but stopped short and turned around. "I remember now. I'm supposed to tell you my cousin employs three servants. Mrs. Finch is the housekeeper. She also does the cooking. Mr. Finch is the gardener and he helps Mrs. Finch with certain household tasks, like stocking firewood and hauling water. And there's Withers, the groom. They all live on the estate, but not here in the house. There are some cottages in the north field.

Considering the size of this place, there probably should be more servants, but my cousin won't hire anyone else. Go ahead and unpack, settle in. You'll want to change for dinner."

All the dresses in Lilly's trunk—the remaining five she owned—were in poorer condition than the one she now wore. Thankfully Alex didn't seem to notice the heat in her face.

"That's right!" he exclaimed. "I almost forgot to show you where the dining room is."

Lilly followed him to the balcony where he pointed down over the railing.

"It's that door there, the one on the left."

"Will you be staying for dinner?" As soon as the words left her mouth, Lilly wanted to take them back. He'd already said he had to leave. It was just she didn't want to be alone with… with…

"Goodness, no!" Alex quipped. "My wife hates this house. She says it gives her the willies. We come here for dinner every Friday, but that's it."

Lilly couldn't help her sudden shiver.

Alex chuckled. "You'll get used to it. I don't even notice anymore."

This was the second time he'd made that comment. She wasn't sure what he meant by it.

"Seven o'clock. Whatever you do, don't be late. My cousin is a stickler for punctuality."

They said *he* used Alex like a whipping boy. She guessed she must have looked stricken, because Alex laughed again. "My wife will probably tell you differently, but Gabriel's not *that* bad. I gotta go."

"Thank you for everything," she said.

"You're welcome. See you Friday." He offered a playful salute and ran down the stairs. By the time he reached the front door he was whistling.

Everything Lilly had heard about her new employer raced through her mind. Supposedly he'd inherited his money from his parents, both of whom were deceased. His ancestors on his father's side—his great-grandfather's family—changed their name and fled their duchy at the onset of the French Revolution. Gabriel Drayton held the title of *Duke*. The castle easily gave credence to that story. But this was just the beginning.

Recluse was the term used most often to describe him. It was also the kindest. They said he was mean, rude, cruel, heartless, an ogre of a man. On the few occasions he came to town, whoever had the misfortune of having to meet with him was left scalded, crushed and terrified.

At first, thinking no one could possibly be as bad as the man *they* described, Lilly had felt a little sorry for him. That is, she'd felt sorry for him until about a month after she'd moved in with Julie. It was one day she would not forget.

She'd been coming from the grocery with a basket of produce in arm. Right away she noticed the finely designed, black carriage parked up the block in front of the bank. Several people were gathered on the sidewalk, forming a small crowd. Hushed murmurs and comments were coming from them, but Lilly couldn't hear what they were saying until she drew closer.

"Poor kid accidentally bumped into him," a man charged. "That monster clubbed him, grabbed him by the throat and threw him into the carriage! I saw the whole thing!"

"Why doesn't someone do something? Get the police!" another murmured. "He'll kill that child!"

A middle-aged woman dressed in little better than rags pushed through, pounded on the carriage door and shouted, "Let him alone! Let him out! How dare you! You fiend! He's done nothing to you!"

The carriage door opened abruptly, catching the woman unexpectedly, causing her to stagger back. Had a gentleman not grabbed her she would have fallen. At the same moment, a teenage boy, whose attire was no better than the woman's, tumbled down the three steep carriage steps. He tripped off the last one, as if he'd been pushed from inside, and landed on his hands and knees in the muddy gutter. Gasps of horror and dismay tore through the crowd. Before the boy could rise, the carriage started to pull away.

Lilly had looked up at the uniformed driver, but his face was hidden well by a turned-up collar and a top hat pulled low. Her attention went again to the boy getting to his feet. His skittish eyes frantically scoured the sidewalk. The woman, who Lilly guessed was his mother, rushed to him but he jerked away. Without a word he took off, darting through curious, horrified onlookers, as fast as he could go.

Lilly knew she would never forget the expression on the youth's face—utter desperation cloaked in pure terror. The dirt stains on his cheeks were cut by trails of fresh tears.

A man with a raised fist sprinted after the carriage, shouting, "Come back here! You'll pay for what you did to that boy!"

Others joined in, yelling again for the police. Still others commented in hushed whispers. More words flew—words Lilly would have preferred not to have heard at all—and one man bellowed, "Deformed freak!"

Later, when she relayed the events to Julie and asked why the man would have said such a thing, Julie told her, "They say he's severely disfigured. Birth defects, I believe. He's a bent, twisted creature, so hideous he's not fit to be caged at a carnival! He may be wealthy, but he's uncivilized and dangerous!"

Lilly had been to town many times since then, but that was the only time she'd seen his carriage. She never openly asked either, yet she heard a lot about him. He was quite the topic of community gossip. Nothing she heard cast him in a good light. If anything, the comments grew more troubling. A shopkeeper told her he abducted boys and kept them chained in the dungeon beneath Drayton Hall to abuse and torture!

Lilly had also heard tales of abuse suffered by his daughter, a child who wasn't even his. They said he'd kidnapped her years ago, molested her nightly—after all creatures like him had sick, disgusting appetites for such things—and kept the poor little girl prisoner in his home.

The one thing about the gossip Lilly found odd was that very few admitted to actually having seen him. One woman who did described him as hairy, extremely large and ape-like.

Regardless of the numerous accusations of wrong-doing, there was not enough evidence for the police to arrest him, and although many tried, nothing could be done for the pitiable little girl. No matter what the story, regardless of the circumstances, the consensus was the same. *He* was an inhuman monster and a menace to society.

Lilly stared across the blood-soaked corridor toward that ominous door—his chambers—and then she turned, entered hers and locked herself in.

The man was an immoral, wicked fiend. He was her new employer.

His name was Gabriel Drayton.

Three

The seven o'clock dinner hour was fast approaching. Lilly hadn't changed her dress, but she had unpacked her trunk. For the last half hour she'd been sitting in her new bedroom in front of the vanity mirror, wondering why she'd been so stupid. Taking this position was most assuredly the worst mistake of her life. She should have held out for another. She'd put out enough applications in town. She and Julie could get by for another month or so if they were careful, and if Jason's creditors didn't keep hounding them. She could beg the landlord for another month's leeway, surely.

She'd twisted and styled her long blond tresses as eloquently as she knew how. She wasn't pretty, not by the standards of the day anyway, but she'd been told many times she was. She didn't want to be pretty, not here—especially not here. Her cheekbones were high and her lips full. Her skin was clear and pale. Deep blue eyes stared back at her, reminding her once more that she wasn't nearly sophisticated enough, let alone brave enough. She shoved her round, wire glasses onto the bridge of her nose. There was nothing wrong with her vision. The glasses were merely a crutch to hide behind, and they helped her look the part she was there to play.

She wanted very badly to run away, down the drive, through the forest, all the way back to the haven of her sister's townhouse. She didn't want to look upon the warped, grotesque form of Gabriel Drayton. She didn't want to talk to him. She didn't want to have anything to do with someone who repeatedly committed violent criminal acts, but who, due to precarious, extenuating circumstances, or failure of the justice system overall, had never been prosecuted as he deserved.

Yet she couldn't help thinking again of the little girl, Charlotte. Lilly's own childhood had left much to be desired. Her father had died when she and Julie were very young. Their mother had raised them as well as she could by taking in washing and sewing, but they always struggled financially and never had much. Regardless of these difficulties, her mother was a gentle soul, supportive and kind to her daughters. One thing Lilly had never lacked as a girl was love.

How awful for any child to have *him* for a father, if he even was her father. All the money in the world could never make up for what poor Charlotte was subjected to daily. Alex told her Charlotte tended to be shy at first. Lilly guessed Charlotte's timidity wasn't her natural demeanor. Rather it was caused by her predicament. Charlotte was starved for affection of any kind.

Putting her own monetary troubles aside, Lilly wanted to help Charlotte. Her fear of *him* needed to be secondary. As a Christian it was her duty to aid the oppressed and show love where none existed. She would not only teach Charlotte to read and write, but give her the warmth and comfort of human companionship—something the child had never known. Softly Lilly repeated the Bible verse that had helped her through difficulties in the past. It gave her courage then and it would do so now: *"I can do all things through Christ who strengthens me."*

At precisely six fifty, she rose from the vanity stool, wishing as she did that she wasn't so petite. Five feet three inches wasn't much to stand up to a man who could, with one hand, haul a teenage boy up and into such a high carriage. Apprehension made her stomach quiver. And then she raised her chin a notch.

As she stepped into the dark, crimson corridor, it suddenly dawned on her that in the last two hours she hadn't heard a voice, a footstep or even the creak of a door. Quietly she passed *his* room and continued on until the carpet ended. The loud clack of her heels on the slate floor echoed.

Taking her time she started down the staircase, treading as lightly as she could. She was about halfway when the front door was flung wide. It startled her so badly she had to clutch the railing to keep from tripping. A round, balding man carrying a long, thin torch barreled in. The door slammed closed behind him with a loud thunk.

"Oh, excuse me, miss," he said, bowing stiffly. "I completely lost track of time!" And then he ran about lighting the wall lamps throughout the hall.

Lilly didn't move until he started up the staircase.

"Beg pardon, miss." He bustled around her. "Ya must be Miss Hawthorne. Welcome ta Drayton Hall. I'm Finch. Excuse me, but 'tis important for me ta git this done. I'm late. Late again!"

"I understand," she said. Her eyes followed him as he scurried up the remaining stairs and disappeared into the red corridor. Only then did Lilly continue on to the dining room. Tentatively she touched one of the heavy iron latches and pushed.

The room, like the entrance hall, was dark and dreary. With the exception of a dining table large enough to seat thirty or more, it was void of furnishings. Three place settings had already been set at the head of the table nearest the entrance. Not quite sure what she should do, she traversed the room to one of four narrow windows, where she could see the forest and the long drive.

The sound of someone running down the stairs jerked her around. A second later Mr. Finch skittered in. With a nod to her, he proceeded to light the lamps. At first Lilly was glad for the lighting. She thought it would provide warmth to the otherwise frigid atmosphere. But then, one by one, shadows began to emerge.

"Me wife will be bringin' out the courses in a jiffy. Mista Drayton and Miss Charlotte will be here soon," Mr. Finch said. He bowed and scurried out.

As promised, Mrs. Finch appeared shortly, arms laden with dishes, which she set between the three place settings. She seemed of an age with her husband and just as round, although she wasn't nearly as fidgety. Her hair was white and piled on top of her head in a thick roll. She introduced herself nervously. Before departing, she added, "Mista Drayton will join ya shortly."

Lilly chose the chair that provided a clear view of the dining room entrance. On top of everything else, because *he* was a duke—she'd never met a duke before—Julie had warned her she'd better address him as *Lord* Drayton. She'd heard a few people in town refer to him that way, albeit in a derisive, derogatory way. She'd practiced a few times, but felt foolish saying it. She was certain she would somehow flub it, and the repercussions would be… she didn't want to think about what the repercussions would be. It was relieving to have heard both Mr. and Mrs. Finch refer to *him* simply as *Mister* Drayton.

The fare Mrs. Finch brought looked as good as it smelled and reminded her she'd had nothing to eat since breakfast. As much as she dreaded the upcoming encounter, her hunger made her wish Mr. Drayton and Charlotte would arrive. Better to get the inevitable over with.

She'd been sitting there, restlessly wringing her hands for more than ten minutes—so much for punctuality—when she heard the distant creak of a door hinge. She couldn't see from where she sat, but she could hear clearly.

…CLACK, click, TAP, click, SCCCRRRAAAPE, click…

The slow, uneven sounds grew louder as they crossed the slate floor. She was able to discern that the light clicks interspersed between the heavier treads were the footsteps of a child.

…SCCCCRRAAA… click… AAAPE, click…

Lilly jumped when a deep voice growled, "Go, Charlotte!"

Whatever, if anything, Charlotte said in reply Lilly couldn't hear. They were moving closer. Lilly rose and scuttled around until she was standing behind the chair. Her heart was in her throat.

"I said go!" the voice grated. "You act like she's going to bite you!"

Lilly grabbed the back of the chair. This time she heard Charlotte's reply very clearly, "Please don't make me!"

"Go!" he barked.

"Pleeease! Daddyyy!" Click, click.

Lilly took a step backwards.

…CLACK, TAP, SCCCRRRAAAPE… TAP, tap, tap, TAP…

They were just outside the door.

"Damn it, Charlotte!"

Lilly was sure a raised, twisted claw was inches away from clocking the little girl. Movement in the shadows made her freeze. She took another hasty step backwards and had to cover her mouth to withhold a scream.

In the darkened opening, outlined by the flickering lamplight, was an apparition, something she could have conjured up after listening to Julie's childhood ghost stories. *He* was huge, an imposing wall of slowly moving black.

TAP! Her eyes darted to the floor. The tip of a polished black cane appeared beside a foot clad in a soled, black leather shoe. It was a casual shoe, the kind one might slip into in the evening.

SCRRRAAPE.

His left foot, in a matching shoe, dragged from behind him until it stopped even with the right one.

Inch by inch her eyes traveled up two black-covered legs to an uncovered hand—*a normal looking hand?*—hanging limply, then across to the right one which was clasped firmly around the rounded end of the cane. Up the tall, black silhouette from there, her perusal met with a narrow black leather belt. Tucked in was a black silk shirt. He wasn't wearing a vest or coat. The tiny black buttons on the shirt glittered in the lamplight. She followed the line of them upward... *diagonally.* His torso was bent, the left shoulder sloped crookedly down from the higher right side. A thin, black silk scarf was wrapped around his neck and tied, like an eighteenth-century cravat, with the ends neatly tucked into his collar.

He had been looking at her. She was sure of it, but when she dared to glimpse his face, he wasn't looking at her. His head was to the side and angled downward toward something outside the entrance. All Lilly saw of him was more silk-swathed black.

He turned. Lilly's fingers curled in until her fingernails bit into her skin. He had a face, but not a whole face!

The top of his head was hidden underneath more black—a kerchief of some sort. Between the kerchief and the scarf around his neck was a silk cloth, rising to cover the entire left side from his jaw, upward along his nose and across his forehead. A small hole cut into the cloth allowed him to see with his left eye. Long black hair draped out from under the kerchief to veil his distorted right shoulder.

The dim light didn't hide the faint shadow of whiskers along his right jaw line, the hollow beneath a pronounced cheekbone, the dark pink of a grimly set mouth, which stood out starkly in contrast to his eerily pale skin. He had a firm, straight nose and deeply set grey eyes that were narrowed in a scowl so harsh it caused creases to form between his brows.

In the same gravelly, clipped tone he'd used on Charlotte, he said, "Welcome to Drayton Hall. I am Gabriel Drayton. Charlotte will join you for dinner." His words were civil enough, but the bite in them told her he didn't mean them politely.

Bit by bit, the terror-laden little girl appeared from behind him. To avoid looking at *him*, Lilly concentrated on the child. Her first impression was that Charlotte was beautiful. Her eyes were a deep brown, opened wide, and her top lip was turned in, bitten nervously between her teeth. Two thin strands of hair, the same dark color as his, had been pulled from her temples into a pink ribbon at the top of her head. She wore a pink dress, fringed with lace. White stockings covered her legs from her calves downward to black, patent leather shoes. The expensive clothes were well made and fit her perfectly.

"Excuse me," Gabriel Drayton snapped.

He moved, shifting his weight on the cane, making his body appear even more hunched. Even so, somehow in that moment, Lilly's trepidation, although still present, was suddenly and oddly stirred. He wasn't big at all. Tall, yes, but not big. If anything, he was actually quite slender. He was also younger than she'd thought he would be. Briefly, she caught his eye and was surprised when his diverted first. But, the hasty look-away wasn't shyness, she realized belatedly. His attention had been drawn by Charlotte.

"*Noooo*, Daddy! Don't go!" the child was staring up at him beseechingly.

"Charlotte!"

Bristling from the harsh tone he used on the little girl, Lilly regarded him again. It wasn't quite as daunting with his focus elsewhere. He was still looking at Charlotte. He didn't say another word.

Slowly, reluctantly, Charlotte turned around.

Lilly took a deep breath and forced a smile for Charlotte's sake. "I promise I won't bite," she said as gently as she could.

...TAP, SCCCRRRAAAPE...

Lilly's focus flew to the doorway, but it was empty.

The dark phantom was gone.

Four

"It's okay," Charlotte said as she moved closer and closer to that ominous door. "He doesn't mind. You only have to knock in the middle of the night and in the morning."

It was Thursday, Lilly's third full day at Drayton Hall, and finally Charlotte was offering information without first being prompted. It was the breakthrough Lilly had been hoping for, and an answer to prayer that Charlotte would eventually open up to her. But, going where Charlotte was leading was the last place she wanted to go.

Instead of beginning the tutoring right away, Lilly had told Charlotte she needed the child's help to keep from getting lost at Drayton Hall. She'd used the ploy as much to satisfy her own curiosity as to break the ice with Charlotte. What she hadn't anticipated was that touring the immense property would take so long. After three days they still hadn't finished. The unused north and west wings had yet to be explored. According to Charlotte, the ballroom was in the north wing. That was one room Lilly would have loved to see, even if it was as eerie and dismal as the rest of the mansion.

Lilly looked down at the bizarre concoction of Charlotte's clothes—a sky blue dress fringed with white lace, bright green tights, complemented by an orange barrette stuck crookedly on one side of her head. If her hair had been brushed it wasn't evident. Today Charlotte's shoes were red. Every morning the little girl appeared in something more outlandish than what she'd worn the day before. It wasn't from lack of a wardrobe. Charlotte's enormous closet was filled to overflowing with beautiful, expensive clothes. The problem was Charlotte had no one to help her dress.

By questioning Charlotte, Lilly had learned of the strictly regimented lifestyle at Drayton Hall. After breakfast they were supposed to have school until luncheon at one. After luncheon they would study until Charlotte's riding lesson with Mr. Withers at three. Charlotte's bath came next—another thing Charlotte had no one to help her with other than Mr. Finch pre-filling the tub and Mrs. Finch depositing towels. After bathing, Charlotte had *playtime* until dinner at seven. Following dinner she joined her father in the parlor until bedtime at nine o'clock.

Everything else Lilly figured out about the stringent household schedule—more specifically *his* bedtime routine—she'd gleaned by listening to footsteps.

"I don't think this is such a good idea." She attempted to stop Charlotte one more time from going into her father's chambers. Charlotte's little hand was on the knob. "I don't want to disturb him."

"He's not in there," Charlotte said bemusedly, and then she pushed the door inward.

The first thing Lilly noticed was darkness. Unlike hers and Charlotte's rooms, his was decorated in the same cold, bleak manner as the rest of the house. Stained walnut covered the one wall she could see. Dreary charcoal curtains hid what looked like the only window.

Charlotte walked over and drew the drapes, hooking them behind iron clips. Sunlight spilled in to reveal the rest of the space. What struck Lilly immediately was the size. Compared to hers and Charlotte's chambers it was quite small. A bulky, four-poster bed dominated the room. Flanking it were end tables. The fireplace, like all the fireplaces in the mansion, was in the corner. In front of it were two ugly brown leather wing chairs and a small coffee table.

Lilly took a step forward and something on the bed caught her eye. It wasn't empty. But, what was in it was the last thing she expected, and completely out of character, both for the room and the man. There were two dolls tucked under the blankets.

Charlotte had an extensive collection of dolls. This much Lilly had discovered the first day. The child's chambers were similar to Lilly's, except Charlotte's were decorated in shades of pink and silver, and filled with more toys and children's books than Lilly had ever collectively seen. She'd asked Charlotte if her dolls had names. Charlotte had introduced each and every one of them.

Before Lilly could ask about the dolls in her father's bed, Charlotte said, "This is the closet."

Lilly followed and peered in. The closet was almost as big as the bedroom itself. To the left were his clothes, neatly arranged and hanging almost the entire length of the wall. He had a lot of clothes, but not nearly as many as Charlotte did. Except for what looked like a handful of white shirts and maybe half a dozen brown trousers, the rest were charcoal grey or black. Several pairs of well-polished shoes and boots lined the floor, all of them black leather. There were also three pairs of loafers like the ones he'd been wearing that first evening. Two identical, simply-made chests-of-drawers were side by side on the wall opposite the door. Next to them was an enormous porcelain tub. To her right was a washstand, neatly laden with a handful of men's toiletries. Beside it was a toilet cabinet.

"Who's in your daddy's bed?" Lilly followed Charlotte back to the bedroom.

"Penelope and Henrietta." Charlotte scurried across the room and half jumped, half crawled onto the high bed. It was a move made with ease, giving Lilly the impression she did it frequently. Charlotte proceeded to pull the blanket back and pick up one of the dolls. "They sleep with Daddy 'cause he's scared of the dark, 'cept I have to tuck them in for him because he doesn't do it right."

Had Charlotte been talking about anyone else, Lilly might have laughed. "Are you scared of the dark?" she asked.

"Not all the time. Only sometimes. I have Henry to keep me safe." Henry was a fluffy, owl-shaped doll Charlotte slept with. "Are you scared of the dark?" she asked.

Lilly wasn't quite sure how to answer. She'd never considered herself scared of the dark, but here in the mansion she was. Every rattle was deafening. Every thud caused her eyelids to pop open. Every creak made her shiver.

The first night had been the worst. After Charlotte excused herself from dinner, she ran across the hall and slipped through a door—later

Lilly had learned it went to the front parlor. That evening, Charlotte closed the door behind her and Lilly couldn't decide whether she should feel unwelcomed or relieved. She went to her room and picked a book from the shelves in her library.

The clock on the mantel said eight thirty when she heard Charlotte come up the stairs. Not long thereafter Charlotte went back down. A half hour later, Charlotte returned to her room.

After that the mansion became eerily silent. With a huff of internal censure Lilly had to tell herself to stop acting like a ninny and change into her nightgown. She set the book she'd absorbed absolutely nothing from aside. She'd just finished unlacing her corset when she heard the distant, but distinct tap of that cane. It was eleven o'clock. The remainder of her changing consisted of a harried, hands-shaking attempt to get out of the rest of her underwear, into her nightgown, and hidden under the thick down comforter on her bed. *He* was nearing the top of the stairs when she buried her entire head.

His sluggish, heavy movements were muffled on the crimson carpet, but she was certain he was moving past his own room, across that corridor, right to hers! Her door was locked, but being that this was his mansion, undoubtedly he had the key!

The breath she held didn't come out of her until she heard a door close. But then, just when her heart finally began to beat normally again, hinges creaked. There was no doubt, this time, he was coming for her! For a second she contemplated hiding in her closet, but then decided it would be better to pretend to be fast asleep.

It took a moment for her to realize the door she heard next was not hers. Moments later his awkward treads crossed the carpet. It wasn't long before he went back to his room. His creaky door didn't open again.

This she'd known because the rest of the night she laid awake listening. The second night had yielded much the same. Her third night, she'd slept, but only due to sheer exhaustion.

He did exactly the same thing every night, leaving his room and going to another, but the dulled noise on the carpet made it impossible for her to discern which room he went to.

Charlotte was staring at her expectantly. "I guess I'm scared of the dark sometimes," Lilly admitted.

Charlotte nodded as if she completely understood. "I will bring you Henry. If you have bad dreams he will sing to you and you won't be scared anymore."

Touched by Charlotte's offer, Lilly asked, "I would appreciate that. But what if you get scared and Henry isn't with you?"

"I won't get scared," Charlotte said. Fastidiously she tucked Penelope back under her father's sheet.

Charlotte's solemn expression broke Lilly's heart. Charlotte was entirely too serious and independent for a six year old. What if she did have nightmares? She should have someone to go to. Someone who didn't yell at her every time he spoke to her, like her father did!

Thankfully Lilly hadn't seen the man at all. He hadn't come to one meal or made an effort to speak with her. But she heard his voice every morning.

The morning after her first sleepless night, she'd been dressed before dawn and waiting in the sitting area of her chambers for some sound—any sound—that would be a sign it was safe for her to venture forth. More than an hour passed before she heard Charlotte skitter across the hallway.

Charlotte's little fist thumped on the wood. "Daddy, time to wake up!"

"Wait!"

Lilly heard his gruff response all the way across the hall and through her closed door.

A moment later, Charlotte said, "Daddy, wake up!"

"I said wait!" he yelled. It was followed by, "Fine! Come!"

All grew silent after Charlotte went into his room. Lilly listened intently for his door to open again, but she heard nothing. It took a long internal discourse, and a glance at the clock noting the designated breakfast hour was almost upon them, to convince herself to go out.

Charlotte had appeared in the dining room shortly after Lilly. Upon seeing Charlotte's outlandish outfit, she'd barely been able to contain her nervous laughter. The second and third mornings had been much the same.

Once again Charlotte interrupted her scattered woolgathering.

"Would you like a piece of chocolate?" Charlotte asked.

Lilly smiled. "Yes, I would like that very much. I love chocolate."

"I only have two pieces left. One for you and one for me."

The last of Charlotte's words were muttered absently. Something had diverted her—something under her father's monstrous bed. Charlotte got down on her stomach and reached far underneath it.

"What are you looking for?" Lilly asked.

Charlotte squirmed her way around and stood up. In her hand she held a long, thin wooden stick. The top end was carved into the shape of a five-point star and had been painted shimmering silver and gold. "I forgot I left this in here. I know magic."

"You do?" Lilly feigned awe.

"My daddy taught me," she said.

Lilly had no response to that. She followed Charlotte back to her playroom and into her bedroom. There, from the middle dresser drawer, Charlotte produced a small red box and opened it. Inside were two morsels of chocolate.

Lilly took the one Charlotte handed her and copied the little girl in popping it into her mouth. It was delectable!

"You have pretty hair," Charlotte said next.

"I think your hair is much prettier than mine," Lilly returned. Charlotte's hair was more disheveled than it had been the day before, and the day before that. Tangled strands fell from the hastily clipped, crooked barrette, offering further proof of her unacceptable lack of care.

"Can you make my hair loopy like yours?" Charlotte asked.

"I'll tell you what," Lilly suggested. "When you're done with your riding lesson, after your bath tonight, I'll brush your hair and fix it just like mine."

Charlotte smiled. It wasn't much of a smile, but it was the only smile Lilly had seen in three days. She was so thrilled, her throat grew tight.

"I have to go now. Withers is waiting for me," Charlotte said and started away.

Impulsively Lilly called out, "Would you mind if I walk with you to the stable for your riding lesson today?"

Charlotte's smile grew. The child was simply beautiful when she smiled.

"Okay," she said. And then she murmured, "You're nice."

It sounded to Lilly like this was the last thing Charlotte had expected. It was all Lilly could do to keep from wrapping the little girl in a warm hug. As they descended the staircase, Charlotte slid her small hand into hers.

Lilly had to swallow before she could find her voice. "Thank you for sharing your chocolate with me. I'll bet you didn't know, of all the treats in the whole world, chocolate is my most favorite."

"Mine, too!" Charlotte chirped.

Mr. Withers, Charlotte's riding instructor and the groom for the estate, was a wiry young man, about Lilly's age with thin blond hair and a wide, friendly smile. Charlotte clearly adored him and the feeling was apparently mutual. In observing their interaction, Lilly drew some relief. At least one person in this awful place provided Charlotte with proper attention.

Mr. Withers lifted her up onto her pony and made sure she was properly secured before leading the little horse around the circular track. Charlotte was beaming happily as she bounced along.

If it weren't for the chill in the air, Lilly would have stayed to watch. Intending to retrieve a wrap, she started back toward the vile mansion. From the rise of a hill she could see the roofs of the six cottages Charlotte had pointed out to her on their outside tour the day before. According to Charlotte, Mr. and Mrs. Finch lived in one of them and Mr. Withers in another. The rest were empty. Lilly could also see the overgrown gardens surrounding the far end of the unused west wing of the mansion. Deeply set within them was another building of some sort. During their tour, Charlotte had passed it by as if it didn't exist. Lilly had wanted to ask about it, but she hadn't.

She entered the mansion through the kitchen, where Mrs. Finch was busily preparing the evening meal. In as friendly a tone as she could, Lilly said hello and asked if there was anything she could do to help.

"Oh no, no thank you, miss," Mrs. Finch murmured.

Mr. and Mrs. Finch weren't nearly as open and amiable as Withers, but Lilly didn't dislike them. Rather than assuming inevitable castigation on his behalf, it was beginning to amuse her how Mr. Finch ran around lighting lamps every night, claiming to be perpetually late. He certainly did an excellent job of ensuring she had plenty of wood stocked by her fireplace to keep her rooms cozy and warm. And he'd brought fresh bath water for her every day without fail.

Lilly would have made an effort to carry on a conversation with Mrs. Finch, but she had tried before with little success. Mrs. Finch barely responded when Lilly complimented her cooking. Intuitively she guessed Mrs. Finch wasn't intentionally rude. She was merely shy. The only thing Lilly had been able to learn in her attempts to speak with Mrs. Finch was that she only prepared meals Monday through Saturday. Sundays were her day off.

Sundays were supposed to be Lilly's day off, too. At least, that's what Alex Drayton had told her when he hired her. For the upcoming weekend, she decided she would leave after Saturday dinner, as soon as Charlotte disappeared into the front parlor.

She would spend the night with Julie and not return to Drayton Hall until Sunday evening. Ensuring Julie was okay was of utmost importance. Her sister would be giving birth around the holidays, little more than three months away. Threats from Jason Gibson's creditors were causing Julie a great deal of stress, and this wasn't good for Julie or the baby. Alex had told Lilly she would receive her wages each week on Saturday morning. Most of what she earned Lilly intended to hand over to Julie.

More than anything, however, Lilly couldn't wait to just get away, even if it was only for one short day. She couldn't wait to put dreary, frightening Drayton Hall behind her. She couldn't wait to be in an atmosphere where she wasn't apprehensive every single second. She couldn't wait to be out from under the invisible sinister force that seemed to scrutinize her every move.

As she made her way along the lower east hallway—a very long hallway—toward the main part of the mansion, her thoughts drifted to the lesson plans she'd made for Charlotte but had yet to use, and guilt settled in. She wasn't doing what she was being paid to do. At least, however, she'd read to Charlotte a few times. Charlotte certainly seemed to enjoy the children's book she'd picked from the shelf in her library. She'd enjoyed it so much, when Lilly asked her to pick a book the next day she'd picked the same one. Lilly had read that same book to her again this morning.

The only other thing she'd done with Charlotte that was remotely related to schooling was the little ditty she'd tried to teach her called the *Addition Song*. Charlotte had listened attentively, but no matter how much Lilly coaxed, the little girl wouldn't sing along.

Absently humming to herself, "One plus one is two, two plus two is four, three plus three is six…" Lilly rounded the corner in the east hallway and stopped cold.

"Get out!" It was Gabriel Drayton, standing half in, half out of a doorway.

Lilly was fairly certain that door went to his study. From the angle she had a clear view of the long fingers of his left hand curled around the doorframe, his right hand firmly holding onto his cane, his warped, black-cloaked form and his silk-swathed head. The only part of his face she could see was the tip of his nose.

Alex was there as well. He'd already taken a few steps out into the hallway. Sounding annoyed, he said, "It was just a suggestion. You don't have to get in such a bother about it."

"Get out!" Gabriel repeated in his gravelly, wicked tone.

"For goodness' sake, Gabriel, it was just an idea." Alex turned around, saw Lilly and nodded politely to her. "Oh, hello Miss Hawthorne, nice to see you."

Gabriel Drayton spun. His cold eyes narrowed on her, but he didn't say anything. With a swift scrape of his left foot, he shoved himself backwards. The door slammed shut.

"Sorry about that," Alex said. "No matter what I say to him these days, I make him mad." He shrugged and grinned. "But enough of that. How are things with Charlotte?"

"Okay." It was all Lilly could think to say. Her eyes flitted back and forth between the study door and Alex.

Alex excused himself, saying he needed to get going. Decidedly spooked, Lilly waited until he was gone, then raced through the hall, moving past that door as fast as she could. She didn't slow down until she was locked in her room, and she didn't come out again until the dinner hour.

While descending the staircase, repeatedly she told herself she had no reason to fear Gabriel Drayton. He was upset with his cousin, Alex, not with her. He had yet to speak with her. Except for today, she hadn't even seen him. If things continued in this manner, she could be Charlotte's tutor without ever having to deal with him at all. As she much preferred.

Charlotte appeared in the dining room in another outrageous collaboration of colors. Lilly took one look at the little girl's still-damp hair, and realized her mistake. She'd completely forgotten her promise. "I'm so sorry, Charlotte," she said quietly. "We were supposed to fix your hair after your bath."

"It's okay," Charlotte shrugged.

"How 'bout I fix it for you after dinner?" Lilly asked.

"Okay," Charlotte said and she smiled.

Their conversation during the meal was, for the first time, more than Charlotte simply answering Lilly's questions. And, for the first time Lilly heard Charlotte laugh. It was the funniest rapid staccato giggle, and it provoked her own. By the end of the meal, although she wouldn't sing, Charlotte was at least humming along to the number song.

They went back to Charlotte's room afterwards so Lilly could braid and style Charlotte's hair. As soon as she finished, Charlotte ran to the mirror and giggled.

"Do you like it?" Lilly asked.

"Yes!" Charlotte beamed. "I have to show my daddy! Do you want to come with me?"

All the good humor in Lilly drained instantly. She took a deep breath. "I don't want to intrude."

"What's intrude?" Charlotte's nose wrinkled curiously.

"It means go somewhere you're not welcome. Perhaps your daddy would rather I don't come."

"He won't mind," Charlotte replied matter-of-factly.

Lilly was stuck and there was not a thing she could do about it. She rose, reminding herself to be strong. She could do this—for Charlotte— because Charlotte was a darling child and deserved so much better. Charlotte took her hand as they went down the stairs. The simple gesture fortified her. Even so, the moment Charlotte pushed open that parlor door, Lilly's stomach catapulted into her throat.

Like the rest of the mansion, the room was a morose, enormous place. There were several lit lamps on the walls and the fireplace was blazing, but shadows lingered. The huge, lion-clawed piano in the corner caught Lilly's eye as much this time as it had when she'd seen it during Charlotte's tour. Lilly had asked Charlotte if she played, and Charlotte said, "Only my daddy plays sometimes."

The man in question was slouched at one end of the dull rust sofa near the fireplace with his cane propped against the side of it and his left leg stretched out in front of him. His left forearm was lying on the arm of the couch with his long fingers dangling off the end. His other forearm was on the cushions beside his thigh, making his shoulders appear even more warped than when he was standing. His crooked torso was extremely lean, so willowy she could almost consider him gaunt. And now that she had a good view of the uncovered side of his face, she could have sworn his skin was even more eerily pale than when she'd seen him before. The area around his sunken, uncovered eye was so dark it looked bruised.

The overall ghostly apparition he presented, she decided, had to be an optical illusion, brought on by the overly large sofa and poor lighting.

His head had been resting against the cushions, but he raised it when they entered. Lilly was certain his eyes had been closed, too. That sinister gaze was now focused right on her.

She wanted to keep looking at him. She wanted to stare right back until she could dispel the element of evil-like mystery that shrouded him, but she couldn't.

"Daddy," Charlotte said brightly. "Miss Lilly is going to play with us tonight!"

"Is that so?" His uncovered eyebrow arched.

"I don't want to impose," Lilly murmured.

"Impose?" He let out a noise—a grunt. He didn't get up but flippantly gestured to the wing chairs across from the sofa. "Make yourself at home."

"Th…thank you." *Why was it so difficult to find her voice?* The last thing she wanted was for him to realize how truly scared she was! She chose the chair closest to the door.

To Lilly's horror, Charlotte scooted up onto the couch right beside him. "Do you like my hair, Daddy? Miss Lilly did it for me," she said.

"It's fine," he muttered.

An awkward silence permeated the room. Charlotte was alternatively fiddling with her fingers and glancing at her father. Lilly kept her focus on the carpet and the intricate leaf-like patterns of rust, brown and black.

Eventually he said, "I thought you brought *Miss Lilly* here to play with you?" There was no mistaking the veiled sarcasm over her name.

Charlotte shimmied onto her knees and leaned close to him. With one hand she moved the hair away from his uncovered ear, tucking it behind. With the other she hid her mouth so she could whisper to him.

Lilly cringed, anticipating the moment he would yell and shove her away.

"Fine. Go on," he said.

Charlotte jumped down from the sofa and skittered out.

The tension in the room could have been cut with a knife. Lilly had absolutely no idea what to say. She picked nervously at her fingernails, wishing she could run out of there as fast as Charlotte had. She counted the brown leaves in the carpet. She counted a pile of imaginary apples in her mind. And all the while she could have sworn he was staring at her with those awful eyes of his. But then, when finally she forced herself to look, he wasn't. His focus was on the fire.

"Where did Charlotte go?" she managed to ask. It was the only thing she could think of to say.

"To relieve herself." His frosty gaze turned on her, and he added gruffly, "And, I suspect, to bring something to play with."

"Oh."

Again silence lingered. This time, Lilly was certain he was looking at her. She counted more leaf-like shapes, and was up to thirty-three apples when his raspy voice caused her to jolt.

"Your room is sufficient?"

His tone told her he didn't care whether it was or it wasn't. "The suite is lovely. Very comfortable. It's much grander than I expected. Your home is very...very beautif—" Nerves were making her babble. She cut herself off as his eyes narrowed.

"How is Charlotte doing with her studies?" he asked.

She forced an apologetic smile, "Well, we haven't really—"

"Yes," he interrupted, "nosing around where you don't belong does take time. I suggest, Miss Hawthorne, from now on you stick to doing what you were hired to do."

He didn't raise his voice at all, but his tone was icy. Lilly could feel the blood rushing to her head. "I'm...I'm sorry..." she squeaked.

"I'm sure you are," he said, then added, "Now."

"Mr. Drayton, I...I am truly sorry."

He didn't reply. But at least he stopped staring. He was looking at the fire again.

The seconds ticked by and Lilly became even more appalled with herself when she felt the burn of tears. Charlotte's return was her saving grace, enabling her to regain some semblance of control.

Charlotte was carrying the marble maze from the dresser in her bedroom. She set it on the end table next to Lilly and withdrew three marbles from her pocket. Happily she chattered while demonstrating how the toy worked. The marbles she set into the small hole at the top caused the wooden pieces to turn and twist, dropping each marble from one to the next until they landed in a cup at the bottom.

"May I try, too?" Lilly asked.

Charlotte handed Lilly one of the marbles and held up another. "I'll take Daddy's turn with this one," she said.

Lilly chanced a glance at him. He looked completely engrossed in the fire, so much so that she thought he probably wouldn't respond even if spoken to. It was quite apparent he had no interest whatsoever in playing with Charlotte's toy.

A moment later, surprising Lilly, Charlotte walked over to her father and stood so close to his leg the side of her petticoated skirt became severely dented. "Daddy, I brought cookies."

"Did you?" He sounded bored.

Charlotte reached into her pocket and withdrew three cookies, one of which she handed to him, and then she skipped across the room to give one to Lilly. "They have chocolate pieces in them."

"Thank you very much," Lilly said.

Charlotte returned to the sofa, climbed up onto it and took a bite of the one she'd kept for herself. "Daddy," she chirped, "Miss Lilly likes chocolate just like me! Will you bring me more chocolate?"

Gabriel wasn't eating his cookie. He'd dropped it on the end table beside him as if he was furious with Charlotte for giving it to him. "No, Charlotte, I won't bring you more chocolate!" he growled.

A surge of protectiveness welled in Lilly. The man's tone was entirely too harsh to use with a child, especially one as sensitive and timid as Charlotte. Rather than appearing upset, Charlotte continued to nibble. She finished the cookie and turned to him again. "What should we play next?"

"Perhaps Miss Hawthorne should retire?" he said.

It was a dismissal. Lilly didn't hesitate. She rose, thankful to be getting out of there.

"Can we play some more tomorrow?" Charlotte's voice was small and despondent.

Lilly wasn't sure whether Charlotte was posing the question to her or to *him*. The only thing she could do was offer Charlotte a smile. She used it to hide the fury she felt—fury toward that...that *creature!*—who was staring at her again! She could have sworn there was a triumphant gleam in his eye. Never in her life had she wanted to hit someone, but she had the overwhelming urge to walk over and slap the exposed side of that awful white face!

Instead she excused herself. He said nothing, not one word of farewell, as any polite person would have done. By the time she reached her room tears were threatening again. But this time they weren't caused by fear or humiliation. This time they were tears of anger. No wonder people said what they said about him! Kicking her shoes off, she told herself she would *never* let an ogre like him make her cry. And so she swallowed until her resolve was firm and her eyes were as dry as bones.

Five

The sleek, black carriage lumbered along the dirty, rutted streets of downtown Havertown. Inside, Gabriel Drayton pressed his palm firmly into the seat beside his hip. It had been a long week, one that put him behind and caused him to miss deadlines he couldn't afford to miss. He wasn't feeling better and the jarring from the carriage didn't help.

He didn't like coming into town, but he took this same obligatory route once a week, although not on the same day and not at that same time. He'd learned that lesson well since returning to live at Drayton Hall. With the curtains drawn he couldn't see outside, but he knew exactly how much longer it would be before he arrived at his third destination.

His first meeting, at least, hadn't been as much of a waste of time as it normally was. The man he'd met with—Dobbins—was a detective he'd been paying for years. Today he'd left with a list. He wasn't quite sure what he was going to do with it, but it was handy information—no matter how unrelated it was to the usual work Dobbins did for him. He'd tucked it in his pocket, where it would be secure until he was home and had a chance to look it over more thoroughly.

His second appointment that morning wasn't worth thinking about at all. He despised doctors. This one had taken his blood, leaving him with an aching cut on his arm.

The carriage turned a corner and hit a sharp rut in the road. Gabriel couldn't suppress the groan he'd been holding in for the better part of the ride. Thankfully his next stop wasn't much farther. As the carriage slowed, he grabbed his cane from where it was propped against the seat and waited for Withers to open the door.

The brownstone townhouse was one block away from the main shopping district, and as usual parking wasn't available right in front. With as much dignity as he could muster, he hobbled out of the carriage, along the uneven brick sidewalk and up the stone steps, all the while pretending to ignore the handful of people meandering about. Some of them stopped to gawk, others looked but quickly turned away, and still others acted like they didn't see him at all.

He didn't bother to pull the bell. He just pushed the door open and shuffled inside. Moments later he was slumped in the high-backed wing chair across from his attorney's cluttered desk. There were stacks of books, papers, file folders, several ink wells and other writing implements strewn across it. For anyone else the mess would raise concerns of disorganization and incompetence. Gabriel knew better. His attorney would know every paper on that desk and exactly where to find it.

Robert August was the only adult left in the world Gabriel trusted, and one of very few he still considered a friend. They'd met at boarding school when they were fourteen. Over the years they'd had countless adventures together, some indiscreet, others casual. Those, however, were all a very long time ago and not worth pondering now.

Rob was behind him, standing in his office doorway, and Gabriel listened to his teasing drawl, "Thanks, darlin'. Is that another new dress? It's nice. I like it."

He was speaking to his housekeeper, Molly Finch. Upon Gabriel's arrival, Rob had gone to seek her out and ask her to bring them coffee. Molly was supposed to cook and clean for Rob, but Gabriel was aware her services extended to more than those of a regular housekeeper. Regardless, Gabriel knew Molly didn't like him. She didn't appear with their coffee until he was in the chair, hidden from view, and she would avoid being anywhere nearby when he departed.

Rob handed Gabriel a steaming mug, then rounded the desk and took his seat in the giant leather chair—his throne—behind it. "I have a new bottle of Jack Daniel's finest. Picked it up yesterday with you in mind."

"No. Coffee's fine."

"Not even to celebrate? Your birthday is next week," Rob said.

Gabriel took a sip of the harsh black liquid. He liked his coffee black. Molly Finch knew that. "When are you going to move? Parking outside is impossible. I'll pay for a new office if you get out of this sorry district."

Rob's features contorted into an anxious frown. Quietly, he said, "You don't look well, Gabe."

"I'm fine."

"Have you seen a doctor yet?"

"I said I'm fine!" For more than a month now Rob had been badgering him relentlessly to see a physician. Rob's thick, dark eyebrows rose, an expression that reminded Gabriel of Alex. It was uncanny how much Rob resembled Alex. An old memory of the three of them out on the town, of being accused by the women they'd met of being brothers, came to mind. How they'd laughed about it. Gabriel was annoyed with himself for thinking of it. Rob's dripping concern didn't help. And he despised that nickname! He'd never given permission for Rob to use it. No one else, including Alex—especially Alex—would have gotten away with it!

"I really hate to ruin your birthday by bringing this up," Rob said, "but by this time next year it won't matter where my office is. You won't need me anymore."

"I don't give a damn," Gabriel hissed. "I don't want the money. I don't want any of it. I never did."

"And Charlotte?" Rob asked quietly. "What about her? How will you support her?"

"I'll give her to Alex and Susan like I should have done a long time ago."

Silence lingered and Gabriel knew exactly what Rob was thinking—the last place Charlotte belonged was with Alex and Susan. In this they both agreed, but it wasn't worth discussing. He expected Rob to come back at him with some disparaging remark, but he didn't. Instead Rob said casually, "It's really not that complicated. At this juncture you still have a fifty percent chance of retaining it all. It won't be terribly difficult to find a woman willing to marry you."

"I'm not willing!"

"Your father was no dummy," Rob said.

"My father was an ass!"

"Your father wanted to preserve the estate and the name, and he wanted you to grow up. He knew exactly what he was doing when he created the trust agreement. What he didn't account for was you being so stubborn," Rob said.

"Bullshit! My father didn't give a damn about me. He never did. You know that."

"You really want Alex, of all people, to get everything?"

"What choice do I have?" Gabriel retorted. "Alex has a son. Alex is happily married."

Rob chuckled. "Happily?" Soberly, he asked, "What did Dobbins report today?"

"Nothing. As always, nothing. He's been following Alex for three years. Alex had nothing to do with the fire."

"I wouldn't be so sure."

"Christ! You're as bad as Dobbins. You people have turned me into a suspicious fool. I fired everyone who worked for me—people I've known my whole life—only to find out they were all innocent. I moved out of my house—the house I loved—for what? To come back to this godforsaken town I despise. I hired strangers—people so sickened by me they won't even look at me—and I'm not allowed to believe anything anyone says, including my own cousin. Must I remind you Alex saved my life?"

"People aren't sickened by you. They're afraid of you. There's a big difference," Rob said. "And Alex pulled you out of the rubble. You were supposed to already be dead. There's a big difference there, too."

"He's like a brother to me!" Gabriel snapped.

Rob let out a heavy sigh. "Gabe, I'm worried about you. Really worried. You're my best friend, and I need my best friend. I've never trusted Alex, and Dobbins is right. You should be suspicious of him. Ever since I've known him he's coveted the estate. It's all he ever talks about. I still can't believe you let him keep a key."

Gabriel didn't bother informing Rob he'd told Alex to give his key to Lilly Hawthorne. It didn't matter anyway. Alex knew the mansion well enough to get in any number of ways without a key. He also didn't bother to remind Rob that since returning to Drayton Hall, all he had to contend with were derelict, undisciplined teenagers. The real threats—the ones he'd received in Philadelphia—had stopped. They'd discussed this enough in the past. The topic didn't need to be regurgitated for the umpteenth time. He said, "Explain to me then, why Alex came by yesterday with the sole purpose of reminding me about the clause in the trust agreement? He had a whole plan laid out for me. He said I should marry Charlotte's tutor."

"Yeah, and he's doing his damnedest to make himself look innocent. He's just biding his time, banking that you'll never marry, or even if you do, it won't be in time." Rob smirked. "I would have loved to be a fly on the wall for that conversation. What did you say to him?"

"I told him to go to hell."

Rob stared. "I hate to say this, but Alex doesn't have a half bad idea there."

"You can go to hell, too!"

Rob grinned crookedly. "Your father would turn over in his grave. You marrying a lowly tutor! If I were you, I'd marry her for that reason alone, just to spite him."

"No."

"Would you change your mind if I tell you I haven't had any new cases come in since last month? You're the only reliable client I have anymore," Rob said.

"No."

"Without you my firm will go bankrupt?"

"No."

"What if I promise to move the office? I'll move to the country—you know how much I loathe the country—where the closest neighbor is miles away?"

"Maybe."

Rob chuckled. "See, the old Gabe I know is still in there somewhere."

"I'm not going to marry the tutor," Gabriel hissed.

"What's she like? Pretty?" Rob asked.

"I don't pay attention to that sort of thing anymore."

"Ha! Right!" Rob chortled.

Gabriel rolled his eyes. "She's disgusted by me, just like the rest of the world."

"And I'm sure you've done everything in your power to alleviate that." There was no hiding Rob's heavy sarcasm.

Gabriel took a sip of his coffee and briefly closed his eyes. He didn't need to remind himself again of Lilly Hawthorne's perusal, or the abhorrence in her expression. She'd turned so green just from looking at him, he'd been sure she was going to vomit.

"Charlotte's not disgusted by you," Rob said.

"Charlotte doesn't know any better."

"Charlotte is the only one in the world with any sense." Rob paused. "You haven't said anything about Dobbins' search for her mother for a while now. Has he found anything more?"

Gabriel shook his head. "Of course not."

"What's the tutor's name again?" Rob asked.

Gabriel opened his mouth and almost blurted it out. Infuriated with himself, he growled, "Why does it matter?"

"I'm curious. Oblige me."

"There's no point. She'd never accept."

Rob smirked. "I wouldn't presume. Is she blond?"

"If you're so goddamned curious, you marry her!"

Less than an hour later, after finally getting off the topic of his perverted inheritance and finishing the business regarding the two properties he'd come to discuss, Gabriel made his way as quickly as he could down the steps to the sidewalk and into the waiting carriage. He was grateful there were no young hooligans lurking about, and even more thankful Withers had found a closer place to park. He usually avoided making eye contact with anyone, but today he did. There was a woman walking toward him with a little girl about Charlotte's age. The woman grabbed the child's hand, spun around and darted away. The little girl's terrified eyes looked back at him over her shoulder.

Gingerly, Gabriel sank into the cushioned seat. Withers shut the door, hiding him within the preferred seclusion of the carriage.

Is she blond?

He let go of his cane, intending to prop it beside him, but it fell, clanking loudly on the floorboards. With a whispered curse, he leaned back and closed his eyes.

The carriage began to move and he automatically braced himself. Aloud he murmured, "Stupid fool!" He needed to be home resting in the front parlor where he wouldn't be mercilessly jerked and jostled. Charlotte would probably take one look at him and run back to her playroom for her magic wand.

Charlotte... the only one in the world with any sense...

Gabriel had one more stop to make before he could go home.

Six

After the scolding from her employer, Lilly awakened determined to begin Charlotte's schoolwork. As the day unfolded, however, she realized the task might not be as easy as she'd thought. Charlotte wouldn't cooperate. She didn't want to learn about letters and numbers. She wanted to learn to braid hair. Lilly ended up letting Charlotte practice on her. One thing led to another and Lilly discovered not only did Charlotte have a much broader imagination than her initial bashful behavior revealed, she could be quite gregarious. If she didn't want to do something she was very effective at avoiding it. Every time Charlotte changed the subject, it was to tell Lilly something more about her father. These ramblings about him only caused Lilly's pity for Charlotte to intensify.

Some of the activities Charlotte claimed to have done with Gabriel Drayton were normal things any father might do with their child, like raking leaves, collecting rocks, planting flowers, and going sledding. Others were amusing. According to Charlotte there wasn't much he could do without her guidance. She'd taught him to swim, to fold a blanket, to diaper her dolls, to shuffle cards, and to dip his pen in the inkwell so it wouldn't make smudges when he wrote. She had to help him read his books, to put on his boots, to eat cookies without dropping crumbs, to make angels in the snow, and to not be afraid during bad thunderstorms.

At one point, while listening to Charlotte's chatter, Lilly began to picture a man with a kindly smile, a devoted, caring parent, a man very much like the one she'd imagined her own father to be, a true gentleman. But then she reminded herself who he really was, which brought to mind how callously and dismissively he spoke to his daughter. Charlotte's stories were nothing more than the wishful ramblings of a neglected, mistreated child. She clearly adored the man. And he, obviously, didn't want to have anything to do with her.

Lilly erased the *D* she'd written on the slate and wrote *B*. "What's this letter?" she asked.

"I'm a really good ballerina," Charlotte said.

"You are?" Lilly feigned awe. "That's wonderful, but what's this letter?" It was the fourth letter she'd written that Charlotte had no interest in identifying.

"Do you want to see my dance?" Charlotte asked.

"I would love to, but I think we should do our schoolwork now. I can see your dance later during playtime. *Ballerina* begins with this letter."

Charlotte's smile widened. "You can come to the parlor tonight and I can dance for you!"

Another evening in the parlor wasn't something Lilly wanted any part of. "What's this letter? *Braid* begins with this letter."

"Will you read me the book one more time?" Charlotte asked.

"I will, but first you have to tell me what this letter is. The word *book* begins with this letter."

"Uncle Alex and Aunt Susan and Mark will be here for dinner tonight. They come every Friday."

"Yes, I know. I'm looking forward to seeing your Uncle Alex again and meeting his wife."

"Mark is three. He's still a baby." Charlotte's expression wrinkled in distaste. "He has a runny nose all the time so you have to be careful when you give him a hug, 'cause his boogies can get in your hair."

"Okay, I'll be careful. Do you know the word *boogie*..."—she couldn't believe she said that—"...begins with this letter?"

"After dinner Alex and Susan and Mark will come to the parlor to play with us. I will dance for them, too!"

The idea of being in the parlor with others—not just Gabriel Drayton—was much more appealing. "Alright, I'll come see your dance in the parlor tonight, but only if you tell me what this letter is."

The smile on Charlotte's face instantly disappeared. Lilly felt like a heel. This child had enough harshness in her life. The last thing she wanted to do was threaten Charlotte, no matter how mild or harmless the threat might be. She relented immediately. "Since it's almost time for lunch, let's go ahead and read."

Charlotte jumped up, seemingly happy again, and skipped over to the bookshelf to retrieve her book.

"B…b…book begins with this letter, do you know what it is?" Lilly prompted.

"It's *B*." Charlotte said this so casually Lilly was certain she'd known what was written on the slate all along.

Not much later they headed to the dining room for lunch. Lilly took her seat and caught a funny smile from Mrs. Finch. At first she didn't realize what the cook was laughing at. Then she remembered Charlotte had done her hair. She had seven lopsided braids, each one coming off her head at a different angle. It was a good thing she wouldn't have to see anyone else until dinner that evening!

While she and Charlotte ate, Lilly couldn't resist asking, "Will your father join us for dinner tonight?"

Charlotte made one of her many faces, the one Lilly recognized as meaning she'd asked a very silly question. "Of course," she said.

"Is Friday the only day your daddy eats with you?" Lilly asked.

Charlotte slurped her soup, loudly, from the spoon. "No, he eats with me all the time."

"But he hasn't been here at all this week. Not even for breakfast."

"Sometimes he isn't hungry and sometimes he likes leftovers and sometimes he likes to eat in the parlor and sometimes he likes to make his own food. 'Cept he isn't a very good cook so I have to help him on Sundays."

"Your daddy cooks on Sundays?"

"Yeah," Charlotte drawled proudly. "Last Sunday we had chocolate cake for breakfast!"

"Chocolate cake for breakfast! My goodness!" Lilly exclaimed, while internally she added another mark to the already extensive list of the many ways Gabriel Drayton carelessly mistreated his daughter.

"It was really, really good. Daddy said it was easiest. But he didn't make it. Mrs. Finch made it."

"What else did you eat on Sunday?"

"Popcorn. We have popcorn on Sunday for dinner mostly 'cause it's Daddy's favorite. Do you like popcorn?"

Lilly smiled to cover her rising anger. "Yes, I do. Is that all you have on Sundays? Popcorn and chocolate cake?"

"Oh no. Daddy makes lots of things, 'cept eggs, 'cause he doesn't like eggs. I don't like eggs either. Sometimes we have pancakes and sometimes we have sandwiches, but mostly we have everything soup."

"What's everything soup?"

Charlotte shrugged. "I look in the pantry and see what everything is there to put in it, and Daddy stirs it all up in the big silver pot."

"What was in the last everything soup you made?"

"Green things and orange things and red things and white things and yellow things," Charlotte said.

Despite her irritation, Lilly chuckled. "Was it good?"

"Not really. But I had cake for dessert so I wasn't hungry anymore. I'm all done." Charlotte slid her bowl toward the center of the table. It was a move she made with her dish every time she finished eating.

"Shall we do some more schoolwork before your riding lesson?" Lilly asked.

Charlotte didn't answer the question. She rose and Lilly followed her out of the dining room and back up the stairs. Instead of going into her own room, Charlotte went past it and then on into Lilly's suite. "I'm supposed to show you something."

"What's that?" Lilly asked curiously.

"The fire escape."

"The fire escape?"

"If there is a fire, it's how you have to get out. After you went to bed last night Daddy said I must not forget to show you. I only almost forgot," Charlotte said.

"Oh," Lilly stammered.

Charlotte led her to a narrow bookshelf against the wall near the fireplace. There, she reached up under an empty shelf. A latch clicked.

"This is how it opens." Charlotte took hold of the shelf with her other hand and pulled it easily. The hinges had been oiled so well they didn't make a sound.

Behind the bookshelf was a rectangular opening—a doorway framed in thick grey stone. The darkness made it difficult to see, but Lilly could tell there was a narrow passage with steep, descending stone steps.

Oh God! Charlotte was leading her to the dungeons!

Charlotte grabbed a lantern from a hook on the wall. "Will you help me light this? I have to show you the way," she said.

The trip down the stairwell was spooky and eerie, and Lilly was certain the whispery tendrils that tickled her forehead and slithered over her ear were hanging cobwebs. Charlotte didn't seem the least bit frightened. They went down for quite a ways before the stairs ended. At the bottom, they turned left, the only way they could go, and they were in a long, narrow tunnel.

"Where does this go?" Lilly asked. "Is there a dungeon?"

"No, it's just tunnels. This one goes to the west garden," Charlotte said. "It echoes down here. Isn't it neat?"

They continued on. Another tunnel joined up with the one they were in, but it was so dark Lilly couldn't see more than a few feet into it. Charlotte began chanting her name and counting the number of times it echoed. "Do you want to try?"

"Lilly!" Lilly called out.

"*...Lilly... Lilly... Lilly... Lilly...*" the tunnel replied.

"Four times!" Charlotte chanted. "Don't be scared, Miss Lilly."

Thankfully, she heard no cries from victims chained to walls. She thought they'd been walking forever when out of nowhere they ran into more steps, this time ascending. It was a short flight compared to the one they'd come down. At the top there was another door, angled diagonally overhead.

"It's really heavy," Charlotte said. A key was stuck in the lock. Charlotte turned it easily and then shoved the wood with both her little hands, grunting with the effort.

Even for Lilly the door was difficult to open. But as soon as it was, sunlight poured in on them. Another stone stairway brought them up and out, and into the middle of an overgrown rose garden. Looking around, Lilly saw they were less than thirty feet from the building she'd noticed from afar—the one near the west wing of the mansion. It was covered with vines and ivy so thick the door was almost completely hidden. There was a small white steeple at the top, which was also barely visible under all the weeds.

"If there is a fire this is how you get out," Charlotte said.

"Does your room have a fire escape, too?"

"It's the same. I'll show you how to get in from my room when we go back."

"What's that building?" Lilly pointed.

"It's the chapel. Nobody goes in there."

That was obvious. It would take hours to clear the overgrowth away in order to simply get to the entrance.

They were on their way back through the tunnel—there were no dungeons, thank goodness—when Charlotte said, "My grandmother used to go in there all the time with my daddy. She died before I was born."

It took a second for Lilly to realize Charlotte was talking about the chapel. "She died when your daddy was a boy?" It was one of the rumors Lilly had heard. *They* said the late Lady Drayton had been so distraught over her son's deformities, she'd killed herself.

"He was ten," Charlotte said. "There is a painting of her, but it got burned up in the fire and it doesn't look good anymore, so Daddy put it in the west wing."

Lilly was confused. "There was a fire here in this house? In the west wing?"

Charlotte shook her head. "No, not here. In our old house in Phildelfa. Daddy builded it, but it wasn't the same after it burned up, so we came here and he brought the painting with us. This house is better than our old house." Resolutely, she added, "And safer. This is the house Alex and Daddy grew up in."

"Oh?"

"Alex says Daddy looks like my grandmother. He doesn't look like my grandfather at all. I look like my grandmother and like my daddy. We have the same hair. Daddy didn't used to have long hair. He let his grow long like mine so we could be twins!"

During the tour of the library, Lilly had seen the portrait of the late Lord Drayton. She couldn't say whether Gabriel Drayton resembled the handsome, middle-aged gentleman. How could she? All she'd ever seen of Gabriel Drayton was half a face.

As they passed an adjoining passageway Lilly asked, "Does one of these tunnels go to your daddy's room?"

"Yes," Charlotte said, "but not that one."

Lilly's next question had been burning in her head all week long. "Charlotte, what does your daddy do all day?"

"Sometimes he goes to town and sometimes he likes to read and sometimes he goes in his study. He does lots of stuff, but mostly he works."

"In his study?"

"No," Charlotte said. "It's a secret, so I can't tell. If I tell you, will you promise not to tell anybody?"

"Yes, I promise," Lilly said.

"In the west wing. Only he's allowed to go in there, but he lets me come in sometimes."

"What kind of work does he do?"

Charlotte shrugged. "He makes pictures of buildings."

Not much later they were making their way back up the narrow stairway. At the top Charlotte solved the mystery of the wooden panel. It was the back of another bookshelf—Charlotte's bookshelf.

Time had flown while they explored the fire escape. The clock on the mantel said Charlotte needed to get ready for her riding lesson, and again Lilly walked with her out to the stable yard.

Later, about the time Charlotte should have been finishing her bath, Lilly slipped into her room and offered to help pick out clothes for dinner.

"How about this one?" Lilly asked the towel-draped child. She held up a beautiful, silk, royal blue dress fringed with lace and pearls.

"With this petticoat? And these stocking? And your black, patent leather shoes?"

"No," Charlotte said, "I wanna pick!"

The vehemence in Charlotte's tone caught Lilly off guard. But it wasn't anger. It was more self-sufficient resolve. Charlotte chose an emerald green dress in lieu of the blue one, orange stockings and a purple bow for her hair. The only thing Lilly had suggested that Charlotte seemed remotely amenable to wearing were the shoes.

"Don't you want to wear white stockings instead of orange ones?" Lilly asked.

"I like orange," Charlotte said. "It's my favorite color."

"I like orange, too, but I'm going to wear white stockings and I thought maybe we could wear the same color?"

Charlotte's eyes brightened. "Okay!" She took the white pair Lilly held.

Soon enough, Charlotte was squirming to reach the buttons on the back of her dress. "May I help?" Lilly asked.

Charlotte turned around and held up her damp hair. "Daddy has to help me sometimes when I can't reach," she said.

Next Lilly offered to brush Charlotte's hair. While doing so, she sneaked in a white bow, rather than the purple one. Until then she hadn't looked at the clock. When she did, she gasped. It was already six-thirty, and she still had to redo the mess Charlotte had made of her own hair!

Hastily, she swept down the hallway to her room. She slipped into her yellow dress, the second best she owned, and buttoned the tiny pearl buttons she'd sewn on the bodice. The buttons had come from one of her mother's two pearl necklaces. The other necklace she clasped around her bare neckline. It wasn't a proper dress for the evening, at least compared to what she imagined Susan Drayton would be wearing, but it was better with the pearl buttons. As she stared at herself in the mirror, making last minute touches to her hair, she found herself so edgy her hands trembled.

The last thing she needed to do was decide what to do about her glasses. She'd worn them all week, but tonight she would be with wealthy people—wealthy, well-bred, people. That was nerve-wracking enough. She wanted to try at least to look mildly sophisticated.

But, *he* would be there! This reminded her she didn't want to be pretty! After expelling a deep breath, she shoved the glasses onto her nose and headed out.

She was the first one to arrive in the dining room. Shortly thereafter, Charlotte joined her. "Aunt Susan and Uncle Alex are always late," Charlotte declared. Several minutes past the designated hour, they heard the loud rap of the iron knocker.

Charlotte jumped up from her seat and ran out. Lilly rose but sauntered slowly to the doorway. Before she reached it, she heard Alex Drayton say, "Hi sweetie! My, oh my, you're getting heavy!"

"Alex! Put her down!" a woman's voice demanded, but her tone changed to one of pleasant surprise, "Why, Charlotte, look how nicely you're dressed today! And look at your hair! My goodness! You look lovely!"

The voice accompanied an extremely striking woman with dark hair elaborately piled on top of her head. Her eyes were dark, her skin pale and flawless, including the generous portion of it exposed by the low cut of her dark purple gown—a gown which molded to every one of her slim, perfect curves.

A young boy—a miniature Alex—was holding her hand. Even he was dressed in a full three-piece wool suit. He was simply adorable.

"Miss Hawthorne, it is good to see you again." Alex settled Charlotte on the floor and grasped Lilly's hand in a warm shake. "I trust you've settled in and are getting used to everything."

Lilly returned his smile. "Yes, thank you."

"May I introduce my wife, Susan Drayton, and our son, Mark?" Alex said.

"It is lovely to finally meet you." Susan extended a perfectly manicured hand. "Alex has told me what a fine teacher you are. I am so pleased you're here for Charlotte. This is a much better arrangement for her than going to the school in town." She lowered her voice and leaned closer. Her next comment was intended for Lilly's ears alone. "Children can be so cruel."

"I am honored to meet you as well," Lilly stammered. "Charlotte speaks very fondly of you." It was true. Charlotte had, today, talked about Susan. She'd told Lilly about the vegetables she didn't like but had to eat at Friday dinners because she didn't want to disappoint Susan.

"Charlotte is a darling." Susan winked at Charlotte, who was beaming.

"Will you sit by me?" Charlotte asked Susan.

"Of course I will," Susan said.

Little Mark scurried over to the table and climbed up onto one of the seats. "Daddy sits by me!" he announced.

"Miss Hawthorne," Susan said, "I do so want to apologize for neglecting you. Last week was terribly hectic." She went on to explain about two charitable organizations she was involved with and the annual dinners she'd had to coordinate. "Now that that's behind me, finally, I would so like for us to become friends. Perhaps we can meet and have tea sometime? There is a lovely tea room on Market Street in town. Or better yet, I can send our driver to pick you up and you will come to our home."

Lilly was struck dumb. She couldn't believe someone of Susan Drayton's ilk would attempt to offer friendship to her. She had no idea what to say. As it turned out, she didn't have to say anything.

Glancing about the room, Susan visibly shivered. "It must be awful for you here. This place is like a dank, dreary mausoleum. I've always despised it—"

"Good evening, Susan," Gabriel interrupted icily.

Lilly spun. Gabriel's flawed, darkly-concealed form caused her to lose her breath. *How had she not heard him approach with that awful scrape of his foot?*

Susan's friendly manner disappeared. One eyebrow rose haughtily and her address to Gabriel contained as much chill as his had to her. "Gabriel."

Lilly looked back and forth between Susan and Gabriel's fiercely aimed gazes. Alex appeared annoyed, but he didn't say anything. Both Charlotte and Mark seemed oblivious.

And then Gabriel moved. Surreptitiously Lilly sneaked glances at him. His attire was no different than it had been the first time she'd seen him. Now, the scrape of his dragging foot assaulted her ears like fingernails screeching across a chalkboard. The sharp tap of his cane echoed. He was leaning so heavily upon it, it wobbled. Her eyes darted to his face. His expression, the part she could see, was closed and cold, revealing nothing.

She'd never actually seen Gabriel walk before. His progress was slow, his movements labored. He didn't bother to politely shake Alex's hand, but went straight for the table and yanked the head chair back. Everyone else took seats, too. Charlotte sat to his right, Alex to his left. Susan took the chair beside Charlotte, and Mark beside Alex. Quickly and quietly, Lilly sat next to Mark.

"Can I say grace tonight?" Mark bubbled. "Charlotte always gets to say grace, and I want to. Can I? Can I?"

"That would be lovely, Mark. You go right ahead," Susan said.

Along with everyone else, Lilly bowed her head and closed her eyes. After a few seconds of Mark's mumbles, she peeked. Seated in the dining room chair Gabriel Drayton's shoulders didn't look quite as crooked as they did when he was upright. She looked up to the scarf around his neck and his facial covering and immediately wished she hadn't. His frosty glare was boring into her.

"…and God bless Mommy and, um, and um, Daddy and, um…um, um Charlotte and um, and um, um, Uncle Gabriel. And um, um, and um—" Mark droned on.

"That's enough prayers!" Gabriel growled.

If looks could kill, the glower Susan threw could have felled him.

"You forgot Miss Lilly!" Charlotte twittered. She bowed her head and said reverently, "And God bless Miss Lilly, the very best teacher in the whole wide world. Amen."

Lilly felt heat rush to her face. *He* was still staring at her.

Gabriel reached for a serving dish, but Susan beat him to it. She served Charlotte and herself and then passed it to him. Lilly could have sworn Susan deliberately let go of the dish before Gabriel had a grip on it. The heavy ceramic plate clamored down right in front of Charlotte, clanging on her place setting and spraying the surrounding area with gravy and pieces of roast beef, some of which landed on Charlotte.

A hiss of fury came out of Gabriel.

"I'm sorry, Daddy. I ruined my dress," Charlotte said.

"It's fine," he snarled while maneuvering the serving dish to an empty spot on the table. Then he swiveled Charlotte's skewed plate to where it was supposed to be.

"Should I go change my dress?" Charlotte looked like she was about to cry.

"It's fine, I said!"

"It's not her fault, Gabriel," Susan scoffed. She reached for her napkin and started to wipe the spills from Charlotte's clothes. "See, sweetie, no harm done," she said to Charlotte. To Gabriel she seethed, "If the children weren't present right now—"

"If they weren't present, what?"

"I would tell you exactly what I think of you!"

"If you have something to say to me, say it!" Gabriel fired back.

"Stop it, both of you!" Alex cut in. "Can't we have just one peaceful meal without the two of you bickering the whole time? You're certainly making a great impression on Miss Hawthorne."

"Miss Hawthorne has every right to know what kind of man she's working for!" Susan spat.

"Susan!" Alex murmured harshly.

"Well, she does!"

"Susan, don't stoop—" Alex started, but he caught himself.

"To my level?" Gabriel turned on his cousin. "Is that what you were going to say?"

Alex threw his napkin down on his empty plate. "Sometimes I don't know why we bother to come here anymore!"

"Neither do I," Gabriel said.

Alex moved like he was going to rise.

"Don't!" Gabriel hissed. "Stay and enjoy. Pretend it's next year." With that, he shoved his chair back, grabbed his cane, and with a heavy hand on the table, rose to his feet. And then he began the arduous process of removing himself from the room.

Staring after him, Lilly noticed his hair was indeed as long as Charlotte's. The thick, straight strands fell out from under the tied kerchief to just below his crooked shoulder blades. It looked like layered velvet.

"Charlotte, stay here." Susan had a restraining hand on Charlotte's arm.

"I'm going with my daddy," Charlotte said soberly.

"Aren't you hungry?" Susan asked.

"No," Charlotte said.

Alex rose. "Gabriel, I'm sorry. Don't leave. Please."

Gabriel didn't acknowledge Alex's apology. He just planted his unsteady cane and took his next deliberate step. Holding her breath, Lilly watched Charlotte, who somehow had escaped Susan's hold, race around the table after her father.

"Charlotte, come back and sit down," Susan said.

"I'm going with my daddy!"

"Stay here with us, sweetie," Susan repeated. "Your daddy doesn't want you with him."

Without turning, Gabriel bellowed, "Finch, bring Charlotte's plate to the front parlor."

Not another word was spoken until Mr. Finch shut the parlor door, enclosing Gabriel and Charlotte inside.

"At least we can eat in peace," Alex smiled as he pulled his chair in. "I'm sorry about this, Miss Hawthorne. It's not fair for you to have to witness our family squabbles."

They weren't long into the meal when Susan looked at Lilly and spoke sorrowfully, "Gabriel didn't used to be like this. He used to be friendly, even charming when he wanted to be. It's such a shame."

"Susan!" Alex glanced pointedly at Mark. "This is not the right time."

Under other circumstances, Lilly would have found it amusing that Susan blatantly ignored her husband. She said, "I worry so much about Charlotte. Gabriel treats her so badly. This is no life for a child, living in this horrid place, with no playmates, no friends. And a father who wouldn't be able to string two kind words together if he tried. Why, he won't even let her go to church!" Contemptuously, she added, "He thinks there is no God." Then her tone grew shallow. "I love that little girl like she was my own. Alex and I both do. She is precious to us. We've asked Gabriel many times to let us keep her, but he won't. I don't understand it. He doesn't care about her. To him she's nothing but a burden."

"Miss Hawthorne doesn't want to hear this," Alex said.

Susan continued, "All I can say is I'm very glad you're here. We've been telling Gabriel for years he needs to hire a nanny for Charlotte, but he won't. She's too young to look after herself the way she does. I know you're not a nanny and I don't mean to imply that you should take on that role. It's just that Charlotte needs the influence of a woman, someone who can suitably guide her. It is so relieving for us to know she will finally have a positive role model. I can already see how attached to you she has become. And I can't tell you how thrilled I am to see her dressed properly for once."

"Susan!" Alex warned again.

This time Susan heeded her husband. Lilly murmured reassurances about her intentions where Charlotte was concerned, but she was grateful when the conversation turned to Mark. The little boy was adorable and quite inquisitive. His funny comments and questions provoked laughter in all of them. He did, however, have a runny nose. Lilly had to hide her grin watching Alex retrieve his handkerchief to wipe it.

They were in the entrance hall, getting ready to depart, when Alex stopped and said, "Give me a minute?"

"What for?" Susan said. "You're wasting your time."

Alex went to the parlor anyway and rapped lightly before peeking in. "I just wanted to say goodnight."

If Gabriel acknowledged Alex, Lilly didn't hear him. She couldn't see him either, but Charlotte came running. She was wearing a blue dress instead of the stained green one. She hugged Alex and Susan, and then Mark, bending awkwardly around him to avoid his nose.

As soon as the door closed behind them, Charlotte turned to Lilly, grinning widely. "Now I can show you my dance!"

The expectation in Charlotte's eyes made Lilly bite back an excuse. She had promised earlier, even if that promise had been made believing there would be others present. The last thing Lilly wanted was to be left alone with Gabriel Drayton again.

Inside the parlor, she saw that he was seated in the same spot, in the same oddly hunched position he'd been in the evening before. This time, however, he didn't bother to raise his head. He just glared at her and drawled, "I see we are to be honored with your company again tonight. Please, make yourself comfortable."

Lilly chose to pretend she didn't notice his derision. Instead she took a seat in the wing chair and concentrated on Charlotte, who was bouncing her way across the room. "Daddy, I want to show Miss Lilly my dance. You have to play the dance song."

Gabriel closed his eyes. "No."

"*Pleeease*," Charlotte's little hand was on his leg, just above his knee.

"I said no, Charlotte!"

"But I told Miss Lilly I would show her," Charlotte pleaded. She pushed at his leg, causing it to rock back and forth.

"Not tonight." This time his voice sounded different. Although still gruff, there was no forceful rush of anger behind the words. There was no rude disdain. Charlotte was still rocking his leg.

The disappointment Lilly saw in Charlotte was her undoing. "Please," she said as amicably as she could, "I would enjoy the music very much, and I've been looking forward to the dance ever since Charlotte told me what a great ballerina she is."

"Not tonight." His eyes opened in slits, but he didn't look at her. He didn't look at Charlotte either, before he closed them again.

"I'll be right back!" Charlotte was already running out of the room.

This is what Lilly had dreaded the most—being left alone with him. She had nothing to say, and it was evident he had no interest in speaking to her either. A second glance showed his eyes were still closed. Lilly took the opportunity to look at him—to really look. In that perusal, it struck her there was something about him that didn't make sense. When standing, leaning on his cane, his right shoulder was higher than the left. Here, slouched on the sofa, it wasn't his right shoulder that was higher. It was the left one. Her eyes traveled down to his lean torso and further to his long legs. The right one—the one Charlotte had been rocking back and forth—was bent at the knee in a normal sitting position. She could see the muscle of his thigh through his black trousers. His left knee was also bent, but at less of an angle. There was no difference in the lengths of his legs. There was no difference in the lengths of his arms. Although they were encased in leather-soled shoes, there was nothing odd about his feet. And his hands... there was nothing wrong with them either. His fingers were long and clean, with neatly trimmed nails. She had expected him to be malformed because that's what she'd heard. Because of that, her mind had played tricks on her, making him appear more debilitated than he was. Obviously there was something wrong with his left leg, but she was fairly certain whatever it was, wasn't a birth defect.

Returning her focus to his face, she saw his eyes were open again. In a slow, deliberate move, he rolled his head against the back of the sofa, leaving her a profile view of the unmasked side of his face. He wasn't deformed at all! Injured, but not deformed! The truth of it hit her like a brick. And then her fury rose. If he wasn't deformed, then his ruthless cruelty was all the worse! This didn't make sense, really, but she thought it anyway.

Charlotte breezed back into the room holding her magic wand high. She skipped right up to her father and began chanting, "*Abra-ka-dabra, alla ka zoom, ikkidy, klickity...*" All the while making arrays of circles in the air. Lilly caught herself cringing in panic when the tip of the star came within inches of grazing his jaw. She imagined him grabbing the wand from Charlotte's hand, dragging her over his knee and whipping her with it. She didn't release the breath she held until Charlotte's wand came to a halt.

Then Charlotte skipped over to her. "Miss Lilly, I can put a magic spell on you, too. I can fix your eyes so you don't have to wear glasses anymore."

Lilly smiled. "Alright."

"You have to close your eyes. It only works if you close your eyes."

Lilly felt the wind from the wand as Charlotte stabbed the air around her and chanted her magic words.

"Open your eyes!" Charlotte said finally. "Now take off your glasses. Can you see without them? Daddy says sometimes it takes a little while for the magic to work."

Lilly folded her glasses and set them on the table beside her chair. Charlotte was looking at her so expectantly, she almost laughed. "Yes, I can see! You're amazing. It's a miracle! Oh my goodness! I can see perfectly again!"

Charlotte grinned from ear to ear and skipped around the room. "See, Daddy! See what I did!"

He opened his eyes and fixed his intimidating glower on Lilly. "Charlotte," he murmured coolly, "how are your studies with Miss Hawthorne coming along?"

"It's Miss Lilly, not Miss Hawthorne," Charlotte chided.

"Miss Lilly, fine," he said.

"I learned lots and lots!" Charlotte climbed up onto the sofa beside him. She was still absently twirling her wand. "I learned to read a new book and I learned mathmics."

"Mathematics?" he prompted.

"That's what I said, mathmics," Charlotte replied.

It was barely perceptible, but Lilly noticed a faint twitch at the corner of his mouth. She almost smiled herself.

"Ask me a number and I can mathmics it," Charlotte said.

"Twenty-five?" he said.

"Daddy!" Charlotte's eyebrows drew together in a stern rebuke. "A little number, not a big number. I've only had school for one week!" She got on her knees and flipped around on the sofa until she was facing him.

"Three?"

"Three and three is six!" Charlotte nodded proudly. "Ask another one."

"Six?"

"Six and six is twelve! Ask another one." Lilly thought the child was precariously close to him. She was practically lying on top of him with her nose just inches from his.

"Nine?"

Resting back on her haunches, Charlotte bit her lip. "Nine and nine is… um… nine and nine is… um… I know, don't tell, I know… it's eighteen! See, I learned lots and lots. Miss Lilly is better than school!"

"I guess so," he murmured.

Charlotte leaned over and asked, "Did the magic work yet? Can I do my dance now?"

All of the gruffness that had been missing a moment before returned. "No!"

Charlotte bounded off the sofa as cheerfully as she'd been when she jumped up onto it. "I'll go get my new book!"

"It's time for bed!" he said curtly.

Charlotte turned back to him. "But we didn't do my dance yet."

"Charlotte, go!"

"Not yet, Daddy, *pleeeease!*"

"Charlotte!" he snapped.

Lilly stood up and held out her hand for Charlotte to take. The forlorn turn of Charlotte's expression broke her heart. She hoped the glare she threw at Gabriel would convey at least some of the contempt she felt for him. "It's okay, Charlotte. I'm sure there will be another opportunity for you to show me your dance."

"Are you sleepy?" Charlotte asked.

"I am. It's probably a good idea for both of us to go to bed."

Lilly had no intention of saying goodnight to Gabriel, and she knew—from experience—he wouldn't offer one to her. With Charlotte's hand in hers she started away, but couldn't resist glancing back. The minute she did she wished she hadn't. Pure hatred—there was no other way to describe it—was shooting out of his eyes like flames and it was aimed directly at her. It caused her entire body to recoil, and she shivered enough for Charlotte to notice.

"What's wrong?" Charlotte was looking up at her.

"I guess my eyes aren't completely well yet. I thought I just saw an evil, awful monster!"

Charlotte nodded soberly. "Daddy says sometimes it takes a little while for the magic to work. But don't worry, monsters are only pretend. Henry will protect you."

Lilly forced a smile for Charlotte's sake, but inside anxiety was building. There was no way Gabriel hadn't heard her foolish insult. Then she heard him murmur, "Goodbye, Miss Hawthorne."

Later, after she'd changed into her nightgown and climbed under the covers, she was still quivering with apprehension. She'd made a horrible mistake with her careless words. There was no way a man like him would let her get away with such imprudence. The consequences would be dire. She was so caught up in her thoughts, she almost missed hearing Charlotte leave her room.

Seconds later, Lilly was sneaking out, tiptoeing to the top of the stairwell, and there she stood. She could see enough over the balcony railing to know the parlor door had been left open. Someone was playing the piano. The melody was lovely, the accompanying harmony in perfect contrast. It made her think of a running brook, washing over the smooth, weathered stones. As the music rose, the brook became a graceful waterfall. She'd never heard anything like it. She'd never been so drawn to or touched by music in her life. When it ended she was severely disappointed.

"Miss Lilly forgot her glasses," she heard Charlotte say.

Lilly didn't wait to hear the reply.

Lying in her very comfortable bed, she told herself she must have imagined that music. The aloof, unfeeling Gabriel Drayton couldn't possibly produce sounds of such beauty.

Seven

The next morning Lilly almost missed breakfast. She'd been waiting to hear Charlotte's knock on her father's bedroom door, but it never came. In a hurry, she left her room and didn't see what was on the floor in front of her door until she stepped on it.

It was an envelope containing money—her first week's wages—and the amount was more than Alex had told her she would be paid. There was also a hastily scrawled note that read, 'The carriage is at your disposal. Withers will drive you.' It was signed simply, 'Drayton'.

The cost of her careless remark was exactly what her worst fear had been. She'd been dismissed. Shame and a deep sense of failure overwhelmed her. Suppressing her emotions as well as she could, she went to the playroom, rapped lightly and entered without waiting for Charlotte to beckon.

Charlotte was in the process of tying on her bonnet. Before Lilly could offer up the farewell she'd come to make, Charlotte announced, "Daddy said we can go shopping in town today!"

Unaware of her suddenly speechless teacher, Charlotte ran over to her dresser and brought Lilly the glasses she'd left in the parlor. "You don't need these anymore, but Daddy said I should give them back so you can keep them in your jewelry box."

"I don't have a jewelry box," Lilly stammered.

Charlotte ran to her dresser again, this time returning with a rectangular red box, which she opened to show Lilly the contents. "Daddy said we can take it with us and have a treat in the carriage!"

Lilly stared in complete astonishment at the brand new selection of chocolates. "I thought he said *no,*" she murmured.

"He only means no if he only says no," Charlotte said.

That made no sense whatsoever. "Oh."

Happily, Charlotte proclaimed, "I'm going to buy a seashell and you're going to buy a jewelry box!"

Eight

It was dark when Molly Finch donned her long cloak and slipped out the back of the townhouse. She had plenty of time, but she hurried anyway, crossing the street to a side avenue. The cool night air whipped through her cloak and she shivered. She didn't like being out in the city at night, but she didn't have a choice. Every Monday she attended these meetings. It was the only time she could get away without Rob questioning her. He was out as well, attending his Bar Association meeting. By the time he returned, she would be long in bed.

Two blocks down she turned left into a narrow alley. Her heels were clicking too loudly on the cobblestone streets. She quickened her pace, running on the balls of her feet. The shriek of a distressed cat had her glancing over her shoulder. Her next turn brought her into an even darker alley.

Her destination was the back entrance to an old tavern on the lower level of a row house. She pushed past the small iron gate, lifted the front of her skirt and made her way up the short walk to the door. There she rapped three times, paused and rapped twice.

It didn't take long for the door to open a crack. The man who answered—one of the bartenders—recognized her, but didn't say anything as she brushed past him. He'd seen her there enough in the last three months to know where she was going.

The men she'd been meeting told her they were brothers, and they were both named John Smith. They were big men. She could have used the term burly to describe them, but because they wore fine gentlemen's clothes, that word didn't fit. They didn't look like brothers either. The only resemblance between them was their size. One had greasy, dirty blond hair brushed over a receding hairline. Internally Molly dubbed him Greasy John. The other had kinky red hair and a fair, but swarthy freckled face. She called him Red John. He was by far the more ruthless of the two.

They were exactly where she expected to find them, at a table at the very back of the bar where the lighting was so dim it was difficult to see anything. Molly sat in one of the two empty chairs.

"You're late," Red John said.

"I'm sorry." She wasn't late.

"We knew you'd be here," Greasy John said. He held out a small cotton pouch with a drawstring pull. "This should cover next week. There's a little more here than last time."

Molly took the pouch and quickly tucked it into the pocket of her cloak. The powdery substance in it was weightless.

"How much is left from the last supply?" Red John asked.

"None. I used it all," she said. "He didn't come this week until Friday morning. I used it then."

"Do you think it's working?" Greasy John asked.

"I don't know," she said tentatively. "I didn't get a good look at him on Friday, but Mr. August said he looks ill."

A crooked half smile turned up one corner of Red John's mouth. "The Benefactor has asked us to speed up the process. He wants it administered twice a week. Since Drayton only goes to August's once a week, you'll need to go to Drayton Hall."

"I can't do that!" Molly interrupted in a harsh whisper. "I've never been there. I don't know where to—"

"Molly, Molly," Red John sneered. "We picked you to help us because of your connections. Don't you think it's about time you pay a visit to Mommy and Daddy? I'm sure it won't be difficult for you to help Mommy serve tea?"

"But what if the cups get mixed up? What if the wrong person drinks it? There's a little girl living there. I can't—"

"We trust you to ensure nothing goes amiss," Greasy John interrupted.

Panicking, Molly rushed on, "But it's easy with the coffee because Mr. Drayton drinks his black and Rob, I mean, Mr. August, takes cream. There will be no way to tell—"

"Molly, you're a smart girl. You'll be able to figure it out," Red John cut her off. "Twice a week from now on. We'll meet back here same time next Monday."

Molly didn't like either of them. Since she'd been working for them, her feelings for Red John had turned to loathing. He was too callous and too demanding and he had no sympathy for the difficulties she encountered. She looked beseechingly at Greasy John, hoping he might say something to help her, but he didn't.

"You didn't pay me yet," she said to Red John.

"Ah, yes," he scoffed. "See Molly, everything is about business in the end, isn't it?" He pulled another pouch out of his inside breast pocket and set it in the middle of the table. The contents jingled.

Molly snatched the money up. This pouch—the heavy one—she stowed in the pocket of her skirt, secure and hidden beneath her cloak.

Minutes later she was hurrying back toward Robert August's townhouse. All the while, she repeated Red John's words over and over in her head: "*It's just business… it's just business…*" What she was doing was just that—business. She didn't know Gabriel Drayton. She knew *of* him. From what people in town said he was a bad man. He'd caused harm to many. He'd even killed boys in his dungeon! And he was using Rob August in the worst possible way, deceiving him, blackmailing him, and Rob—God bless him—was oblivious. Time and time again the John Smiths had told her Gabriel Drayton deserved this. She didn't need to feel guilty about what she was doing. This was well-warranted justice.

The John Smiths had promised her that after Gabriel Drayton's demise, her parents would be taken care of. The Smith brothers said the Benefactor, as they called him, would ensure her parents would continue to be gainfully employed. If, and only if, she did her part.

Three years ago, not long after Gabriel Drayton came to reside at Drayton Hall, Rob had set Molly's parents up as the gardener and housekeeper for him. At the time her parents had badly needed the work. Turning down the offer had not been an option, regardless of having to answer to a merciless tyrant.

Molly loved her parents, but she wasn't close to them, and they rarely spoke. Their relationship had deteriorated after she ran away from home. She'd been sixteen at the time. For two years she struggled. Desperation, fate and a great deal of luck had landed her the position with Rob August. He'd given her a home, plenty to eat, and paid for a much better wardrobe than she'd ever had before. On top of all of this he allotted her a hefty salary, one she'd never imagined in her wildest dreams. For six years she'd been his cook, his maid, his laundress and even, sometimes, his secretary. That wasn't all. She had a very pretty, comfortable room in the attic of his townhouse. But, for several years now she'd been sleeping on the second floor in a much larger bed.

Rob August was just wonderful! He was ideal in every way possible. All Molly wanted—her only real aspiration anymore—was to someday be referred to as Mrs. Robert August. The only problem was that Rob hadn't yet realized she was the perfect woman for him. She had come from a poor family, without money or social status. These things were important to Rob. If she wore stylish clothes, if she looked the part, if she spoke properly, she could be as sophisticated as the people he called friends. She'd worked hard listening to and emulating well-bred speech. She'd bought magazines and studied the fashions of the wealthy. No one would have to know where she'd really come from. She could be as refined as the magnificent Susan Drayton, and once she proved it to Rob, he would be able to ask her to marry him. He would finally love her as much as she loved him.

To be as chic and polished as Susan Drayton, Molly needed money. What she was doing for the Smith brothers provided her with that money. The Benefactor was paying her very, very well. But more than anything, she was doing this for Rob. If left undeterred, according to the Smith brothers, loathsome Gabriel Drayton would ruin Rob completely.

Nine

Lilly's visit with Julie over the weekend turned out to be not nearly as relaxing as she'd hoped it would be. Other than Julie bemoaning how much she missed her irresponsible husband, Jason, her sister seemed healthy enough. The creditors, however, were another issue. Julie had told her one of them came by every day. When Julie had informed him she didn't have the money to pay, the man—Mr. Horace—became belligerent. Lilly knew better than to give Julie the entire envelope of wages she'd received from Gabriel Drayton, but she'd handed over enough to cover a portion of the overdue rent and to hopefully pacify Mr. Horace for a little while. By Sunday evening, she was ready to put the whole mess behind her. As much as she dreaded returning to Drayton Hall, she was almost relieved to see Mr. Withers pull up in the carriage to take her back.

Seeing Charlotte again was a joy. Even so, by the middle of the week, Lilly's frustration was mounting. Not because of Julie, or creditors, or angry landlords this time, but because of Charlotte's prevarications. Every day something came up to keep them from doing schoolwork.

Monday they'd gone to visit the seamstress in town. Charlotte said they had an appointment. Mr. Withers being prepared to drive them led Lilly to believe this was true, and the seamstress was already ready with a dozen or more fabrics to show Charlotte. They returned in the afternoon, just before Charlotte's riding lesson.

Tuesday, because Susan had sent a note asking them to come, they went to visit her. Charlotte seemed exceptionally excited. In the carriage on the way, she told Lilly, "Uncle Alex has pet snakes!" And then she elaborated in detail about the giant cages he kept them in. Once they were there, however, Charlotte spent the majority of the time in

Mark's playroom while Lilly visited with Susan. The snakes didn't come up again.

Lilly liked Susan. For all her wealth and fine-living she didn't seem the least bit pretentious. Her home was tastefully decorated and very grand, although not nearly as large as Drayton Hall. Most of the time while they were there, Susan did the talking, which was fine with Lilly. She really wasn't sure what to say anyway. The truth was she was a little in awe of Susan. That day, by the time they returned to Drayton Hall, it was time for dinner.

Wednesday Charlotte wanted to go fishing in the creek. Mr. Withers had the tackle box, the fishing poles and bait, and a picnic lunch packed and ready for them. Lilly didn't want to give in, but Charlotte said soon it would be winter and it would be too cold.

It wasn't that Lilly wasn't enjoying Charlotte's company. It was that she worried incessantly about receiving another caustic rebuke from Gabriel Drayton. Despite Charlotte's claim that he shared meals with her all the time, he had again, this week, not made an appearance. The morning ritual, in which Charlotte went to his room to awaken him, was the same. So were their evenings in the front parlor, except Lilly hadn't been invited to join them. Although relieved at not having to see Gabriel Drayton, another part of her was bereft at being left out. This she decided was just plain foolishness.

Thursday, after Charlotte's bath, she asked if Lilly wanted to play the piano with her. Lilly had learned to play a little when she was young, but she hadn't touched a piano in years and didn't remember much of what she'd been taught. Even so, she agreed to accompany Charlotte to the front parlor.

"Will you teach me how?" Charlotte said once they were seated side by side on the bench.

"I don't know enough to teach you," Lilly told her. "Have you ever asked your daddy to teach you?"

Charlotte's smile faded. "He says he doesn't know how either."

That made Lilly furious. *Selfish, arrogant man!*

After listening to Charlotte randomly pounding keys, creating a loud dissonant display, Lilly thought her ears would burst. She had to do something. "This is what I can teach you," she said, and she began explaining to Charlotte how to identify the keys A through G by where they were in relation to the sets of two or three black keys. Charlotte seemed intrigued, and Lilly was amazed by how quickly the child caught on.

Soon enough she found herself challenging Charlotte, "Play a *C*, any *C*. *C* is for Charlotte."

Charlotte picked out two, one high and one low.

"How about a *D?*" Lilly suggested next.

Charlotte leaned over Lilly and played a low one. "*D* is for Daddy," Charlotte said.

Inspired, Lilly said, "You can spell *dad* on the piano. After the *D*, what letter comes next?" To Charlotte's frown, while playing the corresponding keys, Lilly prompted, "*D-A-D* spells dad."

Charlotte played the notes after her, repeating, "*D-A-D* spells dad."

"Your daddy's name is—"

"Gabriel!" Charlotte blurted.

"What letter is for Gabriel?"

Charlotte looked at her inquisitively, but Lilly didn't have a chance to respond. The front door knocker sounded. Charlotte was off the piano bench in an instant and running out into the hall. Lilly followed more slowly. She was rounding the parlor entrance when she heard Charlotte squeal, "Sir Rob!"

If Charlotte hadn't said the man's name, at first glance, Lilly would have thought he was Alex Drayton. The resemblance between them was striking, but upon closer look, she noted that where Alex's face had a wholesome boyish quality to it, this man's did not. He was quite the dashing gentleman, with a kindly smile.

Formally, although playfully, he removed his hat and bowed to Charlotte. "It is very nice to see you again, your highness."

Charlotte returned his bow with a curtsy, and giggled as she gave him her hand, which he raised to kiss.

Stooping to one knee, so he was at Charlotte's level, and drawing a freshly picked daisy from behind his back, he said, "How are you, princess?"

"I'm good, my lord," she replied, giggling again.

"Will you introduce me to your teacher?" he asked.

"Yes!" Charlotte beamed. He stood up and she grabbed his hand to drag him over to where Lilly stood. "This is Miss Lilly. This is my Uncle Rob, but I call him *Sir* Rob because I am a princess and he is a knight in shining armor. Uncle Rob fights all the big, bad dragons."

Rob grinned and shrugged. "Somebody's got to do it." Then he politely shook Lilly's hand. "It is a pleasure, Miss Hawthorne. I'm Gabriel's attorney, Rob August, but please call me Rob."

"How come you came to visit?" Charlotte asked.

"I thought I would give your daddy a break so he doesn't have to come into town to see me this week. And I thought maybe I could join you for dinner?" Rob said. "I'm not too late, am I?"

"No, you're not late."

"Where is your daddy? In his study?"

"I'll go find him!" Charlotte was already scampering away.

Rob turned to Lilly again. "It is a pleasure to finally meet you. I've heard great things about you."

From whom? Lilly wanted to ask. Instead she said, "It's nice to meet you, too."

He made pleasant small talk, about the weather and his ride from town, until they heard the distinct noise of Gabriel's approach.

Charlotte appeared first, skipping her way toward them. Gabriel was behind her, but he stopped by the staircase and didn't seem inclined to move closer. "Why are you here?" he demanded in a tone Lilly thought was terribly rude.

"Why are you such a grouch?" Rob retorted, although his tone wasn't harsh at all. He crossed the distance between them, but didn't shake Gabriel's hand. His next comment was a murmur, intended for Gabriel's ears alone, and Lilly couldn't hear it. Gabriel's answer was a scowl. Then Rob said, "I thought I might have dinner with you?"

"I'm not hungry. I'm sure Miss Hawthorne and Charlotte will be glad to have your company," Gabriel said.

Rob shook his head. "Unfortunately, business before pleasure. I need to discuss some things with you, so I guess I'll be skipping dinner, too."

"*Nooo*," Charlotte whined. "Please stay, Uncle Rob. *Pleeease!*"

"Christ!" Gabriel muttered and then with his free left hand he made an elaborate, wholly unnecessary gesture toward the dining room. "Fine!"

Charlotte bounded onward, happy as a lark. Lilly raised her chin and followed. Rob was right behind her. Mrs. Finch was there, in the process of setting the last of the serving dishes on the table. It didn't take her long, and she quietly left.

Assuming Rob August would want the chair to Gabriel's left, where Lilly usually sat, she went around to the other side and sat next to Charlotte.

Gabriel reached for a heavy meat platter layered with shaved roast beef, and he did something that completely shocked Lilly. He served Charlotte. He did it automatically like it was something he did every day. When finished, he passed the plate to Lilly without serving himself. He did the same with every dish, not serving himself until the plate came back around to him. Without mentioning saying grace, gruffly he said, "Eat."

It was hard for Lilly not to stare at him. No matter how hard she tried not to look, her eyes were drawn in his direction. Even though his mask didn't cover his mouth, she wondered whether it would get in his way. But she couldn't tell. He wasn't eating. He was just shoving the little bit of food he'd dished up for himself around his plate with his fork.

"What is so important it can't wait until I'm in town?" he asked Rob.

"I have some papers I need you to sign. We can do that after. I also need to talk to you about one of the Philadelphia properties."

"Which one?" Gabriel asked.

"Cherry Street…" Rob droned on about the particulars of a family interested in renting the place.

While Rob talked, Gabriel finally started to eat. Every bite he lifted on his fork was extremely small, and then he took forever to chew before he swallowed. Lilly didn't think she'd ever seen anyone eat as slowly or pick at their food so much. Even so, his manners were impeccable, and the mask didn't seem to hinder him at all.

At the end of Rob's discourse, Gabriel took a sip of water and said, "Fine."

Rob brought Charlotte into the conversation by asking about her schooling. Much to Lilly's chagrin, Charlotte rambled on, speaking of everything they'd done the last several days, making it quite clear, although not intentionally, they'd done very little schoolwork. "And today," Charlotte continued, "Miss Lilly taught me piano keys."

Lilly chimed in, "I think if Charlotte had piano lessons she would be a natural. She picked everything up so quickly."

"Can you give me piano lessons, Daddy?" Charlotte asked.

"No," he said. Then his icy glare turned on Lilly. "We will discuss this later."

"But Charlotte is so interested. And I really think—" Lilly started.

"Miss Hawthorne," he interrupted coldly, "this is none of your business!"

"Oh, come on, Gabe—" Rob jumped in.

Gabriel's fury turned on his attorney. "And neither is it yours!"

Casually, Rob said, "It's a great idea—"

"No!" Gabriel snapped.

"You *could* teach her."

The lack of fear Rob exhibited toward callous Gabriel not only floored Lilly, it left her slightly in awe. She felt like she was at the track, cheering on a horse race, and Rob was a head out in front.

"No!" Gabriel barked. "Drop it!"

Rob's hands went up in feigned retreat and Lilly was sorely disappointed.

Silence lingered while they continued to eat. Rob broke it by saying to Gabriel, "What's wrong, no appetite tonight? That's too bad. Mrs. Finch is a fabulous cook." There was a hint of sarcasm in the words. He loaded his fork so it was spilling over and took the overly appreciative mouthful.

"I told you I'm not hungry," Gabriel hissed.

Rob chewed and swallowed. "I'm going to come back tomorrow with Harold Brewster."

"No!"

"You need to see him. This has gone on long enough."

"I said no!" Gabriel roared.

Rob shook his head, but apparently, like before, he chose to drop the argument.

A moment later, Gabriel pushed his full plate forward on the table. The move was identical to the one Charlotte made every time she was done eating. "Excuse me," he muttered. "Bring what I need to sign to the front parlor when you're finished here."

Lilly watched Rob's eyes follow Gabriel as he left the room. There was no mistaking his worry, but when he turned back he was smiling, and he chuckled with a teasing quip for Charlotte. Charlotte was still giggling when the awful iron knocker on the front door sounded.

Charlotte started to get up, but Rob said, "Stay here, princess. Your daddy's out there. He'll answer it."

From where they were in the dining room, they couldn't see him, but it was easy to hear his scraping shuffle through the hall. A moment later, the hinges grated and gruffly he barked, "What?"

The next thing they heard was an airy female voice. "Hello! You must be Mr. Drayton. It's nice to meet you. My name is Julie Gibson. May I come in?"

Lilly shot up out of her seat. Why her sister would come here she had no idea! There was no question Gabriel Drayton would be furious over the intrusion, and the repercussions—not for Julie, but for her—wouldn't be pleasant!

Lilly barreled out, but caught herself before fully stepping into the hall. Gabriel was leaning against the open front door in a way that made her think Julie had frightened him. She watched as he transferred his cane to his left hand so he could take Julie's right hand in his.

Julie looked like a pumpkin. She was dressed in apricot and the girth of her waistline looked unusually large. Her sister was all smiles as she pumped Gabriel's hand. "I'm here to see my sister, Lilly. Lilly Hawthorne. She's your daughter's tutor."

Without another word, without waiting for Gabriel to invite her in, Julie breezed right past him. Already she had loosened the ties to her bonnet and whisked it off.

"Miss Hawthorne is having dinner," Gabriel said.

Lilly's jaw dropped. There was no gruffness in his voice at all. He sounded... *friendly?*

"Oh," Julie said. "Well, then perhaps you can help me? I'm in quite a pickle and I'm not sure what to do. Lilly always has good advice. Right now I'm desperate for some."

"Go on," he said.

"My husband is away, you see. He couldn't find work here in Havertown, so he went to Philadelphia, but he hasn't had much success finding a position there either. At least, not yet. One of his associates has been coming by my house and I don't know what to tell him. I'm not sure when my husband is coming home, and I can't give this gentleman what he wants. I've got to think of something to stop him from coming by because it's becoming rather bothersome. Do you have any ideas?"

"Shall I assume what this associate wants is money?" Gabriel asked.

Julie's expression turned sheepish. "Well... yes. As soon as my husband comes back we'll pay the debt. I've tried to tell him, but I don't think he believes me."

"What's his name?" Gabriel asked.

Mortified, Lilly flew toward them. She had to stop this. "Julie, what are you doing here?"

"Oh good, you're here!" Julie heralded loudly. "Mr. Drayton was just helping me."

"Come with me," Lilly took her sister's arm firmly, intending to lead her up to her room where they could talk privately. When she felt

Julie's wavering protest, she dug her fingers in and murmured to Gabriel, "I'm sorry for the interruption."

"Ouch!" Julie shrieked. "Geez, Lilly! Let go!"

"Hello! Are you Miss Lilly's sister?" Charlotte chirped. She and Rob had followed Lilly out of the dining room.

All Lilly wanted to do was get her sister away, but the next thing she knew introductions were being made, causing all sorts of delays. Impatiently she watched as Julie made a huge fuss over Charlotte. Throughout, Gabriel Drayton just stood there, staring at her sister. Oddly enough, for once, he didn't look mad.

Eventually, Rob suggested, "Why don't Gabe, Charlotte and I go on ahead to the parlor. Miss Hawthorne and Mrs. Gibson can join us when they're ready."

"Finch," Gabriel said, "bring coffee and tea."

Lilly turned. She hadn't realized Mr. Finch was standing there. And Gabriel had requested tea... for Julie *and* for her?

Lilly didn't think she could be any more shocked. Then Gabriel said, "Mrs. Gibson, after your tea with us, Withers will drive you home. It's too dark and cold to walk to town by yourself."

Lilly had to forcibly close her gaping mouth.

Once they were alone in the dining room, Julie plopped into one of the padded chairs and said, "Why, he's not at all what I expected. You said he was mean."

It was the only adjective Lilly had been able to come up with when Julie hounded her about him over the weekend. "*Shhh*, keep your voice down."

"He's not mean at all," Julie continued just as loudly. "He's got a bum leg, but he's certainly not deformed. My goodness, I think he's the most fabulous-looking man I've ever seen. And just as nice as can be. It's too bad he has such a terrible case of influenza. I'll bet he's ever better looking when he's not so ill."

"How do you know he has influenza?"

"My goodness, Lilly, I'm not blind!" Julie scoffed. "Poor man. It was quite thoughtful of him to step away like he did at the door so he wouldn't pass me his germs. He's quite divine, isn't he?"

It was on the tip of Lilly's tongue to ask Julie if she was confusing Gabriel with Rob. *Divine*, indeed! Didn't Julie even notice the mask? And Julie was the one who had told Lilly most of the awful rumors about him! Trying to remain focused, Lilly said, "Tell me what happened. Mr. Horace came by again?"

Julie nodded. "I stayed out as long as I could to avoid him, but he must have been hiding outside, waiting for me. He started knocking right after I got home. I told him I didn't have any more money for him. He shoved me and I fell."

"Are you okay? Are you hurt?"

"No, just a little bruise on my derriere, I think," Julie admitted with a grin. "What should I do? I can't stay away from home all the time. He'll be back tomorrow and the next day and the next."

Lilly sighed. "I'll be right back." The quick retreat she intended—to get money from the stash in her room—didn't go as planned. Just outside of the dining room she froze. Rob and Charlotte were nowhere to be seen, but Gabriel was still there in the hall, leaning crookedly on his cane. His eyes narrowed on her. Dumbstruck, Lilly fled up the staircase.

By the time she returned, thankfully, the hall was devoid of any presence. With the envelope in hand, she went back to her sister. "I'll have more for you on Saturday. Give Mr. Horace all of this. It should satisfy him for a little while longer."

"Thank you, Lilly. I don't know what I would do without you."

"Promise me you'll give it to him," Lilly said firmly.

"I promise, but there's another problem."

"What now?"

"Well, the landlord came by and said if I don't pay up all the back rent within two weeks he's going to evict me," Julie said.

"You were supposed to give the other money I gave you to the landlord. Didn't you do that?"

At least Julie had the gumption to look guilty. "Well, no," she said. "I had to buy groceries and I bought a crib for the baby. It's really pretty. It has white lace—"

"Julie!" Lilly admonished. "Your baby won't be here for another three months. Don't you think it's more important to have a house than a crib? If you're evicted, where do you propose to put the crib?"

"Don't yell at me, Lilly. You know how hard it's been for me since Jason left!"

Lilly got up and paced, quietly counting to ten under her breath. "I'm sorry. I didn't mean to yell. But sometimes you don't use your head. Here's what you have to do. Give half of that money to the landlord and half of it to Mr. Horace. You can promise the landlord you'll give him more on Monday. It won't be enough to cover everything you owe, but hopefully it will appease him. You'll have to beg him to let you stay. It's the only thing you can do."

Julie sniffled and swiped at her dampened eyes. "I would very much like to have some tea. Can we go to the parlor now?"

"Don't you want to just go home?"

"What will I do there all by myself? Besides, Mr. Drayton said... oh, I can't remember his name—Walters or Willis or something like that—will drive me home. The later I go, the better. Mr. Horace might be waiting for me."

Julie tucked the envelope of money into her reticule. With one final swipe at her already dry eyes, she pushed herself up and started across the hall. Lilly had no choice but to follow.

In the parlor, Rob August was seated in one of the wing chairs with Charlotte on his lap, and he was telling her a story. Gabriel Drayton was in his usual spot on the couch, but this time he wasn't slouched over. Without waiting for a gesture of welcome, Julie waddled over to the sofa and lowered her bulky self right next to him. They were so close, Julie could have easily reached over to take his hand!

Face burning, Lilly settled into the wing chair next to Rob. He smiled in greeting, but didn't interrupt his story—a story about mud pies, of all things. Charlotte was giggling, and it wasn't long before Julie was, too. Gabriel didn't laugh, but he didn't seem upset either. He wasn't smiling, but for once, he wasn't scowling and his eerie eyes weren't glowering.

Germs, indeed!

Just as Rob finished the story, a petite, dark blond woman came in carrying a tray with a tea pot and several cups on it. She was very pretty.

"Hi, Moll," Rob drawled. He plucked Charlotte off his lap and sent her off to join her father and Julie on the sofa. Then he got up and took the heavy tray right out of the woman's hands to set it on a side table. "Miss Hawthorne, Mrs. Gibson, this is Molly Finch." To Molly he said, "It's nice of you to help your mum."

"The white coffee cup is for Mr. Drayton. Yours is the blue one," Molly said quietly. "I wasn't sure what everyone else wanted so I didn't prepare the rest."

Rob helped Molly serve, including adding the requested amounts of sugar and cream, and then he asked her to join them. Molly declined with a shy smile, tucked the tray under her arm and said, "Good evening, everyone."

The minute Molly pulled the parlor door closed behind her, Gabriel said, "What's your housekeeper doing here?"

"I told her I was coming out and she asked if she could ride along. She wanted to visit her parents. I guess it's been a while since she's seen them. Seemed like a good idea to me, and I didn't think you'd mind. You always say her coffee is better than her mother's."

Gabriel took a lingering sip of the steaming liquid he held. "That it is," he murmured, and then he took another one.

By Molly's attire—an expensive gorgeous silk, rose-colored dress—Lilly thought Molly didn't look like a housekeeper at all. In fact, at first she'd assumed Molly was Rob's wife. Then, when he'd introduced her, she'd thought she must be his fiancée. She'd been shocked at hearing Molly was merely his housekeeper. At the same time she was both intrigued and deeply touched by Rob August's efforts in assisting her. What an extraordinary gentleman he was!

More stories followed from him. Initially they were stories intended for Charlotte—somewhat fantastic—but before long, he moved on to a story about one of his own boyhood misadventures.

Not to be bested, Julie piped up with the tale of Lilly and her getting lost in the woods. They'd ended up sleeping in a tree, or rather attempting to sleep in a tree. Lilly remembered it as a harrowing night full of mosquitoes and spiders and noises that were inevitably wolves and bears. Their mother had gone to the constable, and a search party had been sent out. Very early in the morning, they were found. Julie ended the tale with, "When we got home Lilly grabbed onto momma and wouldn't let go for hours!"

Rob laughed. Charlotte giggled. Gabriel was staring at her. Julie had left out the part of the story where she'd filled Lilly's head with ghost stories all night long. "I was only seven years old," she murmured, but nobody seemed to hear her.

"That reminds me of the time a search party went looking for Gabe." Rob chuckled aloud and went on relaying an event that occurred at the boarding school he, Gabriel and Alex had attended. He and Gabriel were sixteen. Alex was fifteen. One night the three of them broke curfew and sneaked out of their dormitory. Their purpose was to spy on a party being hosted at the dean's house. Gabriel ran off with the dean's daughter, who, as planned, had sneaked out too, leaving Rob and Alex to do the furtive spying.

From their hiding place in the bushes overlooking the dean's veranda, Rob dared Alex to throw a toad into the crowd. Alex did it, hitting a woman right between the eyes. The woman screamed. Rob and Alex fled.

Rob was lucky, but Alex was not. He was caught and dragged back to the dean's house by the earlobe. In front of all of his guests, the dean whipped Alex with a wooden paddle. Meanwhile, Rob went frantically searching for Gabriel, to no avail. Rob ended up sneaking back into the dormitory, escaping punishment entirely.

Gabriel didn't fare so well. After the dean's wife discovered their daughter wasn't in her room, they sent out a search party. She and Gabriel were found in the woods, doing things sixteen-year-old girls and boys should not be doing—at least that was the way Rob described it. Julie laughed and Charlotte giggled, although Charlotte wouldn't have understood Rob's implication. It was difficult for Lilly to contain her mirth, too. Gabriel's expression up until then was blank, but he'd been listening. As Rob continued on with the story, Gabriel's focus turned to the fire.

In what remained of Rob's narrative, Gabriel's father came to the school to convince the dean not to expel his son. The set-down Gabriel endured from his father apparently was much worse than the whipping the dean had given him. Rob ended the tale by saying he'd been glad Charles Drayton wasn't his father!

From other stories Rob told, Lilly learned that Gabriel had saved Alex from drowning when they were young. Years later, Alex won an Olympic medal for swimming. Another funny tale involved Alex's pants catching fire while he, Gabriel and Rob were canoeing.

They'd built a small fire in their boat to cook the fish they'd caught. Because Gabriel was purposely rocking the boat, Alex lost his balance and fell into the flames. Rob and Gabriel splashed him until the fire was out—fortunately only his clothes had been scorched!—but Alex was so mad at Gabriel, he punched him. For a week Gabriel sported a black eye!

The three of them had gone on from boarding school to attend the same college in Philadelphia. More entertaining stories evolved from these years. Rob was charismatic and compelling in the telling. He spoke with his hands and used different voices to portray the characters. With the exception of Gabriel, much of the time he had them laughing.

It wasn't until Rob began to speak of his younger years that a spark of pity for him welled in Lilly. He'd apparently been raised until the age of fourteen in a home for orphaned boys.

"Back when I was a mere scamp of nine, my two best buddies were Cleet and Avery. We were quite the little hooligans!" Rob droned on with a tale of Avery almost being adopted.

He and Cleet came to Avery's rescue by debilitating the wagon that belonged to an ugly man who was going to take their friend away. Together the three boys ran off and stayed away from the orphanage until the money Avery had stolen from the ugly man ran out.

"We were pretty cold and hungry by then," Rob said. "Avery, bless his sorry soul, took all the blame and got the worst beating of his life from the headmaster. It was worse, by far, than the whipping Gabriel got from the dean! Ah, but I miss those two sometimes…"

Lilly supposed Rob would have continued, but just then Molly rapped lightly at the door and peered in. "I've brought more coffee and tea, and warm milk for Charlotte."

As before, Rob helped her. This time, however, there wasn't as much to do. She'd pre-poured for each of them. Methodically she and Rob went about replacing empty cups with steaming, freshly filled ones. Molly had also brought a tray of macaroons.

"Tell more about Cleet and Avery," Charlotte said with her mouth full. "Cleet and Avery are funny!"

It was well past Charlotte's bedtime when Rob finally suggested they wrap up. By then, Charlotte was snuggled against her father. From her drooping eyelids it was evident she was having a hard time staying awake.

Julie said, "I'm having such a great time, I hate to go! But it is getting late."

Gabriel had been the one to say Withers would take Julie home, but Rob was the one who sought Withers out. Preoccupied with accompanying Charlotte to her room, and helping her change into her nightgown, Lilly didn't think any more of Julie. Instead she was thinking of Rob August, wondering if she would see him again. She hoped so… more than she wanted to admit. Tomorrow, she might… he was supposed to come by with a man named Harold Brewster…

That night sleep claimed her so deeply she woke late. The clock on her wall was chiming eight o'clock—the designated breakfast hour—and she was still scurrying about getting dressed. She flew down the stairs to the dining room, breezed through the door and stopped dead in her tracks. Gabriel was seated at the table reading a newspaper.

"Hi, Miss Lilly!" Charlotte chirped.

Gabriel's newspaper crinkled.

"I'm sorry I'm late," Lilly murmured as she slid into the seat to his left.

Without a word he lifted the newspaper high, blocking her out. On the table in front of him was a small plate with crumbs. Charlotte had a larger plate containing fruit, untouched toast, and the remnants of what had once been a slice of ham. From the serving dishes Lilly chose a muffin and an apple.

"I'm all finished." Charlotte pushed her plate away.

Gabriel folded the paper and dropped it on the table. "Go upstairs and get ready for school," he said.

Charlotte scampered off, leaving Lilly with a mouthful of muffin. She could feel Gabriel's stare. Self-consciously she swallowed.

"There are some things I would like to discuss with you. I will be waiting for you in my study at three o'clock today," he said curtly. Using his cane and the arm of the chair, he pushed himself to his feet. He was standing there, towering over her. In a frosty, disdainful tone, he said, "Try not to be late."

It was no wonder Alex had wanted to punch him so badly all those years ago! Furiously she glared at his retreating figure. She was still fuming when she made her way up the stairs to Charlotte's playroom. She didn't like lord high and mighty Drayton at all. The rumors with regard to his hideous character were very much correct. The other rumors, however, were not. She thought of Rob's stories, and specifically the one in which Gabriel had been caught with the dean's daughter. This brought Charlotte's mother to mind.

Many times Lilly had wondered about Charlotte's mother, whether she was dead and whether she and Gabriel had ever been married. Before, because of the rumors she'd heard, she'd assumed he'd raped the woman. No woman in her right mind would willingly subject herself to that monster's attentions. Now, however, she realized Charlotte must have been conceived prior to Gabriel's debilitating injuries. According to Charlotte, there had been a fire at their home in Philadelphia. Lilly wondered if that fire just might be the reason Gabriel Drayton wore that dreadful mask.

Charlotte was waiting for her, huddled on the pink sofa in her playroom, with a book in her lap.

"I want to read this one! It's new!" she announced. "My daddy brought it for me."

Ten

Gabriel's sixth destination was one he'd never been to before. He'd never been in this part of town either. Withers opened the carriage door and Gabriel glanced around before stepping out. The day was cooler. Once he was on the street, he drew his cloak more securely around his shoulders.

The paint on the door of the building in front of him was chipped. There was trash scattered, blown by the wind, along the sides and into the corners of the steps he had to climb. On the second step was a rotten piece of food—a banana peel, perhaps? It was hard to tell. The whole area had a foul, rancid odor.

Heavily he pounded on the door with his fist. In short order, he heard a woman's voice shout some slang language which he internally translated into, "Wait a minute."

She pulled the door open, gasped aloud and took a hasty step back. Such a reaction was typical. This day, however, Gabriel didn't care. If anything, he welcomed it. The woman was missing two teeth. The remaining ones were a cakey brown. Her floral patterned skirt was streaked with lines of grease, or dirt, or… he didn't know what.

Gabriel moved forward and she took another step back. The stench of the interior of the unkempt house was worse than the odor outside. He closed the door behind him anyway. "I'm looking for Mr. Simon Horace."

She cleared her throat. "Who's callin'?"

"A friend," he snapped.

She left him there.

Seconds later, a man—Simon Horace, Gabriel presumed—appeared. The woman was behind him, sneaking peeks over his shoulder. Unlike the woman, Horace was dressed more tastefully in a three-piece suit. His hair had been brushed, but it looked greasy. It was not the kind of grease one would apply to keep one's hair in place. Beady hazel eyes narrowed on Gabriel, but the man didn't make an effort to greet him properly. Gabriel was glad of that.

"What do you want?" Horace demanded.

The slight hesitation in his voice, although well concealed, told Gabriel he was as scared as the woman. In this case, as with most of the stops he'd made, it was to his advantage. "How much does Jason Gibson owe you?"

"What business is that of yours?"

Gabriel didn't answer. He merely glared at the man.

Horace rattled off a sum much greater than what was shown on the list Dobbins had given Gabriel.

"Wrong," he snapped. "Try again."

The sum Horace touted this time was less, although still greater than what Gabriel knew it should be.

"Try again!"

Horace was the fifth of seven known creditors owed money by Jason Gibson, and Horace was the man abusing Julie Gibson. Earlier that morning, Gabriel had gone over the list with Dobbins once again to ensure the names and amounts were still accurate.

Jason Gibson, in Gabriel's opinion, was an imbecile. He guessed that neither Julie Gibson, nor Lilly Hawthorne truly knew the extent of the debts. If Lilly were to hand over her earnings for the next five years, she still wouldn't have enough to pay the substantial amounts Julie's idiotic husband owed.

The next sum Horace quoted corresponded with what was shown on Dobbins's list. Gabriel hadn't expected the man to cow so quickly. He supposed Horace didn't have any thugs lurking in the back room like the others did. In two of his previous stops, Gabriel had found himself surrounded. The second meeting was the worst. One of the thugs had aimed a revolver at him.

With his free left hand, Gabriel reached inside the pocket of his coat and withdrew a thick, bound envelope. "I trust your visits to Mrs. Gibson will cease."

"Only if you pay what's owed."

With a quick flick of his wrist Gabriel chucked the pouch. In an excellent display of fumbling, Horace attempted to catch it and missed. The packet hit him square in the chest and dropped to the floor at his feet. Quickly, he squirmed, bending to retrieve it.

"If you come within a thousand yards of Julie Gibson, I will be back," Gabriel said.

"You have no right to threaten me. I'll go wherever I please!" Horace sucked in air and puffed his chest out. At the same time he fiddled with the envelope, trying to rip it open.

Gabriel released a seething breath. "Another meeting between us will not be in your best interest."

"What are you gonna do, beat me?"

In a flash, the tip of Gabriel's cane landed underneath Horace's thick chin, causing a third wrinkle to appear in the extra skin. Horace took a step back to release the sudden pressure and careened into the woman behind him. Gabriel advanced, increasing the pressure until the woman's back hit the dirty wall behind her. Horace's body pinned her in place. The cane remained crammed against Horace's throat. "If I must," Gabriel hissed.

Horace raised both arms in surrender.

Much easier, by far, than the second meeting, Gabriel mused wryly, lowering the cane. He'd had to advance and parry, using his cane like a sword to knock the gun from the squirrelly character's hand.

"Good day," Gabriel swung around and yanked open the door. Withers was there, by the coach, waiting.

"All the money better be here!" Horace shouted after him.

Gabriel didn't bother to reply. He glanced about as he crossed the sidewalk. Three teenage ruffians—he was fairly certain there were three—were attempting to conceal themselves around the corner of the building at the end of the block. One of them he recognized.

He was one step away from being safely in the carriage when he heard their heavy-footed charge. A rock stung his left shoulder, and it hurt, but he didn't stop moving. "Let's go," he murmured to Withers.

Ever faithful Withers knew what he really meant—*don't close the door for me. We need to move quickly!*

The carriage took off like a shot, lumbering over the rutted street. The crack of another rock hitting the outside slightly to the right of the door sounded. A third glanced off the corner near the left rear wheel. Something else smashed on the roof. The noise of it, however, wasn't as familiar. A ball of mud, Gabriel guessed? He was pretty sure Withers had escaped unscathed, for once.

Other than to give him orders, Gabriel didn't speak to Withers, yet Withers had proven himself to be one of the most loyal people Gabriel had ever had in his employ. And Withers put up with a lot on his behalf. Never once had the young man complained, not about cleaning off the carriage, not about keeping the sporadic schedule, not about being subjected to shouts, name-calling and any other number of obscenities, and never once about being pelted with inanimate objects. The blond man was humble and patient. This was the reason Gabriel had asked him to give Charlotte riding lessons. Withers had agreed without hesitation. Of course, Gabriel couldn't forget, he was paying Withers extremely well.

After checking to ensure his pockets were empty, Gabriel balled up his cloak and opened the carriage door just enough to shove it through. He didn't bother to look where it landed in the street, or watch to see who would be the first urchin to come out to curiously poke at it, or who would eventually steal it.

There were only two more stops he planned to make this day. The next one wasn't close. They needed to go back out to the countryside for a good two miles. Withers knew where to go. Bracing himself, Gabriel rested his head back, arching his neck over the rounded top of the cushion. The black-tarped ceiling of the coach blurred before him and he closed his eyes. He breathed and breathed again, deep breaths, willing himself to find some level of relief. The discomfort of the knot from his kerchief pressing into the base of his skull was nothing compared to the pounding in his head, the cramping in his stomach and the dull, endless ache in his hip. He was almost done, he reminded himself. Almost done.

The coach picked up the pace, an indication they'd left the confines of town. Within seconds the horses were racing steadily onward. He knew by feel alone the second they moved from the open countryside to the section of roadway that went through the woods. It was rougher, rockier, causing the coach wheels to rattle. Absently he reached for the security strap and clutched it.

They were almost to the open countryside again when he grabbed his cane. He was gasping, swallowing, and gasping again and he couldn't control it. He opened his eyes to take in the neatly pleated patterns in the curtained ceiling. Upending his cane, he used it to press through the fabric to the hard surface beyond, once, twice, three times…

On his fourth attempt there was no thud. He barely graced the curtain. The cane dropped. It hit his knee as it fell, clanking to the floor. He squeezed his eyes shut, hoping desperately Withers had heard him.

The coach began to slow and the jolting inside increased, which meant Withers was pulling to the side of the road. Gabriel grabbed the door handle, hauled himself to the edge of the seat and shoved the door open. The carriage bucked as it came to a final stop and the door swung in on him, slamming into his knee and knocking him backwards. Gaining his balance again, clinging to the doorframe, he shoved the door and grabbed for the handle, but missed. At the same time he pushed off with his good leg, intending to step down, but he missed the step too, and catapulted forward. He landed on his knees and his hands, jarring his shoulders and elbows in a desperate attempt to prevent his face from smashing into the rocky, crabgrass-infested soil. But the pain from the fall barely registered. Somewhere in the fog of his mind he was aware of Withers jumping down from the high driver seat and rushing to him.

"Sir, are you alright, sir?" Withers sounded panicked.

Gabriel couldn't reply. The bile he'd been holding back for the better part of the morning refused to stay down any longer.

Eleven

Lilly knocked on the door to the study at precisely five minutes to three. There was no answer. Pacing the hallway outside of it, she waited and waited, and all the while her employer's caustic, *Try not to be late!* replayed in her head.

A half an hour later, under her breath she murmured, "Practice what you preach, you disrespectful boor!" Then she went outside and meandered down the path to watch Charlotte bounce around on her pony.

Earlier that day, for once, Charlotte had been unable to avoid her schoolwork, and Lilly's initial worries had heightened. Alex had told her Charlotte had attended the local school in town for several months. There was no question Charlotte was a bright child. By regurgitating things she'd heard, Charlotte faked it well, but Lilly was pretty certain the little girl didn't recognize any written letters or numbers.

Teaching Charlotte wasn't the problem. Rather, it was the fear of having to discuss her concerns with Gabriel. After much deliberating, she'd come to the conclusion that he wouldn't care, which meant she didn't need to say anything to him at all.

That evening when Alex, Susan and Mark arrived for dinner, Gabriel didn't make an appearance. Charlotte's response to Alex's inquiry about him was a shrug. The meal was pleasant, full of laughter, and Charlotte convinced them to stay and join her in the parlor after dinner. Once there, Alex retrieved the cello from the black leather case he'd brought along. Charlotte's enthusiasm bubbled over as she announced she was going to show them her dance.

What followed was an entertaining evening watching Charlotte and Mark, who wasn't nearly as graceful as his cousin, twirling about the room. The only person who didn't seem to enjoy the festivities was Susan. By the second dance, she appeared wholly bored.

As she listened, Lilly's thoughts turned to Rob August. He had said he was going to stop by with that man—Harold Brewster—but if he did, she hadn't seen him. It was a disappointment. She was still thinking of Rob when Alex's bow screeched across the strings and came to a halt. "Gabriel!" he spouted.

Gabriel was standing in the doorway. "What are you doing?" he growled.

"Do you remember how we used to play duets?" Alex said cheerfully. "I brought my cello because I thought it might be fun to try again. It's been years."

Gabriel didn't respond to Alex. "Charlotte," he barked. "Time for bed!"

"Well, I *was* having a pleasant time here for once." Susan's eyebrow rose.

Gabriel glowered at her. "You hate this house, remember?"

"You're right. I do." Susan gracefully stood. "It's about time we left. Alex, let's go. We're not really welcome here, are we?"

Alex wasn't as easily deterred. "Gabriel, come on, for old time's sake. Besides, this was the only thing I could think of to do to apologize to you for losing my temper last week."

"Put it away!" Gabriel ground out.

With that, Alex's placidity ended. "Susan is right. I should know better. You know, every time I see you, you remind me more and more of your father."

"Get out of my house!"

Alex shoved his cello back into the case so roughly Lilly cringed on behalf of the instrument. He tossed the bow in after it and slammed the lid down. "Susan, Mark, let's go. Lilly, Charlotte, we'll see you later. I do apologize. This is not something you should have to put up with." As he passed Gabriel, in a low voice he said, "It won't be your house for long."

"Get out!" Gabriel roared.

Worried about Charlotte, Lilly wrapped her arm around the little girl's slight shoulders.

"Charlotte, it's time for bed!" Gabriel repeated.

"I want to dance one more dance for Miss Lilly."

"Not tonight."

To appease Charlotte, Lilly suggested reading a bedtime story in her room. Thankfully Charlotte agreed, but the good humor that had been present in her moments before was gone. Taking Charlotte's hand, Lilly led her out.

After helping Charlotte change into her nightgown, Lilly settled on the bed beside her and read Charlotte's newly favored book for the fourth time. When she finished, she closed the book, kissed Charlotte's forehead and said softly, "Goodnight, sweetie."

"Miss Lilly?" Charlotte was looking at her with those round expressive eyes. "Are you going to go away again tomorrow? Like you went away last week?"

"Yes, I have to go to see my sister."

"Can I come with you?" Charlotte asked.

Lilly's blood began to boil. The poor child was desperate to get away from the horrid man she had the misfortune of calling *father*. More than anything, Lilly wanted to say yes, but she couldn't. Not with threats from Mr. Horace and the landlord and all the creditors hanging over Julie's head. "That's not such a good idea."

"Can you come back early on Sunday morning?" Charlotte asked.

"I go to church on Sunday mornings."

Charlotte pushed herself up. "I've been to church before!"

"You have?"

"Yes, with Uncle Alex and Aunt Susan. It's lots of fun! They sing there. I'm good at singing."

Lilly hesitated before daring to ask her next question. "Would you like to come to church with me?"

"Yes!" Charlotte beamed. "Can I?"

"We'll have to ask your daddy."

"He won't mind," Charlotte said.

"Will he want to come, too?"

"He won't go. One time Alex asked him to and he said no. I'll ask Daddy if it's okay for me to go with you." Charlotte's cheerful expression disappeared in an instant. "I forgot I have to help Daddy make breakfast." Then she smiled again. "I'll tell him to get up early!"

"Why don't we talk about this more tomorrow? It's time to get some sleep." She leaned over and kissed Charlotte's forehead one more time. "Goodnight."

Lilly was halfway to Charlotte's bedroom door when she heard Charlotte's covers rustling. She turned back to find Charlotte crawling out of bed. "Where are you going?"

"I have to say goodnight to my daddy."

"But your daddy said it's time for bed."

Charlotte shook her head. "It's only time for bed the second time. The first time means to change into my nightgown."

Charlotte scrambled to her playroom, where she began rummaging around in her toy box. Whatever she was searching for wasn't there. She hastened over to her shelves full of dolls and started yanking them off.

"What are you looking for?"

"My magic wand," Charlotte said. "I don't know where I put it."

Remembering seeing it in Charlotte's library, Lilly went to retrieve it. As she handed it over she said softly, "I'm sorry your daddy yells at you."

Charlotte made one of her faces, the one that meant, *what you said makes no sense.* "He doesn't yell at me."

"Yes, he does. All the time."

"No, he doesn't." Charlotte was resolute. "He only yells at Aunt Susan, and sometimes Uncle Alex. I have to go now." With that she bounded out of the room.

Lilly was reading in bed when she heard Charlotte come back up the stairs. She must have fallen asleep after that because she didn't remember hearing Gabriel, either coming to bed or doing his trek through the hallway. But later, something—an odd noise—awakened her. From her bedroom, she couldn't define it. For a long time there was silence. Telling herself she must have imagined it, she lay back down and closed her eyes. And then she heard it again.

She was out of bed, wrapping up in her robe as fast as she could. When she opened her door her foot slid on something—something that crinkled. It was the envelope containing her wages for the week. Carelessly she tossed it to the table by the suite entrance.

From the darkened hallway, she recognized the noise. The guttural sounds of retching weren't coming from Charlotte's room. They were coming from Gabriel's. Julie had said he was ill, and Lilly had thoughtlessly disregarded Julie's claim.

She remained in the hallway internally wrestling with what to do. Gabriel Drayton may be a rude, uncouth, disagreeable man, but she couldn't just leave him like that. She was almost at his door, ready to knock, when the violent heaving ended. With her arm still suspended, she waited.

The minutes ticked by, but she heard nothing more.

Twelve

Like the week before, on Saturday Lilly and Charlotte headed to town. Withers dropped them off near the shopping district so they could walk along Market Street and peruse at their leisure. For lunch they stopped in a tea shop—the one Susan had recommended. Afterwards, Charlotte said she didn't want to shop anymore. She wanted to take a walk.

The idea suited Lilly. Charlotte skipped along the sidewalk with Lilly following a short distance behind. They turned a corner, walked a block and turned again. The street was tree-lined and pretty. The townhouses were larger, three- and four-story structures, most of which appeared to be businesses with shingles hung out. Because there was much less pedestrian traffic, Lilly didn't have to pay such close attention to her charge. She allowed herself the luxury of taking in the elaborate architecture of the buildings. Then one of the shingles caught her eye. It was the name of the man Rob said he was going to bring to Drayton Hall to see Gabriel—Harold Brewster. After his name were the initials, MD. Harold Brewster was a doctor?

Ahead of her at the next house, a three-story brownstone, Charlotte bounded up the porch stairs. "Charlotte, wait!" Lilly bellowed.

"It's Uncle Rob's office!" Charlotte called out.

Sure enough, the shingle in front read, *Robert August, Esquire*. Suddenly butterflies fluttered in Lilly's stomach.

She had to remind herself that she was too old and too sensible, after having gone through what she did three years ago, to develop a crush on any man. Long ago, she'd resigned herself to the idea that marriage for her was out of the question. It was silly for her to even think of it. Rob, of course, would have no interest in someone like her anyway. And yet, she couldn't help the welling anticipation.

"Come on, Miss Lilly!" Charlotte hollered impatiently.

Charlotte didn't knock. Grunting, she pushed the door inward with such force it slammed into the wall behind it. By the time Lilly got to the top of the porch steps, Charlotte was opening another door without knocking—the one to the left just inside the small foyer.

"Why, it's Princess Charlotte!" Lilly heard Rob chortle. "What a nice surprise."

"We came to visit," Charlotte chirped.

"Very good, because I need to talk to your daddy."

"Not Daddy. Me and Miss Lilly."

"Really?"

To Lilly, he sounded surprised, but not unpleasantly so. She peeked around the doorframe. "I hope we're not disturbing you."

Rob rose from behind his desk and smiled. "Not at all. I'm up to my ears in my latest case and I need a break. All this research has my eyes crossing."

He came out from around the desk, took her hand and kissed the back of it.

"Is Miss Lilly a princess, too?" Charlotte asked.

He winked at Lilly and addressed Charlotte, "What do you think?" Charlotte nodded.

"How's your daddy today?" he asked.

"He's fine," Charlotte said.

"I'm glad to hear it." To Lilly he said, "May I offer you some tea? And cookies, perhaps?" The last was made to tempt Charlotte, whose eyes widened with glee. "Will you run to the kitchen and ask Molly to bring us a plate?" Charlotte took off and Rob gestured to one of two wing chairs opposite his desk. "Please have a seat."

Lilly sat down in one and was touched, when, instead of returning to his desk, he took the other. Pleasantly he made small talk and then asked after Julie, but it wasn't long before Charlotte returned with Molly.

Molly, Lilly noted right away, was again dressed more like a high society wife than a housekeeper. After setting a tray on the table, she politely excused herself.

Lilly nibbled on a cookie as she listened to Rob teasing Charlotte. He had Charlotte giggling hysterically by declaring that someday she would marry a toad—a toad that didn't turn into a prince like he was supposed to!

Charlotte was still giggling when Rob turned to Lilly and said, "What about you, Miss Lilly? Do you have a Prince Charming out there waiting for you?"

There was a twinkle in his eye. Lilly knew he was teasing, and yet her cheeks heated. "There's no Prince Charming for me," she murmured.

"Oh, come now. Someone as beautiful as you I'm sure has a whole string of suitors."

Lilly shook her head. Charlotte giggled yet again. The look on Rob's face turned odd for just a second before he smiled. She knew she couldn't possibly be reading him correctly, but she could have sworn in that moment he looked relieved. Her heart began to beat at a much faster pace.

He started in on Charlotte again, thankfully. Soon enough their tea was empty and the cookies were gone. The grandfather clock in the corner chimed two o'clock. They'd been there for more than an hour!

"We'd better get going so Uncle Rob can get back to work, and so we're not late for your riding lesson," Lilly suggested.

"Charlotte," Rob asked, "before you go, would you mind going to the kitchen and asking Molly to come here?"

Nodding happily, Charlotte scampered off.

"I don't mean to keep you, but I wanted to talk to you without Charlotte being present." Rob smiled briefly before becoming serious. "I know the situation with your sister is dire. I just wanted you to know, if there is anything I can do, please do not hesitate to call on me. The *esquire* behind my name can often help when dealing with… *er*… how shall I put this… unscrupulous creditors?"

Lilly was floored and mesmerized all at the same time. "I can't tell you how much I appreciate the offer, but Julie doesn't have the funds. I could pay you from what I earn from Mr. Drayton—"

Interrupting her, Rob took her hand and ran his thumb over the back of it in what could only be deemed a familiar caress. "You misunderstand. I don't want you to hire me. I mean it as a favor. For a friend."

Lilly was still hemming and hawing in an attempt to express her gratitude when Charlotte and Molly appeared. Embarrassed, she yanked her hand away.

Shortly thereafter, she and Charlotte said their farewells. While they strolled along the sidewalk Lilly couldn't stop the churning in her stomach. She was certainly no expert, but she was sure Rob had been flirting with her! The top of her hand still tingled from his touch.

It was only a few blocks to where Withers had parked. They found him with a bucket of water at his feet, rubbing down the side of the carriage. The distinct odor of rotten egg was wafting through the air. He turned when he heard them and smiled. "Did you have fun shopping?"

"We did!" Charlotte chirped. "And we saw Uncle Rob, too!"

"What happened?" Lilly asked.

Withers rolled his eyes and murmured, "The hooligans again. The Drayton carriage is their favorite target. I'll be done here in a minute."

While Withers finished cleaning up the mess, he asked of Lilly's weekend plans, so he would know when to drop her and pick her up. Charlotte piped in that her daddy had said she could go to church, so Withers agreed to retrieve Lilly from Julie's early Sunday morning. They would return to Drayton Hall, pick up Charlotte and then go on to the church.

Once they were on their way back to Drayton Hall, Charlotte was oddly silent. Without Charlotte's constant interruptions, Lilly took the opportunity to sit back and daydream. Oddly, Rob wasn't the only man who kept coming to mind. She was thinking of Gabriel, too, albeit not in a good way. They were turning up the drive when Charlotte, who had dozed off, opened her eyes. "I'm going to tell Daddy we saw Uncle Rob!"

Lilly forced a smile. She was troubled by how attached Charlotte was to her father. The poor child would probably be eating chocolate cake for breakfast and popcorn for dinner again tomorrow! At the very least, since Charlotte was coming to church with her, Lilly could ensure she had a decent lunch. There was something else, however, at the forefront of her mind. "Charlotte, is your daddy sick?" she asked.

"No."

"But he was ill? Is that why he hasn't been eating with us?"

Charlotte looked perplexed. "No. He's not sick. He was sick a long time ago when I was little. I had to live with Uncle Alex and Aunt Susan because he was in the hopsital."

"The hospital?" Lilly corrected gently.

"That's what I said. The hopsital, 'cause the fire in our house burned him. He's all better now, 'cept sometimes his leg hurts. I'm the only one who can make it better."

Through the window Lilly saw the enormous expanse of dark grey come into view.

"Some people don't like my daddy," Charlotte said. "Uncle Rob says people are mean to him 'cause they're scared of him, and we should feel sorry for them because they're ing-rant, but I don't like those people. You know my daddy's not a monster, don't you?"

Lilly could only hope Charlotte wouldn't notice the color rising under her skin. "Who told you he's a monster?"

"The other children at the schoolhouse. They said he is wicked and they called him mean names. I tried to tell them he's a good daddy, but they didn't believe me. I told Daddy I didn't want to go to school anymore and he said I didn't have to. He said I could have school here at home. That's why Uncle Alex brought you."

Disturbed, Lilly tried to deflect. "That means come Monday, we'd better get to work on learning your letters and numbers so you don't ever have to go back to that schoolhouse. What do you think?"

"Okay," Charlotte smiled, but her smile faded as quickly as it appeared. "You don't have to be afraid of my daddy, Miss Lilly. He won't ever hurt anybody. He's a really good daddy."

The carriage turned into the circular area in front of the mansion.

"Maybe you and my daddy can get married and then you can be my teacher and my momma," Charlotte said.

Revolted beyond measure, Lilly tried to think of a gentle way to put Charlotte off, but Charlotte droned on before she could say a word.

"In church tomorrow we're going to learn about Jesus. I already know who He is. Aunt Susan and Uncle Alex taught me about Him. I'm going to pray to Jesus that you and my daddy get married, so you can be my momma!"

Lilly took a breath. How in the world was she going to get these outlandish notions out of Charlotte's head? Just the idea of marrying Gabriel was so reprehensible, it made her shiver. "Charlotte, you can pray to Jesus for anything you want. But remember Jesus answers prayers in His own way and in His own time."

Charlotte nodded knowingly. "It's okay, Miss Lilly. I won't be upset if it takes a long time for you to love my daddy."

Thirteen

"You're exhausted," Molly said as she stepped into Rob's office with a cup of coffee in hand.

He looked up from the file he'd been studying for the better part of the last two hours. His eyes ached and so did his head. It was very late, but the case he was working on, a new one, was one he couldn't put off. "This contract I'm drafting is due next week. I can't afford to lose this client."

Molly handed him his coffee and then walked around to the back of his chair. The chair was enormous in width, but the back was low enough she could reach over it. Rob felt her touch on his shoulders, gentle at first, but then heavier as her fingers dug in. Wearily he closed his eyes. "You're awfully tense," she said.

"Too much to do, Moll. Just too much to do. But damn, that feels good."

"Is there anything I can do to help?" she asked.

"Keep bringing me coffee. I'm going to be here for a while," he lamented. "After I finish with this, I have some things to take care of for Gabe." He took a sip of the perfectly creamed, steaming brew she'd brought him and leaned back into her massaging hands. "What would I do without you?" he whispered.

"Mr. Drayton makes a lot of work for you," Molly said.

"He's a royal pain in my ass!" Rob smirked. Molly's tender fingertips probed up the back of his neck, into his hair, and he groaned. He was tense, indeed. His law practice was in dire financial straights. Nevertheless, his money difficulties weren't what kept him up at night. He would pull through. He'd done it before, and he would do it again. What was on his mind extended far beyond economic problems. A trip to New York was necessary, but he wasn't looking forward to it. In the last couple years every time he'd been to New York he'd left the busy city angry and unsettled. He didn't want to think about that either. Not now. Abruptly he sat up straighter. "I'm sorry, Moll, but I have to get back to it."

Her hands dropped to his shoulders and rested there. "May I suggest a short break?"

Rob grinned crookedly as he swiveled to look up at her. "Believe me, you're very tempting. But I can't. I really can't."

"Perhaps I can persuade you." She moved around the chair, pushing on the edge of it so it rolled on its wheels, creating distance between it and the desk. Then she leaned over enough to give him a delectable view into the low-cut neckline of her gown.

"Molly…" he tried to warn her, but there was no conviction in his tone, and she knew it. She grinned and leaned closer. The chair creaked under his weight as he eased back. Her full, pink lips came within an inch of his mouth.

"You've been working all day. You deserve a break," she whispered.

Silently, from under hooded lids, Rob watched her take control. And he let her, because… *oh geez*… just because. He gripped the arms of the chair, as she pressed his knees apart and knelt between them. Already his loins were burning in anticipation. Her hands moved fleetingly to the fastening of his trousers. As deftly as always, she made short work of opening them. He watched her draw the length of him between those full, marvelous lips of hers. He watched until his pelvis, of its own accord, rocked up to meet her, and then he closed his eyes and just breathed.

Molly was adorable. He'd thought so from the first moment he saw her standing on his doorstep. She'd responded to the ad he'd placed in the newspaper for a housekeeper. Of all the candidates he'd interviewed, she was the least qualified, but he'd hired her above the others simply because of how pretty she was. He'd always been a sucker for a pretty girl, he supposed, and she was especially lovely with her long dirty-blond curls, her large blue eyes and that pert little nose with a smattering of tiny freckles across the top of it. She had the most intriguing lips he'd ever seen and an enticingly shapely petite body. Yet, he'd had no intention of anything sexual happening between them.

For the first two years of her employment, she'd proved herself to be surprisingly competent. She'd been quick to pick up on his likes and dislikes, and she catered to him very well, preparing his favorite foods, laundering his clothes and ironing his shirts just the way he wanted them. She even primped his pillows exactly the right way, so he could fall into bed without having to adjust them at all. She'd spoiled him almost from day one.

In that time, although he'd still considered her highly attractive, he'd never imagined she would ever be more to him than a housekeeper. Their first kiss had been unexpected. He'd been heading toward the kitchen and she'd been coming out of it with an empty tray tucked against her hip. They rounded the corner, both of them moving at a fairly clipped pace, and collided head on. Everything happened in a split second. The tray slipped out of her hand, and in an attempt to grab it, she tripped. Had he not caught her, she would have sprawled to the floor along with the loudly clanging tray. Her hands clung to his shoulders. His arms were around her waist. Her wide, translucent eyes stared up at him, her luscious mouth was open in either horror or shock—exactly which he wasn't sure—but in that millisecond he was overwhelmed by the soft, lily scent of her perfume. He dropped his head and fused their lips together. He remembered how his heart pounded, how his loins sprang instantly to life. He'd felt like a seventeen-year-old boy with no self-control, and he hadn't cared. That kiss had been simply amazing.

But, he shouldn't have kissed Molly. He shouldn't have because he was in love with someone else—a woman who had been his lover for years. Molly didn't know about her. No one did, not even Gabriel. His lover was someone he could never have. For her, his own value was solely that of a bed partner. Because he wasn't good enough, she'd married someone else.

That day though, Rob had broken off the kiss with Molly and stepped awkwardly back, and he'd apologized, hoping she wouldn't look down and notice the tent in his pants. He'd swallowed hard, trying to tramp down his strange, desperate ardor.

Molly's beguiling eyes never left his. "I'm sorry, too," she said, as if she, rather than he had been the instigator.

"You're very pretty," he said, like it was an acceptable excuse.

Only then did her eyelids lower. Her bashfulness drew him and he wanted to just wrap her in his arms and hold her. The desire had compelled him so badly, he'd had to take another step away.

For days thereafter, he'd lain awake at night remembering that kiss, the softness of her lips, the taste of her, the way their tongues melded so perfectly, her sweet, shy expression afterwards. He'd even wondered what she would do if he went to her room and propositioned her, and he'd almost done it. More than once he'd found himself on the attic stairs. To get Molly out of his head, he'd gone to see his lover.

As the months passed, he'd caught himself watching Molly more and more. While she went about the house doing her duties, he noticed the gentle sway of her hips, the bounce of her curls, the delicate length of her fingers, the curve of her jaw. He'd made up excuses to seek her out, to go to where she would be, just to be near her. And he'd felt like a heathen, because whenever he masturbated, which he did fairly often, he thought of her.

She hadn't been immune to him either. Before the kiss, she'd looked him in the eye. After it, she wouldn't, and it made him sad. He'd never meant to scare her or make her uncomfortable, so he'd decided to ask if she would prefer to seek a position elsewhere. He'd planned to tell her he would provide references and help her find employment with someone who would value and pay her well. To do so would have been easy for him. Due to his flourishing law practice—at that time it had been flourishing—and his connection with the Draytons, he was acquainted with a number of influential people. He'd worked hard to gain a good reputation among them. Nevertheless, the conversation he'd planned to have with Molly never happened.

He could remember well the day he'd received word of the fire that destroyed Gabriel's home in Philadelphia. The missive that came was brief and unclear. Immediately, he sought Molly out and told her he needed to leave right away for the city.

"I'll go pack for you," she said.

Their eyes met. It was the first time she'd looked directly at him in the long months since that kiss. He took trips away frequently. New York and Philadelphia were both places he stayed for days, sometimes weeks. Molly had never accompanied him before, so why he suddenly wanted her with him he didn't know. When he asked if she would mind going too, she replied with no hesitation whatsoever, "Of course I will."

"I don't know how long we'll stay." He'd felt himself shaking, and his voice was unsteady. He'd been unable to finish what he intended to say. "My friend... my friend is badly injured... I don't... I don't know... he could die..."

In the coach on the way they spoke very little. Molly's questions were softly offered and reflected concern. She knew of Gabriel because of the numerous trips Rob had taken to visit him, but she'd never met him. Rob told her he would procure rooms for them at a hotel and that he would go on to the hospital to see Gabriel alone.

It was very late when he returned to the hotel. Molly was sitting quietly on a small settee in front of the fireplace, in his room, waiting for him. She stood when he walked in. She had purchased whiskey. The unopened bottle was on the coffee table along with an empty tumbler. He grinned.

"I thought you might want a drink," she said. "I wasn't sure."

Rob gestured for her to take her seat again and he sat next to her. The fabric on the small settee was pale blue satin, and it matched her eyes. He watched her open the bottle and pour. She handed him the glass and he downed the liquid like it was water. Then he set the glass on the table and leaned back.

"Will your friend be alright?" she asked.

He felt the tentative touch of her fingertips on the back of his hand. Turning to her, he whispered, "I don't know."

She took his hand in hers and squeezed it gently. "I will pray for him. For you."

"I want you," he said bluntly.

She didn't say anything. She just looked at him. All he wanted to do was bury himself deeply in her, so he could forget everything else, so all he had to think about was finding release. It didn't even matter who she was. She could have been any woman. It didn't matter that he would be cheating on his lover, something he'd never done before. He needed a distraction, anything, anyone, to take away the horrid images he'd just seen—images of his unconscious best friend, so grotesquely burned, so horribly mangled, so near death.

So he leaned close and took her mouth with his. If there was any hesitation on her part, he didn't feel it. She had such incredible lips, and she tasted really good, like wine and peppermint. He started to unbutton her dress. He did it slowly, taking his time, baring her creamy, pale skin inch by inch. She did nothing to help him, but she didn't stop him either.

With the bodice unbuttoned, he slid the material off her shoulders, and followed with her chemise, until her breasts were bared to him, and… *oh Jesus*… how mesmerized he'd been. The breasts of the woman he loved were smaller, not nearly as irresistible. He leaned over and took one in his mouth. The other he teased with his fingers. The whole of it was simply sublime.

He drew her to the bed and stripped her, piece by piece, until she lay gloriously for his eyes to devour. And then he buried himself in her just the way he wanted, taking it slow, stopping when he got too close, giving himself more time to gorge and disappear from the world.

When he could no longer hold back, he pulled out and came on her stomach. Afterwards he got up to get something to clean her up, found a small towel, and brought it back with him.

Sitting beside her, he asked if she was alright. There hadn't been a lot of response from her during, and it hadn't really mattered to him. He supposed she'd had very little experience with such things.

Over the years that had changed. Molly was an exceptional lover in every way. He couldn't ask for better. It was just as well. The next time he'd gone to see the woman he loved, just days after Molly and he returned from Philadelphia, she'd told him she was pregnant. The child was her husband's. And she turned him away. Numerous times thereafter he'd been to see her. She still claimed to love him, but she wouldn't let him touch her.

Rob wasn't particularly proud of the way he was using Molly. Sometimes he regretted it, but not right now. Not when she was helping him to relax and forget his worries for just a little while, giving him the break he so desperately needed in such a selfless, magnificent way.

He gasped, gyrated and moaned through the pleasure of it. "I'm coming," he murmured in warning. The orgasm burst from his loins, burned through his chest and washed him from head to toe. Molly didn't take her leave until every last drop of him was spent.

Then he just rested, taking deep breaths, until he could open his eyes again. Smiling he looked down at her, still on her knees between his feet, and he watched her tenderly fix his trousers. "Do you have any idea how good at that you are?"

Molly shrugged in her typical modest way. "Are you less stressed now?"

Rob laughed and sat forward, taking her hands to help her to her feet. "I'll make it up to you."

"I know." Her eyes flashed in promise.

"Can I have a peek, just one little peek?" It wasn't fair, he told himself, as she tugged at the bodice of her dress to give him what he asked for. Because he couldn't help it, he curved his hand around her bared breast.

The woman he loved would never have done what Molly just did for him. Not in a million years would she even consider it. It wasn't fair that he was in love with someone who sometimes he didn't even like.

Wrapping one arm around Molly's waist he drew her closer until her breast was a breath away from his mouth. She leaned in, grazing his lips. But she didn't give him enough time to do what he wanted. She pushed away. Rob grabbed for her, but she was too quick for him.

"Uh-uh, you have too much work to do," she murmured. "You can't afford to get side-tracked."

Groaning, he looked up in time to watch her saunter away. At the door she told him to call if he needed anything.

"You know what I need," he said.

Molly just laughed and disappeared.

It wasn't fair that Molly came from the people she came from. He liked the person she was. He liked the way she teased him. He liked all her demure traits. Even better were the subtly aggressive ones. And she dealt so creatively and enticingly with his odd fetish, which he couldn't control at all. When he was with her he felt extraordinarily virile and as insatiable as he'd been at eighteen. Every second of their intimacy was good—very, *very* good. In that respect they were, without question, *extremely* well suited.

Early on, he'd assumed he would tire of her the way he had with other women he'd been with, but he wasn't tired of her. He wanted her all the time. There were nights when he was traveling that he couldn't be with her. Those nights he felt like he was lost in the desert without a drop of water. She was the only oasis, but no matter how desperately he tried to get to her, running, tripping, crawling, crying out her name, she remained just out of reach.

But he didn't love her. He couldn't love her because she wasn't known among the elite. She couldn't give him another step up into the socially acceptable world he needed to be part of. Not the way his lover could.

Fourteen

Sunday morning was bright, without a cloud in the sky, completely the opposite of how the night had been. Torrential downpours combined with strong winds and booming thunder had caused Lilly a sleepless night at Julie's townhouse. She'd spent most of it alternately hoping Henry, the stuffed owl, was helping Charlotte not to be afraid, and worrying about Julie's situation. Julie needed to find new lodgings and Lilly didn't know how she was going to go about it. The landlord had come by not long after she'd arrived and Lilly had handed over her entire week's wages to the man. But they still owed more.

Before he left he said, "I'll give you three more weeks. If I don't have the rest by then, you're out. I have another tenant ready to move in!"

Three weeks wasn't enough time for Lilly to come up with the money he expected.

Rather than allowing herself to get mired down, she concentrated on anticipating an uplifting church experience with Charlotte. At Drayton Hall, however, she found Charlotte's rooms and the dining room empty. The only other place Charlotte would be was the kitchen, most likely having chocolate cake for breakfast! Gabriel was ill, she reminded herself. Nevertheless, hoping to intercede and see that Charlotte had something healthy to eat, Lilly headed that direction. Just outside of the kitchen, she heard Charlotte's voice, and she stopped in her tracks.

"I wish I was a boy, not a girl," Charlotte was saying. "Can we put peaches in the pancakes?"

"Peaches? Fine," Gabriel Drayton was with her! "Why do you want to be a boy?" His voice was still gruff, but to Lilly's astonishment, it contained very little of his usual disdain.

"Here's the bowl. I'll get the pan while you mix. Don't forget to light the stove," Charlotte instructed, and then she said, "If I was a boy, we could stay here. Since I'm a girl, we have to leave. I don't want to live somewhere else."

"We can't always have everything we want," he told her.

They were silent for a while. Lilly didn't know whether to retreat or go in. She heard the clanking of a pan and vigorous whipping.

"Here's the peaches," Charlotte said. This was followed by the rapid thumping of fruit being dropped onto a counter.

"Whoa… whoa!" Gabriel spouted.

"Good catch, Daddy!" Charlotte chortled.

"Bring me the little knife," he said next.

"This one?"

"Yes, that's the one."

"Can I help?"

"No."

"I'll be careful. I know how," Charlotte pleaded.

"No, Charlotte."

"But it's taking too long!"

"You're the one who wants peaches," he said. "Here, stir this while I peel."

"Do you think Miss Lilly will like pancakes with peaches?"

"I guess we'll find out."

"You can ask Miss Lilly to marry you," Charlotte said.

Lilly held her breath during the pregnant silence that followed. Finally, to her sheer relief he said, "No."

"Why not?"

"Because I said no," he said.

"If you marry Miss Lilly, she can make a boy like Susan made Mark, and then we can stay here."

"It's not that simple," he said. "Time to cook."

Charlotte squealed. Batter sizzled as it was poured into a hot pan. "Let's make one big giant pancake!"

The fizzing continued. "This big?"

"Yes, that big! Why is it not that simple?"

"It's just not."

"But why not?"

"Charlotte!" he growled.

Silence lingered for a moment or two, then Charlotte said, "When you were little did your daddy yell at you?"

There was a brief hesitation before Gabriel answered, "Sometimes."

"He yelled at you when you played the piano, so you were only allowed to play it when he wasn't here."

"How do you know that?"

"Uncle Alex," she said. "Uncle Alex taught you how?"

"Sort of. Time to flip."

"I asked Uncle Alex to teach me, but he said he can only teach me to play the cello like him. I only want to play the piano like you."

"*Shi*—" Gabriel started and cut himself off. "It doesn't look very good, does it?"

Charlotte giggled. "I told Miss Lilly you weren't good at cooking, so she won't mind. How come Uncle Alex was allowed to play his cello, but you weren't allowed to play the piano?"

"Did Alex tell you that, too?"

"Uncle Alex said your daddy wouldn't let you do anything, 'cept study," Charlotte said.

"All done. Hand me that plate."

The fizzing began again as more batter was poured into the pan.

"Is that why I'm not allowed to play the piano? Because you want me to study?"

"No," he said.

"Is it okay if Miss Lilly teaches me?"

"That's fine," he said. "We need butter and syrup."

"I got it already. It's on the table."

Several more pancakes were made. Lilly was about to creep away, to wait for Charlotte in the entrance hall, when Gabriel said, "I think this is enough. Let's eat."

The sounds of Gabriel's shuffle and tapping cane told her they were moving to the table. She heard a bench scrape and the clink of plates being set down.

"Here's your coffee," Charlotte said. "More syrup than that, Daddy! Will Jesus be in church?"

"No."

"Susan says Jesus lives in heaven. Can I go to heaven to meet him?"

"No."

Charlotte giggled. "You're going to meet Jesus in heaven."

He grunted. "Who said I'm going to heaven?"

"Uncle Alex did," she said.

"When did he say that?"

"A few weeks ago. Daddy, what does Jesus look like?"

"I don't know."

"I think you look like Jesus," Charlotte said.

"I look like Jesus?"

"You look like the picture in the church, 'cept Jesus' hair is curlier than yours and you don't have a beard. If you come with us, I can show you!"

"No."

"*Pleeease!*"

"Charlotte, I said no!"

Lilly hadn't moved, so how Charlotte realized she was there she didn't know. "Miss Lilly's here! Miss Lilly's here!" Charlotte bounded up from her seat and Lilly stepped into the room, hoping it would appear she'd just arrived. Charlotte grabbed her hand and dragged her to the table. "We made pancakes with peaches! Do you like peaches? You can sit next to me!"

From where he was seated, Gabriel's back was toward the door. He didn't turn. Lilly rounded him from the left and avoided looking at him until she was on the bench beside Charlotte. When she did look, her first thought was that Charlotte was right. He did resemble the painting of Jesus in the church, with the exception of having half of his face covered. "Good morning," she murmured.

He inclined his head curtly. "Help yourself."

The short stack of overly large, badly misshapen pancakes didn't look very appetizing, but they smelled good. Both his plate and Charlotte's were swimming in syrup. Under Charlotte's chatty directions Lilly took two and dressed them.

"You don't have enough syrup." Charlotte frowned.

"This is how I like them." Lilly took a bite. "They're wonderful!" It was true.

Charlotte giggled.

Bantering with Charlotte while they ate kept Lilly from having to look at Gabriel. Even so, she could feel him staring at her. When she did dare to glance at him, his eyes quickly diverted and it surprised her. "Charlotte," she said, "If we're going to church, we'd better get ready or we'll be late."

"I have to get my coat and my bonnet. I'll be right back!"

Charlotte bounced away and Lilly silently cursed her foolish suggestion. She didn't want to be alone with *him*. "I'll wash up," she said. "It's the least I can do."

"Finch will do it tomorrow," he said.

Their eyes met. "I don't mind."

"Fine."

To avoid conversing with him, Lilly busied herself clearing the table. Even so, she was fairly certain he was staring at her again. Out of the corner of her eye she saw him take a sip of his coffee. Taking a chance, she asked, "Will you consider joining us for church?"

"No."

"I think Charlotte would like for you to come—"

"Let's get something straight," he cut her off. "I don't go to church. Don't ask me again and don't encourage Charlotte to either!"

"Don't you want Charlotte to learn about God and—"

"Miss Hawthorne, I will allow you to warp Charlotte's head with these ridiculous notions you people believe, but that's where it ends. Do you understand? There is no God!"

Stunned, Lilly managed to mumble, "I am very sorry for you."

He rose so swiftly she jumped backwards and knocked the plate she'd just set on the counter into another. The clanking came in unison with the rough slide of the bench scraping across the floor. "As I am for you!" he bellowed.

Lilly raised her chin and walked past him out the door. At first she had no intention of turning back, but once she was in the hallway, she changed her mind. She'd suppressed her feelings about his disservice to his child long enough. He needed a piece of her mind! As she rounded the doorframe, however, everything she wanted to say died in her throat.

He was standing halfway between the bench and the sink with his coffee cup in one hand and his plate in the other. His cane was still leaning against the table. He staggered the two remaining steps and his dishes crashed to the counter. His forearm came down hard beside them and whispered curses flew out of him, *"Oh Christ! Oh shit!"*

Lilly had a clear view of his right profile, his bowed head and cringing features. She didn't think she'd made any noise, but she must have. His head jerked up. "Get out!" he hissed.

Lilly's conviction vanished. She turned and fled.

Fifteen

"How dare you!" Gabriel charged as he ripped his gloves off and sank into the wing chair in Rob's office. He took the proffered coffee cup from Rob's hand and slammed it down on the end table beside him. Hot droplets splashed over the rim, but he ignored them.

"Nice to see you, too." Rob took his seat behind the desk. "What, pray tell, did I do this time?"

"Charlotte was here on Saturday, was she not?"

Rob nodded.

"I'm not going to marry Lilly Hawthorne!" Gabriel snapped.

Laughter burst out of Rob. "So that's why you're in such a tither—Charlotte suggested you get married? Good for her! But I can assure you I had nothing to do with it."

"You didn't put her up to it?"

"No, of course not. Contrary to what you seem to believe, I don't purposely do things to piss you off. That's Alex's job, not mine. Besides, I have half a mind to marry her myself. She is rather incredible, isn't she? I've been thinking that the institution of marriage might not be so bad after all. I'll tell you it's been a long time since I've seen a woman I've been so compelled to get my hands on. I even had a dream about your Miss Hawthorne. It was rather erotic—"

"Shut up!" Gabriel hissed. "She's not a piece of meat, for Christ's sake!"

The corner of Rob's mouth turned up. "Aha! You do like her! I knew it!"

Gabriel grabbed his cane and pushed himself to his feet. "I'm glad you're enjoying yourself so much! If this is how you intend the rest of today to go, there's no point in me staying."

Rob chuckled as he got up and rounded the desk. "Don't be mad. It was the only way I could think of to get you to admit it. I didn't really mean it. Although she is pretty. And she has that thick blond hair you're so partial to. Please sit down. Drink your coffee."

Purposely ignoring him, Gabriel turned his back on Rob and took a step toward the door. In a low, clipped tone he said, "I need you to update my will. Replace Alex and Susan as Charlotte's guardians with Lilly Hawthorne and add a full trust fund to cover living expenses for Lilly for the remainder of her life. You will need to word it in such a way that Alex will have no way to assume control. I'll review it next week."

"Gabe, whoa!" Rob walked around until he was blocking Gabriel's path.

"Is there a problem?" Gabriel growled.

"Yes, there is. First of all, you know the trust agreement is very specific as to what powers you have over the money. Setting up Charlotte's trust fund was easy with Alex and Susan as guardians, but changing her guardian isn't possible—"

"There are loopholes," Gabriel interrupted. "I pay you very well to find them. I'm sure you'll figure out how to make it work. Now get out of my way!"

Rob held his ground. "I know all the loopholes like the back of my hand. It can't be done the way you want."

"Try!" Gabriel snapped.

"Has Lilly agreed to this?" Rob asked incredulously.

"No."

There was a moment of silence while Rob stared at him. "Why are you asking me to do this? Is it because you finally realize Alex is guilty?"

"He isn't guilty," Gabriel said.

"Is it because of Susan?"

"No."

"Have the threats started up again?"

Flinching from a round of cramping pain, clutching his stomach because he couldn't help it, Gabriel barked, "No!"

"Then why?"

"Because I want Charlotte to be cared for by someone who will treat her the way a real mother would. Not Susan."

"Gabriel, sit before you fall down," Rob said. "We need to talk about this rationally."

"Damn it, Rob! Just do it! I'm finished here." Gabriel took a step to the side in order to pass, but Rob moved too, blocking him again.

"I'll stand here all day if I have to," Rob said. "You're not going anywhere until we've talked this through. Let's just for the moment suppose Lilly has agreed. She's only been living in your house for two weeks. You barely know the woman."

"She's good with Charlotte."

"She's good with Charlotte? Listen to what you're saying. Have you lost your mind?"

"So say the masses," Gabriel retorted, cringing again. "You just met her and you want to marry her."

Rob's arms flailed. "I was kidding!" He lowered his voice. "This is all rather pointless. Even if I can figure out how to change your will, it won't matter. By this time next year, the estate will belong to Alex. Any trust fund you set up for Charlotte without Alex as guardian won't be worth a penny. If you're too stubborn to move in here with me, which I'm sure you will be, you and Charlotte will be living destitute in some hovel."

Gabriel didn't say anything. He wanted to shove Rob out of his path, but his head was swimming too badly for him to move at all. Rob was smirking at him.

"Of course the other alternative, and the preferred one I think, would be for you to marry."

"That won't solve the problem!"

"Not the whole problem," Rob said, "but you could work on the rest. Chances are—"

"There will be no chances!" Gabriel hissed.

"You are the most stubborn—"

"Damn you! Drop this now!"

"I won't drop it. I'm looking out for your welfare," Rob persisted.

"Christ!" Gabriel groaned. "Don't you get it?"

Sounding confused, Rob asked, "Get what?"

"By this time next year, I won't be here!"

"What are you saying? You're going to die? I know you've been feeling poorly, but that's a little extreme, don't you think? If you would just go to a doctor. Harold Brewster is right next door. He's good—"

"I have!" Gabriel interrupted. "I've been poked, prodded, bled, stripped and humiliated by every doctor in this godforsaken town. None of them know what's wrong with me, including your neighbor. I'm getting worse. Every day."

"Then we'll go to Philadelphia. There are better doctors there—"

"No," Gabriel muttered. "Your great neighbor told me to get my affairs in order so that's what I am trying to do." He was so dizzy. Too dizzy. "Get out of my way. I have to go… to go…"

"*Gaaabbbbbe!*"

Gabriel felt Rob grab him. He was careening sideways. The thump of his cane hitting the carpet rang loudly in his ears. Somehow Rob maneuvered him enough that he was close to the wing chair. When he dropped he went backwards. His bad hip jarred against the hard arm of the chair as he fell into it. Whether it was the sudden excruciating pain or the increasing fuzziness in his head, he wasn't sure, but he completely blacked out. He was only aware of Rob calling his name, then yelling for Molly.

He opened his eyes to Rob leaning over him, lightly slapping his cheek, and simultaneously shouting instructions for Molly to run next door for Harold Brewster. The front door slammed.

Gabriel shoved at Rob's arm. "Get off me!"

"Oh, thank god," Rob muttered. "Here's some water." He took the glass from a small tray on the end table that hadn't been there minutes before. "Drink this. Do you want coffee?"

Ignoring him, Gabriel tried to pull himself out of the uncomfortable slouch. Stabbing pain in his leg prevented it, so he eased back and squeezed his eyes shut. He heard the glass clink as Rob set it down and he felt, rather than saw, Rob get up and tread an imaginary circle on the carpet. He heard Rob's heavy sigh.

When he could, Gabriel looked up. Rob was standing in front of him, staring down at him. The glassy pools in Rob's eyes caught him completely off guard. "You can…" Gabriel murmured, but stopped to clear the wad of spittle from his throat, "feel free to increase the pay for your position as permanent trustee of the estate. You won't ever have to worry about going bankrupt."

"Fuck you!" Rob whispered. Then he turned around.

Through the haze in his eyes, Gabriel saw Rob run his fingers through his hair and then down his face. When finally he turned back, he said, "I never had a mother or a father, or brothers or sisters, or uncles or cousins. There were boys in the orphanage who were my friends, but we've all long since gone our separate ways. You always say Alex is more a brother than a cousin to you. In all these years, with the exception of allowing Charlotte to call me uncle, which I will add was her idea, not yours, never once have you referred to me that way." He stopped and paused. When he continued, his voice was thick with emotion. "You and Charlotte are the only family I have. And now you come here and spring this… this…" He stopped, flailed around and rasped, "What the hell, Gabriel! What the hell—?"

Gabriel closed his eyes. It was hard to make them open again. When he did, Rob was there, still staring at him. He'd never seen such anguish in Rob's expression. He hadn't known fun-loving, happy-go-lucky Rob had the ability to feel that deeply. "It's not so bad. After I die—"

"You're not going to die!" Rob cut in vehemently. "We'll get you help and you'll be fine!"

The door swung open and wind whipped through the room, dousing Gabriel in frosty air. Molly Finch came running on the heels of the good doctor, Harold Brewster.

Sixteen

Much to Lilly's surprise and pleasure, Rob began coming to Drayton Hall every day. He arrived in the afternoons and spent considerable time with Gabriel behind closed doors. Afterwards he joined Lilly and Charlotte for dinner, and later in the parlor, he entertained them with his stories.

To Lilly's relief, Gabriel didn't attend any of the meals. Although he lounged in his usual spot on the sofa during Rob's first two visits, he stayed away for the third, only making a brief appearance to tell Charlotte it was time for bed. That evening, after Charlotte departed, Lilly found herself alone with Rob.

"I guess I should be going, too," Rob said, frowning. "I was hoping the weather would clear since I'm on horseback tonight, but it doesn't appear it will."

The wind outside was gusting so strongly it caused eerie whistles to sporadically reverberate through the windows. Every time she heard them, Lilly couldn't help shivering. Rob had kept the fire in the parlor burning. The room was warm, yet occasional drafts somehow managed to get into the chimney, causing the fire to dip and blow. Lilly suggested, "There is a spare room at the end of the hall in the east wing."

Rob grinned. "That's certainly tempting."

Why the idea of Rob being in the mansion throughout the night brought Lilly peace of mind, she didn't know.

"Do you play?" he asked with a gesture toward the piano.

"No, unfortunately," she told him.

"Neither do I," he said but his smile didn't fade. "We could do a Gabe? It just might work if we try it together. The bench is wide enough, don't you think?"

" 'Do a Gabe'?" Lilly asked curiously.

"It's a secret," Rob said, rising and taking her hand in his. "Come. I'll show you."

Lilly was utterly mesmerized as she sat next to him on the bench, which contrary to what he'd said, was not nearly wide enough for them to sit together appropriately. In order to prevent himself from falling off, Rob had to keep one arm around her. Every inch of Lilly's skin tingled from the contact.

"Gabe says pick a key, skip a key, skip another key, then skip two keys. You can skip them either by playing two keys at once, or break them and play them separately." As he spoke he demonstrated. What he played didn't sound very good at all. Chuckling, he said, "Well, maybe there's more to it than that. Why don't we start with this one? It's a C, right? You play chords and I'll play open?"

They tried it and it actually didn't sound half bad. They kept going solely because of Rob's teasing encouragement and ended up laughing. As their humor faded, Lilly turned to him. His face was so close to hers, she could see the thicker pores of his whiskers, and freckles on his cheekbones and nose, so tiny that even from normal speaking distance they weren't noticeable. And he smelled good, like lavender soap and coffee.

"That's Gabriel's secret," Rob murmured. "He's never had a lesson, and he can't read a note. He figured out his little skipping theory all on his own. Everything he plays he makes up. Have you ever heard him?"

"Yes," Lilly admitted. "I would have never guessed."

"Nobody can. He's amazing. He can twist things around, change keys and do these runs up and down the keyboard that sound incredibly difficult. He'll tell you it's all just a trick, but I think it's more than that. He's very gifted. It is a shame he was never allowed to formally learn."

"Why is that?" Lilly asked curiously.

"His father—" Rob cut himself off, and started again. "There's a long history of scandal in Gabriel's family, most of it surrounding Gabriel's father, the great and powerful Charles Drayton." He paused and let go of the sarcasm. "You know, it's funny, when I was growing up, all I ever wanted was a father. Then I met Gabriel. I used to come here with him on holiday. At first I was kind of in awe of Charles, and I remember wishing he was my father, too. The more I saw how he treated Gabriel, my outlook changed. I still think sometimes I was better off without a father."

"What did Charles Drayton do that was so terrible?" Lilly asked.

"Most of the time he ignored Gabriel, so it took me a while to notice. I think it was about the third time I was here that I really began to. It was Christmas and Gabriel brought home a paper he'd done. It was so well done the school gave him an award. He was proud and I think he hoped Charles would be, too. It was about hawks. Gabriel had found a baby hawk, just hatched, and he cared for it. He'd built a cage and kept it in our room in the dormitory. Eventually, when it was old enough, he set it free. He spent hours in the library doing research for his paper. Not only did he write about the history and culture of the species, but he told the story of the one he raised. It brought a tear to my eye when I read what he'd written about having to let it go. That silly hawk kept returning, so one night he closed the window, not because he didn't want to see it, but because it was what was best for the bird.

"During dinner Charles read the paper out loud. When he was finished, he tossed it into the fireplace. I remember being so shocked, I almost got up to try to retrieve the thing before it could burn completely. And Charles said, 'That was pathetic. You are an embarrassment to the Drayton name.'

"I remember looking across the table at Gabriel and having no idea what to do or say. After his father left the room, I told him I was sorry. Gabriel just shrugged like it didn't matter to him at all. We've never spoken of it again.

"Many people don't know this, but Gabriel is an exceptional architect. It takes most men decades to develop a name, but within a few years of finishing college, Gabriel had already sold several of his designs. And then he was offered a commission to design a new auditorium at the university in Philadelphia. Gabriel didn't know when he took the job that his father was the primary sponsor for the project.

Opening day, at the ceremony in the auditorium Gabriel designed, his father made a speech. At the beginning he made a joke, saying the only thing wrong with the project was that he had no say in choosing the architect. It was the perfect set up for him to later tell everyone his own son was the brilliant mind behind it all. I remember being excited for Gabriel and anticipating the moment Charles would actually hail him as he deserved. Charles went on to compliment the builders, the dean, the professors, everyone who'd had a hand in the project, including the interior decorator, who'd worked countless hours with Gabriel. All of them were seated in a row behind Charles, and he asked each of them to stand as he recognized them. Charles didn't mention the architect again. Gabriel was the only one on that stage not named or asked to stand. A month later, his father died. Gabriel hasn't drawn since. It's such a shame."

Lilly didn't know what to say. She could only imagine how crushed Gabriel must have been. For the first time since residing at Drayton Hall, she felt pity for him. It wasn't the same as feeling sorry for him for being ill, or for seeing him in pain in the kitchen. This sorrow on his behalf was much deeper. The impact of it was so strong she shivered. And then she remembered what Charlotte had said about her father drawing buildings in the west wing.

"Gabriel would be furious if he knew we were talking about him like this." Rob ran his hand up and down her arm, "Are you cold?"

Lilly shook her head. "I was just thinking maybe you're right. My father died when I was a baby. I don't remember him at all. I spent a large part of my childhood envisioning an imaginary one. A perfect one."

"I didn't know that," Rob said softly. "I guess you and I have something else in common."

That comment was precipitated by earlier conversations in which they'd discovered they had similar tastes in cuisine, books and art. Rob was staring into her eyes. Lilly had been kissed before, but never had she wanted to be kissed as much as she did at that moment. Her focus was drawn to his mouth. And she thought because his eyes moved to her lips too, he was thinking the same thing. She was sure of it. He angled his head. She closed her eyes. And felt…

Nothing. Suddenly he moved, dropping his arm from around her shoulders, to stand up. Lilly opened her eyes.

"I'm sorry," he said apologetically. "The last thing I want to do is show you disrespect of any kind. I admire you a great deal—"

By the way he spoke, stopping abruptly, Lilly was sure he was going to say more, but whatever it was, he withheld. Her stomach churned. An electric current unlike anything she'd ever felt before raised every goose bump on her body.

"I really need to go." He smiled contritely. "If it's alright with you, I'd like to speak with you privately, perhaps on Saturday? Would it be possible to ask Withers to bring you to my home in town? We can have dinner there, together?"

"I would like that," Lilly stammered.

He took her hand and kissed the back of it. The wind whistled through the window behind them, like a musical accompaniment. "I think it would be a very bad idea if I stayed the night." That teasing lightness was in his eyes again. "Goodnight, Lilly," he said. "Until Saturday."

Later, despite how comfortable her bed was, between the thunder and the wind, Lilly didn't think she would ever sleep. But, if she was being honest, the storm wasn't the cause of her restlessness. Rob was. She liked him. She really, really liked him. She'd wanted him to kiss her. The idea of having a private dinner with him at his home… was just… so unnerving and so exciting and…

Lilly rolled over and covered her head with the pillow. She was too old for this silliness! And yet, she still felt it, in the flutters in her stomach and the rapid beat of her heart.

How long she laid there, she didn't know, but it was a while. The storm eventually calmed. The flashes of lightning became so distant they barely lit the room, and she couldn't hear the thunder at all. What she did hear was a sudden, faint shriek.

Because she was so preoccupied, at first she thought the sound might be from a screech owl perched outside her window. But it wasn't a screech owl. The faint wailing noise that followed was clear enough, and it wasn't coming from the outside at all. Charlotte was crying!

Lilly flung her blankets back, slipped into her robe and padded through the sitting room toward the hallway. Before she opened the door, she heard that distinct thump and scrape. It was much too late for Gabriel to be taking his normal nightly walk. Even so, it sounded like he was following that same path.

Lilly couldn't allow her fear of him to keep her from seeing to Charlotte. She opened the door and stepped out, expecting to see his warped, limping form in the darkness. It was dark, but not that dark. He wasn't there, and Charlotte's door was open.

"Daddy! Daddy!" Charlotte wailed. The bed creaked, and just like that Charlotte stopped crying.

Stepping closer, Lilly saw him, outlined by the flickering light from the fireplace. It looked like he was wearing nothing but long underwear, and he was sitting on the edge of Charlotte's bed.

"Where's Henry?" he grumbled gruffly.

"I gave him to Miss Lilly," Charlotte said.

"Did you have a bad dream?" he asked.

"Yeah," she hiccupped. "Can I sleep with you?"

If he responded verbally, Lilly didn't hear it. She couldn't tell whether he nodded or shook his head, but Charlotte clamored out from under her blankets and launched herself at him. He rose, holding her entirely with his left arm. His cane was secure in his right hand.

Lilly crept back into her suite. Peeking through a crack in the door she watched him slowly, but steadily, carry Charlotte across the hall. Her little legs were wrapped around his waist. Her face was buried in the scarf around his neck.

Lilly didn't completely withdraw until he reached his room and hooked his cane around the doorknob to close it. He was indeed dressed in nothing but underwear, and it did nothing to hide his form. He was lanky and thin, but there was no mistaking the lines of muscles in his arms and legs.

Lilly crawled back into bed. Except for that initial shriek, she'd barely heard Charlotte's crying. Had she already been asleep, or had her room not been right next to Charlotte's, she most likely wouldn't have heard her at all. Gabriel, she deduced, must have exceptional hearing to have heard her all the way across the red-carpeted corridor and through two sets of closed doors. As exceptional as his small, muscular backside!

Admonishing herself for the highly uncouth thought, she flopped over and buried her head under the pillow. One mystery was solved. Now she knew where Gabriel went every night—to Charlotte's room.

Lying there, she recalled the horrid rumors about him. People claimed he molested his daughter. But Charlotte had been the one to ask to be taken to his room. No child would ask to go somewhere where they would inevitably be subjected to such horror, would they? The visits he made to Charlotte's room every night were too short in duration for him to be abusing her then.

Lilly should have been relieved, and yet she wasn't. It wasn't that she wished Charlotte was being harmed—she would never wish that kind of terror on any child! But, for some reason, one she couldn't define, she was angry that Gabriel made the effort to check on his daughter every night.

He was supposed to be the horribly rude monster the rest of the world believed him to be!

Seventeen

"I thought Chardonnay? It's a bottle I've been saving for a while. Directly from the Loire Valley in France." Rob grinned.

"That would be lovely," Lilly replied. She had no idea about the value of such wine.

Rob's dining table was tiny compared to the one at Drayton Hall, and the dining room was small, but cozy. There were freshly cut mums in vases on the side hutch. Lilly felt like a schoolgirl, full of knots and butterflies. Even her hands in her lap were quivering.

Rob poured for them both while Molly served their plates. She'd prepared roast duck and its presentation was flawless, like something Lilly imagined would be found at an exclusive, expensive restaurant. It tasted as good as it appeared.

While they ate the succulent fare, the conversation flowed easily and did much for easing Lilly's nervousness. She was just beginning to relax, thinking it wouldn't be as difficult as she'd anticipated to ask Rob for his assistance with finding housing for Julie, when Rob set his utensils down, wiped his mouth and folded his napkin beside his plate. The humor in him disappeared. He was regarding her somberly.

"Lilly, the reason I asked you to come here is because I have something important to discuss with you. It's about Gabriel. This is rather awkward, so please bear with me."

Lilly nodded and set her fork aside to give him her full attention.

"Gabriel, as you know, is very wealthy. He has an extraordinary amount of money at his disposal right now. He has numerous properties and many lucrative investments that continue to increase his wealth daily. There is only one problem. The money isn't really his. None of it is his, not Drayton Hall, not the rest of the properties, not the stocks, the bonds. All of it is held in a trust set up by his father. Gabriel has certain liberties to use the money and the estate until his thirty-third birthday. At that time, the trust expires. Now here's the odd part. Unless Gabriel has fulfilled certain conditions, the money, the property, the entire estate will no longer be his. This is all very complicated. Does it make sense so far?"

"Yes, I understand so far," Lilly replied.

"Gabriel will turn thirty-three in September of next year. He has not fulfilled any of the pre-set conditions and at this juncture, with only a year to go, it is highly unlikely he will be able to. This is all very concerning, not so much for Gabriel, but for Charlotte. Because she was born after Charles Drayton passed, no provisions were made for her. The trust does mention the possibility of illegitimate children, but it specifically excludes them from inheriting anything."

Rob paused and while the silence lingered, Lilly began to feel awkward. "Are you telling me this because as of next year, there will be no money to pay me to tutor Charlotte?"

"Yes," Rob said, "at least, that's one of the reasons for telling you." He paused again. "Are you aware how much your sister's husband owes to his creditors?" To Lilly's stunned expression, Rob added, "I don't mean to upset you. I'm making a huge mess of this. I can only ask that you accept my apology and please hear me out." Rob went on to tell her an amount that was more than she could have ever imagined. They were mostly gambling debts, he said, and then he talked about the money Julie's landlord was demanding.

Lilly looked at her hands in her lap. "My sister will be evicted next week. I don't have enough to cover the back rent. I spent the afternoon looking for places, but nothing affordable is suitable. I thought, because you offered it before, I would ask for your help."

Rob didn't really acknowledge her inquiry. Quietly he said, "Lilly, I really would prefer not to have to ask you this. I would prefer to be able to solve this problem in a different way, but if there is a different way I don't know what it is." He took a deep breath and expelled it slowly. "I also need you to know that Gabriel has no idea we're having this conversation. This is my idea and my doing alone."

"Okay," Lilly said. Apprehension was suddenly making her skin crawl.

"The conditions of the trust require Gabriel to be married and to have produced a male heir by the time he reaches the age of thirty-three. If that does not occur, Alex will inherit the entire estate. Gabriel will be left destitute and so will Charlotte.

"This is what I propose. All of Jason Gibson's debts will be paid in full including back rent to the landlord. A home will be purchased outright in Julie's name, where she can reside with her child without interference. The terms will include the expense of two servants for all of Julie's lifetime and an educational trust fund for the child. A home will also be purchased in your name. The property and location is your choice. Cost does not matter. Monthly income will be paid to you for the remainder of your life as well."

The amounts he quoted made Lilly gulp. It was more per month than she would earn in a year as Charlotte's tutor. It all sounded too good to be true.

"It will be a business arrangement only," Rob continued. "The marriage will take place in a quiet, unattended ceremony. You will have to live with Gabriel at Drayton Hall until he turns thirty-three, at which time your obligation will be complete and you can retire to your new home."

Lilly stared at him. "You want me to marry Gabriel?" Her voice didn't sound anything like it normally did.

"Purely a business arrangement," Rob repeated. "After Gabriel's next birthday, there will be a quiet divorce and you will be free to live the rest of your life as you choose. You can remarry without any changes to your monthly stipend or relinquishment of the property you own."

Lilly took a deep breath. She told herself this couldn't be happening. Rob August, the man she'd been so taken with, and believed might return her feelings, wanted her to marry Gabriel. What a mistake she'd made! "It doesn't make sense," she said slowly. "There has to be a legitimate male heir. A business arrangement wouldn't help Mr. Drayton in that regard at all."

The heightened color that suddenly spread across Rob's cheekbones told Lilly her answer. She would also be expected to bear Gabriel Drayton's child. "Oh," she whispered.

"You're so calm," Rob remarked. "I didn't think you would be."

Lilly blinked. *Calm?* On the inside she was being torn apart, somewhere between fury and utter mortification. "May I think about it?"

"Yes, but understand the decision needs to be made soon in order for there to be time for a child to be conceived and born before next September."

Lilly just looked at him.

"As I said before, Gabriel doesn't know about this meeting. Please say nothing to him until you've given me your answer."

"If he doesn't know about it, then how do you know he will agree to pay for the homes and the servants and the debts?"

"He will," Rob said. "Believe it or not, Gabriel is one of the most generous men I have ever known. That part of this plan will require no convincing from me at all."

That brought Lilly's head up. "Are you saying he might not agree to the marriage?"

"He won't want to, but he will. For Charlotte."

"And the child?" Lilly asked. "If it's a girl what will it mean?"

"The money will go to Alex."

"So chances of this even working are at best fifty-fifty?" Lilly asked.

"Yes."

"And really when you consider how many babies are miscarried, or stillborn, the chances are a great degree lower." She didn't bother saying how many women died in childbirth, or even how long, in some cases, it might take for a child to be conceived. "I would say the chances are less than ten percent."

"I would agree with that," Rob said.

"What will happen to the baby afterwards, regardless of whether it's a girl or boy, assuming it survives?"

"That will be your choice. If you want to keep it with you, you may. You will be made sole guardian and any decisions on behalf of the child will be yours and yours alone. You will even have the choice of keeping Gabriel from having any contact with the child. On the other hand, if you would prefer the child remain with Gabriel, he will raise it. Regardless of where or by whom it's raised, a male child will become the sole heir of the estate upon Gabriel's demise."

"In that case Alex gets nothing?" Lilly asked.

"Yes, that's correct. But Alex doesn't need the money. His father left him a substantial estate of his own."

"Why would Gabriel's father choose Alex to inherit over Gabriel?"

"Alex was the favored child. In Charles Drayton's eyes Alex could do no wrong. As cruel as Charles Drayton was to Gabriel, he was nothing but supportive of Alex. Alex's father passed away when Alex was very young—about four, I think. Charles was the one who insisted Alex come to reside at Drayton Hall. He and Gabriel grew up together. I told you before that the Drayton history was full of scandal. It goes something like this: Charles' marriage to Gabriel's mother, Anne, was pre-arranged and forced upon him by his own father. He didn't want the marriage because he was in love with another—a woman named Beatrice. But Beatrice had left town leaving no word of her whereabouts to anyone, including Charles. Charles's father told him if he could find Beatrice before a certain date, he would reconsider the pre-arranged marriage. Charles couldn't find Beatrice. She didn't come back until after Charles was married to Anne. And then, because Charles was no longer available, Beatrice married his brother, Francis, Alex's father. It is said Charles and Beatrice continued their affair for many years, even before Anne and Francis passed away."

"Oh," Lilly whispered. "They are all deceased now?"

"Actually, no. Beatrice is still alive. She lives in New York. She hasn't seen Alex or Gabriel in quite some time. The last time she came to Havertown was for Charles Drayton's funeral. She's never seen Mark, her own grandson. The Drayton estate owns the property she lives in and pays her a monthly sum which will continue for the remainder of her life."

"Did Charles and Beatrice marry? They could have after Francis and Anne passed away."

"They could have, but they didn't."

For a second all Lilly wanted was her glasses, as if they would shield her somehow. She hadn't worn them since Charlotte cured her eyes with her magic wand. That prevailing thought in the midst of this farce made no sense whatsoever. "Who is Charlotte's mother?" she asked.

Rob sat back in his chair. "Good question. According to the birth certificate her name is Mary Smith, a popular name, which has made finding her extremely difficult. Gabriel has been searching for her for years."

"Does he care for her?"

Rob smiled crookedly. "No. He doesn't remember her. Therein lies part of the problem."

"He doesn't remember her? He had... *relations* with her and he doesn't remember her?"

"He says he doesn't." Rob sighed. "Do you remember the story of the dean's daughter? I told you Charles came to the school to prevent Gabriel from being expelled. In front of the dean, he crushed Gabriel with the set-down he gave him. It was enough to satisfy the dean. After the dean left, Charles paid Gabriel a compliment, if you want to call it that. It certainly wasn't constructive. It was crude and crass, but for Gabriel, who'd been trying his entire life to do something to make his father proud, it meant something. I remember it well. Charles said, 'My worthless offspring has finally developed some balls. We might just make a man out of you yet.'"

Rob took a sip of his wine. "Gabriel has slept with many women. I'm not trying to justify his behavior. But I hope you can understand why he did."

Lilly was completely numb on the inside. "I should go." She didn't know what else to say.

"One last thing," Rob murmured. "If you don't mind?"

What else could there possibly be?

"If Gabriel should die before his thirty-third birthday, all of the housing, income—everything promised to you and your sister—will remain intact. If that should occur, would you be willing to consider being named legal guardian to Charlotte?"

Eighteen

Rob was supposed to come by Friday afternoon, during Charlotte's riding lesson. They were to meet in the stable, at which time Lilly was to give him her answer. Like the week before, he'd been coming by the mansion every day, but this week he hadn't stayed for dinner. For that Lilly was thankful. She didn't want to see him. She wanted nothing to do with him! The one brief conversation they'd had involved determining the time and place of their Friday meeting.

She had only two more days to make up her mind.

While traversing the long east hallway on her way back from walking Charlotte out to the stable, just as she was about to pass Gabriel's study, she heard a voice that struck every other thought out of her head. Her sister was here!

A glimpse into the study showed that Julie was indeed there. She was seated across from Gabriel's desk, and she was rambling about her landlord. Gabriel wasn't scowling. He didn't look annoyed or upset at all. In fact... it couldn't be, could it? Gabriel was actually gazing affably at her sister!

In that split second it occurred to Lilly that there was another way. If only Rob would agree!

Julie stopped talking and Gabriel said, "As I mentioned already, there are two fully furnished cottages here on the grounds. You're free to choose either one. Withers can show them to you this afternoon. Please keep in mind that living here is not convenient to town. You can coordinate with Withers to drive you so long as it doesn't interfere with Charlotte's riding lesson."

Lilly stepped into the room. They both looked at her, and Gabriel's eyes narrowed. "How much will the rent be?" she asked.

"There will be no rent due," Gabriel said stiffly. The amicable tone he'd used when speaking to Julie was gone.

"How long may she stay?" Lilly asked.

"For as long as I own the property." To Julie, he said, "Finch and Withers will assist with moving your things, Mrs. Gibson."

"Thank you! I knew you would help me!" Julie awkwardly pushed her extended girth up from the chair. She was grinning from ear to ear. "I don't know what to say. I'm so grateful!" And then she waddled around the desk, leaned over and kissed Gabriel on his exposed cheek. "You are the nicest man I've ever met!" When she turned back around, she exclaimed, "Lilly, I knew he would help me. I knew it! I told you he would!"

Julie had told her nothing of the sort. Lilly had no idea Julie was planning this!

"Mrs. Gibson," Gabriel said, "I need to have a private word with Miss Hawthorne. Would you mind waiting outside for a moment?"

"I don't mind at all." Julie breezed past Lilly and Lilly stared after her half-dazed. Julie was humming *Amazing Grace.*

"Close the door." Gabriel's harsh voice startled Lilly. "Sit."

Lilly took the same chair Julie had vacated. For a long time Gabriel said nothing. He was just glaring at her, as usual. All she could think was that she could change the decision she'd made. There was an alternative. If only…

"I've been meaning to speak to you for a while about Charlotte," he said.

They'd had a meeting scheduled—the one he'd demanded she not be late for! He was the one who'd failed to show up!

"What do you think of her?" he asked.

The question took Lilly by surprise. "What do I think of Charlotte? She's lovely."

"Do you like her?" he asked.

Lilly's ire heightened. "I adore her. Considering her… environment, she's surprisingly thoughtful, creative, well-mannered…"

His eyes became slits of pure evil. He'd not mistaken her implication. She didn't care if she'd angered him!

"What are your plans for the future, Miss Hawthorne?"

"I don't know what you mean."

"Do you intend to raise your sister's child?"

"To help her, of course. Yes." Realizing where he was going, she quickly added, "I can assure you helping my sister won't interfere with my position here. Charlotte's studies will continue to have my full attention."

"Do you like children?" he asked.

"Yes, very much. It's why I decided to become a teacher."

"Fine," he said. "You can go. Send your sister back in."

Nineteen

Rob arrived at Drayton Hall on Friday, at precisely the time he'd told Lilly he would, and she was exactly where she'd told him she would be—in the barn, seated on a bale of hay. Meeting in the barn was necessary, so as to prevent Gabriel from finding out.

She didn't look at him as he entered. Instead she was staring off through the barn door. From where she was, Rob guessed she could hear Charlotte's distant laughter and catch an occasional glimpse of her on her pony.

After securing the horse he rode, Rob sat on the bale of hay across from her. "How are you, Miss Hawthorne?"

She didn't answer the question. Instead, she said, "There is something I'd like to suggest." After he nodded, she said, "My sister is quite… enamored by Gabriel. I think the feeling may be mutual."

Rob couldn't help it. As awkward as this meeting was, laughter burst out of him. He caught himself when he saw how fixedly she was staring at him. "I don't think so."

"She is the only person I've ever seen him be civil toward."

"You are mistaken," he said.

"How do you know? Have you seen them together? Are you aware he offered her one of the cottages here on the estate?"

"Lilly, I've known Gabriel for a very long time. Please take no offense, but your sister is rather… *er*… flighty. Gabriel has no patience for people like that."

"Perhaps he's changed," she retorted.

"He hasn't," Rob said firmly.

"I'm certain my sister would agree to marry Gabriel. He could say the child she carries is his. If the baby is a boy, Gabriel's problem will be solved."

"Your sister is already married."

"If you can arrange a quiet divorce for Gabriel, why can't you arrange one for Julie?"

"Look, Lilly, I know this isn't what you want to do. I know you're being forced into it. There are any number of reasons why a marriage between Julie and Gabriel will never work, only one of which is a divorce for your sister and her husband. Mr. Gibson would have to be found first. And then, assuming he agrees to a divorce, he would also have to agree to disown the child. Merely listing a father who is not the correct father on a birth certificate, as you know, would be both illegal and unethical, and as such I could have no part of it. Even if Mr. Gibson agrees to disown the child and I can arrange for the divorce in time, it would be obvious the child was not conceived after the marriage between them. He or she would need to be adopted by Gabriel and, like illegitimate children, adopted children are also disqualified."

Lilly briefly closed her eyes. "I guess that's it then. I don't have a choice." She rose from the bale of hay.

Rob stood as well. "I will go and speak with Gabriel now. Is there anything in particular you would like for me to convey to him on your behalf?"

"No." She started to walk away, but turned back when he said her name.

"After the year is over, after the divorce, perhaps you and I could…"

"I think I have been patronized enough," Lilly interrupted coldly.

"Yes, I guess you have," he said quietly. "I am sorry. I truly am." Rob thought for a second she was going to hit him. Her fist was balled tightly. Instead she spun around. This time when he called her name, she didn't look back. Taking hasty steps he caught up to her and continued walking beside her toward the mansion.

"There is one last thing," he said. "I think it would be easier on both of us if you are present when I tell Gabriel what's been decided."

She did stop then, and Rob was shocked by the fire in her eyes. "Easier on you, perhaps," she seethed. "I'm sorry, but I will be unavailable for the remainder of the afternoon. There is no question in my mind, if there's anything of consequence I need know, you'll see to it I'm informed."

That was enough to keep Rob from walking further with her, but he called out, "Do you know where I might find him?"

"In the west wing!" she spat.

Moments later Rob tried the knob to the lower west wing entrance and wasn't surprised to find it locked. He started to turn away, thinking Lilly had purposely misled him. But Gabriel wasn't in the parlor, the library, the kitchen, the dining room, or his study, which left only two options, and he knew Gabriel well enough to know, ill or not, he would never be in his bedroom at this time of day. Not anymore.

He reached up and ran his fingertips along the upper ledge of the doorframe. It didn't take more than a second to locate the key. A peek through the entrance revealed the numerous doors flanking the long corridor. The first one to the left was open. Years ago that room had been Charles Drayton's office.

After returning the key to the ledge, Rob slipped inside and quietly closed the wing entrance behind him. The corridor had not changed since the last time he'd been in it, about eight years before, but the carpet, which had at one time been vibrant in color, looked faded. It didn't take long to determine why. He had to reach for his handkerchief to cover his nose. Dust this thick always provoked a sneeze.

Sniffling, he stepped through the open office door. The room wasn't in as obvious need of cleaning as the hallway, but it too had a layer of dust. Wistfully, he mused, Molly would never let his house be so unkempt.

Dust or no dust, the place contained the same furniture he remembered. To the left was a large, claw-footed desk. To the right was a sitting area with a high-backed sofa. Only two things in the room didn't belong. One was a portrait of Anne Drayton—Gabriel's mother—not hung, but perched on the mantel above the fireplace. Rob remembered the portrait. It used to hang in the music room at Gabriel's house in Philadelphia. He'd believed it had been destroyed in the fire. Although the frame was clearly damaged, the portrait itself was in decent condition. It irked him that Gabriel hadn't told him he'd salvaged it.

To the left of the fireplace was the other thing that didn't belong— a drafting table. On it was a partially completed architectural drawing. Rob walked over for a better look. It was the beginning of what would become an office building. He knew Gabriel's penmanship well enough to recognize it as one of his. There were more drawings, rolls upon rolls of them, filling a round, two-foot diameter tub nearby. A myriad of pens and inkwells were messily left on a small end table within easy reach of the stool, along with rulers and other instruments needed for the craft. They were all worn from use, but they weren't the same tools Gabriel had before the fire.

A half cough-like sound turned Rob around. From the entrance to the room, the high back of the sofa had hidden the front of it. From where he stood by the drafting table, he had a clear view.

Gabriel was lying there. He was on his back with his head propped on a pillow, but angled, so the right side of his face was tucked against the cushion. His long, unbound hair was splayed around him like a fan. The ever-present facial cloth and scarf were draped across the arm of the sofa.

Because of the way his head was turned, Gabriel's scars were clearly visible. Even his horribly damaged ear was in plain view. Despite Charlotte's claims that Gabriel had grown his hair long so he and she could be twins, Rob knew the real reason was to hide his ear and the surrounding areas where hair would never regrow. Since the fire, Rob had seen Gabriel a few times without the covering—he strongly suspected he was the only one who ever had—and he knew Gabriel wouldn't be happy being caught with it off.

For a while, Rob stood there, staring down at his friend. Gabriel's disfigurements, however, were not what kept his attention. What did were the other changes in him—changes that had taken place more recently.

Gabriel had always had a darker complexion, as if he were tanned by the sun year around. Now his skin looked sallow and unusually smooth, making it appear as an almost translucent covering over the more prominent line of his jaw and cheekbones. There were deep, dark circles under his eyes. When open, his eyes appeared red-rimmed and slightly swollen. Even Gabriel's nose looked more boney.

Expelling the breath he didn't realize he'd been holding, Rob took a seat in the chair across from the sofa. Harold Brewster's diagnosis last week, just as Gabriel had predicted, was no diagnosis at all. Rob had, however, listened intently to their dialogue. Gabriel was suffering from headaches, nausea, abdominal cramping, dizziness, confusion and unsteadiness. Other symptoms were discussed as well—disturbing things that people with passing illnesses wouldn't have.

Afterwards, Rob had gone to speak with Harold Brewster privately. He'd wanted some assurances. From the doctor he'd heard things like kidney failure and liver damage, but the doctor couldn't tell him why this was happening. The doctor said, "There's nothing I can do for him." And then he said, "He will be lucky to make it through the holidays."

At best, Rob's dearest friend had three months left to live.

It was a while before Gabriel stirred. He didn't open his eyes at first, but he groaned and rolled his head on the pillow. Hoping not to startle him, Rob said softly, "Hi, Gabe."

"Go away," Gabriel grumbled.

"Why didn't you tell me you were drawing again?" Rob asked.

Gabriel raised a forearm to his brow and left it there, covering his eyes, and his scars. "What for?"

"All these years I've been telling you your talents are being squandered. I guess I was wasting my breath. You must have at least fifty drawings over there."

"Christ!" Gabriel muttered. "It's just a hobby. It gives me something to do. It's not like anyone will ever see them."

"Have you tried to sell any of them?" Rob suggested.

"No."

"I can help. I'd be happy to make contact with—"

"I said no! Drop it!" Gabriel lowered his arm and pulled himself up. Using both hands, he picked up his leg and maneuvered it from the couch, turning his body with it until both his bare feet were on the floor.

Even Gabriel's hands and feet looked unusually gaunt, like skeletons covered with a thin layer of pale skin.

Rob watched Gabriel reach for his kerchief and tie it in place. It was a cleverly designed piece. The cloth that covered the left side of his head and face was stitched into the kerchief. Rob knew Gabriel had several of them, all black, all that he had sown himself. The covering hung there loosely until, with a few quick flicks of his wrist, he wound the scarf around his neck, tied it off and tucked the ends into the collar of his shirt.

"What do you want?" Gabriel said curtly.

"The answer to that question, my friend, is not going to make you happy," Rob said lightly, "so I am going to avoid bringing up what I've come to discuss for as long as I can."

"Good," Gabriel retorted, "then spare me and leave." He leaned back, dropped his head to the cushion behind him and closed his eyes.

"You look better," Rob said.

"I didn't piss blood today."

Rob smiled. "That's the optimistic spirit I like to hear!"

"Yet."

Sighing heavily, Rob asked, "You're not the slightest bit curious why I'm here?"

"No."

"Lilly Hawthorne has agreed to be Charlotte's guardian."

Gabriel's head snapped up and he opened his eyes. "What did she say?"

"She would be honored."

"What else?"

"What else is there for her to say—"

Gabriel cut him off. "You said whatever it is you have to tell me is going to piss me off. What is it?"

Rob smiled sheepishly. "I made a bargain with her on your behalf."

"What kind of bargain?"

"I told her you would pay all of Jason Gibson's debts."

"Already done, for the most part," Gabriel said.

Rob leaned forward and rested his elbows on his knees. Gabriel had shown him the list from Dobbins, but when he'd asked what Gabriel's intensions were, Gabriel shrugged. Rob wasn't surprised to learn he'd tracked down the creditors, but it annoyed him that Gabriel had done so without mentioning it. "When?"

"Last week. I didn't get to them all. I still have to visit the landlord. And one other."

Rob watched Gabriel look away and he wondered exactly what had taken place with those creditors. He knew Gabriel well enough to realize that if he wanted details he'd have to drag them out, and doing so would only anger his friend. It would be better to brush off his own ire and move on. And, something else had just come to mind. "Do you *like* Julie Gibson?" he asked.

"No," Gabriel said flatly.

"Sorry, my mistake." Rob's lips twitched. "Let me rephrase the question. Do you dislike her less than you dislike the rest of the people in the world?"

"She's a flake," Gabriel said. "But she said I'm *divine*. That's one moniker I've never had to live up to before."

"*Divine?*" Rob laughed.

"She's a mess. She needs help," Gabriel mumbled. "And she's about to give birth."

Rob didn't miss the hint of defensiveness in Gabriel's tone. He watched as Gabriel shoved one foot and then the other into his leather house shoes. "Divine, indeed," Rob murmured under his breath. Aloud he said, "You've always been a Good Samaritan."

"The more appropriate term is gullible fool," Gabriel replied, and he winced. "God, I'm thirsty."

"Will the sins of the father ever heal?" Rob whispered. Gabriel was reaching for his cane. "Stay there. I'll get you something. Molly came with me again today. I can have her make you coffee."

"No. Just water," Gabriel mumbled.

Rob gestured to the pitcher on the end table with all the drawing tools. "Is that fresh?"

"Fresh enough."

After handing Gabriel the glass he poured, Rob took his seat again, and watched Gabriel greedily guzzle the liquid, in gulp after gulp, as if he'd had nothing to drink for days. "I hope you didn't think of yourself as a gullible fool when it came to me," he said.

Gabriel didn't reply. He was just sitting there holding the empty glass and staring blankly at the floor. Rob wondered if he was remembering that awful day at the boarding school too—the day they'd met.

For Rob, the first six weeks at the boarding school had been the worst of his life. He'd been plucked away from everything he'd known and thrown into a world in which he was completely lost. The other boys at the school came from wealthy, significant families. They'd had the best education available. They'd been instructed from infancy on proper manners and decorum. They wore tailored clothing and polished leather boots. And Gabriel was one of them.

The stares and sniggers began from the moment Rob stepped out of the taxi hired to drive him there. Everything about him was lacking—everything from his clothes, to his poor manners, to how behind he was academically. He didn't have a fancy watch like they all did. He didn't know the right way to brush his hair. He didn't know how to speak properly. And his stupid nose was always running. Within a few days he'd been given a nickname—*Rob the slob*. It wasn't the only name they called him.

Even as an outcast, it hadn't taken long to figure out who Gabriel was. Everybody knew of Gabriel Drayton. Because of his natural athletic ability, he excelled at every sport the school offered—riding, swimming, track, fencing—and he was popular. When Rob went from the dormitory to class and back again, he walked alone. Gabriel was always surrounded. There were days Rob watched Gabriel walking ahead of him, laughing with the other boys, and Rob wished he were Gabriel. If he were Gabriel he would know the big words in the textbooks when he was made to read aloud in class. He wouldn't flounder stupidly at the chalkboard, staring at the algebra problem he was supposed to be able to solve, while hushed chuckles filled the room behind him. He would have someone to sit with during study hall and someone to pass notes to when the instructors weren't looking. If he were Gabriel, when the boys broke into teams to play stickball, he wouldn't be the only one that neither team wanted. If he were Gabriel no one would call him that nasty word—the one he'd never heard before coming to that school—*bastard*.

The day he first spoke to Gabriel was one of Rob's worst. It all started in the morning session, when he was supposed to write *indefatigable* on the board. But he couldn't pronounce the word, much less spell it. While he stood there, erasing and starting over again, erasing and starting over, sniggers erupted. It got worse when the chalk made him sneeze. He tried to dig the handkerchief out of his pocket and in the process, dropped it. When he went to pick it up, he sneezed again. To contain the dribble that shot from his nose, he whipped his arm up. The chalk catapulted out of his fingers and rolled across the floor. He scrambled to get it out from under the instructor's desk. Because his eyes were watering, he'd misjudged the distance and slammed his head into the hard corner.

The afternoon session wasn't any less humiliating.

That evening he didn't want to go to the dining hall. He wanted to just stay hidden in his room in the dormitory, and he would have, except his roommate—who hated him—came in and told him to get out. In the dining hall, he sat by himself, as always, and listened to the sporadic jeers directed his way. He tried to pretend Cleet and Avery were with him, and they were together in the fort they'd built from scraps of wood at the orphanage. But pretending didn't work the way it was supposed to. It just made him want to go home more. He missed his narrow, lumpy cot. He even missed the chore he despised—collecting eggs from the henhouse. If he could just go home, he vowed he would never complain about collecting those stupid eggs again.

He was still sitting there, with the tray of untouched food in front of him, when the hushed chant began.

"*Rob the slob, Rob the slob, thick as a door knob. Rob the slob, Rob the slob, dressed like a corn cob…*"

He tore off a chunk of his roll and stuffed it in his mouth, but it was hard to make himself chew. Everything he did in this terrible place was wrong. They made fun of him for the way he held his fork and the way he cut his meat. How was he supposed to know which of the things on his plate it was okay to eat with his fingers?

He was trying to swallow when a shadow settled over him. "Mind if I sit here?"

Rob didn't know who it was because he couldn't look up, and for the same reason he couldn't look up, he couldn't speak. He didn't say anything, neither did he nod nor shake his head. Others had asked to sit with him before, but only so they could make fun of him. This boy's intent, Rob knew, would be the same.

"Thanks." The boy's tray thumped on the hard wood as he set it down. Rob saw a pair of long, school-uniformed legs step over the bench seat.

"Look at Drayton! What's he doing? Why's he over there with *the bastard?*" someone chortled.

Rob raised his eyes, just enough.

The most admired kid in his class—Gabriel Drayton—was directly across from him, and Gabriel Drayton had seen his tears.

"Fake a sneeze," Gabriel said in a hushed murmur. "You have a sneezing problem, don't you? Fake a sneeze. Hurry up."

Rob knew what Gabriel was trying to do. He wanted Rob to sneeze so the others would laugh, just like they always did. Rob had no intention of faking it, but then that annoying tickle began on its own.

Three times he sneezed before he could sniffle himself back into control. When he opened his eyes, a handkerchief was dangling in front of his face.

"Here. Use mine," Gabriel said. And then he grinned, took two rolls from his tray and made a show of stuffing them into his pockets. He picked up the untouched one from Rob's tray and tossed it to him. "Come on. Let's get out of here."

It was the first of many times Gabriel had been his *Good Samaritan.*

Gabriel became his guide, his mentor, and before that semester was out, his roommate. From Gabriel he'd learned how to speak, how to dress and how to eat properly. Countless hours they'd studied together, until Rob was no longer afraid of the big words in his books, until he could go to the chalkboard in the front of the entire classroom and work the problems efficiently from beginning to end.

Shaking off the memories, because he knew if he didn't he would probably start blubbering, Rob asked, "Do you want some more water?"

"No," Gabriel said.

Refocusing on his reason for being there, Rob offered up another in a long line of silent prayers. He could only hope he'd done the right thing. For Gabriel's sake, he hoped. He waited another long moment, watching Gabriel set the glass down on the end table beside him and settle back onto the sofa. Then, he blurted, "Lilly Hawthorne has agreed to marry you."

For a long time there was nothing but silence—deafening silence. With each passing second it looked like Gabriel's skin was growing paler. Just when Rob thought Gabriel was surely about to faint, he opened his mouth and took an audible deep breath. In little more than a whisper, he said, "What have you done?"

"I've done what you asked me to do," Rob countered. "I've secured a stable, loving home for Charlotte the only way the loopholes will allow."

"But, I can't."

"If you're married, I can create a trust fund for Charlotte and for your wife. If not, Alex will get complete control." Feeling as if he were about to step off a pirate's plank, Rob flashed his eyes and added, "Perhaps you can enjoy a few moments of her company. Give yourself one last bedroom tumble."

"But, I can't," Gabriel repeated in the same low whisper.

"Why not? Because you're sick?"

The visible parts of Gabriel's features twisted and he growled, "Not because I'm sick!"

Anger boiled up in Rob causing his next words to be harsher than he intended. "My god, man, you make it sound like you are some hideous monster. You have a few scars. So what? If you're that bothered, then don't touch her. All I need to fix everything as far as

Charlotte's guardianship is concerned is a signed and sealed marriage certificate. But it will be your loss and—excuse me for saying this because normally I think you are one of the most intelligent men I've ever known—your own stupidity. If you keep the lamps out, she won't even notice."

Gabriel didn't say anything. He just sat there, staring at the floor. In all the years he'd known him, Rob had never seen Gabriel cry. He wasn't crying. His red-rimmed eyes were dry, but there was something in his expression that made Rob believe he just might be on the verge of it.

"Do you hate me now?" Rob asked tentatively. Gabriel closed his eyes and crossed his arms over his stomach. The gesture scared Rob. "Gabe? Say something. Yell at me or something…"

"When?" Gabriel asked in that same barely audible tone. As slowly as he'd closed his eyes, he opened them.

"Whenever you're ready, but if you decide you want to try to produce an heir, it should be sooner rather than later. I didn't explain everything to Lilly. I led her to believe she has no choice but to share your bed. You could let her off the hook if you want to. Or you could try to make a baby. I will have the marriage license tomorrow."

"How will I… what will I say to her?"

The vulnerability in Gabe's voice floored Rob. "Be yourself. Be the real you. Not this façade of a person you've made up to keep the world at a distance. Contrary to what you've led everyone to believe, your bark is much worse than your bite. Hell, the truth is, you have no bite at all."

"Did she agree because she pities me?" Gabriel asked.

Again surprised, Rob blurted out his first thought, "No, I didn't tell her…" His voice caught and he cleared his throat to cover it. "I didn't tell her how ill you are. I didn't think you would want me to."

After a while, because Gabriel remained there, unmoving, Rob decided to take a chance. "If you're that worried about it, I would be glad to… er… fill in for you, no pun intended. I'll be discreet. She won't know a thing. In the dark I can pretend I'm you—" Gabriel's head shot up and Rob smirked. "No, I didn't think you'd go for that. It's a bad idea. Never mind."

Gabriel's eyes narrowed before he closed them, dropped his head and leaned over his arms.

"Gabe, are you alright?"

"No," Gabriel whispered. "I... I have to throw up now."

Twenty

Rob rolled off of Molly and lay sweating, trying to catch his breath beside her. His limbs felt like jelly, but that wasn't unusual, especially after such a rigorous coupling. There was a moment during it he didn't think he would come at all, not for lack of wanting or stimulation. He was simply too preoccupied, and he'd had to drive himself all the harder to get there.

Normally he did it for her, but this night, while he lay panting, she cleaned his mess off herself. And then she lay down beside him and covered herself up—both of them—with the sheet that had been roughly kicked off earlier. She moved up so her head was on a pillow leaning against the headboard. He was sprawled lower, so when he turned his head to look at her, his eyes were level with her ribs, not that he could see her, covered as she was. "Are you cold?" he asked.

"No, not really," she said.

"Was I too rough?"

Her eyes sparkled. "I liked it."

That made him chuckle. "May I…?"

"I thought you'd never ask." Her smile lightened him instantly, as did the way she moved her arms, crossing her hands behind her head. Adjusting to his side, propping his head on the crook of his arm, Rob tucked one finger in the sheet and drew it down, baring one very lovely breast. He did this to her all the time, afterwards. Because, for some reason, he couldn't get enough of it. There was a part of him that liked this better than he liked the sex, and he really, really liked the sex.

Sometimes, if he was at it long enough, he got hard again, and sometimes he reached down to try to give her some pleasure too, although he didn't think he was ever very successful. When he was engaged so blissfully, it was impossible to really concentrate on anything else. Regardless of those *sometimes* occurrences, more often than not, the reason he did this, as Molly well knew, was to put himself to sleep.

"You have the most gorgeous breasts, you know," he whispered.

"Indeed?"

She was teasing him and it made him smirk. She'd heard him offer similar compliments many times. With his eyes holding hers, he lowered his head and took her into his mouth. But he couldn't keep his eyes open for long, not when he was indulging himself thusly.

He'd tried, once, to do this to the woman he loved, but she'd knocked him away and told him he was sick in the head. With that experience heavy on his conscience, it had taken more than a year to work up the courage with Molly, and even then, in the beginning, he'd only done it in brief stints, afraid she too, would think him sick in the head. But Molly never chastised him. Quite the contrary. Her encouragement often came in the most exhilarating ways imaginable!

After a while, long enough for his arm to have a kink from holding him up, he dropped back to the bed and replaced his mouth with his fingers. Glibly, he murmured, "Do you think there is something wrong with me? Do you think other men like to do this?"

"I wouldn't know about that," she said.

She'd alluded to her innocence a time or two, but she wouldn't divulge anything about her past. Whenever it came up, she evasively changed the subject. Sometimes he wondered about it, and sometimes it bothered him that she wouldn't share her history. Over the years he'd told her many details about his own life, usually at times just like this one. But, as he often reminded himself, her past didn't really matter. "Maybe I have this obsession because I wasn't breastfed as a baby. Maybe there is a latent need in me to make up for what I missed."

"That could be." She moved onto her side, just enough. Her fingers raked through his hair and Rob smothered his laugh, moaning as he drew her in. In pure contentment, he waited for her whispery words to reach him. She would tell him how good what he was doing felt. She would moan and whimper, and she would demand more. And he would give her everything he had. Molly knew. She knew everything he needed to hear, everything he needed to feel. *Oh Jesus, it was good. So sweet.*

"Is it just mine, or is it all breasts you love?" she murmured.

Just yours. The answer came to him instantly. But going there was too dangerous, and he had to remind himself that Molly could never be more to him than she was now. She was just his housekeeper, and a warm body to share his bed. And she was there to appease his peculiar, insatiable fetish.

He remembered the clandestine glances he'd spared to Lilly Hawthorne's bosom, and how he'd wondered what she might look like under her clothes. It told him his initial response to Molly's question wasn't right. He did think about other women. Sometimes. Oddly, though, he hadn't imagined doing *this* to Lilly.

Unbidden, he remembered his offer to take Gabriel's place in Lilly's bed. He still couldn't believe he'd suggested that. Of course he hadn't suggested it because he wanted to have sex with Lilly. He'd suggested it solely to incite Gabriel. And it had worked. He hoped it *would* work.

Molly's question irritated him, because it made him think of other things, and he didn't want to think of other things. He replaced his mouth with his hand long enough to reply, "I'm obsessed with all breasts. What I need is a harem of women—an endless supply so I can gorge myself whenever I want. Only then will I be a happy man. Until then, you will have to do."

Rob didn't care if what he said hurt Molly's feelings. It served her right for asking such a stupid question. She'd opened herself up for it. And someday, as they both knew, this relationship would have to end. When it did… that wasn't something he thought much about. He certainly wasn't going to think about it now.

He wrapped his arms around her and pulled her over so her other breast, the one he'd neglected so far, was within easy reach. If he could clear his mind completely, by letting himself be lost in what he was doing, everything would be fine. He wouldn't have to think about anything. If he kept his eyes closed, he would be asleep in no time. It would be a peaceful, deep slumber, just what he needed…

Oh Molly, you're so good to me. He couldn't say the words aloud because his mouth was so wonderfully occupied, but they came to him. As did that awful comment he'd made. And with it came another realization. Molly was being unusually still, and silent.

Molly was the only woman he'd ever experienced such amazing fulfillment with. There was something about her, something he couldn't quite define. It was almost as if, when he was with her, he was being carried away on a current—a current that was uniquely hers. It was a current that flowed through every facet of their intimacy. Her erotic appetites were perfectly in tune with his. Suckling fetish aside, there were things he liked to do during sex—things others might consider perverted. Not Molly. She was right there with him every step of the way. Everything about her was just… too damn perfect!

But he didn't love her. He couldn't love her! And he was an ass for exploiting her. He was a borderline sadistic, a sick puppy, and the worst kind of person. Not only for hurting Molly with his crude and thoughtless comment, but for so many other things, like purposely leading Lilly Hawthorne to think he was interested in her. He'd deceived her merely to make it easier for him to convince her to agree to his plan for Gabriel. Then he'd bent the facts so Lilly would believe she had no choice but to share Gabriel's bed. What he'd done was twisted and devious. Worse was that if asked to do it again, he would. Without hesitation.

Rob let Molly go. She rolled away and drew the sheet up, and she said nothing. He was a fiend, a deplorable excuse for a human being.

"Moll?" Rob murmured. "I didn't mean what I said the way it sounded."

"I know," she murmured.

Rising up onto his elbow, Rob leaned close and kissed her. Her lips were bloated from the onslaught of bruising kisses he'd given her earlier. He'd been like an animal, savage and cruel, thinking only of himself, never once of her. He was selfish like that. A lot. Just as he'd been minutes ago, using her to assuage anger that had nothing to do with her.

He kissed her again, moving his mouth over hers, opening it. Her response was slow in coming, and when it did, it was fleeting. Rob couldn't remember a time she'd ever denied him. And she wouldn't deny him, even if she wasn't a completely willing participant. His words had been careless and hurtful. But there was nothing he could do or say to change them.

So he rolled away. There was a thickness in his throat he couldn't control. It wasn't because of Molly, but his imprudence and brutality toward her was the catalyst that brought on emotions he'd been holding at bay for far too long. Everything in his life was warped, and he was failing, not just in his law practice, but in his business in New York. His relationships were a mess. Every one of them was cloaked in falsehoods. There were too many secrets and too many lies, and sometimes he didn't know any longer what the truth was. The weight of his bad choices—so many bad choices—was trampling him down. He was so ashamed, so crushed, so ruined. But none of this was new. He'd been feeling this way for a long time, hiding himself in a persona who showed nothing but good humor to the outside world. In the past whenever he needed someone to confide in, to help him when he fell into these dismal places, he'd gone to Gabriel. But he couldn't go to Gabriel now. Not anymore.

He'd never met Gabriel's mother, but recently he'd been thinking about how she died, and how a choice like the one she'd made might be the best thing he could do for himself, and for everyone else. No one would miss him. Molly would be free to marry someone who could love her the way she deserved. No one really gave a damn about him anyway. Not even Charlotte.

A sob fell out of him and he couldn't stop it. Another followed and he turned away from Molly, curling onto his side. It had been a long time since he'd given in to emotions. His eyelids were like a dam, the water seeping through the cracks in the mortar, chipping away until the stone splintered and washed out completely.

"Rob?" Molly's tender touch was there, on his shoulder. He could feel her presence leaning close. "What's wrong?"

"He's going to die," Rob choked.

"Who?" Molly whispered. "Who are you talking about?"

"Gabriel."

As if he'd shocked her, she abruptly withdrew. Rob was too wretched by then to move. His body shuddered as tears suffocated him, until he was gasping through them.

Molly touched him again, tentatively running her hand up and down his arm. "I thought you hated him," she whispered, sounding confused.

Rob knew why she believed that. Molly didn't like Gabriel. She never had. She hadn't known him before the fire, and the few times she had to interact with him since, Gabriel was his belligerent, surly self. Once or twice Rob had told her to ignore Gabriel's grumpiness. He'd told her Gabriel was harmless. But, most of the time when he talked to Molly about Gabriel, he complained. His comments were always flippant, just like the one he'd made earlier this very evening. He'd said, "Gabriel's driving me crazy!" But he hadn't meant it!

"You say he gives you too much grief," Molly murmured.

Rob shook his head and swiped at his eyes. "He doesn't know," he rasped. "He doesn't know who I am. I can't tell him…"

"What? I don't understand," Molly said.

The sobbing came in earnest now, worse than before. Molly's arms were around him, her softness pressing against him, her lily scent engulfing him.

"Molly," he wailed, "what am I going to do? I don't want him to die! He's my brother and I can't tell him! He's my blood and he doesn't know. He's the only family I have! I can't lose him! I can't… *I can't…*"

Twenty-One

By the end of the following week, Lilly was beginning to think the discussion she'd had with Rob was just a bad nightmare. She was certain Gabriel would confront her, but he hadn't made an appearance at all. Like the previous week, Rob came to the mansion every day, except this week he didn't make a point to speak with her. Instead he sequestered himself in some unknown place with Gabriel. This, however, was a blessing, because she really didn't want to have anything to do with either one of them.

Lilly was seated at her vanity, putting finishing touches to her hair when the rapid, insistent rapping at her door alerted her that Charlotte was up and about. It was still very early in the morning—earlier than the time Charlotte usually knocked on her father's door to rouse him. "Come in," she called out.

Charlotte bounced through the suite and into Lilly's bedroom, all the while hailing loudly, "Miss Lilly! Miss Lilly! The seamstress-essess are here!" Her cheeks were bright red with excitement.

"Again?" Talk about wasting money, Lilly thought blandly. Charlotte already had more clothes than she could possibly wear before she outgrew them.

Lilly was imagining the reaction Gabriel would have if she said as much to him when Charlotte chortled, "Not for me. For you!"

"You must be mistaken…" Lilly startled.

Another knock interrupted anything more Lilly might have said. She followed Charlotte through the sitting room. The door to the suite had been left ajar, but there was no one standing in it. Curiously she kept on after Charlotte, out into the corridor.

And there, with his back to the wall, was the dark, formidable presence of her employer. Lilly took an abrupt step backwards.

Gabriel was facing straight ahead, allowing her only a profile view of the right side of his face. In that gravelly voice she was coming to recognize, he said, "Do you want the dressmakers to come up, or would you prefer to meet with them in the front parlor?"

"Either is fine," Lilly stammered.

He pushed away from the wall and set his cane for another step. "I'll send them up. Order what you want. I'll send Finch with a breakfast tray."

"Miss Lilly, you can get a red Christmas dress!" Charlotte declared.

Gabriel didn't say anything more. It wouldn't have mattered if he had. Charlotte was chattering on about dress colors and bonnets and shoes. All Lilly could do was watch Gabriel slowly moving away. She watched until Charlotte grabbed her hand and dragged her back inside her chambers.

The seamstresses were there for hours. Most of it, Lilly spent wishing someone like Susan Drayton, or better yet, Molly Finch, were there to advise her. She didn't know the latest fashions. She didn't know what colors would best suit her hair and complexion. And she had absolutely no idea how many to order. The only thing she could do was heed the recommendations of the dressmakers—and Charlotte— and hope a dozen new dresses, along with various and sundry other necessities, wouldn't be overstepping too badly.

Later, she and Charlotte were in the dining room sharing the mid-day meal when Julie came waddling in to announce that Finch and Withers had brought two wagonloads full of her things. Julie had chosen the cottage next to the one Withers occupied. It was a charming, one-story house with cathedral ceilings throughout, and it was already fully furnished in rich blues and greens.

Lilly and Charlotte spent the afternoon helping Julie decide what should go where. By the time they'd incorporated Julie's furniture and everything else Withers and Finch hauled in from the overflowing wagons, the cottage looked overcrowded. At least Lilly thought so. Julie, on the other hand, seemed quite tickled with everything.

The last item to be brought in was the pretty, silk-draped crib Julie had bought. She followed Withers into her bedroom and told him where to set it up. This took a while, because Julie kept changing her mind. Withers, thankfully, seemed to take all the ordering about in stride. When finally they came back to the sitting room, Withers nodded politely to Lilly and said, "I guess that's it. I'd better get the wagon back and see to the horses."

"I'll come with you," Julie said. "I'm going up to the mansion to speak with Mr. Drayton."

Withers' response brought Lilly's head up. His ever-present smile was no longer there. Instead his forehead was creased. "I don't think that's such a good idea."

"It won't take but a minute," Julie said. "I just want to thank him."

"Perhaps it would be better to wait until tomorrow," Withers suggested.

"I'm sure Mr. Drayton won't mind seeing me today," Julie insisted. "It's really not that far. I don't need a ride. I'll just walk."

"No, Mrs. Gibson! I can't allow it!" Withers said firmly. Lilly had never heard genial Withers speak so adamantly.

Julie looked as flummoxed as Lilly. "But—?"

"He's not to be disturbed anymore today," Withers stated.

"Anymore?" Julie twittered. "But I haven't seen him yet today at all!"

Julie's relentlessness didn't surprise Lilly. Neither did Withers' exasperation with it, especially after everything else he'd done for her so patiently. "He had a difficult meeting in town this morning. He's resting now," Withers said.

"It's been hours since you brought him home," Julie kept on. "You've been with me all afternoon. He must be done napping by now. It's almost dinner time."

"I'm sure he'll be glad to have your company when he's feeling better." Withers cheeks suddenly reddened, and Lilly guessed perhaps he'd revealed more than intended.

"Oh, why didn't you just say that in the first place? I shall make some nice hot tea for him and bring it up to the mansion. I have herbal tea that's good for the influenza—"

"No! You cannot!" This time Withers almost yelled.

Huffing, Julie ranted, "I don't understand what the big deal is, Jimmy! I'm only trying to show him my gratitude!"

Withers took a step away and bowed his head. "My apologies. If there is anything you need help with, please don't hesitate to ask." With that, he turned on his heel and left the cottage.

It was well past time for Charlotte's riding lesson. It was past time for her bath, too. Lilly said as much to Julie, using this as an excuse to leave. A moment later, she was chasing after Charlotte, who was running to catch up to Withers. Rather than driving the wagon, he was leading the horses across the field toward the barn.

"Charlotte, go get your bath before the water gets cold," Lilly called out as soon as she was within earshot. As she caught up to Withers, she said, "I'm sorry my sister is so persistent."

Withers chuckled. "You can say that again."

Lilly grinned. "I didn't know your name was Jimmy."

"James Withers—that's me. Always been called Jimmy up until I came to work here. Your sister asked me my first name and now she won't call me anything different."

That was definitely like Julie. Lilly laughed in spite of herself, but her smile faded quickly. "Is Mr. Drayton alright?"

Withers' hasty glance and stricken expression caused Lilly's apprehension to grow. "I'm not supposed to say anything, miss."

"But you're worried about him?" Lilly prompted.

"Yes, miss."

"What happened?" she asked.

"It's not my place to say."

"Please tell me. It has something to do with Julie, doesn't it?"

"He went to see her landlord this morning." Withers shook his head, as if whatever he was thinking wasn't pleasant. "They were expecting him."

"Expecting him?"

"The landlord's thugs. Mr. Drayton is swift with that cane of his. Uses it like a sword. I've seen him easily ward off four men at once. But today…" Withers' voice trailed off. "I had to shoot off a round to break it up."

Stricken more than she cared to admit, Lilly asked, "There was a fight?"

Withers nodded. "At least this was the last of them. All of Jason Gibson's creditors are now paid in full."

Lilly swallowed hard. "Are you hurt? Did they hurt you?"

"Not me," Withers said.

They parted ways after that—Withers toward the barn and Lilly toward the mansion. Lilly went to her room, where she hastily dressed in her yellow dress. It was time for dinner with Alex and Susan Drayton.

Lilly greeted them as pleasantly as she could, but her heart was in her throat. Alex was the first to ask whether Gabriel would be joining them. The question was directed to Charlotte.

Charlotte's response was a shrug. Lilly waited until Charlotte's attention was redirected to quietly tell Alex, "I understand Gabriel's under the weather today."

Conversation began to flow after that, but Lilly barely listened. She was sure she heard Gabriel's unmistakable tap and scrape. As it grew louder, no one else seemed to notice, but her attention became riveted on the door.

The second he appeared, breath came out of her. It was so loud, she was sure everyone heard her. Regardless, Gabriel appeared no different than he always did. The swollen black eye she expected was not there. Even the grim set of his mouth was normal. As odd as it sounded, she was actually glad to see his fierce scowl. In his typical, bad-mannered way, he ignored Alex's greeting, and didn't say anything until he was seated at the table. When he did, the one simple word was as gruff and rude as always. "Eat."

Thanks to Charlotte and Mark's banter, the meal went along well. That is, until Charlotte announced, "I'm going to have a real momma soon!"

"You can't get a new momma," Mark retorted. "It doesn't work like that."

"Yes, it does," Charlotte insisted. "Miss Lilly is going to marry my daddy, and then she will be my momma! I'll have a momma just like you!"

"Charlotte," Susan intervened, "where on earth did you get such an absurd notion?"

"It's not adsurbed. It's true," Charlotte defended. "Tell them, Daddy!"

All eyes—not just Mark and Charlotte, but Susan and Alex, too—turned to Gabriel. He looked furious, but this was nothing new. His acknowledgment of Charlotte's claim came as a single curt nod.

Alex was the one who broke the stunned silence that followed. His comments were directed alternately between Lilly and Gabriel. "Well… er… congratulations. This is… this is great news. I'm very… er… happy for you."

"As am I," Susan gave them a sweet smile. "When is the big day?"

"The date is not set," Gabriel growled.

For the first time that evening, his fiery gaze locked on Lilly. She wasn't quite sure what to read in that fearsome look.

"This is cause for celebration!" Alex chortled. Casually, as any man might do to a good friend, he slapped Gabriel on the shoulder. Then, whispering like he intended the comment for Gabriel's ears alone, he added, "May I take some credit here? It *was* my idea."

"Excuse me." Gabriel pushed to his feet. "By all means continue your celebration."

To his retreating form, Alex said, "Where are you going? Gabriel, stay."

"What for?"

"This is in honor of you. For your upcoming marriage…"

"No." Gabriel cut him off. "It is an opportunity for you to have a good time at my expense."

The whole room grew silent. Even Charlotte and Mark seemed to pick up on the tension.

"You're wrong," Alex said, but Gabriel was already gone.

The revelry that followed did last quite a while. At first, in the dining room—Susan asked Finch to bring champagne—and then later in the parlor. Gabriel didn't join them.

It was well past Charlotte's bedtime when Alex, Susan and Mark finally made excuses to depart. Lilly was glad. It was a relief to finally let go of the forced smile she'd been holding all evening. And Charlotte was so tired she was falling asleep on her feet. It didn't take long to escort the little girl to her room, help her change into her nightgown and tuck her in.

"Time to sleep," Lilly said as she reached to turn down the lamp.

"I didn't say goodnight to Daddy," Charlotte mumbled.

"It's okay," Lilly said. "He'll understand you were too tired."

"I'm glad you're going to be my new momma," Charlotte said.

"Me, too." It wasn't until she uttered the words aloud that she realized how true they were. She did want to be Charlotte's mother. She just didn't want the other part of what came with that title—namely the husband part. Leaning over, she kissed Charlotte's forehead and said, "I love you," but she doubted Charlotte heard. The precious child was already drifting away.

The last thing Lilly expected when she crept from Charlotte's room was to find Gabriel in the hall. Like the last time she'd come across him there, she took a startled step back.

"Charlotte's asleep. She was exhausted," she stuttered.

"Did you enjoy yourself tonight?" he asked coolly.

Lilly didn't answer. Instead, she said, "Withers told me what you did today to pay off Julie's husband's debts. I hope—"

"I agreed to, did I not?" he interrupted.

It was impossible to express gratitude to such a rude man! The ice in his expression alone made her shiver.

"When did your last monthly begin?" he demanded.

Lilly's jaw dropped. "I… I beg your pardon?"

"You heard me. When did you last bleed? This is not a difficult question."

Heat surfaced from her chest outward, to her neck, her cheeks, into her skull. Even her arms and legs grew warm. "That's none of your business—"

"It is entirely my business," he cut her off again. "Is it not your understanding that the goal of this arrangement is to produce a child?"

"Yes, but—" Lilly started.

"Then answer the question."

"Last week," she squeaked.

"Can you be more precise?"

"Thursday, I think." She couldn't look at him any longer.

He audibly expelled a breath. "Are you regular?"

"I don't know what you mean."

"Are you regular?" he repeated more crudely. "Does your cycle come about the same time every month?"

"Yes, mostly."

He let out another loud breath of air. "The wedding will be Sunday."

That soon! Lilly wanted to tell him she'd made a mistake. She couldn't go through with it.

She was still whirling, trying to come up with any excuse she could, when he said, "Seven nights will be enough."

Seven! That many! She wanted to scream. She wanted to cry, or at least throw something at him. There was no way she could do this. Not seven times! It should only take one, shouldn't it? Every nerve in her body was on end. Every hair on her head hurt. Her skin was crawling.

"If it doesn't work, I won't expect to try again."

Lilly didn't know what to say. It was all so surreal and so unfathomable, and... and Sunday was only two days away! She couldn't say anything. She couldn't speak at all.

"Contrary to what you believe, I don't maul women. We'll do this and be done with it. This marriage is as abhorrent to me as it is to you," he seethed.

And then he was gone.

It was all Lilly could do not to collapse right there, in the middle of the blood-red corridor.

Twenty-Two

Lilly spent the next day helping Julie with unpacking and cleaning and rearranging and everything else Julie wanted done, which really meant Lilly was working while Julie stood nearby ordering her around. For once, at least, she didn't mind. She needed to do something to keep her thoughts off what the following day, or rather the following night, would bring.

In the late afternoon, she headed to the kitchen where she hoped to get away from Julie's harping for at least a few minutes. She was putting away the last of the kitchen wares when Julie waddled in, settled into a chair and said, "What's wrong with you? You've been moody all day."

"Nothing's wrong. What do you mean?"

"I may not be as smart as you, but I can tell something's amiss."

Annoyed, Lilly blurted, "I'm not that smart. If I were smart I would have figured out—" she cut herself off.

Julie didn't know why Lilly had agreed to marry Gabriel. Julie didn't know Gabriel was paying off all of Jason's debts, or any other details of the arrangement, and Lilly didn't want her to know. What she'd told Julie was that she was marrying Gabriel for the monetary stability he could provide.

When Julie had commented that such a rash decision wasn't like her, Lilly told her she was tired of being poor. She told her she liked Drayton Hall and wanted to live there. And she told Julie she loved the idea of being Charlotte's mother.

"I know what's wrong," Julie said. "You're nervous about the wedding night. It's understandable, but you have nothing to worry about."

"How do you know?"

Julie's eyes flashed. "Take it from your older and much more experienced sister. You will like it."

"I won't like it."

"You can't say that until you've tried it." To Lilly's frown she added, "You've had a bad experience. All you have to do is keep telling yourself Gabriel is not that man. Call it intuition, call it what you want, but I can tell just by looking at him, he'll be a very good lover. All you have to do is relax and let yourself feel, and you'll be putty in his hands."

"The last thing I want to be is putty in anybody's hands," Lilly said tersely.

Julie smirked. "Someday you'll want to be putty, trust me. But for now, just remember, when it's with someone you care about, it's quite wonderful."

"I don't care about him!" Lilly retorted.

"Of course you care about him. If for no other reason than he's Charlotte's father and I know you love her," Julie said.

"He doesn't care about anyone!"

"*Au contraire!*" Julie waved her arms in the air.

It annoyed Lilly to no end when Julie used foreign phrases to emphasize her point. "Last night he said this whole marriage is abhorrent to him!"

"Oh." Julie looked perplexed.

For the moment, Lilly didn't care that she was giving away the ruse. She needed to say it. She needed to say it out loud. It didn't matter if Julie was the wrong person to be her sounding board. She turned around and stared at her sister. "I hate him! I really hate him!"

"Well, that's not a very good attitude to have about someone you'll be married to tomorrow," Julie said. "How much longer until Charlotte's riding lesson is finished?"

Lilly glanced at the clock on the wall. "A few minutes. I'll run back to the mansion and help with her bath. Let's talk about something else, please."

"How 'bout paint for the baby's room." Julie separated the two examples of parchment she had on the table in front of her. "I can't decide between blue or yellow."

For a few minutes they did discuss colors, but that conversation didn't last. Julie ended it by saying, "You're obviously too hot and bothered to think about paint."

"What am I going to do?" Lilly murmured. "I can't marry him. I can't stand him. I hate him!"

"He's not that bad, really," Julie coaxed. "He's short sometimes, but that's just because… well, I don't know why, but he's not cold on the inside. I can tell these things."

"He is that bad! He's exactly what everyone says. He is an inhuman monster, a devil pretending to be human, a freak of nature, a—"

"He is not!"

Both Lilly and Julie turned abruptly. Charlotte was standing in the middle of Julie's sitting room, tears bubbling from both eyes. How they'd not heard her come in Lilly didn't know. How much she'd overheard of their conversation Lilly could only guess.

"I don't want you to marry him anymore!" Charlotte cried. "I don't want you to be my momma anymore!" She spun around and took off as fast as her little legs could go.

"Charlotte, please stop." Lilly ran after her. "I'm sorry. I didn't mean it. I really didn't mean it!"

"I don't like you anymore!" Charlotte wailed.

Lilly raced after her, all the way back to the mansion into the east wing entrance and to Gabriel's study. She rounded the door in time to see Charlotte crawl onto his lap. "What's wrong?" he said gruffly. Too gruffly for someone who was supposed to be comforting a distraught child.

"I don't want you to marry her anymore!" Charlotte was hiccupping through her tears and panting from the exertion of her run.

"Why not?" Wet marks from Charlotte's eyes were forming on the front of his shirt.

"I just don't want you to!"

Gabriel didn't say anything. He didn't push Charlotte away either. He just let her stay there while he stared off, out the window. To Lilly his body language was clear. He wanted her to leave.

Because she didn't know what else to do, she did go. In her room, all she could do was hope Charlotte would accept her apology. Or that Gabriel would change his mind and set her free from this insane arrangement.

She was drying her own eyes when she heard forceful pounding on the door of her suite. It jolted her up from her bed. She knew, somehow, before she opened it, who she would find standing there.

He moved right past her, without asking, and slammed the door shut behind him.

Lilly's defensive hackles rose instantly. She took several steps away from him. "You have no right to come in here!"

"This is my house. I have every right!"

Lilly forced herself to return his glare.

"What did you say to Charlotte?" he demanded.

"It was a mistake. She overheard me talking to Julie."

"And what did you say?"

"Does it matter? I will apologize. Where is she? I'll go to her right now."

She started to walk past him, but he caught her arm in a tight grip. "We're not finished!"

Staring at him, she yanked her limb from his grasp. Her entire arm was numb in the aftershocks of his repugnant touch. "She heard me say I didn't like you."

"Is that all?"

The sudden mirth in his tone was wholly unexpected. He was laughing at her! On top of his lack of concern for his child, this only raised her ire. She was so infuriated she had the urge to break something, anything, over his head! "Do you know Charlotte can't read?"

"What else did she overhear you say?"

Ignoring him, Lilly continued, "At first I thought perhaps her schooling in town had been poor. But I've come to realize that isn't the case. She doesn't recognize any written letters or numbers, and she still isn't learning them. I think Charlotte is very bright, but something isn't right—"

"Charlotte has been reading since she was four," he cut her off. "She reads her books to me all the time."

Lilly held her ground. "She has the books memorized. She is merely reciting what she's heard someone else read to her. She's not reading at all."

He didn't move, yet it suddenly felt like he was looming over her. His immediate and intense reaction completely stole her breath.

"My daughter is not stupid or lacking intelligence of any kind! Your implication is way out of line and wholly unacceptable. It is quite clear to me that if any of Charlotte's instruction has been inadequate, it has been yours!"

"I didn't say Charlotte was stupid!" Lilly fumed. "To memorize an entire book after hearing it only a few times proves exactly the opposite. Charlotte is one of the brightest children I have ever met. The only inadequacy in her life has been having a parent who is too blind to see what her real needs are!"

"How dare you!" he raged.

Lilly refused to cower. "Are you aware of why she doesn't want to go to school in town? Do you know what the other children did to her?"

"Yes, I do," he seethed. "The same thing you just did. Too blind? Turn around!"

Lilly did, too shocked by the harshly spoken directive to do otherwise. And there she was, looking at herself in the mirror.

The door to her suite slammed shut. Gabriel was gone.

Twenty-Three

A hastily scrawled note signed 'Drayton' was the means by which Lilly discovered when and where the wedding would be. He'd left it outside her bedroom door for her to find in the morning. It said Withers would have the carriage waiting for her at six o'clock to take her to the church.

Throughout the day, despite her numerous apologies, Charlotte was still upset. She wouldn't share breakfast or the midday meal, and she refused when Lilly offered to read to her. At least, in the few brief dialogues they had, she didn't repeat her previous declaration that she didn't want Lilly to marry her father.

The six o'clock hour was fast approaching when Lilly went in search of something to nibble on. She expected the kitchen to be empty, but it wasn't. Charlotte was there, sitting at the table, and Gabriel was across from her. They both had bowls in front of them and spoons in their hands.

"Excuse me," Lilly murmured softly.

She would have quietly retreated, but Gabriel said, "Help yourself."

There was a big pot on the stove. Lilly meandered over and lifted the lid. Steam wafted out, along with the heavy aroma of beef broth. "It smells wonderful. What kind of soup is it?"

"Everything soup," Charlotte said.

Lilly dished out some for herself—it looked as good as it smelled—and went to the table, where she asked if she could sit next to Charlotte. To Charlotte's nod, she settled in. At the same time, father and daughter simultaneously pushed their empty bowls away. "Please don't feel you have to stay and wait for me," Lilly said.

"We won't," Gabriel said. "Charlotte has something to ask you."

"Daddy said I can come to the wedding tonight. But only if it's okay with you."

"Of course it's okay with me," Lilly replied immediately. "I was hoping you would come because I need a flower girl."

Charlotte looked at her father. "Can I be a flower girl? What's a flower girl?"

"A flower girl helps the bride carry her flowers," Gabriel said shortly. Then he said, "Charlotte, it's time to go."

They walked out together. Before he disappeared entirely, without turning, Gabriel muttered, "Withers will be waiting for you at six o'clock."

At six o'clock, Lilly was ready. By sound alone she knew Charlotte wasn't in her room. Neither was Gabriel in his. She hadn't heard a peep from either of them since the brief meeting in the kitchen, and she was beginning to wonder if Charlotte would be coming along after all.

At the bottom of the stairs, there was still no one in sight. The front parlor was empty. She fisted her fingers once, twice and stretched them out. Slowly she counted under her breath, "One… two… three… four…" At ten, she forced herself to move toward the heavy front door.

Withers was there, as he was supposed to be, at the bottom of the porch stairs standing beside the carriage. "Are you ready, miss?"

Lilly descended the lengthy stone steps and asked, "Where's Mr. Drayton?"

Withers gestured toward the carriage with a quick flick of his head. It was the last place Lilly expected Gabriel to be. Withers opened the door and offered a hand to help her climb in.

Gabriel was there, staring out the opposite window, looking decidedly bored. He didn't spare her a glance. Charlotte was there, too. She was dressed in white and lace. Everything about her matched and looked perfect, including the baby's breath flowers that had been placed in her braided and pinned hair. In her hands she held a lovely bouquet of pale peach roses.

Soberly she said, "I hold the flowers because I am the flower girl. Miss Molly showed me how."

"That's right," Lilly told her.

"Is this dress a good flower girl dress?" Charlotte asked.

"Yes, it's beautiful," Lilly said.

"Do you like my hair? Miss Molly made it for me."

"Yes, you are the prettiest flower girl I have ever seen."

"Really?" Charlotte squeaked.

The carriage lurched and rattled onward. Charlotte's banter preoccupied Lilly enough to keep the nervous knots in her stomach from overwhelming her completely. Except for a few glances toward Gabriel, which made her think he had turned into some sort of statue, she didn't think of him at all.

At the church—the same church Lilly attended on Sundays—Withers helped her and Charlotte alight and told them to go ahead inside. Molly Finch was waiting for them in the narthex. She greeted them both warmly, telling them how nice they looked. Charlotte beamed under the praise.

Lilly expected Gabriel would follow them in, but he didn't. The sanctuary and long aisle in front of them were empty. The minister appeared first, coming in through a side door. At the same time piano music filled the room.

"There's Daddy!" Charlotte whispered.

Gabriel and Rob followed the minister and joined him in front of the altar.

"It's time," Molly murmured. She took the bouquet from Charlotte and gave it to Lilly. Then she handed Charlotte a small basket. "Remember what to do?" she asked softly. To Charlotte's nod, she said, "Go ahead, sweetie."

Resolutely, Charlotte started up the aisle, sporadically dropping pale rose petals in her wake.

"She's so excited," Molly whispered to Lilly. "She doesn't want to make any mistakes."

Lilly had to swallow over the lump in her throat.

"Your turn," Molly said. With a gentle hand on her shoulder, Molly encouraged her to go. "Don't be nervous. You look beautiful. Everything will be alright."

Molly's kind words were exactly what Lilly needed to hear. Taking a deep breath she started forward, one fateful step at a time. The flowers she clutched shook as badly as her knees. She tried to look at Gabriel, but couldn't. The evil he exuded made it impossible. She couldn't look at Rob, either. What she wanted to do was slap that smug smile off his face. This was his fault! He was the one who had come up with the horrible arrangement.

The aisle of the church had never seemed so long, and yet, all too soon, she was there, with her heart in her throat, standing beside Gabriel, staring dumbly at the minister. It would have been so easy to change *I do* into *I don't*, but she couldn't. Because of Julie, she couldn't. Because of Charlotte, she didn't.

The minister spoke, yet Lilly heard none of his words. What she heard was the storm the churning clouds had threatened to produce. It began in earnest pounding and shuddering against the roof of the church. It was an omen, reminding her of the impending nightmare she would have to face.

There was no *kiss the bride* to seal the deal. There was only the minister's tersely stated, "I now pronounce you husband and wife." There was no walk up the aisle with her new husband by her side. There was only Charlotte fluttering, and Molly following. And Withers.

Withers was the one, with umbrella in hand, who escorted Lilly out of the church to the waiting carriage. Then he drove around to the side of the church to pick up Gabriel, too.

On the way back, Charlotte chattered happily about her excellent performance, but eventually, she curled into a ball on the seat. With her father's thigh as a pillow and his cloak as a blanket, she fell fast asleep. Lilly wished she could have floated away too, but there was no way. She was too jittery to sleep, too anxious to let herself sit back in the luxurious seat, too uneasy to even let her eyelids close.

Except for the pattering rain, the carriage grew uncomfortably silent. This was a business arrangement, she reminded herself. All she had to do was lie with him seven times. Only seven. Seven wasn't very many. And then there would be a quiet divorce. She would leave Drayton Hall and live with Charlotte and her baby—if there was a baby—in a beautiful home of her choosing. She would never marry again. She would never want for anything again either.

It took some time for Lilly to force herself to look at her husband—her *husband... oh dear god!* The darkness made it impossible for him to see anything outside of the window, but he was staring out as if he could. This cold, wicked character wasn't a husband—not a true husband. He was an apparition, a phantom that in time would be gone completely from her life.

As if he felt her stare, he abruptly turned. "Would you prefer I come to your room, or would you rather come to mine?"

Lilly shivered. "I...I will come to yours." She could get away from him afterwards. She could return to a place of safety, where she would be alone, without his mauling hands on her. That was something she could hold onto, something to ease the panic.

He grunted. Lilly had no idea what it meant.

Already her skin was crawling. Already the feeling of being helpless and overpowered consumed her. She remembered it well. The only difference was she was going into this willingly. She could already see his black silk covering above her. She could already feel the heaviness of his body on top of hers. He would clamp his claws around her wrists and hold her down. He would...

She squeezed her eyes shut in an attempt to force the images away, but they wouldn't go away. It wouldn't take long. This was the only thought she could cling to. It would only take a few minutes. A few minutes. That was all. One time a day. For one week. By this time next Sunday, it would all be over.

"Eleven o'clock," he growled.

Lilly jolted. His eyes narrowed, and she stared, utterly petrified, into the deep grey depths of them. She could no more control the stammer in her voice than she could the tremor in her hands. "Y-yes..."

His eyes didn't waiver. If anything, the glare became more menacing. "I am quite aware of how disgusting I am to you. It is not necessary to remind me," he snapped.

Had she not been so stunned by his words, her threatening tears would have fallen. As it was, all she could do was swallow.

The carriage halted. They were home.

"Don't worry, Miss Hawthorne," he said roughly, "it is highly unlikely I will be able to perform. You may be spared."

Within seconds, the door opened and Withers was there with umbrella in hand. Vaguely she listened to Gabriel rousing Charlotte. Withers escorted her up the steps to the front door and then returned for Charlotte.

She and Charlotte were in the entrance hall when she heard Gabriel's scraping gait behind them. Charlotte ran to the parlor. Lilly ran up the east staircase. At the top, she glanced back. She was just in time to see the dark-swathed form disappear through the parlor door. She heard his gruff, clipped voice. "Charlotte, time for bed."

There were only one hundred twenty minutes left until the eleventh hour struck.

Twenty-Four

Lilly heard Gabriel coming and she closed her eyes. She was lying on her back in his bed with the blankets pulled securely to her neck. The pillow was soft enough, but she could still feel the hairpins holding her hair digging into her scalp. She'd been lying there for a while, clad only in a pale cream nightgown. The robe she'd tiptoed across the hall in was strategically draped at the foot of the bed, ready for the moment she could slip back into it and flee. Once more, as she'd done over and over since lying down, she quoted her mantra, *"I can do all things through Jesus Christ, who strengthens me."*

Eleven o'clock had come and gone. She was staring at the lamp on the wall by the door. With the exception of the blazing fire in the fireplace, it was the only remaining light in the room. The latch clicked. The door opened. She held her breath and watched Gabriel limp into the room. At first he didn't notice her. When he did he stopped short. Then he just stood there for a long time in the shadows, halfway between the door and the bed.

Finally he cleared his throat and murmured, "It may get chilly, but it will be better—" He cut himself off. "I'm going to put the fire out."

Lilly didn't reply and she didn't watch him, but she heard every scrape of the shovel he used to scoop ashes to douse the flames. Next, he went to the one remaining lamp on the wall and lowered the wick, and lastly to the window, where he released the curtains from their restraints. The room became so dark she could see nothing. On this at least, she agreed. The pitch black would make it easier.

She heard him move around the bed to the other side, and the dull clunk as he propped his cane against the end table. The bed creaked as he sat on the side of it. His shoes thudded to the floor, one at a time. She could see an outline of him, but that was all. He was removing his clothing. His movements were slow, each one deliberate. The bed creaked again as he rose to slip out of his trousers. Lilly closed her eyes.

She felt cool air as he moved the blankets, but a second later she was surrounded in warmth again. He was on his back like she was. Turning her head slightly, she could feel more than see his right profile. Instinct told her his eyes were open, staring at the canopy overhead.

As if he heard her thoughts, he glanced at her. And then he rolled toward her. She felt soft silk graze her bare forearm. Silk? From his shirt? He'd kept it on? He was leaning on his elbow. Her eyes traveled over his silhouetted form. His shirt was still on him, but no longer buttoned. It hung loosely. His mask and scarf were still in place.

"Let's get this over with," he muttered.

Nodding, she stared at where his eyes should be. In the darkness she couldn't tell exactly. Under the blankets, his fingertips grazed her hip and moved downward. The touch was so light it made the material of her nightgown tickle. Slowly he began to pull the gown upward, exposing her shins, her knees, upward, upward, inch by whispery inch.

She lay as still as she could, unable to even blink. Then he touched her skin, inside her leg, just above her knee. It was a breath of a caress, nothing more. A rush of tingles coursed through her and she shivered. The back of his hand brushed against her other leg and she brought her knee up, to move it away. As if in punishment for her pathetic retreat, which she realized belatedly left her more open to him, his whole hand curved around her inner thigh and moved slowly upward, pushing her nightgown with it. His fingers brushed so close to her womanhood, she sucked in air and held it in anticipation of the rough groping to come.

But it never came. Instead the breath-like fingertip trickle moved downward again. The fingertips of his other hand feathered over her temple and into her hair. The bed creaked as he shifted. His presence pressed down, closer to her, leaning over her. Instinct brought her arm up protectively. For a second she was tangled in the open cloth of his shirt, but then her palm was flat against the center of his chest. She felt a sprinkle of hair there, warmth, and through a layer of spongy muscle, the underlying sharpness of bone. At the same moment she breathed in a salty scent softened by something sweet and clean. She took another breath and felt his heartbeat pounding, steady and fast—as fast as her own—reverberating through her hand.

His fingertips trailed up her inner thigh again. This time when he went back down he moved to the outside of her leg and up, over her hip, the bone of her pelvis and the valley next to it, to her lower stomach. It tickled. Goose bumps formed on her everywhere, from the top of her head to the tips of her toes.

She felt a faint swish of warm air on her cheek. The warmth of his touch on her stomach slid down and covered her between her legs. She jerked and pushed at his chest, but her effort was futile. The warm, tender pressure of his hand below didn't move. She squeezed her eyes closed.

Velvety contact met the corner of her mouth and made her lips quiver. The gentle brush of silk cloth grazed her chin. The velvet moved across her mouth, growing heavier. A soft, moist tickle stroked her lips and they opened. There was a taste, warm, musky and sweet, and she suddenly wanted to taste more. Somewhere deep inside her lower stomach, something twisted. It caused her to move, to stretch to relieve it, an action that brought the warmth of his hand in closer between her legs.

He expelled a whispery groan and it triggered another twinge deep inside the pit of her belly. Her hand on his chest opened and slid over more muscle, harder muscle, a small tight nipple and down from there, until she felt the long caging bones of his ribs.

And in that intense second, the warmth between her legs disappeared. His arm moved up her body so quickly she didn't realize what he was doing until he knocked her hand away. All she could do with the displaced limb was fist her fingers in the blankets while he began a slow trek upward along her diaphragm to the center of her chest, and then on to her collarbone. His fingertips were so tender, tickling over her neck and the line of her jaw. His forearm rested lightly across her chest. Then his velvety lips were over hers, still tender, but heavier than before. Her mouth opened under his and she tasted again. It was good. It was warm and sweet and…

His hand moved down from there, over the material of her nightgown, and this time covered her breast. Her lower stomach churned again, and she couldn't stop from arching in reaction. When she did, he let out another one of those groaning breaths. She didn't understand why his bizarre noise would cause the churning inside her to intensify, or why suddenly and appallingly she realized she was wondering what it would feel like to have the warmth of his touch on her bare skin.

As if he had the identical thought, he began to work at the tiny buttons at the top of her bodice. There were four of them. His gentle touch tickled. Within seconds, he pushed the material out of the way, and his hand replaced it, tenderly stroking, coddling, whispering across her skin. While she struggled with the realization that she *liked* what he was doing, another place, a lower place, was begging for that warming sensation, too. She squirmed, wiggling in the bed, and she was sure he read her mind. Again.

He brought his hand down, under the blankets and under her nightgown, up along her inner thigh. He was almost there when she heard herself whine, a whispery cry of anticipation. The noise of it shocked her as badly as the unsatisfied need. His hand was moving on her leg again, but he was going the wrong way!

Relax and enjoy it, Julie's words repeated in her head. But she couldn't relax. There was no way to relax. Her entire body was as taut as a bowstring. When finally he touched her, she uncontrollably bucked and he replied in exactly the way she needed him to. His fingers began a slow, rocking motion. And he didn't stop, not while his mouth left hers, trailing along her neck, her collarbone and lower still. She felt his tongue on her breast. There were too many sensations going on in her body all at the same time. Involuntarily she moaned.

Moments later she had absolutely no idea what came over her, but somehow the need to be touched became desperate, causing her to writhe. Her back arched, her knee came up, and her heel dug into the bed. She yanked at the material of her gown to expose more of herself. He didn't stop. Not with what was happening below or what his mouth was doing above. And she didn't want him to stop. Ever.

In one distinct and utterly fantastic second her insides completely dissolved into water. She melted into the bed, and was wholly unaware at first of the blankets being stripped away, or of him settling on top of her. She didn't notice until she felt the pulsing fullness of him, seeking entry. He was moving slowly, deliberately, deepening the connection a little farther with each gentle push.

His arms slid underneath her and his long fingers wrapped in and over her shoulders, like some strong enveloping hug. Her knees came up of their own volition. At the exact same moment he pressed down hurtling that final seeking thrust as deeply as he could go. It knocked Lilly's breath from her. And she thought it must have done the same to him because he expelled another one of those whispery moans. Like before, she didn't understand why his noises would put her into such a dreamy stupor, but they did.

His cheek against hers was very smooth and soft. His chest rubbed her sensitized skin like a soft towel. Gripping his shoulder, through his shirt, she felt hard muscles straining. Her fingers traced his triceps, and one hand sneaked between his arm and his side, floundering with the cumbersome flap of material, until her fingertips grazed skin.

"N-no…" he rasped. Like lightning his arm came out from underneath her and drew her hand away. He took it with him, entwining their fingers together.

The movement below began again, this time heavier and faster. Lilly could only react by instinct, by doing what felt right and what felt good. With each of his downward movements, she pressed up, over and over again.

Suddenly he made a noise, a real noise, not a whispery moan. This one had depth to it and although not loud, it seemed to come from the bottom of his lungs. It all happened very fast. His plunging increased in speed for mere seconds, and then his entire frame became rigid. His grasp on her fingers tightened. Another sound came out of him, more of a choked gasp than a noise. Then he became still.

His heart was pounding so badly she could feel it inside of her own body. Her fingers still entwined in his were numb from the tightening of his grip. Then, just like that, when she thought she could never find such an intriguing combination of urgency and solace, he let go. He went away, rolling off to sprawl beside her. She heard the shimmer of the blankets as he flung them over his legs.

Lilly lay there listening to his panting breaths. In the darkness, enough of his silhouette was visible for her to see his forearm resting across his eyes. She didn't know what to say. The entire experience had been nothing at all what she'd thought it would be, and she wanted to express some sort of gratitude, but that didn't seem right, so she said nothing.

The urge to reach out and touch him, to turn toward him and lay her hand on his chest, was very strong. Because she wasn't sure if this would be right either, she didn't. She lay still, allowing the cool air to brush over her heated skin, waiting for him to speak.

He was still breathing heavily, still covering his face with his arm when he murmured, "You can go now."

Stunned, Lilly didn't move right away. All the blissfulness she'd felt a moment before disintegrated. Thankfully her robe was exactly where she'd left it. She told herself not to run from the room, but on legs that felt like jelly, she did.

After yanking out the pins and releasing her hair, she climbed into her own bed. Only then did a few tears fall. They came silently, one by one, in perfect harmony with the rainfall outside. But it made no sense. She hadn't the faintest idea why she was crying.

Twenty-Five

"Get out!" Gabriel looked up from the drawing he'd been working on most of the day, but he didn't turn around.

"Darn!" Rob said. "Your bad mood must mean things didn't go well last night?"

Gabriel slammed his pen down and spun around on the stool. "It's none of your business! If you have something you need to talk to me about, wait in the study. I'll talk to you there. Not here. This room is off limits."

"Ah! You want to keep your little hideout a secret. Sorry. I didn't pick up on that these last couple weeks. But since I'm here, it seems rather silly for us to leave. Tell me what happened. I rode all the way over here to find out."

"Christ! You try my patience worse than Charlotte! I'm not about to keel over dead. You don't have to come here every goddamned day to check on me!" Gabriel snapped.

"I'll have to ask Lilly then," Rob baited.

"Fine! Goodbye!" Gabriel spun himself around and leaned over the drafting table. He'd drawn two lines when he said, "I thought you were leaving."

"Well," Rob drawled, "the truth is, I kind of already spoke with Lilly."

"Then go home!"

"Don't you want to know what she said?"

Gabriel dropped his pen again. "No, Rob, I don't want to know what she said!"

Rob let out a heavy sigh. "Since you don't want me to come here, are you going to come to see me in town?"

"I'll be in town Thursday or Friday."

"For whatever it's worth, I'm sorry," Rob said. "I'll see you."

He started to walk away but stopped short when Gabriel said, "For what?"

"For putting you through this. This marriage thing. I guess I didn't realize how difficult it would be for you."

Gabriel reached for his cane and used it to leverage himself up. "What do you want me to say? It hurt like hell? Yes, it did. Are you happy now?"

Rob flinched. "No, I'm not happy now. Of course I'm not happy now. That's the last thing I wanted to hear."

"You asked. I answered. Leave me alone."

Rob opened his mouth but closed it again. Gabriel started toward him. "Where are you going?"

"To the kitchen," Gabriel said. "I'm hungry."

"Really?" Rob's eyebrows rose. "May I join you?"

"No." Gabriel stopped and glared. "Stop hounding me. Stop hovering over me! I'm fine! Just go!"

"Alright."

Gabriel stared at the door until he heard the click of the lock securing the west wing entrance and then he turned to the couch, took the three short steps to get to it, and sat down gingerly. What he'd said to Rob wasn't a lie. He was hungry. It was the first time he could remember physically feeling this hungry in months. What he'd said to Rob about the night before was true too, but not in the way he'd led Rob to believe. He'd expected physical pain, and he'd been surprised by how little there was.

He'd gone into it telling himself he would do what had to be done, nothing more, nothing less. But there, lying beside her, feeling the softness of her skin, and breathing in her honey scent, he'd been overwhelmed with desire. With it came a severe internal demand to ensure her experience was as pleasant as possible, because Lilly was innocent, and he couldn't take that from her in some cold, clinical act. And he supposed there was a part of him that wanted to prove to her, at least in some small way, that he wasn't the monster she believed him to be.

Somewhere in the midst of it, he'd fallen hard. So hard, his chest had burned him. His limbs had uncontrollably trembled. He hadn't expected to feel her body naturally grow ready for his, but it had. He could only wonder, and dare to hope, that it meant she wanted him, too. Not as much as he wanted her—that was impossible—but at least in some small way.

Reality didn't sink in until it was over. All he pictured as he'd lain there afterwards was the way she'd avoided looking at him as she walked up the aisle, and the way she'd recoiled in the carriage. The softness of her skin, the taste of her kiss had sucked him in and deceived him. She hadn't wanted him then and she never would.

Lying there, trying to catch his breath, he'd realized she wasn't the innocent he'd believed her to be, which, in the midst of the intensity of his passion, he'd forgotten. Not that he was some expert when it came to virgins. He'd never been with one before. But he knew enough to know she wasn't one, and it crushed him. His desperate hope had turned him into a fool. Again. Reality was a knife plunged into his gut and twisted over and over.

Throughout the day he'd avoided her. It wasn't difficult. He'd been doing it ever since she'd come to live at Drayton Hall.

Where Rob skulked off to, he didn't know, and he didn't really care. By the time evening settled in, he assumed Rob had long since departed. He waited until Charlotte's bedtime to go to the front parlor where he knew they would be. Outside the door he stopped and listened.

"How about *B?*" Lilly prompted.

A second later Charlotte plucked out the key on the piano.

"Perfect!" Lilly applauded.

"Now *E?*"

Charlotte found one.

"The last letter is *G,*" Lilly said.

Gabriel leaned a shoulder against the wall and let his head drop to it wearily.

"*B-E-G,* beg," Lilly said.

Charlotte repeated it.

"Can you play it again?"

Charlotte picked out the three keys.

Lilly clapped. "That's exactly right!"

Gabriel could picture the proud grin on Charlotte's face, and he told himself again he was glad Lilly would be her guardian. Two nights ago, while he'd been standing outside of Charlotte's room, he'd overheard Lilly tell Charlotte she loved her. The memory had been replaying in his mind constantly. He squeezed his eyes tightly closed to block it out, but he couldn't. There was no question he'd made the right choice for Charlotte. Why then did listening to them together make him feel so wretched?

Lilly prompted Charlotte with more letters. This time *B-E-D*. Charlotte played the notes and repeated the letters after Lilly. And Lilly said, "Now you must play the words as I say them."

"Okay," Charlotte chirped.

"It is time for Miss Charlotte to go to *bed*..." Lilly paused and Charlotte giggled as she spelled out the word on the piano. Lilly continued, "But Miss Charlotte doesn't want to go to *bed*..." Charlotte played the notes, "...yet, so she is going to *beg*..." Charlotte played. "...to not go to *bed*."

Charlotte giggled. Gabriel could hear the humor surfacing in Lilly as well.

"And Miss Lilly is going to *beg*... Charlotte to please go to *bed*... and Charlotte is going to *beg*... Miss Lilly to not go to *bed*."

Gabriel pushed himself away from the wall and rounded the door frame. They were seated close together on the piano bench and Lilly had her arm around Charlotte's shoulders. He watched her squeeze Charlotte in an encouraging hug. They were both laughing. Simultaneously they looked up.

Lilly was smiling. Her eyes sparkled as they met his. In that split second, before Charlotte drew her attention, while she was still looking at him, her smile widened, and it knocked the wind out of him.

He just stood there, feeling stunned and stupid, and weak in the knees, watching Charlotte whisper something in Lilly's ear.

"Charlotte wants to show you something," Lilly said.

Her smile was making his heart pound. He couldn't breathe right. "Fine."

Lilly said, "It's time for Charlotte to go to *bed...*" Charlotte played the notes, "...but Charlotte doesn't want to go to *bed...* so she is going to *beg...* to stay up."

Once again, Charlotte whispered in Lilly's ear.

"Okay," Lilly said, "Charlotte is going to *beg...* to stay up, Daddy..."

As Lilly started on the letters, Charlotte pressed the corresponding keys on the piano, "*D-A-D-D-E.*"

The shock on Lilly's face told Gabriel this wasn't something she'd taught Charlotte already. Charlotte was grinning up at him.

Gabriel started across the room toward them. "And Daddy, *D-A-D-D-E...*" he said lightly, waiting for Charlotte to play the notes, "...is going to tell Charlotte she can *beg B-E-G...* all she wants, but it's still time for her to go to *bed B-E-D.*"

Lilly laughed. Charlotte frowned. And Gabriel caught Lilly's smile again.

Watching his daughter skip from the room, Gabriel consciously had to force himself to take a breath. He had intended to tell Lilly her obligation was complete. The money and property would still be hers, but she need not come to his room again. The words stuck in his throat.

"I'm sure Charlotte will be back down to read a book in a few minutes," she murmured.

All of the friendliness from a moment before was replaced by the same disgust and apprehension he'd seen in her yesterday.

"Excuse me," she whispered. She was already halfway out the door.

Tonight, if she showed, he would do what he should have done in the first place. Get it done. In and out. Fast and clinical. Nothing more, nothing less.

Twenty-Six

With her eyes closed, alone in Gabriel's darkened room, Lilly took several deep breaths and allowed herself to sink more deeply into the mattress. This night, she'd taken her hair down before coming. Not having the pins digging into her scalp only added to the comfort. Upon arriving, she's discovered the fire and lamps were already out. The room was chilly, but the thick down blankets had warmed her quickly. She was entirely too content, especially considering whose bed she was in.

She hadn't slept much the night before. How could she after what happened? It had taken most of the night to sort through everything in her head, and still she wasn't quite sure what she'd felt or what she should feel now. There was a part of her that wanted to experience his touch again. This was the same part of her that, in anticipation of his coming, caused her to unbutton the four little buttons at the front of her nightgown. Under the blankets, her upper body was fully exposed. The cool silk sheet brushed her breasts, tickling them. With her eyes closed she could almost feel his fingers, his mouth there…

In that dreamy state, with warmth surrounding her so blissfully, she began to drift off. In an effort to remain alert, she tickled the roof of her mouth. For a few seconds she was jarred into wakefulness, but it wasn't long before she was drifting away again.

She didn't hear Gabriel come in. She didn't hear him draw the curtains or remove his clothes. What roused her was the sudden cold caused by the blankets being tossed away, followed by his hasty lifting of her nightgown. Whatever gentleness he'd shown her the night before was not present in him tonight.

She was so startled by his roughly prying hands, forcing her legs apart, a shallow cry flew out of her. She pushed at his chest as hard as she could, while trying to squirm away, but his arm caught her around the waist and drew her back. Lilly kept fighting, flailing in a desperate attempt to escape. Somewhere in the tangle, his palm connected with her bared breast. She whimpered, and in that split second he froze.

"Ow," Lilly cried softly again, this time because his arm was entrapping and pulling her hair.

He jerked, taking himself away, all except his fingertips, which trailed along her hairline.

Tears stung her eyes and her voice broke, "Why… why did you do that?"

The pad of his thumb was suddenly there, beside her eye, wiping away the tears. His mouth touched hers, as lightly as it had the night before. "I thought—"

Whatever he intended to say, he never said. His caresses grew tender, causing goose bumps to form on her everywhere. It wasn't long before her body began to react. His mouth moved lower to her chest, where he catered to every inch of exposed skin. Her stomach began to twist, only to flip-flop when he plucked gently at her nightgown and whispered, "Take this off?"

Lilly had never imagined he could have a voice like that, whispery, husky, and tentative, but she didn't need to respond to the query. He was already taking care of it for her. He lifted her enough off the bed so the shoulder straps could slide away. With gentle guidance he extricated her arms. Next, he slid the entire thing downward—down her ribs, her sides, her hips, exposing her inch by inch. He kept going, shimmying down the bed, all the way to her toes.

Where he tossed the discarded nightgown, Lilly didn't know and she didn't care. He was moving up the bed, swimming his hands along the insides of her legs, gently separating them a little more with each tender stroke, and his mouth followed his hands, kissing her ankles, her shins, the back of her knees, her inner thighs, higher, higher. Lilly tensed as the silky fabric of his mask brushed against her most sensitive place.

He made one of those sounds, deep in his throat, the same sound that had so intrigued her that night before. The tickle of fabric became a warm, hot pressure, and he gave her an ecstasy she never could have imagined on her own.

It was magic—his mouth, his tongue, catering to her every need. She began to quake and convulse in sheer rapture. There was no way she could prevent her mewling cries. He took a short break, just long enough to allow the coolness of the night to touch her, just long enough to let her taut limbs sag, and then he was there again, favoring her even more intensely.

Just when Lilly thought she could take no more, he moved up her body and held onto her the same way he had the night before. His entry was easy, so were his movements. He began to shudder, gasping. She felt every muscle in his body clenching. She heard his breathless cry.

Like he had before, within seconds he rolled away and tossed the blankets over his legs. Lilly swallowed in anticipation of a caustic dismissal. He didn't say anything until his panting slowed, and then he murmured, "Y…you are w…well?"

She wasn't quite sure what he meant. "Yes," she whispered.

"G…g…goodnight," he stammered.

It was strange. She couldn't remember ever hearing him stutter before. Lilly sat up and reached for her discarded robe. "Goodnight."

Twenty-Seven

The next night Lilly crept into his room just before eleven with a candle in hand. As she suspected, the fire was already out. All the lamps were doused. Even the curtains were closed. She set the candle on the night table, and standing there in its dim light, she slowly undid the tie of her robe. She had nothing on underneath. The night before she'd left without her nightgown, and although she had others, there didn't seem to be a point to putting one on, not if he was going to remove it. Closing her eyes, anticipating his touch, she slowly ran her fingers through her long, unbound hair. Her intent was to be ready for him in the bed with nothing on at all. She started to lower the silky robe off her shoulders.

"*Mmmm…*" It was a murmur from across the room.

Lilly spun. Veiled from head to toe in glossy black was a tall figure standing near the wing chair. The cane in his hand gave him away. Lilly knew he was Gabriel, and yet…

"Don't. Don't cover up," he murmured.

He was moving toward her, each step slow and deliberate. His dark apparition appeared more clearly as he drew near, closer and closer, until he was directly in front of her, bathed with her in candlelight. The robe he wore was as pitch black as hers was snow white. The sound of his cane dropping brought her gaze up to his eyes. She could see every line of the grey in his irises and they trapped her. He tucked one hand under her breast. His other arm, strong and warm, came around her waist and drew her close, and then his mouth covered hers.

The kiss was long, exploring, more demanding than the ones they'd shared in bed. When finally he pulled back, her knees felt so weak, she thought she just might collapse. His fingers trailed over her shoulder, taking her sleeve with them.

His paralyzing gaze and slowly trailing fingers had her shivering with anticipation, and yet there was this funny sense of power. It felt like she had cast a magic spell over him, like everything he did was happening because he was as entranced as she. His eyes traveled over her skin, following her robe as it shimmered down her legs and pooled at her feet.

"You are… *exquisite*," he whispered.

Unsure, Lilly reached up to his chest and splayed her palms gently against the soft silk. Beneath her hands, he loosened the lightly tied belt of his own robe and shrugged out of it, leaving himself clothed only in his shirt. As before, it was hanging open. Lilly looked at his chest, the thin swath of black hair that covered the center of it, his small round nipples, the lines shaping his pectoral muscles. He was thin, too thin, because she could see the outline of his ribs. Her eyes traveled to his concave stomach and the fine line of hair that began just beneath his belly button and then down from there. She had never seen this part of any man. The sheer size of him, made her breath catch.

Her wide eyes flew to his face. Tentatively, she reached up and laid her hand on the center of his chest again. His heartbeat hit her palm instantly. Looking into his eyes, she moved her hands over his chest, the same way he'd done to hers. She let one hand trail down the center of his body to his stomach, her fingertip following that thin arrow of hair. He began to breathe faster. His heartbeat became more pronounced.

He cupped her jaw and the back of her head, and he leaned close and kissed her again. Within moments he was laying her down on the bed. A quick flick of his hand doused the candle and he was on the bed too, shifting, crawling over her so he was laying on his right side. His caresses were slow. His mouth was playing with the edges of hers, then with her jaw, her ear and the sensitive line of her neck below it.

Lilly tried to reciprocate by touching him. She explored his chest, his ribs, and around to his side. In an instant he caught her wrist and brought her hand back to the center of his chest, "Not there. Just here," he whispered, and captured her mouth with his again.

Remaining in the center of him, Lilly moved lower, to his stomach and lower still until she heard his breath catch. "How do I...?" she wasn't even sure what she was trying to ask.

One of his breathy groans was her response. His hand over hers led her farther. "*Like this...*" he murmured and he groaned again as she copied, without his guidance, what he taught her.

He was kissing her, pulling her toward him so they were lying facing each other. His leg slid between hers and his thigh tickled the part of her that was dying to be touched. Under his caresses, all she could do was writhe, and deepen the urgency of their kiss. So close to that point of no return, she convulsed and fell to her back, at the same time drawing her legs up.

She didn't realize what she'd done until a sudden throaty gasp escaped him. It wasn't the same as the erotic sounds he made. His left leg, entwined with hers, had been forced upward by her movement. Rapidly he slithered away, rolling to his back.

"Did I hurt you?" Lilly murmured.

He breathed in and out, and whispered, "No."

Seconds ticked by. Seconds that felt like forever to Lilly's growing anxiety. "Is it... is it your leg?" Tentatively she touched his silk clad arm.

"Leave it to me to ruin a perfect moment." There was strain in his tone that hadn't been there before, but he moved onto his side, to face her again.

"It's not ruined." Gently she took his hand and drew it to her chest. "I think I am still putty."

The pad of his thumb toyed with her breast. "Putty?"

"Putty," she repeated. "Julie said I would become like putty in your hands."

"And have you," he asked hoarsely, "become like putty?"

Self-consciously she stammered, "I...I think this must be what she meant."

"You've never been putty before?" he asked.

Lilly shook her head, not remembering he couldn't see her. His fingers came up to caress her cheek. Tenderly he moved close and kissed her. "But you've done this before?"

Lilly shook her head again.

There was something different about him after that, something Lilly couldn't define. It was almost like he was giving up his role, like he wanted her to take control. He asked her what she wanted him to do. It was a question Lilly didn't know how to answer. "I want to be putty," was the only thing she could think of to say.

He brought her there, more than once, and when finally she lay beside him, expecting him to settle on top of her, he took her hand and coaxed her up. His guidance and his whispery, "*This way...*" led her to straddle him. As he reached between them to ensure their connection, he whispered again, "*This way...*" His hands moved to her hips. His strength brought her down slowly, deepening their joining bit by tantalizing bit. "*This way... I am putty... ooh... in your hands...*"

While she moved she became aware of him trembling, sweating, and of his vulnerability. He was entirely at her mercy. It was exhilarating and humbling all at the same time. Her movements grew bolder, circling, trying and testing, enjoying the different sensations she was causing within herself. All the while he made those noises—those breathy gasps and moans—that encouraged her and caused everything she felt to be so much more stirring. The pressure grew and she began a steady, sliding rhythm. She was in command of both their pleasure and still drowning in his scent and consumed by his presence.

His climax, when it came, was powerful, and as Lilly felt the severe shuddering of his body beneath her and heard his rippled cry, she felt like she had done something no one else had ever been able to do. She didn't move right away. She just lay still, relishing the warmth of him under her, telling herself her thoughts were ridiculous, and yet she couldn't contain the internal thrill. She was still smiling as she rolled off of him.

"Goodnight," she whispered, sliding out of the bed. Instinct told her he was watching her. She didn't try to hide herself by quickly grabbing for her robe. Instead she reached for the candle and lit it. Only then, in the dim light did she pick up the white silk covering. Taking her time, leaving her nakedness exposed to him, she slid one arm and then the other through the sleeves. "Goodnight," she whispered again.

"*Mmm… mmm…*" was his throaty reply.

Twenty-Eight

By Friday, Lilly was beginning to believe the man she gave herself to every night was not Gabriel Drayton. She was convinced he was an imposter. He was someone pretending to be Gabriel Drayton, because the Gabriel she knew could never be that tender, that gentle, and that capable of making her dissolve into such rapture. She'd thought the first three nights were good. They were nothing compared to the fourth night, and then there was last night…

Just thinking about it caused her eyes to close.

Every day Julie asked about her nights, and every day Lilly blushed like a schoolgirl, but she hadn't given away any of the sensational details. Julie's laughing, "I told you so's," didn't help with the turmoil going on inside. And it didn't help that Julie came by the mansion every day, not to see her, but to request an audience with Gabriel.

A couple of times Lilly overheard Withers putting Julie off by saying Mr. Drayton was not available, but Lilly was aware of at least two occasions Julie ended up with him in his study for more than an hour. Other than their midnight cloaked couplings, Lilly hadn't seen Gabriel at all. Julie's dreamy eyes and endless compliments made Lilly want to kick her—not that she would ever do such a thing!

It wasn't until the end of the week that she was able to put a name to her irritation. When she realized what it was, she instantly denied it. She could not be jealous, could she?

That evening Lilly and Charlotte descended the stairs for dinner to await the perpetually late Alex and Susan, and they ran into Rob. He was coming from the east hallway, where he'd evidently been meeting with Gabriel. While Rob and Charlotte role-played princess and knight, Gabriel appeared from around the back of the stairs.

Lilly glanced at him shyly, intending to return her attention to Rob and Charlotte, but something about him kept her rapt. She had to consciously keep her jaw from falling. She'd been with him every night, but the room had been too dark. Except for the mask, he looked different. His eyes weren't red-rimmed and encased in dark circles. His skin was still pale, and his cheekbones were still pronounced, but the area beneath them didn't look quite as hollow. Even his lips looked healthy, full and warm and pink and Lilly was overwhelmed with the urge to run to him and… and… *kiss*…

"I wish I could stay," Rob said to Charlotte. "I promise to come back and see you next week."

Rob then turned his attention to Lilly. She didn't really want to see him, especially not after the brief encounter they'd had at the beginning of the week. At first he'd been polite, making comments about how well the ceremony had gone, but then he said, "Would it be too impertinent of me to ask how things went for you… *er*… later?" Lilly had been infused with color. By the smirk that had tugged the corner of his mouth, she'd known he hadn't missed it either. Of all the obnoxiously rude things to ask! "It was fine," she'd managed to murmur. And then she'd run away.

Before she realized what he was about, Rob brought his hands to her shoulders, clasped them warmly, and kissed her, first on one cheek and then the other. "I'll see you again soon."

Lilly reeled from the contact, not in a good way. Rob looked up, behind her, to where Gabriel stood, and Lilly turned, too. Gabriel's skin may not have been as white as it used to be, but the malevolence in his eyes was like flying daggers, and they were aimed at Rob.

Rob didn't seem to notice. "Well, Lilly…" he winked, took her hand and kissed the back of it. "I guess this is goodnight. But not goodbye."

Rob was flirting with her? It made absolutely no sense! But Lilly didn't have time to think about it. His departure and Alex and Susan's arrival were simultaneous. By the banter that ensued, it became clear their relationships were well past that of acquaintances. Lilly knew she should have expected it, at least in light of the stories she'd heard, but for some reason their overt friendliness surprised her. Even Susan gushed, insisting several times, despite his protests, that Rob stay for dinner. The only person who didn't join in and appeared impatient with the whole business was Gabriel. He didn't move from where he stood at the base of the stairs. Because she felt awkward and an outsider, and also because she was quite famished, Lilly was glad when the seemingly endless well-wishes came to an end. And she was glad Rob didn't stay.

The moment the front door closed behind Rob, Gabriel started for the dining room. He wasn't moving fast, but faster than she'd seen him move before. His limp was much less pronounced, and his cane was straight and steady.

Moments later they were all seated, passing serving dishes. There was a tension in the air, but it was different. She noticed Susan gazing at Gabriel with a perplexed look on her face. Alex, too, was spending a lot of time glancing back and forth between Gabriel and Lilly. His odd stares were making her uncomfortable. But it wasn't until mid-meal that he blurted, "Knowing Gabriel, the news will never be volunteered, so I guess I'll just have to ask. Have you set a date for the wedding?"

Charlotte grinned proudly and announced, "It already happened. I was the flower girl!"

"When?" Susan looked shocked.

"Sunday!" Charlotte chirped. "We went to the church!"

Lilly thought Alex's head would fall off the way it swung back and forth between her and Gabriel. "Congratulations! Should we have a toast?"

"Yes, we should. I'll go first," Susan said. She raised her glass and waited for the rest of them to do the same. "To Gabriel, my old friend, and to Lilly, my new friend. I wish you both excellent health and much happiness."

"And," Alex added, chuckling, "may your lives be filled with love, passion, and a whole slew of baby Charlottes."

Charlotte's giggles permeated the room. Mark guffawed, too. When Lilly dared to look at him, Gabriel was staring at her. And he did something she'd never seen him do before. She hadn't realized he was capable of it. He smiled.

It wasn't a great smile, just a faint tilt of his lips, but it caused creases to form beside the corners of his eyes, which instead of glaring with hostility, looked warm. There was a twinkle in them that mesmerized. In that second the rest of the world disappeared. They were the only people in the room. All the laughter and the teasing going on between Charlotte, Mark, Alex and Susan became a distant, funny hum.

"We must have a party. A real party in the ballroom with a hundred guests!" Susan declared brightly. "It's the perfect opportunity, and it's been years since you've had a party here, Gabriel."

It felt like Gabriel's eyes were ripped away from her, like someone had reached up between them and tore their connection in half. His smiled disappeared. Tersely, he said, "No."

"But it's a shame that ballroom is never used. It's a magnificent room," Susan protested.

"You hate this house, remember?"

"That doesn't mean I can't appreciate the one decent room in it. Besides it's a good excuse for us to invite Beatrice. I shall write to her straight away."

"No, you will not!" Gabriel hissed.

Lilly startled from his harsh tone.

"Oh yes, I will!" Susan retorted. "Beatrice has a right to know about what you've done. She has a right to know you've married. And to whom!"

It looked like Gabriel was about to come out of his chair. "Be careful, Susan!"

"Don't threaten me," Susan spat back. "I don't know why you dislike her so much. She's always been good to you!"

"And I," Gabriel said roughly, "don't know why you like her so much. She's never done a damn thing for you."

Susan's eyes welled with tears. "You're hateful!" she wailed. "I will write to her and tell her what you've done against your father's wishes, and she will put an end to it! You'll never get away with this!"

Then she turned on Lilly. "He is using you just like he uses everybody. When he's done with you, after he's deceived you into believing he'll keep all the promises he's made to you, he'll chew you up and spit you out, just like the dog he is! I wish Charles were here. Charles would tell you what a worthless loser Gabriel is!"

Gabriel's fist slammed down on the table.

Susan was up and racing toward the door.

Alex rose, too. "Mark, get your coat and go with your mother." While Mark hopped down from his chair and ran after Susan, Alex's eyes remained firmly fixed on Gabriel. His anger was barely contained. The moment Mark was out of the room, he seethed, "If you ever make my wife cry again, I will kill you!"

Lilly wanted to reach across the table and cover Charlotte's ears. Her young eyes were wide as she stared after Alex's retreating form.

"Daddy," Charlotte said, "you made Uncle Alex really mad at you."

Twenty-Nine

Lilly wasn't sure what she should do. The dinner experience had her stomach churning in a wholly unpleasant manner. Gabriel's demeanor after his cousin left was distant, and he excused himself as soon as their meal was finished. At eleven o'clock, clad only in her robe, Lilly went to his room. Instead of getting into the bed, she sat in one of the chairs near the fireplace and shivered, although not from the cold. Susan had said Gabriel's father and Beatrice would be upset by Gabriel marrying her. And she'd said Beatrice could put a stop to everything. Lilly knew exactly what Susan meant. She was too low born, not of the right class to be a suitable wife for Gabriel.

Gabriel was late, which didn't help Lilly's ever-increasing apprehension. It wasn't until well after the eleventh hour that he slipped into the room.

"I'm sorry I'm late," he murmured closing the door behind him. He started toward the bed but stopped short and spun around.

"I'm over here," she said. It was a silly thing to say because he saw her before she said it.

"Why are you over there?"

"I am… I have… I think…" Regardless of how many times she'd rehearsed her questions, she still had no idea how to pose them. "Will there be a problem if Beatrice finds out about our marriage?"

"It's fine," he said vaguely.

Lilly clutched the arm of the chair. "Is it because I'm not… I'm not—"

"It has nothing to do with you."

"But Susan said—"

"Susan said a lot of things," he retorted sharply. "Don't worry about Susan."

"But, I think—"

With an impatient growl, he cut her off again. "Believe whatever you want to believe. I don't give a damn!"

"I thought we—"

"I am leaving tomorrow for New York," he interrupted. "There will be no seventh night. Shall we say there will be no sixth night either?"

Taken aback, and not understanding where his sudden anger was coming from, Lilly simply stared at him.

"You are free to go. I suggest you take advantage of the opportunity."

"But that's not what I—"

"Get out!" he snapped.

Lilly stood up and brushed past him. At the door she stopped and looked back. He was just standing there, staring at the fire. She could feel the fury radiating out of him. "I wasn't worried about what you think I'm worried about. I wanted to—" This time Lilly cut herself off. She couldn't believe she'd almost admitted how badly she wanted to be in his room with him, experiencing all of the amazing wonder…

Growling in a manner she'd learned from him, she slammed the door behind her.

Thirty

Susan Drayton breezed past Molly Finch, barely sparing her a glance, and shoved the door to Rob's office so hard it slammed against the wall behind it.

"Why didn't you tell me?" she demanded.

Rob looked up from the file splayed open on his desk. "Hello to you, too."

"It's not funny!"

The tears in her eyes had Rob out of his chair and out from around his desk. "Hey," he murmured, "it's not the end of the world." Catching Molly's eye, he walked over to the door and closed it to give them privacy.

"You should have told me." She sniffled. "I was so shocked, I didn't know what to say. I didn't know what to do. I made a complete fool of myself."

"I highly doubt that." Rob couldn't contain his derision. "I can't imagine you being anything but charm and grace where Gabriel is concerned."

"He goes out of his way to provoke me!"

Rob's eyebrows rose. "The same way you go out of yours to provoke him?"

"You're supposed to be comforting me, not upsetting me more."

Rob chuckled as he handed her the handkerchief from his pocket. "And you, my dear, are a truly gifted actress."

"My emotions are genuine!" Susan shot back.

"Ha! But alas, I know you too well. And so does Gabriel."

Susan dabbed her eyes and glared at him for a long, hard moment. "Is this the way you treat someone you say you love?"

"I do love you, Susan. I always have and I always will, but as we have discussed, I won't play this game anymore. You have a choice to make."

"Oh, stop it with the high and mighty standards!" she scoffed. "This change of heart doesn't become you, and now we both have to suffer for it. The truth is you don't want me as your wife any more than you want that lowlife housekeeper you screw, or that pathetic mouse of a tutor Alex hired."

They were standing close. Rob stared down into her eyes. Three months ago, after years of putting him off, Susan had suddenly changed her tune. Rob hadn't bought it. Susan never did anything without expecting something in return. He had yet to determine what she was really after. But, at least he hadn't given in to her. Instead, he'd given her an ultimatum. If she wanted him in her life, she had to divorce Alex and marry him. His reasoning had been that if she really wanted him, she would do it. But she wouldn't do it.

"You're wrong," he told her.

Susan rolled her eyes, and as she often did, changed the subject. "Why do you dress her up like that? She's a housekeeper, not a debutante. It's ridiculous."

"I don't control how Molly dresses. I think she looks nice."

"She makes you a laughingstock."

Rob chose to ignore her stabs at Molly. There was a part of him that wanted to wrap Susan in his arms and kiss her until she was breathless. It had been a long time since he'd kissed her. A very, very long time. There was another part of him that wanted to throw her down on the floor and forcibly subdue her, as if raping her would finally rid him of so many years of pent up emotion. Her lack of response—rejection once again—made the persistent ache inside of him, the one related to everything about her, grow so acute it became physical. He knew, however, that doing what he wanted wouldn't work. Not with Susan. So he approached from a different angle. "I suggest you be careful with your comments about other women, especially Charlotte's tutor. Remember who she is now… *Lady* Drayton."

"What a pathetic farce!" Susan harrumphed. "Did you tell Beatrice? She can put a stop to it."

"She won't," Rob said blandly. "Beatrice doesn't give a damn about the conditions in the trust agreement. She couldn't care less who Gabriel marries."

"I know! I know!" Susan flailed. "This is all Alex's fault! Where did he find that annoying, useless mouse anyway?"

Looking at Susan's distraught expression, Rob said, "I really am at a loss here, Susan. I don't understand why you're so upset. It leads me to believe perhaps you do still have feelings for Gabriel?"

"Never!" she hissed. "I can't stand him."

"Then why?"

Susan plopped down in the chair behind her. "Because now that he has a wife, there is no chance he'll ever give Charlotte to me."

Rob took the seat next to her. "Probably not."

"I could kick myself for saying all those nice things about Lilly Hawthorne right in front of him. It's so unfair," Susan said.

"Trust me, whatever you said has had no bearing on any decisions Gabriel's made regarding Charlotte," Rob drawled.

Susan's eyes narrowed. "He's already changed his will, hasn't he? He's already made that mouse her guardian?"

Rob sighed and nodded. The tears that welled in Susan's eyes were as genuine as tears from Susan could be. He knelt in front of her and reached for her hand. "Hey, hey, don't worry. Remember who I am."

Susan sniffled and used Rob's handkerchief. "Trustee."

He offered her a sly smile. "Exactly. What Gabriel doesn't know won't matter when he's gone."

"Gone? He's leaving? Where's he going?"

Rob made his voice completely bland. "No. Gone... as in dead."

Susan's eyes widened. "What do you mean, when he's dead?"

"You know how sick he's been. He's dying, Susan."

Susan's high-pitched laugh sounded more like a cackle. "Gabriel will never die. That's the most ridiculous thing I've ever heard. He gets too much pleasure out of pissing me off to die. Besides he's like a cat with nine lives..."

As she spoke, Rob's expression grew more serious, so serious that her humor faded away. "I talked to two of the doctors he went to see," he said.

Susan visibly paled. "What's wrong with him?"

Rob shook his head. "They don't know. They can do nothing for him. One of them told me he won't last through Christmas."

Susan rose instantly from her seat to pace the room. "My god! There has to be some mistake!"

"No mistake. I thought you'd be pleased," Rob said casually.

She turned on him and raged, "How can you say such a thing! I can be a selfish bitch sometimes, as you so readily like to remind me, but I would never wish that upon him. There was a time when he and I were good friends! There was a time when he and I… when I… Oooh! Maybe you're the one I should hate!"

"And then you'd be taking the chance of losing Charlotte altogether. I think not, my love. I think you'll continue to string me along for as long as it suits you." He tried to cover his bitterness behind a sarcastic drawl, but for once, he wasn't entirely successful.

Susan stared at him for a long, tense moment, and she said very calmly, "I will eventually forgive you for saying such nasty things to me because I love you. Right now, however, I am too angry to look at you, so I am going to leave." In a very elaborate display of swishing skirts, she flounced toward the door.

"Susan," he called after her, hating the way his voice caught over her name. "I'm sorry." It came out as a desperate plea. It was all he had left to give.

"I know," she replied quietly. "I know it's your frustration talking, not you. And I know it's my fault because I'm not strong enough to deal with the scandal of leaving Alex. For that, I am sorry. I love you, Rob. I always will."

He watched her close the door, then he rounded his desk, sat down and dropped his head into his hands. *Scandal?* It was just an excuse. The truth was, according to what she knew of him, he didn't have superior blood running through his veins. He didn't have money seeping from every pore. He didn't have a legacy and an inheritance to pass on to whatever heirs he might someday sire, because he wasn't a Drayton. For Susan that condition was the only one that mattered.

Thirty-One

It was Beatrice's letter that prompted Gabriel's trip. He was not going to circumvent any damage Susan could cause by getting to Beatrice first, or even to prevent Beatrice from protesting his marriage. She could if she wanted to. According to the trust agreement, Beatrice had final say on the suitability of any spouse he chose. Rob had written to inform her of Gabriel's impending nuptials. As far as he knew, Beatrice hadn't replied to Rob. But she had sent Gabriel a letter asking him to visit. In it she'd written she had something important to discuss with him about his cousin. About Alex.

Through the window of the coach he watched the bustling traffic. To get through it, his driver had to stop and start repeatedly. Gabriel didn't like cities, but this one—where the Statue of Liberty greeted people—he didn't mind. He didn't mind because when he stepped out of the coach, no one would pay attention to him. Even if someone did, they would shrug off the shock, and go on their merry way. People here were so used to seeing things that the rest of the world would consider a freak show, his appearance wouldn't faze them. Ahead of him Beatrice's Manhattan townhouse came into view.

Gabriel had sent her a telegram earlier telling her when to expect him. Her butler didn't answer his knock. She opened the door for him herself, which meant she'd been waiting for him. She looked the same as she had the last time he'd seen her. The only way he could describe her was flawless. She was fifty-three years old, but she had an ethereal appearance that made it impossible to tell. Her Italian-cut, hunter green gown was the latest fashion and accompanied by costly and elegant gems. He didn't recognize the dress, but the jewelry he knew. They were all pieces given to her by his father.

Gabriel had known Beatrice his entire life, but memories of her always brought to mind a single one-on-one conversation. It was the day of his mother's funeral. He was sitting on a stone bench in the garden, alone, because he didn't know where else to go or what to do. There were adults everywhere, a good distance away, walking around, talking, eating, drinking. No one was paying attention to him. Beatrice came and asked if she could sit with him. He didn't want her to, but he nodded because he knew saying no would get him in trouble.

Speaking softly, she'd told him his mother had loved him very much. She said the angels that floated around on the clouds watched over the people on earth that they loved. All he had to do was look up at the clouds to know his mother was up there smiling down at him. She put her arm around his shoulders and drew his head to her breast. She stroked his hair and dampened the tips of her soft white gloves on his cheeks. She told him it was okay for him to be sad.

His father had interrupted them. That part of the memory, like so many others, he chose not to think about.

"Please come in out of the cold," Beatrice said. She smiled, but it didn't look true. Her smiles never did.

She walked ahead of him to her parlor and told him to make himself comfortable. Her butler appeared with tea.

"You don't like tea, do you? Coffee, black, if I remember correctly?" At his brief nod, she gave instructions to her butler. She was so polite, it was sickening. Once the butler departed, she set her tea aside and said, "How have you been?"

"Fine. And you?"

"Well enough, thank you. And Charlotte? How is she?"

"She is well."

They would go through the whole family list. It was the same dialogue they had every time he saw her. Had it been a year? At least that. She asked about Alex, Susan and Mark and he answered the same way for them all. He would have much preferred to skip the pleasantries.

"And Rob? How is Rob?" she asked finally.

She always asked about Rob last. She knew him, of course. Rob had been to Drayton Hall often during their school years, and after them as well. She knew Rob was his friend and his attorney, and Charles had been very supportive of Rob when he'd started his law practice. After he'd had his obnoxiously controlling trust agreement drawn, Charles had appointed Rob to be the trustee of it. Gabriel assumed naturally that Beatrice asked about Rob because Rob was responsible for ensuring she received her monthly stipend. "The same," he replied.

"He wrote me of your marriage. I'm happy for you, Gabriel."

Gabriel eyed her warily. Her sentiment seemed genuine enough, but with Beatrice it wasn't easy to tell.

"Susan wrote to me, too," she said.

That was no surprise, but before he could spout out a defensive retort she said, "Regardless of the powers given to me by the trust agreement, I want you to know I have no intention of interfering in your life—"

The butler appeared with the coffee. After he left, the room grew uncomfortably silent. Beatrice didn't extrapolate further. He'd known she wouldn't enforce her powers. For her to do so would have been so out of character it wouldn't have made sense, and Beatrice was too strong-minded to do anything based solely on what Susan might say. Even so, relief poured through him. He took a sip of the steaming coffee. It was good, but not as good as Molly Finch's. "Your letter said you have something to discuss with me."

"Yes," she said softly. "No doubt you're wondering what is so important you needed to come all this way. I wanted you to come because I am worried about you."

Gabriel didn't hide his surprise. "About me?"

"I believe someone may be trying to harm you again," she said.

Gabriel smirked and shook his head. "I don't think so." She was looking at him with an odd expression on her face. Gabriel didn't know what to make of it.

"I am not quite sure how to begin," she said. "I've made a lot of mistakes in my life. Too many mistakes, some of which I am ashamed to admit. Every day I regret things. Things I can never undo. I realize now withholding this from you has caused, and still has the potential to cause, too much damage. I am getting older and I can't afford to have any more regrets."

Gabriel waited patiently while she took a sip of her tea.

"I wasn't a very good mother," she went on. "I have a son I am not proud of. But the fault is not his. It is mine. I have recently learned some things that lead me to believe he intends to hurt you."

This wasn't news. "I already know, and I can set your mind at ease. Alex had nothing to do with the threats or the fire in Philadelphia."

Her hands trembled as she set her tea cup back in the saucer. "I'm not talking about Alex," she said quietly.

"I've received no threats," Gabriel was wholly confused. As far as he knew, Alex was Beatrice's only child.

"No, but I have," she said. "Please let me explain. Years ago, before you were born, I loved your father. He wanted to marry me, but I was afraid, so I ran away to my uncle's home here in New York. While I was gone Charles married your mother. I didn't know, when I left, that I was going to have a child.

"The birth was difficult and I don't remember much of it. The infant was taken from me, and later I was told he died. But it was a lie. He is alive and well. He is your father's son."

Gabriel couldn't have been more stunned. "Go on," he murmured.

"I didn't know about his existence until he was thirteen years old. He was living in a home for orphaned boys. It was me who convinced your father to provide funds to give him a proper education. I told your father he was the son of my cousin. Your father paid for everything I asked for without question. He never knew the truth."

"I believe my son—your brother—is the one responsible for the fire in your home in Philadelphia. When you survived and no further threats were made against your life, I told myself it couldn't have been him. I didn't want to believe it was him. As your father's first born, he feels he is entitled to the estate."

Beatrice reached over to a small decorative box on the end table, opened it and withdrew a folded piece of cream-colored parchment. Gabriel took the opportunity to say, "The trust agreement excludes illegitimate children. It wouldn't matter anyway. Alex is specifically named."

"Yes," Beatrice agreed, "but there are ways around the conditions in the agreement. The only caveat is you have to be dead. Please take a look at this."

Gabriel took the paper. He wasn't quite sure what to say. "Is he… your son… is he here in New York with you?"

"No," she replied. "He doesn't live here, but he has a business here—a business he's been running under a name that's not his own. Here in New York he's developed a whole new identity for himself. He calls himself Charles Drayton, II."

Gabriel unfolded the parchment. "What's his real name? Where does he live?"

"He lives in the same town you do and you know him well," Beatrice said. "His name is Robert August."

Thirty-Two

For Lilly the weeks Gabriel was gone were both relieving and upsetting. They were relieving because of the horrible, heated exchange they'd had before she'd fled his room. They were upsetting because of Charlotte, whose increasing despondency made it clear she was missing her father dreadfully. As the days passed with not one word to let them know when he would return, he became the primary topic of Charlotte's chatter. One day, as pity for the child welled, Lilly apologized for Gabriel's failure to say goodbye. He certainly hadn't said goodbye to her, and naturally she assumed he'd shown the same lack of courtesy to his daughter.

Charlotte regarded her as if Lilly had lost her mind, and then she said crisply, "He did say goodbye to me. He always says goodbye."

During those long weeks, Rob August came by several times. On his first few visits, Lilly remained aloof, but slowly she began to warm to him. Not because he was attentive toward her—he wasn't, really—but because of the way he teased and played with Charlotte. Charlotte basked in his attention. Clearly she adored him.

Often Rob joined them for dinner, and so did Molly Finch. The more time Lilly spent with Molly, the more she liked her. It was nice having another woman to converse with, and Molly was so kind and gentle with Charlotte. A suggestion was made—Lilly couldn't remember who made it—that Molly accompany her and Charlotte on a shopping expedition. Molly seemed as eager as Charlotte. The following weekend, Withers drove the carriage to Rob's townhouse, where Lilly and Charlotte joined Molly. From there, the three of them spent the day meandering along Market Street, going from shop to shop. They didn't buy much, just a trinket or two for Charlotte, but

Lilly learned a lot about current fashions. The outing was so enjoyable, the three of them collectively agreed they needed to do it again.

As was the custom, Alex, Susan and Mark came every Friday. The first Friday after Gabriel left, Susan pulled Lilly aside and apologized for her outburst the week before. She didn't offer any explanation, but she did say she was sorry for offending Lilly. She hadn't meant to. With that tension resolved, evenings with Alex, Susan and Mark became especially pleasant. Charlotte certainly relished them.

Three weeks to the day of Gabriel's departure, on Saturday morning not long after breakfast, Withers came to let them know he'd received a telegram from Gabriel. He would be going to pick him up from the train station in Philadelphia that very day. Charlotte begged to go along, and neither Lilly nor Withers could come up with a good reason to refuse her.

Left alone, Lilly had nothing better to do than roam the huge mansion. Clad in one of her new dresses, a flowing, lavender thing with lace sewn over the bodice, Lilly felt a little like Cinderella. The final delivery of her new clothes and shoes and undergarments and everything else she could ever possibly need had been made a few days before. Having such an elaborate and beautiful wardrobe was dizzying. As she made her way through the hall, she thought of the two rooms in the mansion she was the most curious about—Gabriel's west wing office and the ballroom. Pretending to dance, she swung to and fro, causing her skirts to swivel about her legs. Laughing, she decided to go to Gabriel's office first.

She didn't expect the west wing to be locked. Frustrated, she yanked on the knobs, jiggling both doors. Disappointment rolled through her. But then, just as she gave one last good yank, to her surprise a key fell from the doorframe ledge above.

Moments later, peering inside, she saw that the hallway was similar in length and décor to the east wing, except it wasn't clean. There was a trail in the dust on the carpet thick enough to reveal footprints. The footprints led to the first door on the left—a door that had been left ajar.

The first thing in the room to draw Lilly's focus was the portrait perched on the mantel. The frame had been burned. The woman illustrated was beautiful and, Lilly guessed, probably in her twenties when the portrait had been made. There was something in her eyes, something that held Lilly's attention. She couldn't really define what it was, except perhaps sadness—deep, overwhelming sadness.

The next thing to draw her was the drafting table and the drawing laid open on it. She had no real experience with architectural work other than the few prints she'd seen at the teachers' college, but she had always thought it a fascinating art. Beside the lines depicting the building were a number of figures and equations. The building was to have twelve floors. She was highly impressed. Wanting to see more, she pulled out one of the rolled papers from the circular tub. It had several layers to it including a finalized drawing of the building as it would appear when complete. The drawing was so well done she thought bemusedly that she could walk right into the picture itself. She rolled it back up and put it away. Then she withdrew another.

Lilly took her time perusing several of the plans, most of which were office buildings. But there were houses, too—grand homes intended for the wealthy. There was one in particular she was extremely taken with, and she spent time imagining what each room inside might look like fully furnished and decorated.

After returning the intriguing house to the tub, she picked up the drafting tools one by one. It was easy to imagine Gabriel sitting on the stool, leaning over the table, working with them. In her daydream she was coming into the room, to bring him coffee, perhaps? His back was to her, and she saw his long, flowing hair, not constricted by the kerchief of his mask. He had such soft, beautiful hair. Memories of the way she'd run her hands through it hit her hard. She could still feel the softness threading her fingers, feel the way it brushed across her skin… *oh dear!*

Closing her eyes, Lilly concentrated on her daydream—*not the memory!* In the daydream, Gabriel would swivel slowly on the stool. First his right profile would come to her, the line of his jaw, the curve of his cheek. The corner of his mouth would be turned up in a smile, and then he would keep turning…

To distract herself, she went to the desk and plopped down in the big chair behind it. She tried to open the top drawer and found it locked. That wasn't a surprise. The next thing to do was hunt for a key. She found it more easily than expected. It was under a thick rock paperweight on the desk. Pleased with herself, she opened the top drawer. Neat writing tools and stationery were ready to be used. The next drawer revealed nothing interesting. There were a number of inkwells. The third drawer had a stack of letters in it. They were opened, but still stored in their envelopes. The one on top was addressed to a building in downtown Havertown. The addressee was a man named Andrew Wentworth.

Curiously she slid the correspondence out. It was a letter from a law firm in Philadelphia. It said the client, who was unnamed, was pleased overall with the prints. There were only a few changes being requested. It went on to list what those were. Then it said that despite Mr. Wentworth's refusal to meet with him, which he wasn't pleased about, and the delays Mr. Wentworth had caused by returning the prints late, which he was also not pleased about, the client had another project he wanted to hire Mr. Wentworth for, because his work was superior. A proposal would follow. The letter warned if Mr. Wentworth continued to refuse to meet with the client in person, and if the next project had any delays, it was doubtful the client would hire Mr. Wentworth for another. The last paragraph of the letter said the payment for his most recent design had been deposited into Mr. Wentworth's account in Philadelphia. The amount caused Lilly's jaw to drop. The letter was two months old.

An hour later, Lilly found herself still reading letters. Andrew Wentworth, it seemed, had been selling his work through the Philadelphia law firm for at least the last three years. He'd sold more than twenty-five drawings, most of which were office projects. There were two cited as personal residences. The amounts paid for the prints were more than Lilly imagined an entire house would cost.

From reading the letters she also discovered the law firm managed Andrew Wentworth's bank accounts and other personal documents, but they had never met him. The earlier letters contained offers to send a coach for him. Apparently those offers had been refused. In subsequent correspondence they offered to come to him. The letters thereafter didn't mention meeting him again, as if his attorneys had given up trying.

Troubled, but not quite sure why, Lilly went back to the drafting table. The half-completed design lying open had no name shown. But the completed drawings from the tub did. She pulled out several wondering how she could have missed the signature and seal in the bottom right corner of each page. All of the drawings had been done by Andrew Wentworth.

No, they weren't! Lilly opened another one—an identical one to one signed by Andrew Wentworth. The signature on this one was Gabriel A. Drayton. But she didn't have time to contemplate any of this further. Through the window she caught a glimpse of the carriage pulling up the lane. Withers was back!

Frantically she worked at cleaning up the mess she'd made. The last three letters were still open on the desk. They needed to be refolded and inserted into their envelopes. The drawing she'd just opened needed to be re-rolled. She didn't start consciously breathing again until everything was in order and she was standing at the west wing entrance with her hand on the knob, hoping against hope no one would see her come through it. She waited, listening intently. Hearing nothing, she opened the door and slipped through.

All she had to do was lock it, which she did quickly, and then somehow put the key back, all the way up...

"Hello, Lilly."

Lilly spun. Gabriel's tall dark figure was not more than ten feet away in the shadows under the recesses of the stairs. It was difficult to see him clearly, but there was no mistaking his deep gravelly voice.

He moved forward. One step, another, coming closer and closer to her. She was caught. And he looked furious and... *oh my!*

She was suddenly and intensely dumbstruck. She'd thought the last time she'd seen him in the light of day he'd looked better. Now, three weeks later, he looked like a different person entirely. There was a darker tinge to his skin, as if he'd spent considerable time in the sun. His formerly gaunt features had filled in. And his limp… he was using his cane, but his left leg wasn't dragging. It was gliding across the floor to catch up to the other one. His shoulders were square and straight. Even with the mask, he looked tall and strong, and so… *beautiful!*

And so enraged!

"Did you find whatever it was you were looking for?" he asked icily.

His awful, evil voice hadn't changed! Why, after all this time, after what they'd done so intimately together, was she suddenly as timid and afraid as she'd been the first time she met him? "I was… I am… I…"

"Don't bother to apologize. I can't fire you now. Although I would prefer you didn't, I can't keep you from snooping. But I will take that key."

She took a step toward him and dropped it into his outstretched palm. "How was your trip?"

"Fine," he said curtly.

"It's good to have you home. We've missed you."

"Have you?"

The derisive scowl that accompanied the question made it clear he didn't believe her. She raised her chin and forced herself to keep eye contact. "Where is Charlotte?"

"Getting ready for her bath."

Lilly found herself caught in the glittering silver of his eyes. She tried desperately to make herself stop trembling, but worse to keep from reaching out and touching him. Gruff tone aside, she wanted him to greet her like he would if he really cared for her, to smile at her, to take her in his arms and kiss her hello. "I'm late," she whispered.

"For what?" he snapped.

Lilly didn't have a chance to clarify her comment. A ball of pink came rolling around the corner from the east hallway.

"Gabriel! You're home!" Julie bellowed. And then she launched herself into his arms, her hard round stomach jamming into him so fast and unexpectedly, he had to sidestep to regain his balance. "I'm so glad to see you! Golly, how we've missed you!" She let go of him, only to raise up onto her tiptoes and give him a kiss on his exposed cheek. Clasping his hand, she said, "You look so much better. I'm so glad to see it!"

Gabriel didn't say anything. Not that he could get a word in if he wanted to. Julie was rambling about her cottage, asking Gabriel to come see what she'd done to it. She talked about the forthcoming holidays and how her baby would be born about that time. Then she started giving him a day by day account of everything that had happened while he was away. As if he would be the slightest bit interested in their mundane routine!

Lilly had to walk away. She couldn't listen any longer.

She huffed her way up the stairs, straight to Charlotte's room, and there, she knelt beside the tub and helped Charlotte wash her long hair—hair that was almost as soft and silky, and long, as her father's.

"Daddy brought me lots and lots of books to read! See over there!" Charlotte's hand popped out of the tub, her little finger pointing, causing a spurt of water and bubbles to fly out and splatter on the carpet.

There were, indeed, two enormous stacks of books on Charlotte's desk.

While Charlotte played in the tub, babbling happily about all the rest of the things her father had brought her—chocolates, a new doll, building blocks to make castles with, a new pair of riding gloves, a chalkboard—Lilly took the time to look more closely at the books. There were plenty of children's stories, but most of them were textbooks on phonics, grammar and arithmetic. A couple of them covered basic science and history. There were even a few selections to help with early Latin and French. The entire ensemble was extraordinary, and more than Lilly had hoped to have to help with Charlotte's studies. Fleetingly she wondered if Gabriel had picked them himself. There was no question a great deal of thought had gone into the purchases.

Something moved, a shadow creating a sound so miniscule it was almost impossible to hear. Lilly turned toward the door for a better look, but there was no one in the doorway, and the little bit of the corridor she could see appeared empty. Shrugging, she went back to helping Charlotte.

Charlotte was still happily chattering while Lilly toweled her hair dry. "Daddy got you a present, too," she said, "Because he forgot to get you one at the wedding. I'm not allowed to tell you what it is."

"Excuse me, Miss Charlotte, Missus Drayton." It was Mr. Finch, peering in. "I hope I'm not disturbing, but I want ta hang this here chalkboard. Mr. Drayton said there's a wall in the playroom where I should put it."

"Yes, of course. Come in," Lilly stammered.

Wrapped in towels, Charlotte ran over to show Mr. Finch where to put the chalkboard. It was good Charlotte took charge. Lilly's head was still swimming over Mr. Finch's use of her new name.

Mrs. Drayton. Not until this moment had she thought of her new name. She had noticed, albeit belatedly, that Mr. Finch and Withers had been addressing her as *ma'am*, rather than *miss*. Mrs. Finch hadn't addressed her at all, which wasn't unusual. But no one, until now, had called her *Mrs.* Drayton. Even Julie, who never missed an opportunity to tease, hadn't said anything!

The chalkboard was quite a big thing, at least six feet in length and four feet from top to bottom. Mr. Finch hung it where Charlotte told him to. Then he produced a small bucket containing chalk and two hand erasers. The chalkboard was a fabulous idea and would be extremely useful for teaching Charlotte.

Lilly Drayton. My name is now Lilly Drayton.

Lilly didn't feel different. She didn't even feel married, really. And yet, now that the name was out there, she couldn't stop saying it over and over. When she headed to her room to dress for dinner, she was still saying it. *Mrs. Lilly Drayton. Mrs. Gabriel Drayton.* If he was a duke, then that would make her a duchess, wouldn't it? *The Lady Lilly Drayton.* Of course she would never use such a title, but it was fun to pretend!

Preoccupied with similar silly thoughts, she swept into her room. And froze.

An enormous vase of red roses was set on the table in her sitting room. Easily, there were three dozen of them. At this time of year, flowers like these were difficult to find, unless one paid an exorbitant amount of money for them.

No one had ever given her flowers before. Awestruck, she leaned in and breathed deeply. The fragrance was wonderful and strong enough to envelop the entire chamber. When she stepped back to admire them better, she saw that below the canopy of flowers was a red box, the same size and shape as the box of chocolates Gabriel had given to Charlotte. On top of it was another box. This one was long and slender and covered in black velvet. On top of it was a small white calling card.

In Gabriel's bold scrawl, it said, 'For my wife.' It was signed simply, 'Drayton.'

Lilly took a moment, quickly setting aside the black box for the red. The first piece of chocolate was so good she had to have a second one, and a third. And she wondered at herself, and the odd apprehension churning her stomach, caused by that small, ominous, black velvet box. She was afraid to touch it.

After her fifth piece of chocolate, she forced herself to set the red box down and pick up the black one. The moment she lifted the lid, her jaw fell. Her fingers went so numb she almost dropped it. Staggering backwards, she fell into the closest chair.

Sparkling jewelry, the likes of which she'd never seen in her life, was nestled in the soft, white interior. There was a necklace of amethysts and diamonds, woven together like purple flowers with crystal leaves. Matching earrings, the kind that would dangle beautifully, were lying in the middle of it.

Lilly could barely breathe. Eventually, she touched it, carefully tracing the gemstones with a fingertip. Amethysts were her birthstone, and she wondered how he would have known. She'd never told anyone at Drayton Hall her birth date, not even Charlotte. Either Julie had said something to him, or it was pure coincidence.

It took her a while to find the nerve to take the velvet box to her vanity. There, as if it was a delicacy that could break with the slightest jarring, she lifted the necklace. Her hands were trembling so badly, she bumbled the tiny clasp several times before she was able to close it. And then she looked at herself in the mirror. It was extraordinary, the most *exquisite…*

Exquisite… why, of all words, did that one come to mind? Gabriel had used it to compliment her in his bedroom, more than once. Briefly Lilly closed her eyes, remembering. Again. She would never forget… his tender touch, the taste of his kiss, the warmth of his breath on her skin…

What followed in her mind wasn't a memory at all. She saw herself, in candlelight, standing beside Gabriel's bed, wearing nothing, except the necklace. Gabriel was holding her hand, his fingers tender as they drew hers to his mouth. The kiss that grazed her knuckles was soft, lilting. But his eyes, those tantalizing grey depths, were gazing into hers. The fingertips of his other hand inched along the side of her face, along her jaw, the touch so light it almost tickled, down her neck, trailing across her skin, following the inner line of the jewels. "*…exquisite…*" he whispered in that husky, deep voice, while he bent his head, closer, closer, until his mouth was on her skin, in the hollow just above the *vee* created by the necklace.

Lilly had to shake her head and fidget to return to the present.

Somehow she managed to put the earrings on as well. And then she stood there, staring at herself in the glass for a long time. The ensemble changed her. It turned her into something more than a country bumpkin. She wondered if others would think the same, or if they would see her as a fraud, dressing up in something that was entirely too good for her. Even so, thinking of the new dresses in her wardrobe, she knew exactly which one would go perfectly with the jewelry, and how nice it would be, come Friday, to have dinner with Alex and Susan and for once not feel so unsuitably attired.

Now all she had to do was figure out a way to thank… *her husband.*

Thirty-Three

Molly was in the small yard behind Rob's townhouse, taking the sheets she'd laundered down from the clothesline. She was blissfully humming, thinking of Rob, but that was nothing new. She thought of him all the time.

He seemed happier again. Much of the despondency that had festered the last several weeks was gone. Just a few days before, he'd received good news—a sudden turn of luck for his paper business in New York. He'd told Molly, more than once lately, he was afraid the paper mill was doomed. There weren't enough customers. But, not any longer. The minute he'd received the telegram from his business partner, he'd come running to find her.

"Molly! Molly! You'll never believe this!" He'd taken her in his arms and kissed her breathless. His ardor hadn't ended there. Molly grinned remembering how they'd ended up on the kitchen floor.

Molly knew Rob was still terribly upset and worried about Gabriel, but the sudden windfall from New York had lifted his spirits tremendously. In the last few days, even when he talked about Gabriel—which he did constantly—he'd sounded less dour.

He'd left not long ago, to go to the post, to send the response to his partner, Stebbens. The evening before, with her in his office, he'd deliberated over it for hours. He'd asked her to sit and then he asked for her opinion. She'd been thrilled beyond belief. Rob shared his law cases with her all the time and he spoke often of his paper mill, but never before had he asked for her advice! Not like this!

Lost in her heady musings, Molly didn't hear the presence come up behind her until she heard the low, rumbling voice, "Miss Finch."

Startled, Molly spun, clutching a sheet to her chest. Even though she'd only ever seen the man in the darkened recesses of the bar, she knew who he was right away—Greasy John. "Wh…what are you doing here?" she stammered.

"You didn't show for our last meeting," he said. His eyes were squinted, either in deference to the sunlight, or he was angry.

"Something came up. I couldn't get away." That was true enough. Rob had decided not to go to his Bar Association meeting. He'd wanted to go to Drayton Hall again and she had accompanied him.

"My brother is not happy. You've not been living up to your end of our bargain," Greasy John said.

"Mr. Drayton is away. He's been gone for several weeks. How can I do what I'm supposed to do if he's not here?" Molly defended.

"My brother wants to see you tonight."

"I can't. I have obligations. But I don't need to come. I have plenty with what you gave me already. Please go. You can't be here. Rob, I mean, Mr. August, will be home any minute."

"Let this be a warning, Miss Finch. You need to do what you're being paid handsomely to do. If you don't, my brother will come after you, and you don't want that to happen."

"I will do it. I will," she said. "As soon as Mr. Drayton is back in town. I promise. I will."

"Don't let us down, Miss Finch. You will be sorry if you do." With that, he turned and walked away.

With her basket full of sheets, Molly ran back inside and locked the kitchen door. Then she ran through the house to make sure the front was locked, too. It was.

Leaning against the door, she closed her eyes. She couldn't believe Greasy John had come here! And if Rob were ever to find out what she'd done… *oh god…* she couldn't even bear to think of the possibility.

To calm her frazzled state, she went back to the kitchen and began methodically folding sheets. But her mind was plagued, as it had been from the beginning. She should never have agreed to this. It was the most foolish and reprehensible thing she'd ever done. No amount of money was worth a life, even if it was the life of a wicked criminal, and someone she despised. It didn't matter what kind of man he was. If

Gabriel Drayton died, she would be a criminal, too. She would be a murderer!

She'd done it for Rob, because she'd thought he hated Gabriel, and she'd believed the John Smiths when they told her Gabriel was trying to ruin Rob. A month ago, she'd held Rob in her arms, listening to him sob in anguish. His pain had been more heartbreaking than anything she'd experienced in her life.

After that, there was no way she could go through with the poisoning. Not because she cared about Gabriel, or even because of the guilt, but because she could never, ever allow Rob to suffer. Hearing that Gabriel was his brother, that they were both sired by the same man, had been shocking enough. Realizing how deeply Rob cared for Gabriel had brought her to her knees.

But Molly was no fool. She knew if she failed to show at their Monday meetings the John Smiths would find someone to replace her. The only way to protect Rob was to keep Gabriel out of danger. To do that she had to keep attending those meetings, collecting the nasty powder and pretending to use it. What no one could ever know was that every last ounce of poison she'd been supplied with in the last month, she'd safely disposed of.

The danger now, which she didn't yet know how to handle, was that eventually the John Smiths and the Benefactor—whoever he was—would realize Gabriel Drayton was no longer going to die.

Thirty-Four

Eggs.

Cringing from an involuntary shiver, Gabriel cracked the eggs he'd retrieved from the pantry on the edge of the counter and dumped them, one by one, into the sizzling pan on the stove. Charlotte would be strolling in any minute. Lilly would be behind her, if not with her. He supposed Julie would appear as well. It was probable she would be going to church with Lilly and Charlotte, and Withers, who had apparently been attending services with them lately.

Did Lilly like eggs, he wondered? Had she liked them when she was a little girl?

"Sunny side up, just like you," Cook used to say to him. She'd made them for him sunny side up whenever his father wasn't present, because it was the only way Gabriel could eat them without gagging. If his father was home she scrambled them, but always undercooked, runny and bland, and he would have to choke his way through until his plate was empty. His father had a big, black mongrel of a dog named Joffy back then. Gabriel had become fairly adept at sneaking bites to Joffy for the few seconds, here and there, when his father's eye wasn't on him. Cook, he was certain, purposely didn't notice. She'd seen him, too many times, sitting there, struggling to swallow each horrid bite. She'd felt sorry for him, but like the rest of the world she couldn't oppose his father's demands.

The whole sordid thing had begun as soon as his father caught wind that he didn't like eggs. Up until then, his mother had kept his secret. Not that it needed to be a secret. While his mother was still alive, his father was rarely home, and even when he was, he never joined them for breakfast. Why his father suddenly decided to show up for morning meals, Gabriel never understood. But he remembered.

It was the day after his mother's funeral. He was ten years old. He and Alex were in the dining room when his father sauntered in. Cook had fried two eggs for Alex because Alex liked eggs. Gabriel's normal breakfast fare consisted of buttered toast and four strips of bacon. The austere, terrifying man—Charles Drayton—smiled at Alex and said good morning to him. But then his attention turned to Gabriel's plate. "What's this?" he bellowed at Cook. "This is what you feed him? He needs eggs!"

"He doesn't care for eggs," Cook said.

His father glared at the robust woman Gabriel had always thought smelled like sweet corn. "You go make this boy a plate of scrambled eggs. Use three eggs, do not beat them before you cook them and do not overcook them. No salt or pepper."

Gabriel could still distinctly recall Alex's wide, fearful stare.

Cook returned moments later with a plate heaped with yellow and white, watery foulness. To Gabriel it looked like vomit. He took one small bite and gagged so badly the clump of it came back up onto his plate.

His father laughed, and Gabriel pushed his plate away, thinking he would be spared after all. Then his father said, "Oh no, you don't!" And he shoved the plate right back under Gabriel's nose. "You eat those eggs, boy! You eat until that plate is clean." He grabbed Gabriel's fork and filled it with the smelly mess Gabriel had just spit up. "Eat!" he shouted, shoving the fork into his hand and forcing his fingers to curl around it. "You will eat three eggs every morning. If you don't, Cook will serve you eggs for every meal. I don't care how many it takes. I don't care if you have to eat so many eggs you begin to stink of them, but you will eat them!"

For years, Alex had sat across from him eating whatever he wanted, while Gabriel ate disgusting, putrid eggs. On his twelfth birthday, his father said three was no longer enough. He was to eat four from then on. Gabriel forced down each awful bite, every single day, until his father sent him to boarding school. After that he only had to eat eggs when he came home for holidays. Thankfully that wasn't very often.

What prompted him to make eggs now, Gabriel didn't really know. That wasn't true. He did know—Lilly. He doused them with salt and pepper, and doused them a second time, and then a third for good measure, and he fried them until the yokes were hard and the edges black and crispy.

"Happy good morning, Daddy!" Charlotte came skipping into the kitchen. She came right up to him and stood on her tiptoes to peer into the pan. Her nose wrinkled. "You made eggs?"

"They're good for you," he mumbled.

"I don't like eggs," Charlotte said.

"You only say that because I don't like eggs." Charlotte was glaring at him, and rightly so. But he scraped one small, very well done egg out of the pan and set it on a plate, added a piece of toast and a couple strips of the bacon he'd fried earlier and handed it to her. "Eat."

"You don't mind if I join you?" Julie Gibson was just as chipper as Charlotte, except Julie's opinion of his breakfast fare was quite different. "Oh, lovely! Eggs! Just what I was craving! And made exactly the way I like them!"

Gabriel shivered. It had nothing to do with the cold.

"I don't like eggs," Charlotte whined from where she sat on the bench. She was holding her fork backwards in her hand and poking the white part of her egg with it.

"But they're good for you." Lilly smiled as she came quietly into the room.

Gabriel liked that about her. She was quiet, not at all like her zealous, overly loud sister. They didn't even look alike. Where Lilly was blond with blue eyes, Julie was dark with brown eyes. He turned his attention to Julie, who came to stand beside him. Looking down at her, all he could see was her protruding belly. "How many would you like?"

"Two will be perfect. If you have enough?"

"There's enough." He'd made ten of the damn things. "Help yourself to coffee or tea."

While Julie went about getting the rest of her meal together, Gabriel could feel Lilly's scrutiny, but he didn't look at her. "I suppose you want some, too?" Peripherally he noticed the way she bristled. "Help yourself," he growled. And then he took his time putting together his own plate.

He sat next to Julie, across from Charlotte, and stared down at the one paltry egg he'd given himself. The last time he'd eaten an egg had been before his father died, eight years ago.

"These are excellent!" Julie rattled. "Charlotte, you must try them. You'll like them! They're quite the best eggs I've ever had!"

Charlotte wasn't having anything to do with this, Gabriel realized, up until Lilly sat down beside her and dug into her own eggs with well-mannered relish. Only then did Charlotte attempt to take a bite. Her jaw worked like the egg was stuck to the roof of her mouth, and just when Gabriel thought she might regurgitate, her expression changed completely.

"Daddy!" she squealed. Her grin lit up her entire little face and made her dark eyes sparkle. "This is yummy! Momma, I like them!"

Barely able to breathe, Gabriel watched his daughter devouring the rest of the small egg he'd given her. She was calling Lilly *momma?* But of course, she would be. She'd been excited about the wedding, not because of the marriage itself, but because Lilly would become her mother. Yesterday, in the carriage on the way back from Philadelphia, she'd chattered about Lilly, referring to her as Miss Lilly, not momma. Pointedly he looked at Lilly to see her reaction. There was none, which told him Charlotte must have been calling her *momma* for a while. Did she mind? He couldn't tell, and he hated that he couldn't tell.

Deliberately stalling, he cut his egg into pieces. Then he loaded his fork, jabbed it into the hard, crumbling yoke, closed his eyes and shoved the bite into his mouth. The first thing that hit his tongue was the salt, then the pepper. He chewed once, twice and swallowed quickly. The salt and pepper made it bearable, but he'd overdone it. Chancing a glance at Lilly, he saw that she wasn't quite as enamored with his skills as a chef as Charlotte and Julie seemed to be. Of course she would be too polite to say anything. Briefly he contemplated demanding her opinion, and then cursed himself for the fool he was. Why did it bother him so much that Charlotte was calling Lilly *momma?* Why did it make his heart twist in his chest every night at bedtime when he heard Lilly telling Charlotte she loved her? Last night Charlotte had responded in kind.

Before that, earlier in the evening, he'd seen Lilly coming down the stairs for dinner. He'd been coming in from the east hallway, hidden from her in the darkened shadows behind the stairs. She hadn't seen him. She hadn't been wearing the necklace he'd given her. Not that he thought she would, or that she should have. *Hell*, he didn't know what he thought, but he'd been… what? Furious, piqued, irritated? He hadn't gone to dinner. Instead he'd gone to the west wing and rummaged through drawers and drawings to see what exactly she'd been into. If she'd touched any of his things, he hadn't been able to tell.

He chanced another glance at her across the kitchen table. Did she care for the gems, he wondered? Probably not. The only jewelry he'd ever seen her wear was a string of pearls. The diamonds and amethysts had been a poor choice. He should have gone with his gut and bought her literature. He'd had several books picked out, but he'd put them back.

Christ! He needed to get her out of his head!

Thankfully, before he could say anything to further doom himself in her eyes, Julie started talking. She was still talking after Lilly dished up seconds for Charlotte and much later, after all their plates were cleared.

"Withers will be waiting for us," Lilly said, cutting Julie off mid-sentence. Gabriel had to turn away to hide his mirth. "Come, Charlotte. We don't want to keep him waiting, and we don't want to be late."

"Okay, Momma," Charlotte chirped.

Gabriel watched Charlotte grab hold of Lilly's hand. Together they headed out.

"Will you come with us?" Julie tucked her arm in his, and she said something else, but he didn't hear it. His eyes were stuck on Lilly's back, and the way she'd styled her hair. It wasn't all up on the top of her head the way she normally wore it. She'd left long curls trailing down her back, to where they fit between her shoulder blades, which were distinct beneath the pale green gown she wore. He remembered having his hands in her hair, the soft texture of it, the way it twisted around his wrist, the way it tickled across his face, his chest. He remembered following the curve and dip of her shoulder blades with his hands.

He tore his eyes away. "What?"

"Are you coming to church with us?" Julie said. "What a treat! I'm so pleased—"

"I'm not going to church," he interrupted briskly. Julie's question had caused Lilly to look at him over her shoulder, but he didn't return her stare. "I'm going into town. Withers will drop me first."

"Oh." Julie's bottom lip pouted out, but her wide smile returned just as quickly. "At least we'll have your company for the carriage ride."

Gabriel leaned on his cane and let Julie lead him through the mansion. He tried to avoid looking at Lilly ahead of them, but his eyes were drawn to her. She moved with such ease and such poise. There was a quiet dignity about her that had intrigued him from the first. Nothing about her appearance disclosed her lowly past. She walked as if she'd been born to privilege. Not that he cared about such things, not like Rob did. His eyes followed the line of her lovely blond hair, to her narrow waist, to the flair of the bustle. He knew exactly what was hidden under that bustle. And how good the softness and warmth of her flesh felt in his hands.

Stop it!

The wind was whipping harshly as they left the manse and made their way to the carriage, and he was thankful he'd secured his kerchief well that morning. He felt Julie's arm tighten around his. Her dress plastered itself to her rounded stomach. Even her petticoats didn't keep it from molding to her legs. The wind did the same to Lilly's dress, then hooked it under the hem and lifted. As Withers gave her a hand into the carriage, Gabriel caught a very nice view of one lovely, stocking-clad leg, all the way to the knee. Quickly he looked away.

Between Charlotte and Julie's chatters, there wasn't a chance to say a word during the drive. Gabriel preferred it that way. He didn't even have to listen. He spent the majority of the time staring out the window. At least, with his eyes occupied by the passing scenery, he didn't have to look at *her*.

He didn't want to think about her, which of late, seemed impossible. She was always on his mind, especially at night. But right now, he couldn't think about her. Now he needed to have all his wits about him for what was to come. His trip to New York had taken much longer than intended. After learning what he had from Beatrice, there had been too much to do. Consumed and driven, he'd come up with a plan and brought it to fruition. Under any other circumstances, it would have taken much longer, but he managed to get what he'd wanted to accomplish done in record time. He'd traveled to Philadelphia and back to New York again before finally returning to Havertown. Fortunately, in the short time he'd been in Philadelphia, he'd been able to deal with several other things, and people, he'd been neglecting for far too long. Those things, like Lilly, were things he couldn't afford to think about. Not now.

So early on a Sunday morning, the streets in the heart of town had very little traffic. Withers pulled up to their destination without having to double park. Without looking at any of them, Gabriel offered a curt *good day* to the other occupants of the carriage and climbed out.

Withers had jumped down from the driver's seat to open the door. His collar was turned up to ward off the cold, but his cheeks and nose were bright red. "Shall I wait until after the church service to come back for you, sir?"

Gabriel stared up at the townhouse in front of him wondering if the occupants would be awake at this hour. Withers wanted to attend church. Far be it for him to be the cause of the man missing out on his religious fix for the week. If nothing else, the indoor warmth of the church would give Withers a chance to stop his teeth from chattering. "Fine."

"Very good, sir. It will be about two hours."

"Fine." Gabriel started forward, leaning into the blustery wind, across the sidewalk, and up the six, steep brick stairs to the small porch. There was a knocker on the door, but he used his knuckles instead. Behind him, he heard the carriage pull away. His stomach was churning, but it was not the kind of discomfort that came from his illness, or even from having forced himself to eat a repellent egg.

It dawned on him that in all the years he'd been coming to this place, he'd never knocked on the door before. Being this time of day, and a Sunday, most likely it would be locked. Even so, he didn't bother to check. For some reason, the idea of barging in the way he normally did felt wrong. Despite the cold and the wind, his hands were clammy with sweat.

Christ! His heart was pounding so loudly he could feel it in his head.

Two hours. He would have to be here for two hours.

He wondered whether Rob liked eggs. He couldn't recall in all the years they'd known each other ever seeing Rob eat eggs. Eggs were served at the boarding school all the time. Like him, Rob usually chose other things. Rolling his eyes at having such a strange thought at such a time, he rapped at the door to Rob's townhouse again.

Robert August was Charles Drayton's son. Rob was his brother.

For as long as he could remember, Gabriel had thought of Rob as his best friend. He'd shared more of his innermost thoughts and secrets with Rob than with any other person in the world. He'd relied on Rob more times than he could count. He'd trusted Rob with his life.

But none of Rob's apparently sincere amiability or heartfelt concern, which of late, had been relentless, was genuine. It was all a great ruse, designed to humiliate and deceive, torment and destroy. He knew this because Rob had written it in the letter Beatrice had shown him.

Rob, his best friend, despised him. And Rob, his best friend, was paying someone a great deal of money to murder him.

Thirty-Five

"Someone's knocking on the door," Molly said.

"Don't stop, darlin'." Rob groaned, curling his fingers into her hips. She was where he liked her best. On top, and he was so close, so close… "Damn, damn! Who the hell would show up at this hour?"

"I'll go see." She slid off him and skittered, in all her glory, to peek through the curtain at the window. "It's a black carriage. It's pulling away."

With his gaze on much more appealing things, Rob wasn't really listening. "Get your cute little ass back here. I'm not finished yet."

She giggled as she raced back and flounced up onto the bed. Palming her backside, Rob helped her to straddle him and draw him in. Then he was squeezing her soft flesh in perfect time with each creak of the bed, and gazing at her gorgeous breasts.

Jesus! His mouth was watering from just gawking at her. The second his load was spent he was going to throw her down and latch on to those stunning morsels again. All day long he was going to indulge like the starving glutton he was, until she couldn't take it anymore. And in between he was going to fuck her, and fuck her again, until she couldn't take that anymore either. She could beg him to stop all she wanted, but there would be no mercy for her. He was going to hold her down, tie her up if he had to, and ravenously abuse her until night came around again, and then he was going to light every lamp in the room, and greedily and voraciously abuse her some more.

When the rap at the door came a second time, Rob hissed, "Ignore it!" He wasn't ready to let the combined reality and fantasy end. Not yet…

"What if it was Gabriel Drayton's carriage? What if Gabriel is at the door?" she murmured.

Rob squeezed his eyes shut. Whoever was on the porch wouldn't have been visible to Molly from the window. There was no way she could know for sure who was out there. Rob had been to Drayton Hall at least a dozen times in the last three weeks hoping there would be some word from Gabriel. No one knew where he'd gone. All Withers could tell him was that he'd dropped Gabriel at the train station in Philadelphia. Rob had even gone to see Alex, but that dreaded interchange had left him with no answers either. Unless Alex was lying…

"I have to let him in. He can't stay out there in the cold. Not as sick as he is." Or, God forbid, what if whoever was on his stoop wasn't Gabriel? What if whoever was out there brought bad news? "Let me up."

The rap at the door came again. This time whoever it was used the knocker.

While Molly helped him into his robe he silently cursed the ruining of their day. Not that what he'd been fantasizing about would happen quite that way. Not if he got lucky. To her he said, "I'm sure it's nothing. Wait for me." Another look at her slender, delectable body made him groan aloud. "I am not done with you yet."

"I can tell." One of her shapely eyebrows rose. "You may want to wait a minute."

He followed her gaze to the jutting tent in his robe.

"Down boy," she teased.

"You play a dangerous game, darlin'," he threatened, stifling his laughter. Eyes flashing, he shoved her backwards until she fell onto the bed. "Don't move. This is the view I want when I get back."

Molly's eyes sparkled as she reached under the pillow and slowly withdrew a thin blue scarf. A second followed the first. She trailed them, one after the other, seductively across her chest. Rob's mouth gaped and his breath came out of him in a silent whoosh. Blood returned to his loins in a razor-sharp rush. He *was* going to get lucky today! This was what he'd really wanted! This was what he'd dreamed of. Oh, the memories—such glorious memories—to be so sweetly revisited. "How many of those do you have hidden under there?" he choked. *Say six. Please say six…*

"Seven," she whispered demurely.

One bare foot rose off the bed and pressed into the center of his chest. At the same time she took hold of a scarf, twisted the ends around her hands, and then in one wily move, jerked it taut.

Rob gulped hard. All too soon she would be winding that scarf around his ankle. He could already feel his muscles stretching, his joints straining. He was writhing, thrashing against those unyielding constraints, arching off the bed, unable to cry for mercy because he was gagged, unable to anticipate the next sweet torture she would inflict upon him because he was blindfolded.

Oh Jesus, what was she going to use the seventh scarf for? He forgot completely why he was standing there, until the foot on his chest shoved him. He staggered back. Molly was laughing at him.

The door knocker sounded again. Rob was alternatively moaning and chuckling as he forced himself to tramp down the inexorable erotic anticipation and saunter out of the room. By the time he reached the bottom of the staircase, his good humor was replaced by anxiety. He quickened his pace through the small foyer, turned the lock and yanked open the door.

The wind whipped around the black-cloaked figure standing on the porch and hit Rob like a brick, full in the face. "*Jesus!*"

"No. Sorry. It's just Gabriel. May I come in?"

"Gabe! What the hell!" Rob exclaimed. "Get in here! It's freezing!"

Gabriel barely limped past the door before Rob slammed it closed. Turning around he saw Gabriel looking up the staircase. From where they stood, he could see part of the open door to his bedroom, and he caught the tail of Molly's robe disappearing back inside of it.

"I apologize if my timing is… *uh*… inconvenient," Gabriel said.

"Fuck you!" Rob said, and he grabbed Gabriel, wrapping both arms around him. For a long moment he held on, taking deep breath after deep breath, trying desperately to rein in an overwhelming shot of emotion. Gabriel wasn't returning his hug, but Rob didn't care. Being demonstrative had never been part of Gabriel's make up, and since the fire, he'd become even more impervious. Rob was content enough Gabriel didn't shove him off.

"God, it's good to see you!" Rob pushed back, but kept a hand on Gabriel's shoulder. "Sorry it took so long for me to answer the door. You woke me up."

Gabriel's visible eyebrow rose and his eyes briefly glanced downward. "Really?"

Rob laughed, and adjusted his robe, not that it did any good. "Where the hell have you been? When did you get back?"

"Yesterday. I went to see Beatrice."

Stunned, Rob just looked at him. Gabriel didn't hate Beatrice. He didn't even dislike her, but Rob was well aware Gabriel couldn't stand to be near her. Indirectly he blamed Beatrice for his mother's death.

"Would you mind if I sit down? My leg is bothering me."

Gabriel's murmur shook Rob. "Of course. Sorry, I'm not thinking straight. Go, go, make yourself comfortable. I'll have Molly make us coffee. Then we can talk. I can't believe you're here!"

Instead of going to Rob's office, Gabriel dragged himself toward the sitting room. Rob wasn't surprised to see the severity of Gabriel's limp. It had been growing progressively worse since the onset of his illness.

While Rob went about making himself presentable, it occurred to him that Gabriel had never been in his sitting room before. Every time they met in this house, they met in Rob's office. Gabriel's choice surprised him. He was even more surprised by Gabriel's demeanor. Although subdued, he was almost being friendly. Something was wrong.

Or—he couldn't believe he hadn't thought of it until this very second—perhaps there was news of a more pleasant, infant-related nature?

It didn't take long for Rob to return fully clothed and coiffed. He found Gabriel seated casually in a chair near the fireplace, still with his heavy cloak on. He looked up the moment Rob entered.

"Molly's bringing muffins and coffee. Geez, it's freezing in here."

After lighting a fire and ensuring it was properly stoked, Rob sat in the wing chair opposite Gabriel and regarded his long-time friend. Gabriel wasn't meeting his eyes, and that was highly unusual. Something definitely wasn't right. "How are you feeling?"

"Cold," Gabriel said. "The fire is good. Thank you." An expression of gratitude from Gabriel was rare indeed. Rob almost laughed, but he didn't have a chance to comment before Gabe spoke again. "It seems I've dodged a bullet."

"What?"

Their eyes met. "I'm not sick anymore."

It took Rob a moment to find his voice, and even then he found himself stammering, "But… but… are you sure? How do you… how do you know? You've been to a doctor?"

"Two doctors. In New York. They both told me I'm in excellent health. Whatever I had was a virus of some sort." Gabriel ran his palm up and back over his outer thigh, a gesture Rob had seen countless times. "There's nothing wrong with me anymore except the obvious. This damn leg may hurt like hell, but it won't kill me. It's always worse in the cold. You know that."

Staring at Gabriel's face, Rob saw what he'd been too preoccupied to notice before. The pallor, the gauntness, the redness in Gabe's eyes was gone. Gabe looked like himself again. Suddenly Rob found his throat tight. "Oh, Jesus! I think I'm going to cry," he mumbled.

"What for?"

"Because of you, you dumbass! I've been out of my mind worrying about you. No one knew where you were. You didn't tell a soul where you were going! I thought… I thought you'd come up with some crazy plan to go off by yourself to… to die. Which is exactly the kind of thing you would do. I… I didn't think I would ever see you again." The way his voice kept catching, Rob thought he just might not be able to contain his blubbers after all.

"Sorry to disappoint you, but I had no such plan."

Rob shook his head, let out a heavy sigh, and briefly pressed his fingers into his eyes. "I'm so glad to see you. I am so damned relieved, Gabe, I can't even breathe." He wanted to haul Gabriel out of the chair, grab onto him and not let go. He wanted to run to Molly, swing her around in his arms, and shout at the top of his lungs.

As if he'd conjured her up out of thin air, there she was, fully dressed in another one of her new gowns, this one a deep rust color, perfect for the season. There was a tray laden with coffee and muffins tucked under her arm. She was a welcome interruption, enough of one to help Rob get his emotions under some semblance of control. "Thanks, darlin'," he drawled, waving her in.

She set her burden down on the coffee table between them, and Rob was struck, as he so often was, by how pretty she was. As badly as he wanted to see Gabriel, Rob hoped his friend wouldn't stay too long. He caught Molly's subtle smile and the promising message in it— *Patience, Rob. Even better things come to those who wait.* What could be better than what already awaited him? She did *not* just mouth the word *seven* to him, did she? Rob cleared his throat.

"If you would like anything else, please let me know," she said in her dainty, lilting voice before turning to leave.

Rob's eyes were still gazing after her when Gabriel murmured, "She's good for you, you know."

Startled, Rob turned back abruptly.

"You stare after her all the time," Gabriel said, still in that very quiet, odd tone. "You don't even realize you do it."

"She puts up with me." To hide his sudden discomfort Rob forced a chuckle. About a year before, one night at Drayton Hall, after Charlotte had long been in bed, he and Gabriel had tied one on pretty well. In that condition, he wasn't able to shut up, and he'd said some things about Molly that he wished he hadn't. He didn't care that Gabriel knew he was having sex with her. Hell, back in their youthful, exuberant days, they'd practically competed over exploits with women. What he regretted was telling Gabriel, in detail, not only about his obsession with her breasts, but some of the more unusual things they did together. Then like a complete buffoon, he told Gabriel he was madly in love with her. Because he'd been too inebriated to make it home that night, he'd stayed at Drayton Hall. The next day, while they sat in the dining room nursing hangovers with coffee and greasy bacon, he told Gabriel what he'd said about his feelings for Molly wasn't true. He'd blamed his confession on his drunkenness.

Rob took a long draught of his coffee—perfectly prepared by the amazing lady herself. Whispering, so she wouldn't overhear, he said to Gabriel, "She's a fantastic fuck."

"She's more to you than that," Gabriel said.

"No, she's not." Rob didn't want to have this conversation with Gabriel. Not now. Not ever. Loving Molly wasn't an option and it never would be. "How was your homecoming with Lilly?"

Gabriel gingerly pushed himself forward in his chair and reached for his coffee. Rob was faster, leaning over to pick it up and hand it to him. "I'm sorry I'm not a very good host," he said. "Would you like a muffin, too?"

"I had breakfast," Gabriel said. "I made eggs."

"*You* ate eggs?"

"Lilly thinks I don't feed Charlotte well enough. Eggs are healthy."

Rob laughed and leaned back in his chair. "Speaking of Lilly… any… *er*… special news?"

"It's too early for that."

Rob shook his head. "You've been gone three weeks. If there is no baby, her womanly curse would have happened by now. If it hasn't, if she's late…" Rob let the rest of what he was going to say trail off. Gabriel wasn't looking at him again. Obviously the cause of Gabe's diffident behavior was not news of Lilly being pregnant. The odd foreboding in his chest told Rob Gabriel's mood wasn't caused by the return of his health either. "Regardless, I'm sure she was glad to see you."

"I doubt it," Gabe said curtly, much more like himself. His tone made Rob smile.

"Who's fault is that? My advice to you is to wine and dine her and treat her like a queen. You could even do something about that awful, dour bedroom of yours. Dress it up. Make it more inviting."

"I like my bedroom the way it is."

"Right," Rob drawled. Then to change the subject, he said, "Tell me about your trip. You saw Beatrice? How's the ice queen?"

Gabriel's response was slow in coming. "That's what I came to talk to you about. She asked me to stay with her for a few days, so I did." He paused. "She told me some things…"

Rob's pulse suddenly sped up. He couldn't imagine Beatrice would give away his parentage. She was the one who had insisted on the secrecy. If she'd planned to tell Gabriel, she would have consulted him first. He was sure of it. But the way Gabriel left the sentence hanging made him wonder. The idea that Gabe might know made him apprehensive. At the same time he wanted everything out in the open. He was tired of hiding, tired of the lies. "What things?"

"You're not going to like this," Gabe said.

"If that's the case, better to spit it out and get it over with."

"Perhaps." Gabriel hesitated again. "Beatrice believes you've been embezzling from the trust."

Rob laughed. He couldn't help it. The accusation was preposterous and he was certain Gabriel would agree. But when he looked up, Gabriel wasn't laughing. Gabriel's eyes were filled with suspicion. "I haven't," Rob bristled. "You know I haven't."

"You manage the funds. You're the trustee. You have more power over the money, and easier access to it than I do. Beatrice said you've been stealing from me for years."

This was not the Gabe Rob knew at all, and he hated the defensive hackles that rose up in him. "I swear to you, I haven't. I don't know why Beatrice would say such a thing. I have spent your money, but only as you've asked me to. Gabe, you're my best friend. You mean more to me than anyone else in the world. I would never betray you. You know I wouldn't."

"I don't mean more to you than Susan."

Rob closed his eyes. None of this made any sense. That bitch—his *mother*—knew damn good and well he'd never taken a dime of Drayton money! That she would tell Gabriel about his relationship with Susan enraged him even more. He could only wonder what game she was playing. There was no doubt it was a game. In the few short years he'd known her, he'd come to realize she was a master at manipulation. It was a good thing she lived so far away, because at that moment he wanted nothing more than to strangle her. Mother or not, God help him, he would have if she were here in the room with them.

His hands clenched into fists. Forcing a deep breath, he reminded himself to stay in control and not let his anger cause him to say something he would later regret. Gabriel might be skeptical, but Rob was sure, in the end, he would not believe Beatrice's claim. He and Gabriel had been friends for too long. They depended upon each other, trusted each other. He let out air and murmured, "I certainly didn't expect to be talking about any of this today. Way to rain on my happy Gabe's-home-and-he's-well-again parade."

"I don't give a damn about Susan," Gabriel said. "If you really care about her as much as Beatrice thinks you do, I feel sorry for you. I'm just surprised you never told me," Gabe said.

"Nothing's happened between us in years," Rob returned bitterly. He took another sip of his coffee, unsure what, if anything more, he should say.

"I'm not here because of Susan. There's something else I need to discuss with you." Gabriel moved again, positioning himself in the chair so he was leaning almost completely off his bad hip. His eyes glittered.

"Do I have to hear it?" Rob asked.

"Beatrice wants me to appoint a new trustee."

"But you're not going to?" Gabriel was looking at him and not saying a word. "You do believe me, Gabe? You know Beatrice is just trying to cause trouble, don't you?"

"I can't afford to take chances."

Rob felt his stomach drop. "What are you saying? You're taking her word over mine? You're firing me?"

"Yes," Gabriel said.

"As your attorney, too?"

"Yes."

"Have you already appointed a new trustee?"

"Yes."

Rob got up, because he couldn't sit anymore. "I need a drink," he mumbled and headed out. He went to his office to the stash he kept there—Jack Daniel's finest. He remembered offering it to Gabe for his birthday… how many weeks ago had that been? His hand trembled as he poured, and still trembled as he downed the harsh liquid.

When he could, when he was calm enough, when his heart was no longer hammering, he went back. Gabriel was still there, in the same chair, still in his cloak, but he was reclined and staring at the fire. "I am at a loss here. What exactly does all this mean? What do you want me to do?"

"Box up the files and records. I will take them with me when I go."

"Alright," Rob said, but he didn't leave. He just stood there. When the silence between them got too heavy, he said, "And us? How does all of this affect our friendship?"

Gabriel looked up. "It's over."

Fury took over, consuming Rob completely. The force of it cut through his chest so sharply he had to look down at himself to be sure a real knife hadn't just been plunged into him. "What about everything we've been through together? It means nothing?" Gabriel's lack of response was his answer. Rob was shaking and he couldn't stop it. "That's it, then? You're taking the word of a woman who's made your life hell over mine? We're through? Just like that?"

Gabriel took the watch out of his pocket and looked at it briefly. "You have an hour to get everything packed."

"Damn you! You son of a bitch! You fucking son of a bitch!" With a ferocity he couldn't control, Rob grabbed the closest thing within reach—a ceramic figurine, one of Molly's angels—from the table beside him and threw it. It crashed, shattering instantly on the stone hearth of the fireplace.

He saw Gabriel jolt and sit up abruptly, as if he expected Rob to hurl something else, whatever it may be, at him next. At least Gabriel was no longer unaffected by all of this. Turning on his heel, Rob stomped to his office and slammed the door behind him.

Molly found him there, sitting on the floor leaning against his filing cabinets. Until she came in, he'd been unable to make himself move. With her help, they collected every last file, filling two crates with endless piles of documents. Over the years, since being appointed trustee, Rob had made numerous notes. He included all of them. Spitefully, he divested his office of every last thing that had anything to do with Gabriel Drayton, including the photograph he'd kept of himself, Gabriel and Alex that had been taken in front of their dormitory at college, and the other one—the one of Charlotte. He'd left himself with nothing. Nothing to remind him of Gabriel or anything related to the Drayton name!

Timing couldn't have been better. The carriage pulled up outside just as he stacked the two cartons in the foyer by the door. Malevolently he carried one of the boxes out himself, dropping it at the curb so it slammed down with a loud crack. Withers ran up into the house to carry the second one and Rob brushed past him on the stairs, purposely bumping him. And he didn't care. He didn't give a damn about anything!

Most of all he didn't give a damn about Gabriel, who was standing in the foyer, balanced on his cane, still wearing that blank, unreadable expression. Their eyes met. "So this is it?" he spat bitterly. "Is there anything else you want to accuse me of? Go ahead!"

Gabriel didn't move, but his eyes became strangely dark.

"What? You have nothing more to say before you shut me out of your life?"

"I do," Gabriel said quietly. "I do have one more thing to say to you."

In all the years they'd been friends, even when they argued, which was more times than Rob could count, he'd never wanted to hit Gabriel, but he wanted to hit him now. He wanted to hit him so badly he had to twist his arm behind his back. It took every last ounce of energy to restrain that fist. "Get the hell out! You fucking asshole!"

"I love you," Gabriel whispered.

Rob staggered as if he'd been struck. He couldn't breathe at all.

Speechless and frozen, he watched Gabriel make the slow, one-step-at-a-time descent down the porch steps. His black cloak billowed out behind him, while he leaned into the paralyzing wind and limped across the sidewalk to the carriage.

The second the carriage disappeared from view, Rob slammed the door and turned around. Molly came to him, as he knew she would. She put her arms around him and tried to hold him, but he shoved her away. For hours he locked himself in his office. Even Molly wasn't allowed to intrude, despite her numerous attempts. He didn't eat. But he drank, and he drank.

After the darkness of night had fallen, he went to his bedroom and stripped. He lay down and waited for Molly. He wanted to fuck. He wanted to fuck until he didn't have to think about anything. Until his mind became a void of nothing.

He watched her enter, watched her disrobe. She sat on the side of the bed and he grabbed her. He threw her over, forced her onto her hands and knees and he took her. But it wasn't enough. Roughly he flipped her over, put her legs up onto his shoulders and jammed into her again. And he couldn't stop. He was going insane, turning into a madman, wanting to hurt someone, anyone. It didn't even matter who. All he needed was for someone else to feel as badly as he did.

And it was working. It was working, until he looked at her.

In Molly's eyes, he didn't see the pain he wanted to see. Instead he saw his reflection—the reflection of the pathetic excuse of a man he'd become. He saw violence and hatred and everything else he despised about himself. Shrieking out the anguish, he came down on top of her, wrapped his arms around her, and buried his face in her neck. He felt her return his embrace, clinging to him as ferociously as he was clinging to her.

Molly knew. She always did. She knew the badness of his heart. Except in her blind innocence, she didn't recognize it as badness. She believed in him, worshipped him, stood him on a pedestal. Instead she should take the damn pedestal and pummel him with it until every bone in his body was broken, because that's what he deserved. Slowly, tenderly now, he rocked with her, holding onto her beauty and her surrender, clutching her tightly, afraid to let go.

It was better this way. It was so much better than what he'd been trying to achieve through brutality. In this he finally, finally began to feel the solace he so desperately needed.

"I'm sorry, Molly. I'm sorry," he whispered, choking over the words. Her fingers were in his hair, lifting his head, bringing his mouth to hers. Her taste and scent surrounded him. Her ardor numbed his limbs until he could no longer feel them. Below, the deep, sluggish rhythm droned on. The intensity built, stacking higher and higher until the heat in his loins became enflamed. It burned. It burned until he began to melt.

And the melting was so good, so very good, shrouded the way he was. He'd never felt anything like it. All he wanted, as they both became silent and still, was to stay right where he was. Forever.

"Moll?" he whispered. "Molly?" He wanted to tell her not to move, to keep holding onto him, but he couldn't get the words out. He didn't have to. She already knew what he needed. Her arms around him were unyielding.

And he realized in that moment he'd done something with Molly he'd never done before. He'd never done it with any woman before.

He had come inside of her.

Thirty-Six

Lilly's plan to thank Gabriel for the gifts didn't happen quite the way she wanted. The evening he'd come home from his trip, he hadn't joined them for dinner, or in the parlor afterwards, not that she could have said anything there, really, with Julie and Charlotte present. The next morning, he'd made breakfast. His eggs—a surprise—had been too salty for her taste, but at least he'd tried. After that, he rode with them in the coach to town and back, but again Julie and Charlotte's presence made it impossible to properly thank him. His surly mood hadn't boded well for seeking him out afterwards either.

Sunday evening, like the previous one, he didn't come to dinner or to the parlor. Lilly only saw him once, in passing, while she was on her way to the dining room. Tersely he'd said, "I won't be joining you. I have things to catch up on." By midweek, he'd made himself so absent, life felt no different than while he'd been away.

Of course Julie was in the mansion daily, looking for him. In Lilly's opinion Julie was making a nuisance of herself. The knocks Julie made on his study door were not answered, and it was somewhat satisfying that Julie hadn't been any more successful in gaining an audience with him than Lilly. Three times she'd gone to his study, all to no avail. If Gabriel was not just ignoring the knocks, and truly was not in the study, she could only assume he was in his west wing office. Drawing his buildings? Or, copying the designs of an architect named Andrew Wentworth?

She thought about going to the west wing, but that idea was dismissed as quickly as it came. Based upon his clipped comments, his west wing office was off limits. This made perfect sense if he was indeed engaged in the illegal activity of *stealing* another architect's designs. Obviously he'd stolen the man's correspondence.

Perhaps he was a thief. But, she still wanted to express gratitude for the flowers and the chocolates and the incredible jewelry. She wanted to thank him for the books he'd brought for Charlotte, too.

By Thursday, Lilly had another idea. Rather than verbally expressing herself, she would give him something in return. But what? What would a man who already had everything he could possibly need, and money enough to buy anything he wanted, appreciate? Eventually she decided to make something for him. She'd been knitting a baby bonnet, booties and a blanket for Julie's baby, and they were almost complete. There would be time during Charlotte's riding lesson and bath, and in the evenings after Charlotte went to bed, to make something for Gabriel, too. If she was diligent enough she could even have it completed by Christmas—it was hard to believe the holiday was already less than six weeks away!

After much deliberation Lilly chose to make a sweater, one he could wear around the drafty mansion on cold winter days. Not that he would like it, or ever wear it. Nothing she could create would be good enough for someone like him. But her resolve was firm—she was going to make him a sweater, even if he threw it away with the trash.

On Friday afternoon, while Charlotte was having her riding lesson, Lilly rummaged through her trunk to find leftover yarn. She was immensely pleased to find a ball of black—the only appropriate color for Gabriel. It wasn't enough for the whole sweater, but she could get started. On her next shopping trip with Charlotte she would get more. The only fairly daunting task left was to determine how big the sweater should be. They only way she could think of to do that was to borrow one of his shirts. He had enough of them in his closet. He would never miss one.

Gabriel was nowhere to be seen, and he wouldn't be, not at this time of day. Nevertheless she found herself tiptoeing across the corridor to his room. Once inside she shook her head at her own silliness. Everything was as it should be, empty and quiet. Three of Charlotte's dolls were tucked under his ugly grey blanket. The equally ugly curtains had been drawn back, letting in just enough light for her to see.

Remembering the nightgown she'd left all those weeks ago, she thought she would take a moment to search for it. There was no sign of it near the bed, or in the drawers of the end tables. She didn't see it hanging in his closet either. All of the belongings in his dresser were neatly folded, but her nightgown was not among them. Sighing in disappointment—it was her favorite nightgown—she meandered over to his washstand.

Shaving equipment was lined up behind the water basin. In the drawer she found a toothbrush, a hairbrush, and a myriad of other toiletries including a bottle of cologne that looked unused. There were several other random things in there, like scissors, a pen, and a handful of coins. It was the only drawer containing his possessions that wasn't neatly organized, and it made her smile.

Next she went to the huge, lion-clawed tub. The porcelain was so clean and white she could see her reflection. On the wall behind it was a thick wooden bar. It wasn't an unusual spot to place a rack for towels, but there were no towels on it. What made her reach out across the tub and touch the bar, she didn't know, but when she did she saw the cracks in the tile. Upon further inspection she realized it was a door of some sort. The latch, hidden at one end of the towel bar, was similar to the latches that controlled the bookshelf doors to the fire escape in her and Charlotte's rooms. She clicked it and pushed. The door opened. In order to actually pass through it, one would need to either move the tub, or step in and out of it again. Because it was too heavy to move, Lilly climbed in and out, and then she was inside the dank, narrow space.

There, she found something she never expected to see. High up in the rafters, above her head, were a dozen or so thin bottles. Not bottles, she realized. They were vials and they were all identical. She reached up to retrieve one. The label read, *Morphine*. The date on it revealed it was only a few months old.

The memory of Gabriel staggering in the kitchen came instantly to mind. More than once she'd seen him run his hand up and down his thigh. His limp was sometimes more prominent. She thought of the night in his bedroom when she'd accidently jarred his leg. She thought of Charlotte and her magic wand. Gabriel was using morphine because of his leg.

She put the vial back, stepped into the tub and pulled the bar to close the door, but it wouldn't stay closed. The latch wasn't catching. Lilly's heart began to pound. If she couldn't get it shut, Gabriel would know she'd been in his room!

After several more tries, including slamming it once or twice, she told herself to calm down and take a more intellectual approach. There had to be a reason the latch wasn't working. The door had been secure when she'd discovered it. Within seconds the problem became apparent. There was a dowel holding the bar in place that was sticking out. Pushing it back to where it was supposed to be wasn't difficult. With the correction made the latch caught easily. Even so, it was a reminder that she needed to stop dawdling and get what she came for.

She moved to Gabriel's rack of clothing and began fingering through his shirts.

"Snooping again? What are you looking for this time?"

Gabriel's growl spun her. She hadn't heard him come in. She had no idea how long he'd been standing there. And that icy glare of his was aimed right at her. If looks could kill she would be prostrate on the ground.

"No...nothing..." she stammered. "I...I need to borrow a shirt. For Charlotte, a school game..." It was a pathetic excuse at best. Why, oh why, did he have to be so terribly intimidating?

"Is that so?"

"Yes."

"Fine. Take what you want. What's mine is yours. Isn't that how the saying goes?"

She could have done without the arrogance and sarcasm. What was it her mother used to say? Smother your enemies with kindness? She yanked one of his dozens of shirts off its hanger, probably more roughly than she needed to. He wasn't really an enemy, was he? Even if he was a thief? "Thank you. This one will do nicely. Excuse me." She intended to brush past him, but didn't get that far.

"Charlotte's books are acceptable?" he said.

Lilly smiled. She couldn't help it. "They're wonderful. I could not have asked for better. They've kept us busy, and the chalkboard was an excellent idea." She would have gone on, unable to hold back her own enthusiasm, except he cut her off in his normal brusque way.

"And Charlotte? She is learning her letters and such?"

"She's doing better," Lilly said. "Charlotte has an exceptional auditory memory. She uses it to compensate for what she's missing visually. She does it so well she's fooled me several times. It's almost like she doesn't see letters on a page at all. It's as if she sees a distorted version of what we see."

"And how do you propose to fix this problem?"

"I don't really know," Lilly admitted. "Repetition. And more writing, which forces her to form the letters on her own. The chalkboard has come in quite handy." To his continued glower, Lilly raised her chin. "She will learn, Mr. Drayton."

"My name is Gabriel," he snapped. "You are my wife. I expect you to use it."

Flustered, Lilly murmured, "Yes, of course." Once again she tried to slide past him, only to be stopped again by his gravelly voice.

"Should I have a doctor out to see you?"

"There's nothing wrong with me."

"You said… you said you're late," he accused. "Are you still? Late?"

His odd stutter over the question surprised her. All week she'd believed he'd misunderstood her fleetingly made comment. "It's too early, I think, to know for sure."

"Fine. You will inform me as soon as you are… *sure*."

Bristling again, Lilly couldn't hold back any longer. "I will be glad to, if you are available, but you're never available."

"I told you I had things to do. Running this estate takes a considerable amount of time. Being away put me behind."

"Well then, if you *were* behind, and you're now caught up, it would be nice for you to spend some time with your daughter. She misses you—"

"That is between Charlotte and me, and it's none of your bus—"

Lilly took a step toward him and interrupted right back. "On the contrary. It is entirely my business. It would be beneficial for you to take a greater interest in her life. You could start by helping her with reading. There is plenty of time in the evening after dinner to do so. That is, if you are indeed caught up with all of your estate demands, and are able to resume your previous schedule!"

"Charlotte calling you *momma* does not give you the authority to tell me what to do, least of all, how or in what manner I interact with my daughter!"

Lilly raised a haughty eyebrow. "Is it not my place to look out for her best interests?"

He leaned toward her. "Tell me, dear lady wife, do you always intrude into other peoples' lives like this, or is it just mine?"

She couldn't help it. Her jaw dropped. "I am not intruding on your life! I am thinking of your daughter! Believe me when I tell you intruding on *your* life is the last thing I will ever want to do!"

"Then why the fascination with my things?"

"I am not fascinated—!" This time Lilly cut herself off, and charged, "What did you do with my nightgown?"

She stunned him. For once. He straightened instantly. "I put it in the laundry. Mrs. Finch didn't return it to you?"

"No," Lilly said.

"I'll see to it. You'll have it by the end of the day."

"Okay," she said.

"Fine," he said.

As Lilly moved past him she had the urge to fling his shirt at him. Knitting a sweater for him was a ridiculous idea anyway. He wouldn't want it. He'd never wear it and he'd certainly never appreciate the time and effort she put into making it.

"Lilly," he said, stopping her in her tracks. She'd almost gotten away! "This is for you. I...I should have given it to you before I left for New York." Surprised by the non-abrasive timbre of his voice, and even more by the way he stuttered, Lilly turned around. He was holding an envelope, and she realized belatedly it had been in his hand all along. "I was on my way... I was going to leave it in your room."

Lilly took the envelope but she didn't open it. She couldn't resist one final rib. "So you could snoop through *my* things?"

His eyes narrowed. Whatever gentleness had been in him a moment before was gone. "If there is a child, you will mention it to no one, except me. Including your sister. Is that clear?"

"You can't stop—"

"You're not to mention it to your sister! You're not to mention it to anyone. Except for church, no more trips to town for you or for Charlotte."

"How dare—"

"If I find out you've been to see Rob August again, your *church* privilege will be taken away as well. Do you understand?"

"Perfectly!" Lilly hissed, and she stormed out, unwilling and unable to listen to any more from the rude monster. So much for buying more yarn to make him a sweater! She'd be damned if she'd waste her time making anything for the ungrateful, boorish clod!

Thirty-Seven

Thief of architectural drawings or not, Gabriel wasn't the clod, Lilly thought. She was.

She fastened the amethyst and diamond necklace around her neck. The earrings were sparkling in the mirror. But her reflection didn't hold her attention this time. What did was the envelope on the vanity table in front of her. Inside was bank account information. He'd opened two bank accounts, both in her name, the day after they'd married. The combined balances were staggering.

She should have looked in the envelope before arguing with him. If he, by chance, showed up for dinner with Alex and Susan tonight, she would apologize. And she would thank him too, for the jewelry and the flowers and chocolates. Tentatively she touched the necklace, running her finger along the inner edge low on her chest. She'd put it on every day just to look at it, and every day she'd dreamed of his touch on her skin.

What was wrong with her? Lilly jumped up from her seat. She owed him nothing. She'd agreed to this arrangement for Julie's sake, not for her own. She was supposed to be provided with funds. She'd just mistakenly believed she wouldn't receive them until after their *quiet divorce*.

When she looked in the mirror again a shiver raced through her from head to toe. It wasn't caused by fear or revulsion. It was caused by the way her skin tingled, by the way her lower stomach twisted.

He was two different people. That was the only answer. The man who was so generous and thoughtful, the man who created the wonder and rapture she'd felt in his arms was not the same man who spoke to her so harshly. In bed he used his tongue in ways that made her quiver just thinking of them. Out of bed that tongue was a crude reminder of what he really was—an evil, heartless creature who cared nothing at all for his child!

She was a dimwitted fool for being unable to control her flippant feelings. One minute she despised him. The next he did something munificent. As she headed out of her room she glanced at the closed door to his dreary room. A part of her wanted to scream at him. Another part wanted to reach out and touch him. Just touch him.

At least, she mused as she descended the staircase, her attire this night couldn't be faulted. The gown was stunning by itself. With the complementing jewels, it was even more incredible. She'd taken special care with her hair, drawing it up in an elegant chignon, similar to one she'd seen on Molly Finch, the one she'd been copying more often of late. Long strands were hanging down her back. It was the first time in her life she could remember feeling completely confident about her appearance.

There was no one in the hall, but she could hear Charlotte in the parlor. And Gabriel was with her. For a second Lilly contemplated going to join them, but she hesitated.

"Come on, Daddy!" Charlotte chortled. "I'm hungry!" The door to the parlor swung inward. Gabriel was looking down at Charlotte and she knew he didn't see her until Charlotte chirped, "Momma!"

His head jerked up and his eyes roved over her, from the floor upward then back again. When he finished the first perusal, he did it again, this time settling his gaze briefly on the necklace. Self-consciously Lilly plucked at it. Their eyes met. And held.

"Daddy, doesn't Momma look pretty?" Charlotte yanked on his arm.

He didn't answer Charlotte's question verbally, but his head dipped in a curt nod. Lilly was still trying to recover from the prickling sensations his slow, appreciative perusal caused. She was unable to do anything but stare back at him.

He took a step toward her, and another. Lilly didn't see his limp at all. All she saw was his eyes, his dark and intriguing presence, moving closer.

Whatever his intentions were, however, she would never know. The knocker from the door sounded and the hall was suddenly filled with greetings.

"Miss Hawthorne. Oh, I'm sorry," Alex shook his head and grinned apologetically. "I mean Mrs. Drayton. You are stunning!"

Lilly smiled tentatively.

"Yes, quite lovely," Susan said. "Shall we go to the dining room? Alex? Charlotte? Mark, come along."

Lilly was still in the same place, feeling flustered, watching the children, and Alex escorting Susan.

"Lilly?" Gabriel was a step away, and he still startled her. He was holding out his left hand for her to take. "Shall we?"

"I've been meaning to thank you," she managed to murmur, "for the gifts."

"The necklace suits you," he whispered, leaning closer. "Do you like it?"

This was the raspy voice she remembered from the bedroom. Once again she found herself trapped by his gaze. Her hand was suddenly in his. His fingertips grazed her palm, tickling, sending more goose-bump raising chills. Then his fingers slid between hers, entwining them together. He'd held her hand that same way—in his bed! She felt his strength, and an unexpected, yet sublime and suggestive tenderness. Lilly's stomach clenched. Her toes curled. Her breath quickened.

"Daddy! Momma!" Charlotte called out. "Why are you taking so long?"

Startled, Lilly yanked her hand out of his. "We're coming. I'm sorry." It was all she could do to get her bearings again. Because she had no other choice, she strode forward, leaving Gabriel to follow. At the door to the dining room she looked back. All the sultry warmth she'd seen in him a moment before was gone.

At least dinner was pleasant. Gabriel and Susan even seemed to get along. They didn't acknowledge each other much, but they didn't fight. While Lilly sat there, absently listening to the random dialogue, it dawned on her that Rob August hadn't come to share a meal with them all week. She found it odd, especially considering how many times he and Molly had been at Drayton Hall while Gabriel was away. Since Gabriel had forbidden her to go to town, the plans for Molly to accompany her and Charlotte on another shopping excursion would never come to fruition. Gabriel's pointed comment that she and Charlotte not see Rob reminded her of the way Rob had stormed out of his house last Sunday morning carrying a crate. Withers had collected a second one. Rob had come to the side of the carriage, but he hadn't peeked in to say hello. He hadn't even acknowledged Charlotte, which wasn't like the overly amiable person she knew him to be, especially where Charlotte was concerned.

Lilly wouldn't have dared to ask Gabriel about his dealings with Rob. It was none of her business, but she couldn't help wondering if they'd had a falling out. She couldn't help wondering what happened to those crates that had been stowed on the back of the carriage contained. She was still thinking about Rob and the crates when Charlotte announced it was time for them to go to the parlor.

After the evening festivities, when Gabriel told Charlotte it was time for bed, Lilly excused herself. But she didn't go to bed. Gabriel was playing the piano and he continued to play long after Charlotte was settled for the night. Dressed in a warm, white cashmere robe—part of her new wardrobe—Lilly slipped out to the stairs and sat down with her back propped against the railing. As it had the first time she'd heard it, Gabriel's music captivated her. She stayed where she was for a long time, even after her eyelids grew heavy. With her arm tucked under her head, she lay down on the steps. Even with the hard slate stairs under her she was exceedingly comfortable. The incredible sounds doused her in tranquility.

She didn't remember hearing the music stop. But she was dreaming of Gabriel's hands on her skin, on her back, tracing the line of her spine. The pressure of his touch grew, turning from a light caress to a serene massage, melting every muscle in her body. It was so nice, so...

"Lilly?"

Her eyes popped open. The lamps along the staircase were lit, but the light was very dim. All she saw was an eerie silhouette—a dark, imposing figure looming large just a few steps below her.

She shrieked and bolted upright, scrambling somewhat to get to her feet. The abrupt terror fell away as she recognized the apparition.

"Are you ill?" he said gruffly.

"No. I'm sorry. You just scared me."

"Why are you sleeping out here?" he asked.

"I'm not sleeping. I'm listening. I mean, I was listening. I must have fallen asleep. Your music is really beautiful."

He didn't say anything.

"I didn't mean to scream," she murmured again, turning around. Whether it was the dimness of the light, or that she wasn't fully awake, she didn't know, but she missed the step and tripped. She landed on her hands and jammed a knee into the sharp corner of the stair so hard a soft cry flew out of her.

There was a funny thump of noise, and then a repeated clanking, but Lilly didn't know what caused it. Terribly embarrassed, all she cared about was standing up again, and getting away from Gabriel. Before she could move, she felt a light touch on her back, at her waist. His presence was so close beside her she could feel the body heat emanating from him.

As she straightened, he took her hand. His other hand was still firm on her waist. He was on his knees, on the step, but he lifted her. Lilly floated to her feet, feeling more like a feather than a deadweight buffoon. Gabriel didn't stand. He was still kneeling there, looking up at her. Shadows from the lamps played across the right side of his face, and Lilly's stomach fluttered. He was so terribly attractive!

"You're okay?" he murmured.

"Yes," she whispered. Her knee was still smarting, but she barely felt it. His hand slid out of hers like a breath of air. Her whole arm and shoulder tingled from it.

She started to turn, to go to her room, when she noticed his cane lying at the bottom of the staircase. Belatedly she realized it was the cane she'd heard clanking its way down the slate stairs. He'd dropped it to come to her aid.

She saw him reach for the railing to pull himself to his feet, and something changed in his face. "You dropped your cane," she said. "Let me get it."

"Leave it!" he barked.

"But I can get—"

"Leave it!"

She did leave it.

She was lying in her bed, unable to sleep, thinking about the morphine, thinking about his tender touch, thinking about him stealing architectural designs, thinking about the money he'd given her, thinking about his demand that she not go to town, thinking about everything he'd done for Julie, thinking about the way his face lighted when he smiled, thinking about his neglect of Charlotte. Her thoughts were still spinning back and forth from the bad to the good and back again when she heard him go to Charlotte's room the way he always did. Long after he'd returned to his own chambers she was still thinking—thinking of everything that was just... *him*.

Thirty-Eight

The first snow of the season came in late December, a few days before Christmas, on the same night as the full moon, dumping more than a foot of powdery white on the valley. The farthest thing from Charlotte's mind that morning was school. She wanted to make a snowman, and could speak of nothing else while she, Lilly and Gabriel ate breakfast.

"Will you, Daddy? Will you help me make a snowman for Christmas?"

Gabriel lowered the newspaper he was reading and looked from Charlotte to Lilly and then back again. "You have lessons."

"Can't I skip lessons today? *Pleeease?*" Charlotte whined.

"That's up to Momma, not me."

Lilly couldn't help smiling, and she turned away. It was the first time Gabriel had referred to her that way, and although it sounded funny in his deep, gravelly voice, she liked it. Probably more than she should have. It was all she could do to hide her reaction. "I think it will be fine to skip school for a few days. We'll call it a Christmas break."

A month ago Lilly would not have agreed to give Charlotte a day off. But Charlotte's schoolwork had improved drastically. This was due primarily, not to Lilly's own diligence, but to Gabriel's.

For the last several weeks, with the exception of a few trips to Philadelphia which required him to stay overnight, he'd been more present in their lives than ever before. He appeared for dinner often and even breakfast a handful of times. In the evenings, in the parlor his focus was on Charlotte. Lilly had to admit it was quite intriguing watching their interaction.

Up until then, she'd never really observed him with Charlotte. The few times she had seen them together had been too brief. The fondness

Charlotte harbored for him was obvious. There was nothing new there. But, over time, Lilly couldn't help wondering whether she'd been wrong about his detachment. Regardless of how silly or ridiculous Charlotte's statements or requests were, or how relentless, Gabriel always responded to her. The latest of Charlotte's obsessions was building blocks. She asked Gabriel for more repeatedly. His response was always the same, "No, Charlotte, I won't buy you more blocks!" But then he did buy them.

Once, during the time Charlotte was supposed to be taking her bath, Lilly found Gabriel and Charlotte together in her playroom, sprawled out on the floor together building a tower.

Gabriel's attention to Charlotte didn't end with the blocks. Their evenings in the parlor developed into a routine of sorts. Every night, Gabriel played the piano while Charlotte pirouetted about the room. Next they played with whatever toy Charlotte brought down from her playroom. She actually had Gabriel holding dolls a couple times! At Gabriel's first call for Charlotte's bedtime, Charlotte ran up to change and returned with a book. She tucked herself beside Gabriel on the sofa and read to him. Lilly couldn't say Gabriel was patient with Charlotte. She'd heard him bark at her too many times for that. He was demanding. If she said a word that wasn't exactly right, he stopped her, pointed his finger under the word and made her to sound out each letter until she had it right. At first, Lilly thought Gabriel was too gruff, but seeing the results—Charlotte actually learning—Lilly's opinion was changing.

And, to supplement the reading, he and Charlotte had come up with a letter system on the piano that wasn't even close to being musically correct, but it utilized every letter of the alphabet. At first Lilly had been skeptical, but within a few days, Charlotte had begun to spell words that a few weeks earlier she would never have been able to figure out. Her progress was, to say the least, miraculous.

But the ultimate question still remained—did Gabriel really care about his daughter? He tolerated her. He endured without complaint, but the irritation in his expression and the gruff stipulations made it difficult to tell. Honestly, Lilly didn't know.

Charlotte interrupted Lilly's musings. "Daddy is good at building snowmen! We made a snowman last year and he was so big it took days and days and days for him to melt!"

Lilly laughed, and her eyes settled on Gabriel. But not for long. They never settled on him for long. Their eyes met and she looked away. She had to.

"Come with us, Momma!" Charlotte twittered.

"As tempting an offer as that is, I really should check on Julie. Last night she wasn't feeling well." It was true. Last night, Julie had come to the mansion complaining of an ache in her back. She'd looked miserable and not at all like herself.

It wasn't long before Charlotte and Gabriel, clad in coats and scarves and warm gloves, were on their way outside. Lilly took her time getting ready for her jaunt across the field, and then she took another moment to peek into the parlor at the decorations she and Charlotte had used to adorn the room. There were red bows on the windows, wreaths on the doors, garland draped over the fireplace mantel, a crèche she'd found in Julie's things set up on the sofa table. The only thing missing to give the room the full effects of holiday cheer was a tree. That, however, would be rectified soon enough. Withers was going to bring them a tree on Christmas Eve.

There were so many things Lilly would have liked to do to the horribly dreary room to make it more inviting, but it wasn't her place, or her right. She needed to be content with the little they'd done. All of the decorations were homemade thanks to Julie, who, for all her faults, was extremely creative. For once Lilly had no complaints about Julie's tendency to hoard things. The endless supply of craft materials in Julie's stash provided everything they'd needed, and it had been quite fun assembling ornaments with Charlotte.

Gabriel's only comment about their decorations had been a cryptically clipped, "They're fine."

In Julie's stockpiles Lilly had also found several balls of black wool yarn—more than enough to knit a sweater for him. She'd deliberated over whether to make it several times. The irritated part of her wanted to be able to caustically say to him, "I'm sorry I don't have a Christmas gift for you, but I wasn't allowed to go to town to get one." The other part of her—the one she couldn't shake off, no matter how hard she tried—insisted she get started knitting, lest she not finish in time.

On her way across the lawn she passed him and Charlotte. The bottom ball of their snowman was coming along nicely. Charlotte was laughing, attempting to pile and pack snow on top as Gabriel slowly rolled the thing. Lilly caught herself smiling, and then became annoyed for warming toward Gabriel. Again!

She was almost to Julie's cottage when Withers came out of it. Why he would have been inside Julie's cottage at this time of day roused her, but she didn't have time to dwell on it. Withers' anxiety was obvious. His hands were wringing. "The baby is coming. Julie said I should ask you to come."

Lilly found her sister dressed in her nightclothes and robe, pacing back and forth in her bedroom. "This is no fun!" Julie whined, arching her back.

Wryly Lilly looked at her sister. "Shouldn't you lie down?"

"Mrs. Finch told me when the contractions began I should walk around. It will help the baby come faster."

"Where is Mrs. Finch?" Weeks ago, Mrs. Finch had agreed to assist with the birth. That is, she'd agreed to assist after Mr. Finch informed them his wife had midwifed many times.

"She was here, but she went back home to get some towels or something. She said it will take several more hours," Julie said. "I just hope she's wrong. I hope this baby comes very soon."

Julie's hopes, however, were dashed. Twelve hours later, long after darkness had settled in again, the baby was still not born. According to Mrs. Finch, everything was going exactly as it should. She was calm and surprisingly reassuring, especially for Julie, who was in such discomfort.

Lilly spent most of the time doing her best to soothe Julie. Withers ran numerous errands, bringing sustenance for all of them, warming water, stoking fires. Lilly was aware, through Withers, that Gabriel had come by to ask after Julie, but Lilly didn't see him. She found herself wishing there was a piano in the cottage and he was there, playing it.

She'd been listening to him play from the steps every night. But, as soon as he stopped, she quickly retreated to the safe confines of her suite. She hadn't thought he knew, until two nights ago.

Two nights ago, Charlotte had run out of the parlor on her way to bed, and Lilly got up to follow.

"Lilly?"

Her name, spoken in Gabriel's husky whisper, stopped her in her tracks. She turned back.

"You don't have to sit on the stairs. You could... you could stay..." he stammered, sounding oddly humble. But then his reticence flip-flopped into the usual caustic growl, "Never mind!"

"I just need to tuck Charlotte in," Lilly murmured, though she wasn't sure he heard her. He was already moving away.

After kissing Charlotte goodnight, Lilly crept back down the stairs and tiptoed into the parlor. Gabriel's eyes were closed, his head was down and he was pounding away at the keys. This wasn't how he appeared when he played Charlotte's dance songs. Now he was consumed. The piece was discordantly minor and intensely riveting. It was a brewing storm, thunder crashing, wind whipping, lightning striking. The storm grew steadily worse, destroying everything in its path. It was so mesmeric Lilly's knees began to tremble. To keep herself from collapsing to the floor, she dropped into the wing chair. From there, because of the immense raised lid of the piano, she couldn't see Gabriel at all.

The piece droned on, bespeaking of a terrified, tormented soul, unable to find the slightest bit of hope. And then at the brink, when it seemed all would be lost, when the bass notes were so heavy they vibrated up through the floor, through her legs and into her chest, everything changed. Whispery sounds began to fall from the upper registers of the piano, fleetingly running downward, bringing not just hope, but a deeply heartfelt tranquility. It was so emotionally powerful, and so beautiful, Lilly could have cried, and she supposed maybe she did, a very little bit.

When the piece came to an end, Gabriel moved on to another. He played for a long time. Some of his music she'd heard before, but most of it was new. Regardless, all of it held her in its grip, evoking emotions from deep within. She found herself wondering, not for the first time, if the music drew and soothed him as much as it did her. It must, she'd reasoned, otherwise, he wouldn't play as often as he did.

It was very late when he ended it all. It was odd, too, because she'd never heard him finish quite that way before. He just stopped, mid-piece. That, and the sudden growl he made as he rose, startled Lilly. She sat upright in the chair.

He moved out from behind the piano. "Oh!" The word came out of him more as a gasp.

He hadn't known she was there. Worried she'd misinterpreted the stuttered invitation he'd made earlier, and that he was angry, she rose quickly. "I enjoyed it very much. Thank you." And she'd fled.

Another contraction brought Lilly out of her daydream.

Well after midnight Mrs. Finch announced it was time for Julie to begin pushing. Lilly supported her sister the way Mrs. Finch instructed as well as she could. Julie was drenched in sweat and screaming with each horrid push. Despite Mrs. Finch's words of reassurance, Lilly didn't think Julie could take anymore.

The wailing cry from Julie's baby began almost from the moment the tiny body slithered the rest of the way out. "Ya have a little girl," Mrs. Finch said. Julie began to cry, holding her hands out, desperate for her child to be in them.

Mrs. Finch worked tirelessly, taking care of the umbilical cord, the afterbirth and everything else that needed to be taken care of. She gave Julie a sponge bath and changed her bed sheets. Finally, once the baby had its first feeding, Mrs. Finch swaddled her and put her in the cradle beside the bed. Not long thereafter, Julie fell asleep. Mrs. Finch told Lilly she was going home to get some rest and that she would be back in the morning.

Exhausted and emotionally drained more than she cared to admit, Lilly thanked Mrs. Finch and walked her out. Then she went back to the bedroom and stared at her sleeping sister for a long time. It was amazing that after all Julie had been through, she appeared so content. She didn't look the least bit the worse for wear. Even so, fear overwhelmed, as Lilly wondered how the birth of her own child would go. She wasn't as brave as Julie. She was afraid she wouldn't be able to go through with it at all.

Lilly lowered the lamps and crept from the room. Rather than going back to the mansion, she'd decided to spend the night on the small sofa in the sitting room. It wouldn't be right to leave Julie or the baby alone. But first, she needed some tea—just one simple cup of tea—to help calm her tumultuous emotional state. Without it, she would never be able to relax. And sleep would be impossible.

But then, when she stepped into the kitchen, she was barely able to contain a startled shriek.

Gabriel was seated at the small table. She hadn't heard him come in. She hadn't known he was in the cottage. Abruptly, awkwardly, he rose to his feet.

"I didn't mean to scare you. Withers told me—" He cut himself off and said, "Tea?"

"Yes."

"You're tired," he said.

There was something odd about his attire. His facial covering was in place, but the scarf around his neck looked different. It took a second for Lilly to figure out why. It wasn't tucked as tightly into the collar of his shirt. The buttons there were open, leaving the scarf hanging loosely—loosely enough to expose a tiny patch of skin at the base of his throat. She started for the stove and the tea pot sitting on it.

"No," he murmured. "I meant... I meant... I will bring it to you."

Unsure, Lilly nodded, but floundered briefly before heading back to the sitting room. There she sank down onto the little sofa. Her legs felt like cooked pasta, ready to buckle under her. Her head ached, her stomach was churning and she thought her eyes couldn't even see right. In the dim light of the kitchen lamps, Gabriel had looked so... pure and solid and she didn't even know what...

He limped into the room with a saucer in his free hand. He brought it right to her, the tips of his fingers brushing hers as he handed it over.

The cup rattled on its saucer. To prevent it from spilling, she set it down on her lap. In those seconds while she willed her body to stop trembling, Gabriel did something she never expected. He sat down beside her, not at the other end of the small sofa, but right next to her, so close she could smell his scent, feel his warmth. Before she knew what he was about, he took the saucer from her lap and leaned across her just enough to set it on the end table.

"*Shhh*," he whispered, and his arm came around her shoulders, drawing her close to him. Cradled against his chest that way, her tears came in earnest. She could do nothing to prevent them or stop them. They rolled from her eyes and made her entire body shudder. The only thing that kept her upright was Gabriel's strength surrounding her like a wonderful, velvet blanket.

"I'm sorry," she managed to mumble. "I don't know why I'm crying."

"It's okay," he whispered. "It's okay to cry."

After a while she was aware of the wet spots on his shirt she'd created. He hadn't moved, hadn't uttered a sound, hadn't complained. All she could hear were the faint sounds of leaves rustling in the wind outside and the occasional hoot of an owl. All she could feel was the thump of his heart under her cheek.

That Gabriel could be capable of such compassion and such selflessness didn't register. What did was that she felt her headache fading away. She felt her limbs becoming like jelly. The churning in her stomach changed to nervous butterflies. There were no tears any longer, just peace and comfort and…

"Gabriel," she whispered and raised her head to look at him, to see the line of his shadowed jaw, to see the pulse at the base of his throat.

He angled his head and their eyes met. She could feel his warm breath on her skin. She could see the paler grey streaks in his eyes. She could see every eyelash. They were long and thick and dark, outlining his eyes in such a perfect way, and how had she never noticed them before?

Her lips parted of their own accord. All she knew was she suddenly couldn't breathe. But what was stealing the air from her wasn't terror.

It was something very different. Her eyes dropped to his mouth, taking in the fullness of his bottom lip, the slight thickening skin at the center of his upper lip, the ridge where his skin turned from tan to pink. Her fingertip touched him there and trailed along that ridge. She arched back a little farther, felt his breath rush out of him and her eyes closed.

Then his soft fingers fluttered over and held her cheek. His lips met hers. At first it was just a fleeting, gentle caress, but it didn't stay that way. Lilly heard herself whimper. She heard his breath again, rougher this time, almost a moan. She knew the sound. She'd experienced it before, and it was no less enthralling this time.

What followed was amazing. Lilly clung to him, feeling nothing, nothing at all, except pure rapture. When he moved, she thought for a moment he was pulling away. Her fingers fisted in his shirt in protest, but she wouldn't have needed to. He wasn't leaving. He was turning, adjusting, steering her gently to deepen their incredible connection. She felt his fingers in her hair, brushing through it. She felt his ardor intensify and she gave into it completely. His taste and touch were so sublime she couldn't think. She didn't have the ability to do anything else. Nothing, except submit to more of this wonder…

She never heard the door open. She didn't hear anything. Suddenly Gabriel's mouth wrenched away from hers. His body stiffened. Lilly's eyes opened. She was looking at his jaw. His head was turned toward the cottage entrance. Only then did she feel the brush of cold air, and the click as the door was pushed closed.

It was Withers. "I'm sorry. I…I…er…uh… I came to make sure the fires… to make sure they don't go out… for Miss Julie's baby… I'm very sorry."

Withers' cheeks were candy-apple red. Lilly averted her eyes so as not to embarrass him further. Only then did she realize where her hand was, tucked into the open front of Gabriel's shirt. She could feel the ridge of his collarbone under her palm, the hard muscle where his neck connected with his shoulder under her fingers. Instantly she withdrew.

"It's fine, Withers," Gabriel said. He waited until Withers disappeared into the kitchen, then asked her, "You're staying the night here?" His eyes were veiled, but glistening as they stared into hers.

"I have to be here in case the baby wakes," Lilly managed to say.

"Is there anything you want from the house?"

She couldn't think. "A change of clothes. Something to sleep in."

"Fine." He just kept looking at her, searching her eyes with his own. Not moving. Not saying anything.

He didn't move until Withers returned, arms laden with logs. Then he grabbed his cane and pushed himself up. "When you're finished here, meet me in my study," he said to Withers, who nodded and went about stoking fires.

The loss of Gabriel's close presence sent a chill running through Lilly. She watched him limp the short distance to the door and she wanted to call him back, but he slipped through it before she could. She was still staring after him when Withers said, "Is it okay for me to go into the bedroom?"

Lilly told him to go ahead. Not long thereafter he left, supposedly to meet with Gabriel. Lilly was still sitting on the sofa, holding the empty tea cup on her lap when Withers came back. This time he was carrying a small trunk. "Mr. Drayton said I should bring this to you."

The trunk contained everything Lilly had asked for, and then some. Gabriel had packed her hairbrushes, lotions, toothbrush, everything she would need to take care of herself for the night and the day that followed. Had she put together a bag for herself she would have forgotten half of it.

She was in a daze, unaware of her surroundings, unaware of anything. Nothing mattered anymore. Nothing at all... except that kiss.

Thirty-Nine

"I've brought yer mail, sir," Finch said.

Gabriel looked up from the papers on his desk to see Finch roll into the room. He took the small stack of letters from Finch's hand. "Is Charlotte still with Withers?"

"Yes, sir."

Finch bowed to him as if he were some kind of royalty. The old man had been making the gesture since day one of his employment, more than three years ago. In the beginning, Finch's bows had annoyed him. After a while they began to amuse him. He was still half smirking as he watched Finch scurry away. Rob had hired the Finches for him, after his friend had convinced him to move back to Drayton Hall, just weeks after he'd been released from the hospital.

Gabriel let out a sigh and absently rubbed his left thigh. It had been his own foolish pride that had kept him in Philadelphia after the threats began. He'd received ten of them over the six-month period before the fire. He'd laughed about them. The pathetic, cryptically written proclamations of his imminent death were ridiculous. He certainly hadn't taken them seriously. Rob had accused him of thinking he was invincible.

But he wasn't invincible. The fire had proved that well enough. One of the threatening letters had stated that fire would be the means to his end. The fire set in his house had been deliberate. Whoever had done it wanted him to die. The scars of his own stupidity for failing to heed those threats would be his to bear for the rest of his life.

Gabriel had spent the morning with Charlotte to allow Lilly time with her sister. This afternoon he'd left his daughter in Withers' care, hoping to take care of a few matters he couldn't afford to put off, namely correspondence from Dobbins. About Rob.

Gabriel hadn't seen Rob at all in the weeks since he'd removed him as trustee of the estate, but he knew everything Rob had done. Twice he'd been to Philadelphia and once, for several days, to New York. In Havertown he'd gone to the bank, the clothiers, the jewelers, the butcher shop and the bakery. He'd bought a new horse—an Arabian. Several evenings he'd attended social engagements, all with people he merely tolerated for the sake of his law practice. He'd gone to Alex and Susan's house as well. That time Alex had been home, but Susan was out. Once he'd taken Molly to the theatre. He'd been to see the minister at the church three times, but not during regular church services. He'd gone to the courthouse for hearings and trials and to the law library at the University. A handful of clients had come to his office, all of whom, Dobbins said, were above board.

None of those activities were unusual for Rob, except perhaps the visits to the minister—Rob wasn't a particularly religious man. None of them troubled Gabriel. What did were the trips Rob had made to Drayton Hall. Ten times in the last four weeks, he'd come by, six on horseback and four by coach. In every case, he'd stopped at the end of the drive, never venturing further. After waiting several minutes, he'd continued on.

The letter Beatrice had shown Gabriel was so incriminating it couldn't be ignored. It was written cryptically, but the innuendo was readily evident. Beatrice had told him she'd found it in a satchel Rob had inadvertently left behind during his last visit with her. In the letter, the writer was hiring two men—men he was acquainted with—promising them an enormous sum of money to dispose of *the target* in a manner of their choosing. The target was *a wild boar*. The only stipulation was that the target's demise had to appear to be an accident. The letter was signed C.A. D--------n.

Charles Andrew Drayton, II, was the name Rob was using in New York. He had bank accounts in that name. Six years ago, he'd started a business there—a paper business. In the beginning it had been fairly lucrative, but in the last two years that had changed. While in New York, Gabriel had met with Rob's business partner, a man named Stebbins. Stebbins knew Rob only as Charles Drayton, and referred to him as Charlie. Under other circumstances Gabriel would have found this amusing. Their father would never deign to allow anyone to refer to him thusly. Such a nickname would have been beneath the heinous old man.

Their father. How strange it was to think of. How strange and…

He couldn't think of it. He couldn't because it made all of this so much more agonizing.

After discovering Rob's paper company had steadily been losing customers, through his own contacts, and through the contacts of Charles Drayton, Senior, Gabriel had secured several new clients for the business—popular publishing houses. If the paper mill continued to run efficiently, within the next several years, Rob—or rather Charles Andrew Drayton, II—would became a very wealthy man.

At first, upon learning of Rob's parentage, and hearing Beatrice's suspicions, Gabriel had scoffed them off as utter nonsense. But after deliberating over that horrid letter, his anger had begun to set in. The parchment used for that letter was the same parchment Rob used in his law practice. It was the same parchment that had been used for the death threats Gabriel had received in Philadelphia. That parchment had been made by Rob's paper mill. In addition, the penmanship was identical. Gabriel knew Rob's handwriting. What he couldn't figure out was why, after all these years he'd never made the connection between Rob's handwriting and the original death threats.

There were times, since his return from New York, Gabriel had been unable to control his temper. He'd thrown vases, plates, glasses, the water pitcher, and a heavy paperweight across his father's office, breaking them on the fireplace, the wall, or whatever else they happened to hit. He'd ripped up drawings he'd spent months working on. He'd paced the halls, the stairs, his study, and his father's office, walking and walking until his leg ached so badly he could no longer bear to stand. Somewhere along the line his fury had shifted into guilt.

He'd gone riding, something he hadn't done since the fire, forcing himself to endure the pain of it. And it hurt. Badly. But he refused to stop. He'd wanted to feel that pain. He'd needed to feel it, because he deserved it! No matter how desperately he searched his mind, he couldn't figure out what he'd done. All he knew was that he'd caused Rob to suffer so horrendously, Rob had not just turned against him. Rob loathed him enough to kill him.

The day he went riding, he'd run his mount to excessive speeds. He'd taken jumps he would have never considered before the fire when his equestrian skills had been at their finest. In his rage, he'd wanted the horse to throw him. He'd wanted to be thrown, and killed. Then, Rob, the vile betrayer, the one person in the world Gabriel had always believed truly cared about him, would have what he wanted!

Gabriel barely remembered returning to the stables, but he remembered falling off the horse and landing in the dirt. He'd lain there in the dark, gasping, retching, groaning. He didn't know how long he'd been that way. What he knew by then was that the pain was so excruciating he couldn't get up. Withers had found him and helped him. Withers had practically carried him back to the mansion.

As the days passed, the guilt had turned into denial. There had to be some plausible explanation for the letter. Memories had swarmed him, good ones, bad ones, old ones, recent ones. He and Rob had been through too much together. They knew too much about each other. Rob had been so distraught over the news of his illness, he'd had tears in his eyes. Thereafter Rob's concern had been evident in his almost daily visits. Rob had almost cried again when he'd learned the illness was no more. The letter, Gabriel was sure, was exactly what it appeared on the surface—a planned hunting excursion, nothing more.

Because the letter was with Rob's things, it had never been delivered, which meant if it really was a cryptic call for murder, and even if at one time Rob had been upset enough to want him killed, he hadn't gone through with it. The old threats—Rob couldn't possibly have written them. They were too pathetic, too tactless and the prose too clumsy. Gabriel knew Rob's ability with words. Rob wrote with much more finesse.

What if… what if someone else had put the letter in Rob's things for Beatrice to find, solely to implicate Rob? Or what if Beatrice had planted it herself? Gabriel was well aware that Beatrice's feelings for him were not exactly warm. Nevertheless there was nothing she would gain by his death. There was no motive. Except perhaps, hatred. But then, why would she accuse her own son? A son she purportedly felt a tremendous amount of guilt over for having abandoned as an infant?

Rob was his *brother!*

Gabriel couldn't think about this anymore. His mind was becoming so twisted, his thoughts were a baffled mess of insanity. He had to stop thinking about it! Just stop!

He took a sip of his coffee. It had cooled, and he needed more, but he downed what remained in his cup. Then he squeezed his eyes shut and breathed out. He hadn't been sleeping well, but last night, it hadn't been thoughts of Rob keeping him awake. Last night, long after he'd checked on Charlotte, he'd waited up for news of Julie's baby's birth. It was well after two o'clock when Withers came to tell him the child was a girl.

"Mrs. Gibson is well?" Gabriel had asked him.

"I believe so, sir," Withers had said.

Gabriel had been relieved by the news, so much so he'd felt his muscles slowly unclenching. He hadn't realized how tense he'd become.

"I saw the baby, sir," Withers had gone on. The man had been grinning, and rambling as if he couldn't help himself. "She's a little tiny thing, but cute as a button. Mrs. Finch wrapped her up in a pink blanket and put a pink bonnet on her head. She opened her eyes and looked at me. Blue as the night sky they are—"

"I'm glad to hear it," Gabriel had cut in. "And Mrs. Drayton? She's still there?"

"I believe she intends to stay the night," Withers had said.

So Gabriel had gone there, to Julie's cottage, in the middle of the night. Not because of the baby, but because of Lilly. He didn't understand why, but he'd needed to see her. Just see her. He'd crept quietly into Julie's cottage and listened to the quiet treads he knew were Lilly's coming from beyond the closed door to Julie's bedroom. He'd gone to the kitchen, made tea and waited, thinking of his last trip to town and the stop he'd made at the office of an interior decorator.

Burgundy, Gabriel had told the man. According to Charlotte, Lilly's favorite color was burgundy.

She had appeared in the kitchen doorway like an angel, dressed in pale blue that matched her eyes. She'd been an ethereal vision, not real. But before she could turn away, he'd seen her tears.

"Tears are for babies! Are you a baby, boy? Don't you dare cry!" His father had yelled at him. He'd been sitting on the bench in the garden. Beatrice had been beside him.

"He's just a boy," Beatrice said to his father and then she turned back to him. Her hand was on his back, rubbing in circles. "It's okay to cry, Gabriel. You go right ahead and cry. It's hard to lose your mother. I know you miss her—"

"It's *not* okay!" his father bellowed. "She doesn't deserve tears, least of all from her pathetic welp!" Up until then, Gabriel hadn't looked at his father, but then he did, just in time to see his father's arm swing. The open-handed blow was hard enough to make his head spin. It stung like the devil. "Don't you dare cry, boy, or there will be more where that came from!"

It was the first and last time his father had ever struck him for crying.

In Julie's cottage, to Lilly, he'd heard himself say, "It's okay to cry." The words had sounded hollow to his ears, like they'd been spoken by someone else. Yet he'd found himself unable to let go of her. The desire to comfort had consumed him to such an extent he'd begun to tremble from it. He'd pulled her close, wrapped his arms around her and just held on.

While holding her, he'd thought, as he had many times, that they'd failed to create a child. She would have known by then. She would have said something, but she hadn't. And he wondered if her tears were, at least in part, caused by sorrow over it.

It didn't matter, he'd told himself. It just didn't matter! He'd held her, finding contentment in a strange, surreal way that was unlike anything he'd ever known. He hadn't wanted to let go. He hadn't been able to.

He'd felt her stir, felt her lean away and he'd loosened his hold. She'd turned toward him and looked up, and he'd become trapped. Desire of an entirely different nature had shot through him. The intensity of it had been swift and disorienting. He'd gazed at her, paralyzed, unable to breathe, watching her eyes drift across his face and settle on his mouth. And then she'd touched him there. The invitation of her eyelids drifting closed and her lips parting had overwhelmed him.

He'd been devoured by that kiss, so carried away on the current of it, he'd lost sense of everything else in the room. He'd felt her clinging to him, felt her hand slip inside the buttons he'd forgotten were open on his shirt. Her tender touch had been directly on his skin, burning through him. Never in his life had he been so staggered by a kiss. Never in his life could he remember wanting like he'd wanted right then. Never in his life had he been so intensely enraptured by one particular woman.

Even now, sitting in his office, thinking of her had him leaning back, closing his eyes, as if he could return to the cottage, as if he could conjure her up out of thin air and have her in his arms, have his mouth slanting over hers. This time he would do it better. He would touch her, unbutton the tiny buttons at the front of her dress, slide his hands under the cloth. He knew the curve of her shoulder, her breast, the softness of, the taste of, her skin. He knew her heat, her perfect, silky warmth...

Gabriel sat up abruptly and grabbed the stack of letters Finch had brought him. He couldn't believe he'd been sitting there fantasizing! He was not sixteen anymore!

Roughly he ripped open the top envelope. It was nothing—a missive asking for money, a fundraiser for something. Probably one of Susan's many projects. Discarding it to be dealt with later, he moved on to the next one. It was from the law firm he used, but nothing that needed his immediate attention. The third envelope went straight to the waste basket. It was an invitation to a formal affair hosted by a well-respected family. His father had been particular friends with the gentleman of the house. The fourth envelope contained a single sheet of cream-colored paper of a heavier weight. He yanked it out and unfolded it absently.

Drayton,

Your time has come.

Christmas day you will suffer and die.

The fires of Hell await you.

Gabriel dropped the note like it scalded him. His breath came out in a rush. It was the same parchment, the same penmanship, the same poorly written prose.

He was a fool, a stupid, pathetic fool! The letter didn't surprise him. What did was the amount of time that had passed since that awful meeting with Rob. He'd convinced himself Rob was innocent. He'd planned to confess everything to Rob, to share what he suspected, to explain why he'd accused Rob of embezzlement and removed him as trustee. He was going to tell Rob he knew Rob didn't write that letter. Rob would forgive him his folly. They would sit in Rob's office, discuss it all over a glass of Jack Daniel's finest and laugh about it.

But he was wrong! Again!

Gabriel dropped his head into his hands. "Damn you, Rob," he choked out. "Damn you!"

Forty

Julie was remarkable. Lilly couldn't believe within three days, after having gone through the ordeal of childbirth, she was up and about, graciously turning down Lilly's offers of assistance. Julie wanted to care for her daughter on her own. Lilly had expected the opposite from her irresponsible sister, and she had to admit she was highly impressed by Julie's fortitude. Not only that, but Julie looked wonderful. Her eyes were sparkling. Her skin was glowing. Seeing her now, it was hard to believe she'd been embroiled in the misery of labor not so long ago.

"Do you think Gabriel will come?" Julie asked. Again.

"I don't know." The only thing about Julie that was annoying Lilly was her persistent requests for Gabriel to visit. She'd passed along two messages through Withers, but so far Gabriel had not responded. Withers, who'd been popping in to check on Julie every hour or so, last reported that after her riding lesson, Mr. Drayton had taken Charlotte out to play in the snow.

"Will you go ask him?" Julie prompted.

"I've already asked him. Withers has asked him, too," Lilly said, deflecting. "I want to run to the mansion for something. Will you be okay on your own for a few minutes?"

Julie's eyes narrowed. "I'm fine and you know it. You don't have to cater to me like a mother hen."

Lilly hid a smile and headed out. It was colder than she'd realized and the snow was still coming down, trickling in delicate drops. It was so beautiful and so peaceful, Lilly couldn't help herself. She began to spin. She kept going with her arms spread wide, her head thrown back, eyes closed, mouth open. The flakes fell like tiny nips of rain on her face, her eyelids, her tongue, instantly melting. She felt lighter than air.

The desire to dance, to just revel in the pleasure of it all, was inspired. Tomorrow was Christmas Eve! How perfect it would be if Gabriel were beside her, if he put his arms around her, drew her close. How perfect, if they were circling under the stars together, if he lowered his mouth to hers...

"Momma, look! Look what me and Daddy did! We made snow angels!"

Startled, Lilly came to a bobbling halt. Charlotte was running down the hill toward her. On the small rise of ground behind her Gabriel was sitting in the snow with his long legs stretched out in front of him. How she had not noticed the two of them she didn't know. They, on the other hand, had to have seen her spinning around, acting so childish and silly! Despite the cold, her face was suddenly overly warm.

Charlotte caught her hand and dragged her toward the hill.

"Look at mine!" Charlotte beamed as she gestured at the mess of flattened snow. Lilly was glad for the distraction. With the memory of... that incredible kiss... still fresh in her mind, she found it hard to look at Gabriel.

"Daddy! No!" Charlotte shrieked, "You're sticking your elbows in. Now your angel has holes in its back!"

He was indeed leaning back on his elbows. Lilly could barely contain her laughter as she watched him lie down and flap his arms. She had the sudden urge to lie down in the snow beside him, to reach out and take his hand in hers, to roll toward him, to...

"You fixed it!" Charlotte praised happily. "Daddy, you have to be careful when you get up, so you don't make more holes. Give me your hand."

Gabriel dug around in the snow to find his buried cane, then reached for Charlotte's outstretched hand. Charlotte yanked until he made it to one knee. Either his cane or his foot slid in the snow. He went sideways and Charlotte went with him. As they rolled, Charlotte scooped snow in her mitten and smashed it to his cheek. He growled and reciprocated, and then he was tickling her. Charlotte screeched and giggled. And Gabriel... oh my... Gabriel was smiling!

Whatever semblance of snow angels they'd made were completely lost in the playful wrestling. "Truce," Gabriel called out. Without getting up himself, he picked Charlotte up and deposited her on her feet. To Lilly, who was trying to help Charlotte brush the snow off her coat, he asked, "Everything is… is okay?"

"Everything is just fine," Lilly said. His question was referring to Julie and the baby, she knew that, but her answer had more to do with her. She was infused with happiness and she didn't even really know why. Her soul felt invaded by it. It was heady and wonderful and she didn't want it to ever end. "Would you both care to see the baby? Julie has asked if you would visit."

"Yes, Daddy! Please!" Exuberantly Charlotte jumped up and down.

"I don't know if it's such a good idea. Perhaps we should wait a few days," Gabriel said. "We've talked about this, Charlotte."

Charlotte's expression fell.

"It's okay. Really." Lilly held out her hand for Charlotte to take. "Come."

They went toward the cottage, arms swinging between them, when Charlotte called out, "Come on, Daddy! Hurry up!"

Lilly glanced back to see Gabriel plant his cane in the snow, and using it, roll to his knees. His movements were awkward and somewhat unsteady as he hefted himself the rest of the way to his feet. Lilly looked away. She should have offered to help him, given him her hand, something, but she hadn't thought! Behind her she could hear him shuffling along, following them.

"Daddy, you're covered in snow!" Charlotte giggled as they reached the door to the cottage.

Lilly turned. Charlotte was right. Following Charlotte's lead, Lilly lightly brushed snow from his shoulder. Both of them were covered, as were his coat sleeves. Lilly busied herself taking care of his arms while Charlotte went around and batted his back. At the same time, Gabriel bent forward to reach his thighs and knees. As he straightened, their eyes met.

She couldn't look at him. She just couldn't. Quickly, she stuttered, "Shall we go in?"

The moment she heard them enter, Julie called out from the bedroom, "Gabriel! Gabriel, is that you? And Charlotte? Oh, do come in! Come see!"

Julie was propped up on pillows, holding the newborn in her arms. As she stepped over to the bed, Charlotte's eyes grew round.

"What do you think, Charlotte?" Julie asked.

"It's a real live baby!" Charlotte squealed. "Look, Daddy!"

Gabriel was hovering by the bedroom door. "Gabriel, please come in. It's okay. I don't mind," Julie coaxed.

Gabriel didn't move, but his expression contained the same innocent curiosity evident in Charlotte. Looking at him, Lilly was struck by the similarity of his mouth, the line of chin, the shape of his eyes to his daughter. How had she not noticed before? The resemblance wasn't just obvious. It was almost uncanny. Charlotte was merely a smaller, daintier version of him.

"I named her Gabriella. After you," Julie said. "We wouldn't be here, so safe and comfortable, if it weren't for you."

Lilly couldn't tell whether Gabriel was touched by this or not.

"Would you like to hold her?" Julie prompted.

Gabriel shook his head, while Charlotte chirped, "I would! I would! Can I, Daddy?"

"You won't hurt her. Come." Julie wasn't talking to Charlotte. She was talking to Gabriel.

Something in his expression changed. Lilly couldn't tell what it was exactly. But she thought he suddenly looked oddly pale.

"We should go," he mumbled. "Charlotte, it's time to go. You can come back and see the baby another time."

"Oh, please don't go!" Julie called after them, but it was too late. Charlotte, for once, didn't argue and followed her father out. Somewhat taken aback by his abruptness, Lilly watched them through the window until she could no longer see them.

It was well past Charlotte's bedtime when finally Lilly decided to head back to the mansion. She was heeding Julie's advice. After so many nights cramped on the little sofa in the cottage, she was looking forward to a long, leisurely respite in her comfortable bed. Withers had promised to check in on them periodically, as he'd been graciously doing, so Lilly didn't need to worry about Julie and the baby.

Thanks to Mr. Finch, the hallways within the mansion were lighted, so it was easy to see. Just as she rounded the staircase into the hall, she heard the piano. She was tired, but as always, the beautiful tones summoned her. She couldn't resist peeking into the parlor.

Gabriel was absorbed in his music. Slowly she approached, her heels barely registering on the ugly carpet. She wanted to watch him, to see his fingers as they glided over the keys, to be close to him, to tell him how poignantly the melodies affected her.

The piece he played ended just as she reached the curved side of the instrument. Gabriel looked up.

"I heard you playing. I hope you don't mind…" she stammered.

"I'm sorry," he murmured.

"What for?"

"For leaving the cottage the way I did. I'm… I'm not good with babies. I don't know… Charlotte was only a few days old when… I… I couldn't… I didn't know how…"

Lilly closed the distance between them. She was beginning to recognize his stutters. They indicated his insecurity, and his fear. She was humbled, and astonished, and supremely touched that he would open up to her this way. "Charlotte adores you," she said quietly.

"I didn't care for her the way I should have," he said. There was such self-reproach in the comment, a lump formed in Lilly's throat. She reached out to him, intending only to offer comfort.

But before she could touch him, his demeanor changed. The scowl returned, and he stood so quickly, the heavy piano bench tipped on its rear legs. Gruffness fanned out of him, seeping not just into his words, but in the sudden stiffness of his frame and the way he whipped his cane around and planted it.

"You think there's a God?" he seethed. "What kind of God would give Charlotte to someone like me? I regret to inform you I won't be playing any more tonight."

He brushed past her. Lilly caught him by the arm and held on, causing him to fling around. Yet he wouldn't look at her. All she could see was the covered side of his face.

"What kind of God would give Charlotte to someone like you?" she said softly. "An extremely wise one."

He took a breath and another. His cane thumped to the floor and in that same second he took her head in his hands and brought his mouth down on hers. She felt the brush of his silk mask against her cheek, felt the ruthless fury in him, and she grabbed on, fisting her hands in the silky material of his shirt. The kiss was bruising and powerful. As he roughly hauled her against him, her arms snaked up around his neck, under his velvet hair. She clung to him, holding on for her life, digging her fingers up under the tie of his kerchief, as far as they could go. Her head was swimming. Her knees threatened to buckle. Her center was a poised bow string ready to let the arrow fly.

As abruptly as he grabbed her, he let go, and Lilly stumbled back.

"You're lucky!" His breath was coming in waves, heavy and frantic like her own. "You're lucky there is no ch—!"

"*Hush!*" Lilly cut him off. Whatever he intended to say was undoubtedly some awful comment so intrinsic to the part of him she didn't like, and she had no intention of listening to him. Instead she flung herself into him. She felt his startle. She felt the momentary loss of balance in his brief sidestep. She wrapped her arms around him and pressed her body as close as she could. "Don't speak! Don't say anything! Just… just kiss me!"

His hooded lids dropped the second before he covered her mouth with his. She felt his hands on her back, in her hair, releasing pins from it. It cascaded over his fingers and she felt, more than heard, his beleaguered breathing. She felt the tension in him turn into something else. The kiss changed, too. It was still demanding, but no longer seeking submission. Now he was pleading with her, begging her hungrily. She knew because she felt the same. He wanted her. He wanted more than just a kiss. Just as she did.

She was swaying in his embrace unable to control her ardor, desperately running her hands over him in frenzied need. She remembered this well, the weakness of her limbs, the pressure between her legs. This was lust, she realized, and it was wonderful. She wanted him to be with her, molding her to him, filling her body with his own.

In the next instant he was gone, leaving her empty and open, spinning and falling against the piano. With each passing second he moved farther away. He said something. She couldn't hear the words, but she didn't have to hear to know whatever he said was self-effacing.

"Gabriel, come back!" He was going through the door, about to disappear. "Gabriel!" she called out, but he didn't stop.

Lilly took several deep breaths, in an attempt to gain control over her trembling limbs and her languid head. She started to go after him, but as she pushed away from the piano her toe bumped something—his cane, lying on the floor. Stunned, she became riveted on the door. He'd walked away without using it. He'd been limping, yes, but not more than usual. And he was long gone.

She picked up his cane. Her fingers whispered over the rounded end, feeling the smoothed indentations in the wood from so much use. Then she slid around the piano and dropped to the bench. Skip a key, skip a key, skip two keys. Always start on C. Don't touch the black keys. She knew from watching Gabriel he never started on C, and he used the black keys all the time. Lightly Lilly fingered the keys, playing her notes, C-E-G-C. She fiddled, desperately hoping Gabriel would come back. He would have to, wouldn't he? If for no other reason than to retrieve his cane?

She stayed where she was, hoping the noise she made from fiddling on the keys might beckon him. But it didn't. He didn't return.

Forty-One

Lilly spent most of Christmas Eve with Charlotte at Julie's cottage, sitting in the rocking chair with Gabriella. There was a little piece of heaven in holding a baby. Withers appeared mid-morning, to tell them he'd just returned from dropping Mr. Drayton in town.

It amused Lilly immensely watching Withers make a fuss over the baby. He seemed completely smitten with her. But he didn't stay long. He had another mission. An important mission, so Charlotte declared— to find Christmas trees, one for Drayton Hall and one for Julie's cottage. Charlotte was going with him.

Lilly was at the door with Charlotte, helping to button her coat, while Withers, who had been swinging Gabriella about, returned her to Julie's arms. Lilly looked up in time to see Julie rise to her toes to kiss Withers' cheek. Then, as he turned, he flung a wink over his shoulder.

The minute the door closed behind Withers and Charlotte, Lilly turned on her sister. "I saw that!"

Julie's cheeks turned crimson. "I know what you're thinking. I'm married, and it's wrong of me to encourage him. I didn't try to. It just happened. But Lilly, I think I love him."

"How long has this been going on?" Lilly was stunned.

"Since I moved here," Julie admitted.

"I thought you loved Jason?"

Julie set her daughter in the cradle and threw her hands up dramatically. "I suppose I do. But Jimmy is different. And he is quite good at… certain things…"

Lilly's jaw dropped. "You've slept with Withers?"

"It just happened," Julie repeated. "I didn't plan it or anything. After the first time, there didn't seem to be any reason to stop. I felt so ugly being as big as a house the way I was. He told me I was beautiful pregnant."

"Does he know about Jason? Does he know you're married?"

"Of course he knows," Julie said. "He was there, you know, when Gabriel paid off Jason's creditors."

This surprised Lilly. She'd thought Julie was blissfully unaware.

"They weren't nice. Those men," Julie went on. "Gabriel stood up to them. Some of them hurt him."

"Yes, they did," Lilly said.

"Jimmy didn't want me to know at first, but I made him tell me. Jimmy thinks very highly of Gabriel. You're lucky to be married to him."

Lilly didn't say anything.

"Do you love him?" Julie asked.

Unable to answer, Lilly went to retrieve her sewing box and settle on the sofa. With Christmas only a day away, she still had quite a bit of work left to do on Gabriel's sweater.

"Do you love him?" Julie asked again.

And again, because she didn't know what to say, Lilly remained silent.

Julie grinned. "Eventually you'll see sense."

The slight wasn't worth her ire, or her sudden defensiveness. She didn't know what to think about Gabriel. She thought about him enough. Many times her musings were related to his touch, but more recently they included other things, like his music, like the way he coached Charlotte, like the way he'd sacrificed to pay off Jason's debts. Of course, he was being compensated for doing so—through her bearing him a child. She hadn't told him of her condition. She wasn't quite sure how to.

Lilly was very glad when Julie flounced off to the kitchen. She didn't need Julie's scrutiny or her advice. She just wanted to be left alone to get done what she needed to do.

By mid-afternoon, Lilly had made decent progress on Gabriel's sweater, but she was still far from finished. There were button holes yet to darn and buttons to sew on. Julie and Gabriella had settled down for an afternoon nap. Except for the crackle of the fire the cottage was very quiet. It reminded her of a few nights ago, when Gabriel sat beside her, here on this same sofa, how he'd held her in his arms while she cried, and what that comforting hold had led to… that kiss…

For a minute she closed her eyes. It wasn't a smart thing to do. She couldn't afford to keep reliving that infinite moment. Besides that, she was tired enough to doze and she couldn't afford to do that either. As it was, when the door bounced open, she startled.

"Mrs. Drayton, ma'am." Withers came in, stomping snow off his boots.

Charlotte skirted around him, tracking more snow. "Momma! Momma! We have two trees. A little one for Miss Julie and a great big giant one for our house! We put the big tree in our house already. It's in the hall, but we still have to set it up in the bucket!"

Lilly swept the not fully completed sweater, together with yarn, needles, thread and buttons into her sewing box.

Soon enough, Julie's tree was up and decorated. It was time to go to the mansion and work on the other one. The tree Withers had dragged in was exactly as Charlotte described. Easily it was four times the size of Julie's. Thankfully, Mr. and Mrs. Finch were there to help hold the monstrosity upright while Withers secured the base. They set it in front of the window next to the fireplace. The next job was to retrieve the box of ornaments Charlotte had helped make. Lilly had stowed the box in the closet in Charlotte's bedroom.

By the time the decorating was complete, it was well past Charlotte's bath time. Lilly sent her up, but didn't follow right away. For a moment she stood back admiring the display. It wasn't too bad, even if a little empty. The tree was just too big for the paltry number of ornaments they'd been able to put together.

She was glad Gabriel wasn't home. She was sure he would think the whole thing was awful, just as she was sure he didn't really like any of the other decorations she and Charlotte had so painstakingly set about. Unfortunately there was nothing she could do about it, at least not then. She still needed to finish his sweater, and the day was quickly getting away from her.

She raced up the stairs to her room, sewing box in hand, but stopped short just inside her doorway. There was a white envelope on the small table, the same table where Gabriel had left the roses and the amethyst necklace. Under the envelope was a thin, black felt box. Gabriel wasn't home yet, which meant he must have put it there for her before he departed this morning. There was nothing written on the envelope, but on the note within, Gabriel's stark penmanship jumped out at her.

It read, "With regard to my deplorable behavior last evening, I beg your forgiveness. I am truly sorry." At the bottom of the page was a single line. "These reminded me of your eyes." There was no signature.

Lilly's hands shook as she picked up the felt box. The ensemble of jewels inside included a necklace, bracelet and earrings. The gems themselves were smaller in size than the amethysts, but the quantity was more, the settings more intricate and delicate. The stones were pale, translucent blue aquamarines and simply stunning.

Carefully, Lilly carried her new jewels to her vanity. In front of the mirror she put them on. Now, more than ever, she needed to finish his sweater. Charlotte would have to see to her own bath. Hastily, she retrieved her sewing box. But time was not on her side. Before she could make much progress, Charlotte came barreling in asking if Lilly would do her hair. The dinner hour was fast approaching and Alex and Susan were expected.

At precisely seven, adorned with the aquamarines, Lilly followed an exuberant Charlotte out of her room. Alex and Susan had already arrived, but there was no sign of Gabriel. Charlotte, insistent upon showing off the tree, grabbed Susan's hand and dragged her to the parlor. Alex and Mark followed, leaving Lilly to enter last. Before she was fully into the room, Susan and Alex's laughter echoed.

"Where on earth did you get those ornaments?" Susan asked.

"Momma and I made them!" Charlotte said proudly.

"Surely your father must have others stored in this old place somewhere? Could you not find them?" The condescending words were barely out of her mouth before her eyes darted to the doorway. "Ah, Gabriel. You're here. We can eat."

"Daddy! Daddy! See our tree!" Charlotte chortled. "Do you like it, Daddy? Do you?"

Lilly turned around slowly. Gabriel was standing in the doorway, still in his heavy, winter cloak. His one exposed cheek was reddened from the cold. He was removing his gloves.

"It's fine," he said curtly.

Lilly followed the entourage out into the hall—brushing past Gabriel in the process—and on into the dining room. They were taking their seats when Gabriel came in. He'd taken his cloak off, but his cheek and nose were still tinged. It wasn't until he sat down that she noticed his gaze on her. He was looking at the jewelry, lingering on each piece. Finally his eyes rose to meet hers.

To express her gratitude Lilly smiled. Gabriel didn't smile back, but she really didn't expect him to. He looked tired, she realized. And there was something else, too, though she couldn't put her finger on it. Throughout the meal he was quiet, but that wasn't unusual. By the end of it, Lilly still didn't know what was wrong. But instinct told her there was something, and whatever it was, must be dire.

After dinner they all retired to the parlor. Rather than sitting in the wing chair where she usually sat, Lilly went to the sofa. Gabriel was the last one to come in. By the way he briefly stopped when he saw her, she knew her choice surprised him. She'd hoped he would sit beside her, but he didn't. Instead he started for the piano. This, of course, made Charlotte quite happy. For her, it meant a night of dancing.

Gabriel played several pieces to which Charlotte and Mark bounced around the room. At one point Charlotte grabbed Lilly's hand and pulled her to her feet. She had danced with Charlotte many times, but never while Alex and Susan were present. Still, the inhibition that plagued her earlier wasn't with her tonight. The last piece Gabriel played was a flurry of sound, demanding the dancers spin. Lilly came out of it dizzy and laughing, close to the piano. Looking up, she caught Gabriel's eye.

Drawn to him, she meandered the remaining distance, rounding the corner of the piano, where she could see his hands. His fingers were long and graceful as they caressed the keys. It was no wonder he was so good with his hands in other ways. Feeling color rise to her cheeks, Lilly forced those thoughts aside. She felt Gabriel look up and when he did he brought the piece to an end.

"Sit with me?" he whispered.

"This is a treat," she said quietly for his ears alone as she settled on the bench beside him. "I can try to learn your secret pattern."

"I'm playing in the key of F#. The notes to play are F#, A# and C#."

He started in and Lilly was content sitting next to him, feeling the warmth of his arm against hers. "You're not just playing F#, A# and C#," she accused.

Without missing a note he said. "Play whatever you want to play, but only those three keys."

Lilly did, tinkling in the upper registers. And he was right. As long as she stuck to those three particular keys, there was nothing discordant. In fact, the high sporadic notes added an element to the piece that reminded her of twinkling night stars. It was also music she'd never heard him play before and she said as much.

"We're making it up as we go," he murmured.

After a while, he nudged her and whispered, "Time to end."

She followed his lead until he stopped playing entirely. What met them was applause from everyone in the room, including Charlotte and Mark.

Caught up in what she and Gabriel were doing, Lilly didn't notice Susan's approach until the bedecked, fashionable woman was standing close enough to reach out and touch her. "That was one of the most lovely pieces I've ever heard you play, Gabriel," she complimented. "Bravo!"

Gabriel didn't acknowledge Susan at all. To Lilly he said, "Next we're in the key of G, which is G, B and D, and the key of D, which is D, F# and A. We'll do eight counts of each and switch back and forth."

Lilly wasn't sure exactly what he meant, but it didn't take long to catch on. The only thing putting a damper on what could have been an enjoyable experience was Susan's close presence. Even so, as they ended the piece, she murmured to Gabriel, "What you do is amazing. I'm having so much fun! Thank you."

"It's all patterns," he said, shrugging. "Once you know what notes fit with others, you can play anything you want. This time let's use A, which is A, C# and E... and E, which is E, G# and B. We'll play the same music we just played, in a different key."

But they didn't play it. Susan interrupted before they could begin. "It's lovely, really, but don't you think we should have some carols? It is Christmas Eve. Charlotte would like to sing."

"No," Gabriel said.

Susan's austere eyebrow rose. "You do know how to play Christmas carols, don't you, Gabriel? As remarkable a musician as you are? Carols are basic. Anyone who plays can surely play them."

Susan was goading him, Lilly realized. Gabriel wouldn't know Christmas carols. He didn't play anything except his own compositions. Having never had instruction in reading music, he wouldn't have been able to learn them. And Susan was well aware of that. Lilly found herself bristling protectively on Gabriel's behalf.

Before Gabriel could answer, Alex jumped in, "Let's give Gabriel and Lilly a break. They've entertained us long enough. How 'bout I take a turn on the cello? I know a few carols. The kids can sing along."

That's exactly what happened. Lilly followed Gabriel to the sofa and sat next to him. She sang along with the children, trying not to let her bad humor toward Susan show. She was glad when Alex announced they needed to get going. It was past Charlotte's bedtime and Mark was already asleep on the floor.

"I'll take Charlotte up," Lilly said to Gabriel after they were gone. But then she added, "Thank you for the evening. It was wonderful. Perhaps we can play music together again sometime?"

Charlotte was heading up the stairs, and Lilly started after her, but she stopped when Gabriel said her name.

"Lilly," he hesitated, stuttering. "I have something... a gift, if you will..."

Lilly called to Charlotte that she would be up shortly. Then she hastened to the parlor, only to find Gabriel in the process of retrieving an envelope and a large, rolled and banded paper from a cabinet drawer. She took a seat on the sofa and waited for him to join her.

He handed her the envelope first. Lilly opened it and removed the folded paper. It was a legal document—a deed to property. She recognized it as being similar to the one she'd signed when she and Julie had sold their mother's house.

"The tract has forty-eight acres. It's not far, about an hour's ride from here. I thought perhaps Withers could drive you and Charlotte to see it tomorrow."

"You bought land for me?" Lilly was incredulous.

"If you don't like it, you can choose something else."

She was supposed to purchase her home—the one she would move to once the arrangement was finished—with the enormous amount of money he'd already given her. "But—"

"The property has a rise of ground. I thought… this…" His voice trailed off as he handed her the rolled papers.

Lilly set the deed aside. Carefully she removed the tied band and unrolled the parchment. Her breath caught as her eyes settled on the first page. It was a drawing of a house, an incredible house with two spires, rounded windows, and a porch wrapping around the front and side. It was situated perfectly on a hill. A weeping willow tree near the bottom of the hill shaded a lovely pond. Beyond the house were rolling fields and mountains in the distance. It was the most picturesque setting for a home she'd ever seen. It was simply magnificent.

Unable to breathe, she moved the top page aside. The next page contained the layout of the first floor interior of the house. The sizes and shapes of the rooms appeared very similar to the house plans she'd been so taken with in Gabriel's office—the drawings done by the architect, Andrew Wentworth.

"Excuse me," Gabriel said and he rose. "It's yours to do with as you wish."

"Gabriel—?"

"I…I have to retire for the evening," he said. "Merry Christmas." Then he was gone.

Lilly looked again at the drawing and the box in the lower right corner that contained the signature and seal. She expected to see Andrew Wentworth's name, but it didn't say Andrew Wentworth. The seal and the architect's signature stated very clearly, *Gabriel A. Drayton.*

After tucking Charlotte in, Lilly returned to her room and changed into her nightgown. Only then, comfortable in her bed, with her sewing box on one side of her and the drawings on the other, did she take the time to really study them. She loved the house. There was nothing about it that displeased her.

She was still perusing the drawing, one floor at a time, when she thought she heard the distant sounds of the piano. It was past midnight and Gabriel had already done his trek to Charlotte's room. Normally at this hour, he was in his room.

Curiously Lilly rose, quickly donned her robe and crept out to the balcony. The doors to the parlor were closed, but the sound coming from behind them was definitely the piano. He was picking out a melody, one note at a time. It was a melody Lilly recognized—the Christmas carol, *Silent Night.*

He played through the melody several times until he was no longer hesitating between notes. Then he began to accompany it. There were a number of discordant sounds. With each he went back to the beginning and started anew. This went on and on, until finally he played through the entire song. *The First Noel* was next.

Lilly listened to him picking, working through the melody, then the accompaniment. Every time he played something that sounded off, Lilly caught herself cringing empathetically. Yet, as with *Silent Night,* eventually he made it through.

When he started on the third carol Lilly realized he was figuring out the same set Alex had played earlier on his cello. This one, *It Came Upon a Midnight Clear,* seemed to give him more trouble. He was halfway through working out the accompaniment when a loud, discordant noise shuddered out of the piano.

Lilly jolted from the harshness of it, but she knew exactly what caused the noise. She'd heard it similarly done by Charlotte, except not nearly as loudly or as abruptly.

Gabriel had just slammed both of his fists onto the keys.

Forty-Two

Christmas morning Lilly overslept. If it weren't for Charlotte barging into her room, she would have kept sleeping. "Hurry, Momma! Hurry! Saint Nicholas left lots and lots and lots of presents under the tree!"

Lilly promised she would be downstairs very soon, and she tried to get up, but nausea had her moaning and remaining right where she was. It took a few minutes for her stomach to finally settle. She had stayed up too late, but at least she'd finished the sweater. All she had left to do was wrap it. That could wait. Charlotte's Saint Nicholas presents were far more important.

Charlotte wasn't exaggerating. The area under the tree was stuffed full of parcels wrapped in all sorts of colored paper. Not only were there presents for Charlotte, but for Withers, both Mr. and Mrs. Finch, a few for Julie and another small pile for Gabriella. Gabriel was sitting in his usual slouched position at the end of the sofa. At some point in all the chaos—Charlotte opening her gifts, Mrs. Finch bringing tea, and Withers coming to tell them the carriage was ready to take them out to Lilly's land—Gabriel disappeared.

"Is he not coming with us?" Lilly asked Withers.

"No, ma'am."

She didn't see Gabriel again on Christmas day. With all of the new toys to occupy her, Charlotte didn't seem to notice his absence. Later in the evening, while Charlotte was still occupied with her new toys, determined to find Gabriel, Lilly went meandering through the mansion.

He wasn't in his study. Boldly she went to his west wing office. He wasn't there either. Lastly, she knocked on his bedroom door. There was no answer.

It was cause for a sleepless night. She couldn't get Gabriel out of her mind, but this time her thoughts about him were different. She was worried, and she wasn't quite sure why. The same instinct she'd had before, telling her something was wrong, was still with her. No matter how much deliberating she did, however, she couldn't unravel the mystery. Dawn was just breaking when finally she fell into a fitful sleep.

In the morning, because Charlotte wasn't in her room, or in the dining room, Lilly headed to the kitchen. There she came upon Mrs. Finch rolling dough. "I overslept again," Lilly said contritely.

"I found this here this morning," Mrs. Finch said. She went to a nearby cabinet and withdrew a folded paper. "I believe 'tis from Mista Drayton."

Absently Lilly took the paper. "Where's Charlotte? Have you seen Julie and the baby today?"

"Julie and little Gabriella are getting along just fine. Charlotte is with them. What can I git ya fer breakfast?"

"I'm not terribly hungry. Perhaps just a biscuit?" Lilly murmured.

"Of course."

To save time, rather than going to the dining room, Lilly sat at the table in the kitchen. Mrs. Finch brought her a cup of tea to go along with her biscuit. She nibbled on the biscuit and took several sips of tea before setting the cup aside. Only then did she turn her attention to Gabriel's note. Why she was afraid of what it might say, she didn't know, but she was afraid. Taking a deep breath, she forged ahead, carefully unfolding the note.

My dearest Lilly,

Please accept my apology for being remiss in ensuring your comfort while you have been residing at Drayton Hall. This is your home and therefore should be outfitted to your liking.

An interior decorator—Mr. Earnest Wilkerson—is to arrive this afternoon at one o'clock. I have engaged his services to make renovations to the front parlor, dining room, library and entrance hall. If there are any other rooms or areas you would like to redecorate, please inform Mr. Wilkerson. Make as many changes as you like. I trust your judgment implicitly. The only room I prefer to be left alone is my office in the west wing.

This project is not intended to be a burden to you. Rather I hope you will enjoy yourself giving Drayton Hall a more pleasing appearance, as you so thoughtfully did in decorating for Christmas. This place has never looked better. I do realize this will take your time from Julie, Gabriella and Charlotte, and for that I apologize.

Thank you for making this year special, Lilly. I will never forget it.

Faithfully your servant,

Gabriel

Taken aback, especially in light of the foreboding that had kept her awake all night, Lilly leaned back and almost fell off the bench. She was pleased beyond measure. How many times had she walked through the halls of this mansion thinking of ways to make it more appealing? She couldn't believe he'd done this! No matter what she chose, fabrics, patterns, furniture—he trusted her judgment. He'd been pleased by her efforts to decorate for Christmas! There was nothing he could have said to compliment her more. Long ago, Susan Drayton had said Gabriel *used* to be charming. With an internal giggle, Lilly mused, he still was!

After having lunch with Julie and Charlotte and determining Charlotte was not overstaying her welcome, Lilly went back to the mansion to meet with the interior decorator. The meeting was everything she'd hoped it would be. The man informed her that Mr. Drayton's instructions were to entirely strip the rooms and redo them. He showed her endless swatches of fabric, as well as drawings depicting draperies, carpets, furniture, and every possible need the mansion could have. Thereafter, together they went room by room, discussing, and in some cases, finalizing plans.

Lilly's only disappointment was that by nine o'clock that evening, there was still no sign of Gabriel. Even Withers didn't know where he was. After putting Charlotte to bed, Lilly wandered through the mansion, imagining once again the changes that would take place in the next weeks. Drayton Hall would no longer be a dull, uninviting place— a mausoleum, as Susan Drayton had described it. It would be open and friendly, and beautiful!

She was just closing the door of the library behind her when she heard the distinct tap and scrape. Her smile grew the minute she saw Gabriel rounding the corner into the east wing. In her excitement, she had to catch herself from running to him.

"You were in town on business?" she asked as soberly as she could.

"Yes," he said. "Your sister is well?"

"Very well," Lilly grinned. "Charlotte spent most of the day with her. She seems to enjoy Gabriella almost as much as her new toys. I think Charlotte will be disappointed to have to get back to her lessons tomorrow."

"Excuse me. I need to… I need to change, wash up."

"You must be tired," she said, noting that he did appear to be. She saw it in the crooked angle of his shoulders, the droop of his eyelids, and that same anxiety-laden despondency she'd noticed before.

"I won't be long. I would like to have a word with you," he said.

"Certainly. Shall I wait for you in the front parlor?"

He nodded briefly and then moved on through the hall and around to the staircase.

In the front parlor, Lilly flounced down on the sofa, irritated beyond measure. Their interchange had been so dreadfully formal. She was nervous, of all things! And the way she'd rambled on about Charlotte and the baby was just... just dim-witted. What she should have done was thank him, and tell him how much she appreciated everything he'd done for her, and for Julie and Gabriella and Charlotte. She should have told him how thoughtful it was of him to have gifts for Mr. and Mrs. Finch and Withers.

Gabriel wasn't the man she'd first thought him to be. The truth was he was far from it. Perhaps he was a little gruff. And that mask of his didn't help, giving him the appearance of a sinister brute. But on the inside...

On the inside, he was gentle and kind and generous. What she wanted to do was touch him, kiss him, show him how much she... *loved* him. Did she love him? Did she, really? Oh, how did one know? How did anyone come to grips with such an overwhelming emotion?

Gabriel shuffled into the room. Despite the discomfiting thoughts, Lilly did her best to smile as he sat beside her. She saw him rub his leg. She'd seen him do the same many times. It reminded her of the vials of morphine she'd found in the alcove behind the door to his fire escape.

"I presume the meeting with the decorator, Wilkerson went well?" he asked.

It was easy to set aside her momentary angst to answer this question. With animation, she shared the details. They were going to start with the parlor and work their way through, ending with the entrance hall. If furnishing and material orders arrived on schedule, the renovations should be complete within two months.

Gabriel made no comments while she relayed these things to him. In closing, and because she was beginning to feel awkward again, she hedged, "I hope you like what I've chosen."

"I will," he said.

Silence lingered and Gabriel turned away from her. He was rubbing his leg again. Mustering her courage—it was now or never— Lilly forged ahead, "Thank you, Gabriel, for everything you've done for me, for everything you've given me. The jewelry, the house, the land. I couldn't ask for better. And thank you for what you did for Julie. I...I don't quite know what to say. Words don't seem to be enough."

Gabriel's acknowledgement to this was made by a single curt nod. He still wouldn't look at her.

"I have something for you—a Christmas gift. I wanted to give it to you yesterday, but I couldn't find you." The wrapped parcel was where she'd left it, under the Christmas tree. It was the only package remaining. Quickly she retrieved it and sat beside him again.

Gabriel's hands trembled as he took the parcel from her. He was exhausted and in pain, that was all, she told herself. Certainly receiving a gift wouldn't cause him to be nervous. But as soon as the thought came to her, she wasn't so sure. He was just sitting there, staring at the pretty red bow, not touching it at all.

"Please don't expect much," Lilly said modestly. "I hope you like it."

"I do," he murmured.

The vulnerability and blatant sorrow in those two simple words caused her breath to catch. Swallowing, she tried to be flippant. "You can't say that until you open it."

He was still trembling as he untied the bow, then delicately ripped the paper. He was so careful and took so long, Lilly had the urge to reach over and tear the wrapping off for him. She was thankful she withheld her impatience when a moment later the neatly folded sweater was in view. He touched it, running a fingertip along the line of ebony buttons.

"You made this?" he asked softly.

"I did. I thought perhaps it would be useful now that winter is here. I also have a confession to make."

This caused him to look at her sharply, and Lilly smirked.

"The reason I needed a shirt from your closet wasn't because of a game with Charlotte. I needed it to measure your size."

Gabriel laughed. He actually laughed! Lilly couldn't believe it. His grin lifted the exhaustion from his eyes, showed off the dimple beside his mouth, and the amazing bone structure of his face. When his laughter faded, as she gazed into his beguiling, expressive eyes and asked, "Will you try it on?"

Without a word, he slipped out of his jacket. She found it odd that he was wearing a jacket. He usually didn't. Carelessly he tossed the jacket over the arm of the sofa, and then he reached for the sweater. There was no carelessness in him when he lifted the sweater. He was being so fastidious, holding it up by the shoulder seams, she wondered if he thought it might fall apart.

Painstakingly he slipped his arms through the sleeves, first the left, then the right, and moving so slowly, she was sure he would never get the sweater fully put on. Finally, he pulled the front lapels together and began buttoning it from the bottom up. Then he just sat there, head bowed forward, looking down at himself

"I know it's not exactly your style," Lilly found herself stammering. "And it's not as grand as something made by someone with more skill. It's okay if you don't like it. I won't be offended. I'll understand."

Gabriel closed his eyes, turned his head away, and mumbled something she couldn't hear.

"I'm sorry. What did you say?"

Whatever it was, he didn't repeat. He didn't say anything, and he still wouldn't look at her. But he took a breath, deeply, and when it came out of him, he shuddered.

The realization of what was wrong was so shocking, Lilly gasped. "Gabriel, it's just a sweater, and a mediocre one at that."

She barely got the words out before he spun and caught her face gently in his hands. His lips met hers. The kiss was very soft, and all too brief. He let her go abruptly. Lilly opened her eyes to find him pushing to his feet.

Standing there, with his back to her, he said, "Tomorrow I'm leaving for New York. I don't know for how long. Perhaps a week." And then he started away.

"I'll miss you," Lilly said, rising too.

His momentary pause in step told her he'd heard her. She hoped he would turn around, but he didn't. Never had she imagined he would have such an emotional reaction to her gift. She was still stunned speechless. Even so, she traipsed after him, stopping at the parlor entrance. From there, she watched his slow progress up the mountain of stairs, one lonely step at a time.

She wanted to go after him. She wanted to have him look at her—really look at her—so she could see in his eyes the evidence of what she'd heard in that emotional shudder. She wanted to tell him about the child she carried. His child.

But she didn't know how. All she could do was watch until he disappeared around the wall that would take him into the red corridor upstairs, and to his room, where he would remain behind a door she couldn't breach.

In the morning, once the nausea passed, she was in a much better frame of mind, at least one that wasn't so filled with self-doubt. She intended to seek Gabriel out, and say everything she'd been too tongue-tied to say the night before. No longer was she ashamed, but rather she was excited. That feeling only intensified when she found the note he'd left on the table inside her suite.

The idea that he'd been in her rooms during the night, rather than frightening her, titillated her. A warm quiver ran through her at the very thought that he might have even come into her bedroom. He might have been watching her while she slept…

The note had no greeting or signature. It had two simple lines. "I will treasure it always," and "I will miss you, too."

Forty-Three

He wasn't dead.

Despite that caustic note proclaiming Christmas to be the date of his death, he'd survived.

It was funny to Gabriel that no one had commented on the increased number of Dobbins' security guards surrounding the estate. Not even Withers questioned the two armed men that had escorted the carriage during the Christmas day trek to the land he'd bought for Lilly.

Gabriel had sent the lot of them—Lilly, Charlotte, Mr. and Mrs. Finch and Withers—away on purpose. While they'd been gone, alone, he'd waited for something to happen. But nothing had happened. The next day, again he'd waited for some unknown folly to cross his path, but again nothing happened. Then he'd gone off, surrounded by bodyguards to New York, via the train from Philadelphia.

He'd told Lilly he would be gone a week, but he hadn't been able to keep himself away quite that long. He was home again. It was New Year's Eve and he was still breathing.

Standing in the middle of his bedroom, Gabriel took one last look around. An unexpected knock on the door caused his pulse to speed up. Upon his arrival, the first thing he'd done was ask the whereabouts of Lilly and Charlotte. They were apparently both with Julie and the baby, in the cottage. And that was good. Next, he'd given strict instructions to Finch and Withers that Lilly and Charlotte were not to be told of his homecoming, or his whereabouts. Not yet. Then he'd gone to his room. If Finch or Withers had let on, he would dock their pay, or something...

"Who is it?" he called out.

"Finch," came the slight, muffled reply.

Gabriel let out a sigh of relief. "Come."

The letter he'd received from the interior decorator told him everything within the mansion was coming along nicely. Gabriel only cared about one room, and it wasn't one Lilly was responsible for. The changes to his bedroom were to have been done discreetly. Any deliveries were to have been made when Lilly and Charlotte were not present.

Everything was in place. He'd made the bed himself with the linens that had been left folded on top. He'd had a few finishing touches to apply—some things he'd bought on his own—sprays of flowers for the mantel, several softer pillows to primp the bed a little more, a vase on the coffee table with three dozen red roses in it.

"It looks nice, sir," Finch said.

On the tray Finch carried was a glass pitcher and two tall glasses. Every day Finch hauled water for Gabriel's bath. Every day he filled the basin in the washstand. And every day he brought a tray with a pitcher and glasses. This water was for Gabriel to drink in the event he was thirsty at night.

"There be someone here to see ya, sir," Finch said.

Gabriel wasn't really paying attention as Finch deposited the pitcher on the table next to his bed. He was staring at the flimsy draperies falling from the bed canopy. They were tied back at the posts, but if he let them down, a very private cave would be created. One he wanted to share so badly...

"If you don't mind me sayin', sir, 'tis a good improvement," Finch said.

"Do you think she'll—" Abruptly he cut himself off. "You said someone's here? Who is it?"

"Oh, sir, yes, sir. 'Tis Mrs. Drayton, sir. She's waitin' fer ya in the front parlor."

"Mrs. Drayton?" The first woman who held that particular title to come to mind was Lilly, but she was always on his mind of late. The second was Beatrice, but knowing Beatrice, she would never come to Drayton Hall. Especially now. "I'll be down."

"Very good, sir." Finch bowed and headed toward the door.

"Finch, you may let my wife know I'm home now."

With Finch out of the room, Gabriel looked around once more. Then he took one of the roses and laid it on the lacy pillow, the one where she would lay her head.

Gabriel was in no hurry to reach the front parlor and his unexpected visitor. The moment he saw who was waiting for him, he rolled his eyes. Susan was elegantly dressed in dark purple—her favorite color—and adorned with jewels to the extreme. The low cut of the gown almost exposed her completely. "What do you want?"

"Don't be rude, Gabriel. I need to talk to you," she said.

"You'll be here for dinner tonight. Whatever you have to say can wait until then."

"This can't wait," she persisted. "I'm concerned about Charlotte."

"Charlotte is fine. There's nothing to be concerned about. I'll see you out."

Susan didn't take his hint, but he would have been kidding himself to think she would. Susan was the most tenacious and demanding woman he'd ever known. How Alex could stand to be married to her, he didn't know. How Rob could want her...

"Are you sure you've done the right thing?" Susan said. "Marrying this... this tutor, what's her name, Lilly Hawthorne? She comes from as good as trash—"

"Be careful, Susan!" Gabriel hissed. "If you've come here with the sole purpose of maligning *my wife*, then get the hell out!"

Susan moved through the room until she was but a pace away. "You look like you're feeling better."

"I'm fine. What do you really want, Susan? I just got home. I have things to do."

"Gabriel, please. This is important to me. You know how much I love Charlotte. Rob told me you've appointed *that woman* as Charlotte's guardian."

"I have. This conversation is over." He started away.

"You've made a mistake. Charlotte belongs with me!" Susan said.

Gabriel turned back. There was desperation in Susan's voice that wasn't typical for her. She was wringing her hands nervously, something else he'd never seen her do.

"It has been my observation that Lilly's influence has been, without question, the best thing that has ever happened to Charlotte," he said. "Does that mollify you? Now you can go."

Susan's eyes pooled, shimmering before him, but Gabriel wasn't fooled. He knew Susan well enough to know it was all for show.

"Get over it," he said briskly.

Susan sniffled and dabbed at her eyes with a handkerchief she pulled from her reticule. "Do you love her… this… this Lilly Hawthorne woman? Do you?" she asked.

Squinting in amusement, Gabriel said tersely, "That's a rather odd question. According to you I don't love anybody."

As quickly as her eyes filled, they dried. "You are a bastard!" she seethed. "I really do hate you!"

"I am well aware of that. Good day, Susan."

"Did she give that to you? That vile sweater you're wearing? It doesn't suit you. You look common."

Gabriel spun toward the door. He had every intention of leaving her there, but she caught his upper arm with both hands and forcibly pulled him back.

"Get off me!" he barked.

"Do you love her?" she screeched.

He attempted to yank his limb from her, but her grip was tight. Despite her delicate appearance, Susan had always been a strong woman. "Let go of me, and get the hell out of my house!"

"Why are you doing this to me?" she wailed. Her eyes filled again.

"I'm not doing anything to you. Let go!"

"I was supposed to be your wife. Your father wanted you to marry me! I was supposed to share your bed and bear your children! What was so wrong with me? Why didn't you want to marry me? Why didn't you love me?"

"Christ!" Gabriel was completely caught off guard by what she did next. She pounced on him, causing him to lose his already precarious balance and stagger backwards. It was all he could do with her weight against him to remain standing. Curses flew from his mouth as his foot clipped the edge of the open door. It swung closed as he slammed into the half of the door that was already closed. He was still cursing when she covered his mouth with hers.

Her kiss was as bold as he remembered. Her hands were on his head, her fingers flitting around his ear and into his hair with enough pressure to make his head tilt. Her mouth angled over his, and she wasn't shy with her tongue. Then her hand moved, down between their bodies. Her touch between his legs was rough and seeking, but it didn't last.

Abruptly she pushed away. "Damn you!" she screeched. "Damn you, and your cold unfeeling heart and your insipid self-control! I know you still want me. You can pretend all you want, but I know."

Gabriel didn't have a chance to refute her. She flew at him again. This time she grabbed his belt with one hand and shoved the other inside his pants. At the same time her mouth clamped over his.

She broke the kiss to murmur, "I love you." Then she took his hand and pushed it into the low cut bodice of her gown. There was very little fabric between her exposed skin and her nipple.

"I have always loved you," she said huskily. "Tell me you love me, Gabriel. You can't deny you want me. I have the evidence right here. Tell me, Gabriel, tell me you love me and not her. Tell me…"

Forty-Four

Lilly was with Julie and Charlotte in Julie's sitting room, putting together a puzzle—one of Charlotte's many Christmas gifts—when Withers popped his head into the cottage.

"Ladies," he nodded. "Charlotte, it's time for your riding lesson."

"I thought you went to town to pick up Mr. Drayton?" Julie asked.

Withers shrugged, but his eyes twinkled mischievously. "He was delayed and told me to come on back. Said he'd hire a coach to bring him later."

That made little sense, but Lilly didn't question it. "Go ahead, Charlotte. We'll have to finish the puzzle another time."

Disappointed, but easily redirected, Charlotte went about getting her coat and hat. Moments later, she skipped out the door. Withers was behind her, but he stopped before pulling the door closed. He looked at Lilly and said in a hushed tone, "Mr. Drayton is home. I thought I'd keep Charlotte distracted for a little while."

Lilly's smile was instantaneous, as was her blush. Withers pulled the door shut and Julie started giggling. "Jimmy is fabulous, isn't he?"

Lilly got up, and took her time slipping into her coat, hat and gloves. The minute she stepped out of Julie's cottage, however, she was running. She was as giddy as a schoolgirl, with no self-control. He'd said a week. But he'd come home early!

There hadn't been one second during the time he'd been gone that he wasn't in her thoughts. She'd been so absent-minded, she'd barely been able to concentrate on Charlotte's lessons. Several times Julie had to repeat things she'd said, because Lilly hadn't heard her. She was exhausted from the sleepless nights—nights plagued with euphoric imaginings. Of Gabriel!

He was home! He was home! She wanted to shout to the heavens. A million times she had dreamed of his homecoming, of running to him, of sitting down with him, of taking his hand, of having him take her in his arms and kiss her, and eventually, when they would come up for air, she would tell him about their child.

Oh, the distance to the mansion had never seemed so far! Once she finally reached it, however, she slowed her pace. Now, walking briskly, she headed through the east wing hallway. A quick glance into the study revealed he wasn't there. Her next stop would be the front parlor. Hastening her steps she rounded the corner into the hall. At first, she didn't hear the whispery voice—a woman's voice, but when she did she froze.

One of the double doors to the parlor was open, not much, just a crack, but it was enough. Through it Lilly had a perfectly clear view of Gabriel leaning against the closed door, and a woman in purple. Her body was tight against his. Her mouth was a mere inch from his. Her hand was down the front of his pants. Her other hand was on top of his, covering his long fingers, which were buried inside the low neckline of her dress.

"I love you," the woman said in a seductive whisper. "I have always loved you. Tell me you love me. You can't deny you want me. I have the evidence right here. Tell me, Gabriel. Tell me you love me and not her. Tell me…"

Lilly didn't wait to hear, or see, any more. She fled up the staircase and slammed herself inside her room. There, she raced to her bed and fell onto it. Her head was pounding, but that was nothing compared to the wrenching in her chest. Tears welled in her eyes and she couldn't make them stop, no matter how much she told herself he didn't deserve them.

He was hateful, vile! He *was* the unfeeling monster the world believed him to be. He was a thief, a cheat, and a liar! He was with Susan Drayton! And he'd been wearing the sweater Lilly had made for him!

Somewhere in the time she spent wallowing, she was able to convince herself she didn't care. If Gabriel wanted Susan, he could have her! Charlotte's knock, after her riding lesson, reminded Lilly that her sole purpose in being here, in this awful mansion, was for Charlotte. Charlotte needed her. Julie and little Gabriella needed her, and they were the people that mattered. Not *him.*

Because of the holiday, Alex and Susan were expected for dinner. With determined resolve Lilly rose from her bed. Getting through the evening would not be easy, but she would be damned if any of them— least of all Gabriel—would know of the anger and turmoil going on inside of her. To them, she would appear calm, quiet and collected. She would center her attention on Charlotte and little Mark.

As for the foreseeable future, there were only six months before the baby would be born. In that time she needed to secure a residence, a place where she could live with Charlotte and the baby, preferably as far from Drayton Hall as possible. She no longer had any interest in the land or the house Gabriel had given her. She wanted nothing from him! And since he didn't really care for his daughter, it followed that he wouldn't want the baby she carried either. When the time came for her to move to her new home, she would do everything in her power to keep Gabriel from ever laying eyes upon their child!

By the time she reached the hall, despite her determined resolve, her stomach was little more than a tightly woven ball of knots. Charlotte was with Gabriel in the parlor, but joining them was out of the question. The doorbell rang, as if in answer to prayer, and Lilly was able to let out the breath she'd been holding.

Charlotte came bounding out of the parlor to answer the door, and Lilly heard Gabriel, but she didn't look at him. Instead she focused on Alex and Mark. It didn't escape her notice, however, that Susan hadn't changed her clothes. She was still wearing that deep purple gown. Briefly, Lilly's eyes were drawn to the low-cut front. Gabriel's hand had been there, stuffed under that expensive silk.

As much as she didn't want to, she was forced to acknowledge Susan's, "Hello, Lilly," from a distance. If Susan had approached her, or attempted a more affable hello, Lilly didn't know what she would have done.

Raising her chin, she said all the appropriate greetings to Alex and Mark, and although she tried, she wasn't able to avoid Gabriel. He was moving toward her.

The glance she intended to give him turned into a stare. Unlike Susan, he had changed his clothes. Never had she seen him wearing anything but black, but tonight he wasn't, at least not entirely. His wool trousers were a dark grey. The shirt he wore was white, with the ends of his black scarf tucked neatly into the collar. Over the shirt was her sweater.

He was close, just a few steps away when Susan suggested, "Shall we go in to eat?" There was no way Gabriel didn't hear her, but he acted like he didn't. His eyes were on Lilly and didn't stray. "Are you well?" he murmured quietly. "Charlotte said you were feeling poorly."

By the concern etched in his expression, she could have sworn he really cared. But she knew better! This was simply an act. To hide his affair with Susan.

"I'm fine. Just a little tired." She could do this. She could play their deceitful game as well as they did! Because she knew Susan was watching, she took a step toward him and another, until she was so close all she had to do to kiss his cheek was rise up onto her tiptoes.

As she settled back on her heels, she caught his smile and the glint of his eyes. The warmth there was so genuine, for just a second she was sure, like his concern, it was real, too.

"I missed you," he said in that husky whisper.

"I missed you, too," she forced herself to say.

He held his hand out to her and said hesitantly, "Would you... would you... I know I'm slow... if you would prefer to go ahead without me..."

Instead of taking his hand, Lilly tucked her arm through his. She was on his left, so most of his face was hidden from her, but she could see his faint smile. This was indeed a game—a horrid, fake pretense. "Shall we?" she murmured.

She truly didn't mind their progress, deliberate as it was. What she did mind was the reaction her traitorous body had to touching him. It didn't help that the wonderful scent of him was filling her head. The problem was she'd spent too much time daydreaming of being close to him. Now that she was, every inch of her was infused with awareness. Silently she damned her foolishness. She should have no feelings toward him at all!

In the dining room, thankfully she was able to let go of him. She started for her seat next to Mark, where she always sat when Alex and Susan were in company.

"No," Gabriel said, startling her. He moved to stand behind the chair Alex usually sat in, the one corner to his seat at the head of the table. And then he pulled the chair out. "Lilly, please sit here."

By asking her to sit beside him, rather than in the seat farthest away, was he trying to show her honor? As Gabriel pushed the chair in under her, she briefly caught Susan's eye. But there was nothing in Susan's expression to indicate she was displeased by this show from Gabriel. If anything, the wealthy woman appeared mildly smug, as if she knew some great secret, which, of course, she did!

Gabriel surprised Lilly yet again, however, when after ensuring Charlotte was served, instead of passing the plates counterclockwise past Charlotte to Susan the way he usually did, he changed the direction and passed them to her first.

They hadn't made it far into the meal, most of which Lilly was having a difficult time finding an appetite for, when Charlotte announced, "Daddy has a special surprise for Momma."

Ignoring the glare that flew out of Gabriel directly at Charlotte, Alex chortled, "Oh? I wonder what it is?"

"I can't tell," Charlotte said. "Daddy said if I tell, I'll ruin the surprise. Momma has a surprise for Daddy, too."

This startled Lilly. She had no idea what Charlotte was talking about. She certainly had no surprise for him, other than the news of her pregnancy, a secret Charlotte did not know. No one knew. Not even Julie.

"We'd better not say anymore about it," Alex conceded, eyes twinkling. "Your momma and daddy will have to exchange their surprises for each other later." Then he added bemusedly, "Gabriel, I must say, nice sweater. I like that look on you."

Lilly's eyes went straight to Gabriel, to see his reaction. There wasn't one, at least not one she could decipher. She didn't want his surprise, no matter what it might be. And he... he would undoubtedly be disappointed by her news, not that she had any intention of telling him a thing. Not any longer!

By the time they headed to the parlor for post-dinner festivities, Lilly was exhausted. As desperate as she was to beg off, she couldn't think of a satisfactory excuse. The one thing she was able to do that Gabriel wasn't happy about—she noticed the spark of disappointment in his eyes—was let go of his escorting arm as they passed the chair she usually sat in. He'd wanted her to share the sofa with him. Never again would she do that!

Most of the evening was spent listening to Alex and Charlotte make up fantastical tales of knights and dragons. This, of course, reminded her of Rob, and his continued absence. But he wasn't worth dwelling on, any more than Gabriel was!

Although she tried to pay attention, Lilly missed the content of much of the chatter. She couldn't concentrate with Susan in the room. And Gabriel kept staring at her! This was why she supposed she was startled when Gabriel said, "Charlotte, why don't you play your piano words for us?"

That suggestion obviously delighted Charlotte, who lit up and ran over to the big instrument. Then she insisted Alex, Susan and Mark join her there. Within minutes she was spelling their names and using them in sentences, creating more stories.

Much to Lilly's chagrin, while everyone else was otherwise occupied, Gabriel came to sit in the wing chair beside her. Lilly tried to pretend she was engrossed in listening to Charlotte. She certainly didn't want to speak with him!

"I want to apologize for being away so many days," he said quietly. "I didn't intend for the trip to take so long."

"I understand." Lilly copied his hushed tone.

"Are you chilled?" he asked.

"No," she said. But she was trembling.

"I'll have Finch bring tea, or hot chocolate?" he suggested.

"I wouldn't mind a glass of wine." She hoped, if nothing else, the alcohol would calm her.

Gabriel surprised her yet again when he rose, went to the sideboard, and poured the glass for her. As he served it to her, their fingers touched. Looking at him, however, was a mistake. It made her throat tight. Swallowing hard, she busied herself taking a sip of the aromatic sampling. It was dry, perfectly suited to her mood and quite good. She took another sip and watched Gabriel sit down and rub his thigh. Thankfully he didn't say anything.

By the time Charlotte was finished showing off her musical words, Lilly was finished with her glass. It was potent stuff. One glass of wine didn't usually affect her so strongly, but then again, she hadn't eaten much at dinner. Already she was mildly light-headed, but at least the wine was doing what she'd hoped it would. The tension in her was slowly ebbing away. In its wake was renewed determination to not ever let Gabriel know that she knew about his affair with Susan. Susan loved him, and although Lilly hadn't stayed long enough to hear him respond in kind, she knew he must have. He'd been touching Susan in such an intimate way. Just as she had been touching him!

As the nine o'clock hour approached, Gabriel told Charlotte it was soon time for bed. Taking the opportunity to make her own excuses, Lilly murmured, "I think I'll head up, too." But no one seemed to hear her. Not even Gabriel.

The production of farewells took forever. Alex surprised Lilly by kissing her on the cheek and telling her she looked lovely. When he stepped away, Lilly caught Gabriel's eye. He'd been watching them, and he was scowling. She was glad his attention was taken by Charlotte so she could escape. She was almost to the foot of the stairs when Gabriel called her name. She glanced back. Alex and Susan were by the door, already in their coats.

Gabriel was limping toward her. Lilly faced the stairs and waited. She felt his presence and his warmth close in behind her, and he touched her. It was just the whisper of his fingertips across her bared shoulder, so lightly done it tickled. She closed her eyes, and his breath grazed her ear.

"Come to me tonight," he whispered. "Not because you have to, but because you want to."

Low in her stomach something twisted and she peered over her shoulder. His eyes were shaded, half closed, but they weren't hiding anything. What he wanted was right there, plainly visible. And so was something else—an openness she'd never seen in him before. It shocked her and she reacted by inclining her head briefly. His gaze moved to her lips and lingered there, hungrily, before returning to her eyes.

Unable to take another moment of this torture, Lilly tore herself away. But she didn't run. She couldn't let him know how eager she was to be away from him. At the top of the steps, although she told herself not to, she looked down over the balcony railing.

Alex, Susan and Mark were long gone, but Gabriel was still there, staring after her.

In her room she quickly changed into her nightgown, crawled into bed and pulled the thick comforter to her neck. Less than two hours separated her from eleven o'clock—the time he would expect her. God help her, she wanted to go!

But, how could she, knowing what she did? That very afternoon, he'd lain with Susan. Their love was no doubt precluded due to her being married to Alex. But how long ago had the affair begun? How long had it been going on? And poor Alex, who was so devoted to Susan, was being betrayed not only by his wife, but by his cousin—a cousin who, according to Rob, Alex thought of more as a brother! They'd grown up together!

Lilly flounced down on her bed. If she went to Gabriel tonight, while he made love to her, would he be thinking of Susan? Had he been imagining she was Susan when she'd been with him before? It had been of utmost importance to Gabriel that there be no lighting. Lilly had assumed this was because he didn't want her to see his face. But, even if the fires had not been doused, she wouldn't have. He'd never taken the mask off. It only followed that the reason he'd been so adamant about the room being dark had nothing to do with him, and everything to do with the person beside him.

The idea that she was his substitute—a substitute for Susan—both humiliated and sickened Lilly. She was crushed, and yet, as pathetic as it sounded, she still craved the feelings he'd evoked. Perhaps he did love Susan, but Susan wasn't his *wife*. It didn't matter that their marriage was just a convenient arrangement. She held a position Susan never could.

Wives had the right to request intimate attentions from their husbands, didn't they? According to Julie they did. Her mother had once told her husbands did to their wives what they wanted. Husbands could choose to please or ignore their wives. Husbands could take mistresses if they wanted. Julie had taken Lilly aside and told her their mother's viewpoint was old-fashioned. They didn't live in the dark ages any longer. Wives had a right to faithfulness. But what kind of faithfulness was it when a husband had, mere hours before, been with someone else?

By eleven o'clock Lilly's thoughts had flip-flopped so many times she had no idea what she was going to do. All she knew was that she was sick at heart. And it was a hurt so deep and heavy, she didn't know if she would ever be able to crawl out from under it.

Forty-Five

The room was perfect, as perfect as he thought he could make it. The fire in the fireplace cast it full of warmth and shadows. A plate of chocolates flanked by two white tapered candles sat in the middle of the small table in the sitting area. The bottle of wine was encased in ice on the side table. Sheer lace drapes fell in waves from the canopy surrounding the bed. The silk burgundy spread shimmered like water in the dim lamp lights. The rose he'd laid on the pillow earlier was still in place.

"Please, come," Gabriel whispered under his breath as he lowered himself into the wingchair by the fireplace. "Please, just be late."

She was supposed to have been here when he came in. She was supposed to have found the roses and the chocolates and the books he'd brought for her, all before he arrived.

Impatience had demanded he give her only a few moments before joining her. When he'd entered the room, a scant three minutes after eleven, his rapidly pounding heart had fallen hard to his ribs. She wasn't there. The room was empty.

Restlessly, he cursed the popping of the fire, which drowned out the sound of a door latch—*was it?*

His pulse increased to the same rapid pace it had been before, and he sat up, listening intently. He should have left the bedroom door ajar, he should have… *Christ!*

When she walked in, she couldn't find him like this. He was a mess. Never in his life had he been this nervous, with anticipation shifting between pure terror and desire so unquenchable he thought he would die from it. He forced himself to lean back, to appear relaxed. His mind rehearsed again the first words he would say, and he changed them. Again.

But the only thing looming was silence. The footsteps he'd thought he heard hadn't materialized. The click of the latch had been nothing more than his imagination playing tricks on him!

The entire time he'd been in New York, all he'd been able to think about was her. He'd wanted the bedroom to be finished, as a surprise. For her. Not because he wanted her physically—God only knew how much he did—but because he wanted to see her, to talk to her, to be in her presence. Bedroom decorations notwithstanding, he would have been completely content sitting with her in the front parlor all night long, or here, by the fire.

After he'd taken care of the room and told Finch to let her know he was home, he'd hoped she would come to him. How many times had he imagined her smile of greeting, and the quiet, tender voice he heard every night in his dreams, murmuring, "Hello, Gabriel. I've missed you."

He'd spent hours dreaming of her, of taking her hands, of kissing her cheek, of listening while she shared the events of the week. But instead of coming to him, she'd gone to her room.

He'd walked past her door several times, debating whether to knock. Charlotte had come in from her riding lesson full of giggles and chatter and everything else that made Charlotte Charlotte. Instead of engaging his daughter, like a heathen, he'd sent her into Lilly's room, to spy for him, to find out why Lilly wasn't coming out.

A moment later, Charlotte had returned. She'd shrugged and said, "Momma's tired."

Gabriel had tried to take it at face value, tried to ignore the nagging voice in his head telling him something was wrong. Later, when he'd seen her at the bottom of the stairs, just as Alex and Susan arrived, she'd seemed distant. But then, she'd kissed him and told him she'd missed him. His fear had dissipated.

Throughout the evening he'd been unable to take his eyes off her. She'd been so lovely, wearing the aquamarine jewelry he'd given her. She'd chosen a gown of shimmering iridescent blue satin to complement it perfectly. With her incredible hair, her soft skin, her amazing eyes, and that smile, just gazing at her had kept him breathless.

In his entire lifetime he could never remember feeling so awed and riveted simply by looking at someone.

Lilly wasn't just someone. She was his wife. His *wife!* The concept was staggering and… *oh, god…*

The idea of marriage had always been abhorrent to him. Married, he would become the cheating louse his father had been. Memories of his mother swarmed him. As a boy, he'd thought she was beautiful. He remembered the way she'd stroked his cheek with the back of her fingers, how she tucked the blankets around him, the way she laughed when he said something silly, the way her soft voice vibrated when she sang to him, they way she'd held his hand with her thumb stuck through his fingers. Sometimes, even now, her scent would drift through the air and into his senses.

He knew it was just a hallucination—the pathetic, wishful tricks of his mind—intended to twist the knife of guilt deeper into his gut. For years he'd hated his mother for deserting him. It took him many more to realize how much she'd shielded him from his father, and how daunting and humiliating a task it had to have been for her.

For as long as Gabriel could remember, his father had flaunted his lover, Beatrice, in his mother's face. He'd paraded Beatrice on his arm to social events, all but ignoring his wife, who trailed behind, holding Gabriel's hand. If Charles glanced at his mother, it was only to castigate her in some subtly vicious way. *Stand up straight! Don't embarrass me tonight! Must you bite your lip like that?* The stinging rebukes were endless. His mother's grip would squeeze around Gabriel's fingers. Her nails would dig into his skin deep enough to leave marks. She never realized she did it.

There wasn't a time Gabriel could remember his father ever paying compliments to his mother, let alone speaking to her affably. Theirs was a relationship based upon avoidance, from both sides. Even so, as bad as the obligatory public displays were, the private interactions were worse. Because the shouting hurt his ears, Gabriel ran. He hid, sometimes in his room, sometimes outside, and sometimes when he couldn't make the voices in his head stop, he just kept running—running and running until the stitch in his side was so painful he thought he would vomit. His mother wasn't worthy of the Drayton name. Unlike Beatrice, she had never been good enough for Charles Drayton.

The great Charles Drayton—such a well-respected man, someone to be emulated, admired, sought after. Within days of Gabriel's mother's death, Beatrice, Charles's preferred companion, had come to live at Drayton Hall. Why his father never married Beatrice had always been a mystery. What had become clear was that his father wasn't any more faithful to Beatrice than he'd been to his wife.

Charles had liked women. He'd been a tireless flirt. Charming had been the word used most often to describe him. Gabriel could remember listening to his father's silky flattery, seeing his suave, clandestine caresses. It wasn't unusual for his father to invite younger women to their home and entertain them privately in his west wing office.

Beatrice had turned Gabriel into her pawn. She would send him off to the west wing, touting some made-up excuse as to why he needed to go in there, and then he had to report back to her the things he'd seen. The images that flitted through Gabriel's mind—images of his father in various sexually deviant positions, often with more than one woman—still sickened him.

Boarding school had saved Gabriel from having to spy for Beatrice. Nevertheless, he was aware his father's passions didn't diminish while he was away. If anything, as Charles aged, he became more insatiable and unforgiving.

Gabriel remembered, too, the intimate caresses his father had imparted to Susan—the brush of his fingers over her shoulder, a tap on her behind, a whisper in her ear—all done when Charles thought no one was watching. Although Gabriel had never actually seen them, he was fairly certain Susan had, at one time or another, been enclosed with his father in that west wing office.

Susan was nineteen when Gabriel met her. He was twenty-three. By then, he'd known for years he was afflicted with the same demented appetites for the opposite sex as his father. As much as he hated it, his father's blood was in his veins. The women were easy and plentiful, and he never hesitated to take what was so readily offered. Sex had become his pinnacle pleasure, and the manifestation of his true value as a man.

He'd been attending a small gathering at Drayton Hall, by obligation, not by choice, when his father introduced Susan. The daughter of a well-respected peer of Charles', she was quite striking and audaciously intelligent. Charles had pushed her at Gabriel from day one. The old man had been adamant they marry. By doing so, Gabriel would elevate his lowly, incompetent self, and finally be worthy of bearing the Drayton name.

At first he'd been mildly intrigued by her, until snippets of her true nature began to surface. Gabriel's refusal to marry Susan had as much to do with his distrust of her as it did his suspicions that she was one of his father's many lovers. The heated discussions he'd had with his father about her weren't worth remembering. In most of them, he'd stood silently while his father reiterated time and again the same criticisms Gabriel had heard his entire life. He was a disappointment, an embarrassment, the pathetic spawn of a manic, repulsive woman. The only way he could improve himself would be to marry someone with superior blood—someone like Susan.

Christ! Why was he sitting here, thinking about Susan? He still couldn't believe she'd had the audacity to show up for dinner, not after he'd roughly shoved her away—the only way to get her off of him—and then kicked her out of Drayton Hall. He'd hoped she would come up with some fictitious malady and beg off. He should have known better.

All evening it was all he could do to be remotely civil toward her. He wondered what Alex would say if he told him what Susan had done. He wondered what Alex would say if he knew about Susan's affair with Rob.

Susan's behavior today convinced him once and for all, no matter how hasty his decision to replace Susan as Charlotte's guardian had been, it was the right one. Not just because Susan was a selfish manipulator. It was the right thing to do, because Lilly was so competent, and so perfect…

Gabriel leaned his head back and squeezed his eyes shut. *"Lilly. Oh, Lilly."* Did he say her name out loud? He wasn't sure. *"Please come. Please."*

Who was he kidding? Lilly wouldn't come, because she didn't care for him any more than Susan did. Could he blame her? Would it matter to her if he told her he just wanted to sit with her and watch her eat chocolates, share a glass of wine? Would it make a difference if she knew he wanted to tell her about his trip, and the boys at Bridgton Academy he'd gone to see, to talk about Charlotte, and Julie's baby, and politics, and God help him, God?

He wanted to trace the curve of her cheek with his fingertips, lightly kiss her lips. He wanted to release the pins from her hair, see it flowing down her back. He imagined slowly stroking through the soft waves. He wanted to see her in profile, the line of her jaw, the tip of her pert little nose. He wanted to see her eyes close, her lashes flutter as he slowly worked the brush through…

Gabriel sat up abruptly. Good god, what was he thinking? He wanted to *brush* her hair? Never in his life had he ever imagined doing such a thing, to any woman. But he did want to. His hands itched to. To Lilly and Lilly alone. And he would.

If she came to him tonight…

She's not coming, you besotted sop! Go to bed and be done with your pathetic wishes. She doesn't want you! She never did and she never will! To her this is an abhorrent arrangement. Nothing more. You mean nothing to her!

It was two a.m. when he set his empty glass aside. He'd filled it three times, after having given in to the temptation to open the bottle. Every noise had caused him to jump, to stare hopefully, in earnest anticipation, toward his bedroom door, waiting, waiting for the latch to click. In the last hour he'd let the fire die to cinders.

"Stupid fool," he whispered under his breath as he made his way to bed—the side he normally slept on. There he stripped to his underwear, leaving his clothes on the floor by the bed. Second thought had him reaching for the clothes, taking them to the laundry hamper. She would think him a slob, which he could be at times.

If she came to him tonight...

Back at his bed, he stared off at nothing. Then he rose and fixed the blankets back the way they'd been before his first attempt to get under them. He took another moment to smooth the silk and ensure the pillow with the rose on it was fluffed the way he'd originally had it. He went around to the other side of the bed, the left side. Until those nights with Lilly he'd never slept on the left side, nor had he since. But he would.

If she came to him tonight...

Lying in his bed, under the new, shimmering bed clothes, he wondered for the umpteenth time if she would like them.

She wasn't coming so it didn't matter! She was right not to come here. After all he had his father's blood running through his veins, and like his father he was incapable of committing to any one woman.

Why then had he shoved Susan away? It wasn't like he'd had a stream of liaisons since the fire. The only woman he'd touched since the fire was Lilly. Why did just the idea of being with someone other than Lilly turn his stomach to such an extent he felt nauseous from it?

Lilly was his *wife*, a position warranting honor, a treasure to be revered and cared for, for the rest of his life. His mother should have been valued like that. His father should have shown her respect, given her the dignity and the authority she deserved. How Gabriel had wanted that for her! How he'd plotted and schemed and tried his damnedest to get his father to say something kind to her. Just once. But he'd been a stupid boy, never able to come up with anything good enough.

Gabriel clutched his head with both hands and pressed the heels of them into his eyes. He held them there until bizarre designs and colors floated behind his eyelids. Not for the first time, he thought, it was a good thing he hadn't made Lilly pregnant. It was better that she wasn't carrying his child. Better for her. Better for the child. Because he wasn't a good father. He'd neglected Charlotte. He would have to tell Lilly that...

If she came to him tonight...

Releasing the pressure, he grabbed for his mask, intending to yank the damn thing off and set it aside, like he did every night. But he stopped abruptly and pushed it back in place, taking the time to ensure the knot in the scarf around his neck would hold. She couldn't see his face. No matter what, she could *never* see his face!

If she came to him tonight...

Sleep didn't claim him until just before dawn. With it came the recurring nightmares of children—terrorized, screaming children. There was a little boy who looked much like Alex had when he was young, the dark hair brushing his brow, the pale blue eyes wide with unabashed fear. The group of them ran from him, except for Alex, who turned back.

Alex was still as a child, but older, with a dagger in hand. Gabriel didn't know how he got there, but he was trapped under something, something heavy, and Alex was hovering over him, holding that knife. He was choking... he couldn't breathe...

"I warned you," Alex said. "But you laughed at my letters. You laughed at me. You cuckolded me! Now you shall pay!"

SWISH... SWISH... SWISH...

Gabriel awakened with a start, jolting upright in the bed so fast, pain lanced through his hip and down his leg.

That sound—that horrible sound—wasn't a weapon slashing into his chest. He heard it again.

TAP... TAP... TAP...

Someone was knocking at the door!

Oh god! She was here! She'd come to him! No! Not yet! He wasn't ready!

Clumsily he tugged at his mask. It had become askew during his tossing and turning. His heart pounded. He couldn't breathe. But he tried to get up, gasping through the agony.

TAP... TAP... TAP...

"Daddy! Daddy! It's morning! Time to wake up!"

To be continued...

One Fine Man

Elizabeth Courtright

CHAPTER ONE

January 1889

She'd done a terrible thing!

Molly Finch glanced at her employer, Robert August, seated beside her in the hired coach, and watched him, for what must have been the fifteenth time, turn to stare out the small rear window.

"Is he still there?" she asked softly.

"Yes, damn it," Rob hissed. He was disgruntled and rightly so.

They were being followed. The horseman was keeping several paces back, too far for them to identify clearly, but Rob was fairly certain it was the same man who'd been trailing them since they left the confines of downtown Havertown. This wasn't the first time in the last month they'd noticed being followed. Rob believed whoever it was, was pursuing *him*. Molly knew better. The man wasn't after Rob. He was after *her*. And she knew exactly who he was.

"Don't worry, darlin'. I'm going to get to the bottom of this." Rob took her hand and entwined their fingers. Squeezing gently, he added, "Today."

The conviction in his tone caused Molly's pulse to surge. "What are you going to do?"

"I'm not sure yet," he said as he slipped across to the opposite seat and knocked on the box to tell the driver to pull over.

Molly didn't need to look out the window to know where they were. Lately, this jaunt through the countryside was something Rob did almost every day. More often than not, he asked her to accompany him.

The coach rumbled over frozen, muddy ruts, jostling its passengers as it slowed and came to a stop right in front of an elaborate iron-barred gate— the imposing entrance to the property known as Drayton Hall.

Rob drew his cloak more securely around his shoulders. Too impatient to wait for the coachman to clamor down from the driver's seat and open the door, he grabbed the latch and pushed. Molly wanted to call out to him, to tell him not to get out, to stay inside, but she didn't.

"Wait here. This won't take long," Rob said over his shoulder.

A shiver coursed through her from the swath of chilly air that blew in. All she could do from then on was peer out the window to watch Rob battle the blustering weather and make his way to stand behind the coach. The wind was so strong it caused the tails of his cloak to flap out behind him like a flag on a pole.

He made an impressive figure, waiting for the tracker to pass by. But then again, to Molly, Rob was always impressive. No matter whether he was traversing the floors of a courtroom, or seated behind the stately desk in his office. He could be mounted on the new thoroughbred he'd purchased a few weeks ago, or sprawled comfortably in bed reading a book. In repose, he liked best to be on his stomach, one arm tucked up under the pillow.

Thinking of him that way, despite the current unsettling circumstances, brought on a wistful smile. Molly had fallen for Rob's charms from the very first day they met. It was hard to believe it had been almost seven years ago.

He'd been such a gentleman and so very attractive with his dark hair and blue eyes when he answered her knock. And he'd been unexpectedly kind, serving her a cup of tea complemented by a plate of peppermint sticks. Propriety wouldn't allow her to partake of the sweets. She hadn't been there to eat. She'd been there to be interviewed. But then, he hadn't asked many questions. All he'd wanted to know was whether she could clean, do laundry, cook and make coffee, and he'd asked if she would mind taking care of the shopping. After that, he took her on a tour of his townhouse.

The front rooms on the main floor served as his law office. The kitchen and scullery were in the rear, overlooking the small yard and alley. His bedroom was on the second floor, and hers, if she wanted the position, would be on the third, in the attic. That cozy room with its quaint dormer windows and slanted ceilings had been hers for a while, but she didn't sleep there any longer. Rob's sudden ardor, almost four years ago, had been a surprise, but not an unwelcomed one. By then, she'd been too deeply entranced to refuse him anything.

Becoming Rob's housekeeper had provided Molly with the opportunity to rise above the dismal hand God had dealt. No one she associated with these days knew of her lowly, pathetic history. Not even Rob. He did know her parents, but that was as much as she would ever reveal of her past. She was no longer a foolish, spoiled girl, running from an embarrassing, immigrant family. She'd worked hard to rid herself of the accent, to show that she could be dignified and well-mannered like the wealthy first-class people Rob admired. And Rob had noticed. At least he'd noticed enough to want her in his bed.

In the beginning she'd believed their intimacy would lead to more, that someday Rob would ask her to marry him. As time passed, she came to realize the issue wasn't her speech and behavior, it was her appearance. Rob paid her well, but not well enough to transform her wardrobe into that of a high-society lady. To be truly refined, and an acceptable wife for Rob, she needed money. Last summer, she'd been offered that money.

She had beautiful clothes now—more fashionable dresses and stylish hats than she could ever outwear. She had lacy, enticing unclothing, and distinguished jewels. She had dainty slippers and fancy boots, beaded gloves and colorful scarves by the dozens. But, taking that money had been the worst decision she'd ever made.

The entrance gate to Drayton Hall was a reminder of what she'd done and what she was still supposed to do. If Rob ever found out... *oh god...* she couldn't bear to think of what would happen if Rob ever found out!

Six months ago, Molly hadn't understood Rob's obsession with Drayton Hall, or the people who lived there, but she understood now. Because of the surrounding woodlands, no part of the grandiose estate could be seen from the road. The elaborate mansion house, which to Molly resembled a dank, medieval castle, was so far up the lane from the gate, even when peering through the bars, it wasn't visible.

Molly was glad of this. The last thing she wanted to do was look upon the daunting grey towers. Worse, however, would be running into any of its residents. It wasn't that she didn't like them. Two of them she did like, and she pitied them. Lilly Drayton had been hired to tutor Charlotte, a lovely, precious child. Within a month of her employment, Lilly had been forcibly coerced into marrying Charlotte's wicked father.

Not for the first time, Molly shuddered just thinking of what poor Charlotte and Lilly endured at the hands of that monster. Gabriel Drayton was rumored to be ruthless and cruel, and Molly knew all too well how true that reputation was. The man was callous and vengeful, a hostile tyrant without mercy or feeling of any kind. But this wasn't the worst. The worst were his perversions, which were so appalling, just thinking about them made Molly feel sick.

The horrid man even looked like a fiend, garbed as he always was in black. With his wielding cane and hitching step, his long dark hair and the hideous mask he wore, he wasn't just creepy, he was disconcertingly petrifying. Molly had despised him from their very first meeting, not just because he deserved to be despised, but because of what he'd been doing to Rob.

For many years, long before he'd hired her, Rob had been the attorney for the Drayton estate. He'd also been the trustee under the trust agreement that controlled the Drayton's numerous holdings and assets. But there was much more to Rob's relationship with Gabriel and the rest of the Drayton family than merely these important offices.

Learning Rob's life story had only entangled Molly's heart more. As an infant he'd been left in a basket on the porch of an orphanage. He didn't even have a name. The headmaster dubbed him August, because the day he'd been found was the first day of that month. For thirteen years of his life, he'd lived in that horrible, inhumane place. But then, when he was fourteen, he'd been whisked away to boarding school. The funds for his education had been donated by an anonymous person, the same person who paid for his post-secondary schooling. It wasn't until he finished law school that Rob discovered his patron's name—Charles Drayton.

Charles Drayton had been impressed by Rob's acumen and ambition. He'd hired Rob as his attorney, and appointed him trustee. Charles gave Rob a jumpstart on his law practice by loaning him money and introducing him to elite, influential people. More than once, Rob had commented that if it weren't for Charles, he would have never become a successful gentleman and counselor.

Molly would have liked to have met Charles, but sadly by the time she came to be with Rob, Charles was already gone. Rob had shared with her that he'd learned of his parentage at Charles' funeral. That bombshell had been thrust upon him by Beatrice, Charles' longtime mistress.

Once, Molly had overheard Rob and Gabriel talking about Beatrice, and they'd referred to her as the 'ice queen.' Beatrice lived in Manhattan and never ventured to Pennsylvania to visit. Molly had only one encounter with the woman.

It was shortly before the holidays last year. Rob had asked her to go with him to New York. He'd wanted to confront Beatrice over something she'd purportedly said to Gabriel. During that meeting, she'd denied the allegation, and Molly had believed her. Even so, she'd left the Manhattan townhome thinking the 'ice queen' epithet was pretty accurate.

In Molly's opinion, it certainly was a heartless thing to do to reveal information of such life-altering proportions at a funeral. Not only that, but Beatrice had demanded Rob's secrecy. And Rob, bless him, had kept the secret. He'd never told Gabriel. He'd told no one, except Molly.

Beatrice was Rob's mother, and Rob was Charles Drayton's illegitimate, first-born son.

Gabriel Drayton was Charles's second son, his only legitimate child and sole heir—loathsome Gabriel, whom Rob had considered his closest confidante and best friend. Over the years, Molly had watched Gabriel make Rob's life pure hell. He'd brutishly instigated adversity with Rob's peers. He'd discouraged new clients from hiring Rob. He'd carelessly caused more headaches and strife than anyone could be expected to endure, but Rob, in his unerring loyalty had been too blind to realize it. Rob laughed over the rumors about Gabriel, refusing to believe a word of them.

But then, last fall, for no fathomable reason, Gabriel made up a horrible, quite ludicrous accusation, claiming that Rob had embezzled trust funds. Because of this, Gabriel had cut off Rob's livelihood and all but destroyed his law practice. He'd callously fired Rob and removed him as trustee of the Drayton estate.

Fortunately, Rob had his paper mill business in New York. This venture, unbeknownst to Gabriel or anyone else except Molly, Rob had started years before with a partner named Stebbins. The mill, however, hadn't taken off the way Rob and Stebbins had hoped. They got by, but profits had never been abounding. Recently that had changed.

During their trek to New York before Christmas, after seeing Beatrice, Rob had taken Molly to meet Stebbins. A few weeks before, out of the blue, two publishing houses had called at the mill. According to Stebbins, who knew the paper business inside and out, clients of this magnitude never sought services without first receiving a solicitation. Regardless, the new business was secured, and because of it, revenues were expected to be substantial. So far they'd been pouring in quite well.

Molly needed to stop fretting, and instead concentrate on the here and now. The follower was gaining ground. Because of how the roadway was surrounded by forest, both on the left and the right, there was nowhere for the rider to veer off. Through the window, she could tell he'd slowed his pace—the horse was merely walking—but even so, within a minute or two, he would pass Rob, who was still stoically facing off with the gale-forced winds.

Straining her eyes, Molly tried to make out the pursuer's features. It wasn't easy due to his outerwear. To ward off the cold his hat had been pulled low and the collar of his coat was turned up sharply. Not one shred of his hair was visible. Even so, she knew he was one of two men—one of the two who had hired her to do the unthinkable.

For a while, every Monday evening, while Rob was occupied at his bar association meeting, she'd gone to see those men, the John Smiths, in a sleazy tavern in a grim, unkempt part of town. At these rendezvous the John Smiths gave her two pouches. One was filled with money. The other contained a deadly powdery substance.

And she'd used it. It didn't matter that she'd been lying to the John Smiths, telling them she was still doling out the dosage, when in truth, for months now, she hadn't been. It didn't matter that the man whose coffee she'd repeatedly tainted was no longer a client of Rob's, or that her parents worked for him. It didn't matter that he'd done unconscionable things to Rob. It didn't even matter that he was a sick, perverted monster, who preyed upon boys, keeping them prisoner in the dungeons of Drayton Hall to slowly torture and maim.

It didn't matter that Gabriel Drayton was evil incarnate. If she had killed him, she would be as bad as he was! She would be a murderer!

But Gabriel was still alive, and because he was, the John Smiths were after her! With her heart in her throat, she watched through the paltry rear window, as Rob boldly stepped in front of the oncoming horse.

Even above the loud gusts whipping through the trees, she could hear Rob bellow, "Why are you following me?"

"I'm not," the rider said, and he pulled on his reins to direct his mount around Rob.

In the next instant, Rob grabbed the man and dragged him off the horse. From inside the coach, Molly screeched so loudly she was sure Rob heard her, but if he did, he didn't acknowledge it.

Rob was a strong man. This Molly knew from the definition in his muscle—muscle she was quite familiar with—but never had she seen him act with such aggression or violence.

The horse took off as Rob shoved the man to the ground. He had a knee pressed firmly into the pursuer's midriff, and a hand clasped tightly at his throat to hold him immobile. With his free limb, Rob reached under his cloak. When he pulled his arm out, there was a revolver clutched in his grip!

Molly knew Rob had guns. He had two of them. But she'd never seen him carry them, and she'd never seen him use them. Because of the way Rob's cloak flapped, it kept blocking Molly's view of the rider's face. She didn't know yet if he was Greasy John or Red John, but based upon how submissive he'd become, she guessed he had to be Greasy John. Red John, she was sure, would have put up more of a fight.

"Whoa, Mister!" prone Greasy John implored. "I don't know who you think I am, but I ain't been followin' ya. I don't know who you are!"

"Liar!" Rob hissed.

He leveled the revolver and thumbed the hammer. That ominous c-l-i-c-k was loud enough for Molly to hear inside the coach, and she gasped. She wanted to scream, "No, Rob. Don't!" but she couldn't.

"Tell me who hired you?" Rob snarled.

"I swear to God, I ain't followin' ya! I swear, man! Let me go!" Greasy John begged.

He pleaded more, but the words were lost to the wind. Whatever he said didn't pacify Rob. Instead of letting go, Rob pressed the barrel of the revolver under the brim of Greasy John's hat, right to the middle of his forehead, and then Rob started counting, "Five... four... three... two..."

"Alright, alright!" Greasy John cried. "I have been following you!"

"Why? Who hired you?" Rob demanded.

"I report where you go, that's all. I swear! I don't know any more than that!"

"Who do you make your report to? Who hired you?" Rob repeated.

"Dobbins," Greasy John said. "I work for Dobbins."

Molly was so startled by this admission, she had to clasp the seat to keep from toppling out of it. This couldn't be right! She knew of

Dobbins. He was a prominent detective in town, and known to be firmly law-abiding. Often he worked closely with the police. Rob had hired him a time or two to help with law cases. It made no sense that criminals like the John Smiths—and there was no doubt in Molly's mind that both men were the worst kinds of criminals—would associate with someone as upstanding as Dobbins.

"Tell your boss to expect a visit from me," Rob said. Letting go, he stood up.

"You ain't gonna shoot me?" Greasy John warily pushed to his feet.

Rob was situated between Greasy John and the coach in such a way that Molly's view was still hindered. The only part of Greasy John she could see were his arms, raised in surrender. But Rob wasn't aiming the revolver any longer. It was hanging limply at his side.

"Go on, get out of here," Rob said. "You'd better catch your horse."

From the window, Molly couldn't see the horse at all. She'd heard its clip-clops after Rob wrestled Greasy John off, but they'd faded and she'd been too riveted by Rob's actions to pay attention to the animal.

"Are you going to shoot me in the back?" Greasy John countered.

"Sorry," Rob chortled. "I have no interest in spending the rest of my life in prison. I'm no murderer."

"That's not what I heard," Greasy John blurted, and he barreled past.

Molly caught a brief glimpse of Rob's jaw-dropping astonishment. Her focus, however, wasn't on Rob. It was on the fleeing man. He ran right by the coach, perfectly in her line of sight, and she saw his face quite clearly.

He wasn't Greasy John.

Thank You...

All proceeds from the sale of this book benefit the Third Chance Foundation.

The Third Chance Foundation is a nondiscriminatory, nonprofit corporation that provides postsecondary scholarships to foster and adopted children. Our sole purpose is to help today's youth achieve career goals and follow dreams. We believe there is no aspiration too trivial or undeserving.

Our scholarship funds are raised through book sales. For more information, please visit us at www.thirdchancefound.org. The more books we sell, the more scholarships we will provide!

We thank you for your contribution. By purchasing this book, you have changed a life!

THIRD
CHANCE
FOUNDATION
Buy a Book. Change a Life!

About the Author

"It was hard to keep a straight face!" says Elizabeth's mother of the tales Elizabeth wrote as early as six years old. Her parents sure got a kick out of them anyway!

Today, this diehard romantic owes her inspiration and imagination to her family. Proceeds from the sales of her books benefit the Third Chance Foundation, a non-profit organization which provides scholarships to foster and adopted children, like her own. She and her husband of twenty-two years—her knight in shining armor—amidst their chaotic house full of kids and pets, consider themselves extremely blessed.

Connecting

Elizabeth enjoys hearing from readers! Your questions, comments and feedback are most welcome. Please feel free to visit Elizabeth's website at www.elizabethcourtright.com. Reviews can also be posted on Amazon or at www.thirdchancefound.org.

To contact Elizabeth directly:
Elizabeth@thirdchancefound.org

Other Titles
by this Author

In this series:

One Fine Beast

One Fine Man

In the Grace Series:

Concealing Grace

Saving Grace

Healing Grace (forthcoming)

Other Novels:

Moonlit Haze